FAIR GODS

AND

FEATHERED
SERPENTS

A SEARCH FOR THE
EARLY AMERICAS'
BEARDED WHITE GOD

Terry J. O'Brien

First Printing: July 1997
Second Printing: November 1997

International Standard Book Number:
0-88290-608-9

Horizon Publishers' Catalog and Order Number:
1079

Printed and distributed
in the United States of America by

**Horizon
Publishers
& Distributors, Incorporated**

**Mailing Address:
P.O. Box 490
Bountiful, Utah 84011-0490**

**Street Address:
50 South 500 West
Bountiful, Utah 84010**

**Local Phone: (801) 295-9451
WATS (toll free): 1 (800) 453-0812
FAX: (801) 295-0196**

Internet: www.horizonpublishers.com

It is the secret of the world
that all things subsist,
and do not die,
but only retire a little
from sight,
and afterwards
return again.

—Ralph Waldo Emerson

MYSTERY MAN ARRIV

ROM ACROSS THE SEA

CONTENTS

Part 1
A Mystery Discovered

Part 2
Fair Gods in Far Places

4. The Serpent Sheds an Ancient Skin . . 59

The legends extend farther back in time as other heroes surface.

5. Bearded Visitors in South America . . . 81

Extraordinary tales from the jungles, mountains, and deserts of South America.

6. Fair Gods in North America 98

An ancient, bearded, white visitor leaves a trail from Alaska to Canada and other parts of the United States.

Part 3
The Theories:
Searching for Bearded Visitors

11. Lost Tribes in a Promised Land 188

Explosive discussions challenge suggested visits from Israel,
but supporting evidence increases the controversy.

12. Christ Before Columbus 209

Bewildering parallels between Christ and the culture heroes
challenge traditional beliefs.

Part 4
Unravelling the Mystery

13. The Universal Nature of Culture Heroes 235

The role of natural phenomena and universal responses in creating
and expanding white-god legends.

LIST OF ILLUSTRATIONS

Unless otherwise noted, all illustrations and photographs are by the author.

INTRODUCTION

Of all the American heroes, who was the greatest? Was it George Washington, Abraham Lincoln, John Kennedy, perhaps Albert Einstein? How about Martin Luther King, Simon Bolivar, Benito Juarez, Eleanor Roosevelt or Eva Peron? Every nation on the North and South American Continents can list men and women of strong impact. Many of these individuals were great only within their own countries, while others transcended borders and still inspire us today.

But of the many noteworthy individuals produced by the Americas, only one had a power so pervasive that it has touched every corner of the continents and the life of every inhabitant. One figure alone has given rise to accounts of accomplishments so great that they eclipse the deeds of all the other heroes of the Americas combined.

Indian legends, from the Bering Straits in Alaska to Cape Horn in South America, tell of an amazing white, bearded "foreigner" whose contributions in the distant past were so remarkable that they eventually penetrated every culture of the Americas then, and still endure today. So revered was this person that huge monuments were erected to his honor. His symbol, the feathered serpent, is still found today in ceremonies, paintings, carvings, and architecture throughout all the lands of the Western Hemisphere.

Although a belief held by many is that Columbus was the first to visit the Americas from the Old World, Indian legends say the white visitor travelled across the oceans long before the Italian navigator, or even before the Vikings whose pre-Columbian visit is undisputed. The various legends claim this stranger brought with him a high culture and established advanced civilizations, then departed as mysteriously as he arrived. In the hearts of these diverse and scattered people he fixed a promise that he would one day return to rule and enrich their lives.

Spanish explorers and missionaries were the first Europeans to encounter and record the strange tales of this mysterious culture hero. The scholars who followed puzzled over the meaning and identity of the ancient visitor, whose promise to return virtually opened the door to the conquest of the American Continents, thus ultimately affecting every inhabitant. Speculation about the identity and origin of the bearded hero was rampant. Some said he was Greek, some said Egyptian, others insisted he was from Atlantis. Many strongly believed he was of the Lost Tribes of Israel, or a Christian Apostle, or Christ himself. But while colorful rumor was intriguing, it eventually receded into the shadows of conquest and colonization brought by the more recent bearded white visitors from across the seas.

Early European colonizers of the Sixteenth Century had less interest in native gods than in native gold. Through subsequent centuries this great hero of the Americas remained lost in archives and seemed in danger of being forgotten by all but a few isolated Indian tribes who quietly guarded his sacred memory.

Then, in the 1800's, the situation changed. A wave of archaeological excitement uncovered imposing monuments from the Americas' ancient past: pyramids, temples, large works of sculpture, and painted ceramics. With these discoveries came renewed interest in the pre-conquest builders who had created these magnificent objects. Fortunately, along with the ruins and artifacts, several manuscripts emerged that had miraculously survived the Conquest and time. They spoke of powerful heroes and myths who had inspired the creation of these fantastic works of art now visible once more.

Scholars began the difficult task of unravelling intriguing mysteries hidden for so long, and foremost among these riddles was the ubiquitous legend of the bearded white man. Dressed in a long robe and sandals, he had reportedly crossed the ocean eons ago, alone or in company with others of his kind, bringing a cultural shift to the ancient North and South American peoples.

Ongoing dramatic archaeological discoveries, the discovery of startling parallels between Old and New World cultures, and contemporary speculations about visitors from outer space and prophecies concerning events of the third millennium make the age-old mystery even more spellbinding. Many nagging questions continue to surface:

- Who was the mysterious visitor, and why did he come?
- What is his origin?
- How did he get here?
- When did he come?
- Was there more than one bearded culture-hero?
- How many of ancient America's cultures did he influence?
- Will he return?

Had early recorders preserved more of the traditional Indian histories and legends, many of these debates could perhaps be resolved. Still, in spite of the wanton destruction of many ancient libraries by explorers and overzealous missionaries who tried to obliterate the native cultures and beliefs and replace them with their own, a surprising amount of information is available. Much of it is found in what has survived of tribal legends, but some comes from surprising contemporary discoveries.

Fair Gods and Feathered Serpents brings together the many stories about the white visitor, called by various tribes and cultures *Quetzalcoatl, Kukulcan, Viracocha, Ioskeha,* and a host of other names. It unravels, as well as reveals, some of the confusion created by the various legends and the puzzling combination of bird and serpent identified with him. It examines startling recent evidence and unexpected answers that scholars and modern scientists are providing for the questions that have perplexed investigators for nearly five hundred years.

Fascinating clues, which today are rapidly increasing, will entice the reader to join this search for a solution to the oldest and most baffling mystery of the Americas: the identity of the fair, bearded visitor from across the sea, and the feathered serpents by which he or they were everywhere identified.

Acknowledgments

Of course I take full responsibility for any errors and misconceptions found in the book. But to minimize them, I have been fortunate to receive valuable assistance and advice from scholars and friends who, although they did not always agree with me, did their best to put me on the right track. Among them are:

- Many Native Indians of North America, Mexico, Guatemala, and South America who awakened me to their beautiful cultures.
- Dr. Robert Carmack, Gillett Griffin, and Merle Greene Robertson for invaluable scholarly insights, suggestions and corrections.
- Dr. Linda Schele and Dr. Peter Matthews, who shared with me many enlightening hours at Tulane and Palenque.
- Dr. Robert Wauchope who, shortly before his death, reviewed my proposal.
- Peter and Roberta Markman for stimulating conversations, and for introducing me in person to Joseph Campbell.
- Dr. George Carter and Stephen Williams for offering challenging insights and new material.
- Dr. Robertson and members of the Tulane Seminar who initially issued the challenge, and who rightfully said I would never finish.
- Nancy Rayl, Jean Messingale, and Marie Rose for invaluable suggestions to make the book readable.
- Many friends who accompanied me to the ruins and asked questions, including Dr. Jess Groesbeck; I appreciate their lifelong friendship, support and inspiration.
- Bob and Carol Hummel, Donna Lloyd, and Diane Mitchell for encouragement and for adding to the challenge.
- Family and faculty for their patience, and
- Students of my Pre-Columbian art class for inspiration, encouragement and questions.

Others who graciously gave of their personal time and insights were Drs. Henry Nicholson, Chris Donnan, Michael Coe, Ignacio Marquina, Cyrus Gordon, Giles Healy, Mendel Peterson, Richard Dody, Paul Cheesman and John Sorenson. Also, I appreciate insightful conversations with Robert Marx, Maria Reiche, George Stuart, Alfred Bush, Trudi Blom, Duane Erickson, David Diel, Wayne May, Russell Burrows, Horatio Rybnikar, Charles Platt, John Wadsworth, Cordell Anderson, Phil Leigh, and the Coshocton Museum staff.

Of course, I am indebted to my long-time associate, Duane Crowther, the President and Senior Editor of Horizon Publishers, for having the courage to publish the results.

How This Book Was Written

As a youth, I was intrigued by stories of a mysterious, bearded white visitor who preceded Columbus to the Americas. Some people suggested any number of trans-oceanic visitors, while others insisted he was Christ. These answers, devoid of explanation, seemed too easy, and I wanted to know more. I searched for books on the subject, but found mainly isolated articles and scanty chapters buried in ponderous volumes of detailed histories, or fantastic speculations on the origins of American natives. A few later offerings provided inspiring or fanciful tales, but appeared one-sided and simplistic. Many lacked helpful references.

Disappointed, I looked in vain for years for a more complete and balanced treatment about the identity of the fair god; it didn't exist. I waited for someone to write it; no one did. Finally, encouraged by my students, I decided that in spite of my admitted inadequacies, I would do it—I would write the book I had always wanted to read. By this time I had lived among Guatemalan Indians for several years and visited over 250 ancient sites in North America, and from Mexico to South America. I participated in Maya conferences at the jungle site of Palenque, attended classes from scholars in anthropology, and collected and read countless books on pre-Columbian cultures. All this raised more questions.

A summer at Tulane University in Donald Robertson's N.E.H. seminar on Mesoamerican studies introduced me to colleagues and anthropologists. They met my seemingly innocent proposal to write a book about the mystery man of ancient America with astonished laughter. "You can't do it," they insisted. "You are not trained in anthropology," "There's too much," and "You'll never finish" were their typical comments.

Their doubts became my challenge, and I took them on. Now, twenty years later, the book is done. Although I teach a college course in pre-Columbian art, I'm still not a trained anthropologist, and true to my friends' predictions, there was too much and I will never finish. But for now, it is done. From this labor, I have resolved many nagging questions. Others still linger.

This book is not written for scholars, yet it attempts an academic foundation. It is written in popular style for the curious layman who seeks intriguing insights and a balanced perspective on this compelling mystery. It is for those who do not have time for, nor access to, overwhelming amounts of confusing and often contradictory material on the subject. Much of it is out of print and difficult to find.

Some readers, convinced that the bearded hero and his role in the Americas' native cultures developed in complete isolation from outside influence (*Isolationists*), will be disturbed by any suggestions of foreign contacts. Others, open to possible influence diffusing from non-native sources (*Diffusionists*) will be eagerly receptive. Sadly, promoters of one side or the other on this issue of the identity of the bearded white god too often succumb to either wild speculation or to narrow dogma, refusing to entertain alternative answers. But alternative answers do exist for most questions on the subject, and those who are willing to consider the broad range of options in the light of solid evidence often find surprising results.

I imagine that many readers will want conclusive answers, and may feel irritation with what appears to be ambivalence. But my purpose in writing is to open windows, not to shut them. I am interested in presenting the broad picture fairly, not just advocating one narrow view. Thus, I find it necessary to focus upon the details of one side, reverse them to show the other side, then, perhaps, reverse again. This allows readers to make up their own minds, or impresses upon them the difficulties of such decisions and the hazards of leaping to early conclusions. Where I feel conclusions are merited, I will suggest them, and at the end of the book I draw several (don't look ahead). But, for most of the book, my approach is: let the reader decide.

Although I have documented this work carefully and extensively, I do not pretend to cover all available sources—there are too many, (Sorenson and Raish, for example, have published an impressive 5600 references alone with a recent updating of 1200 more). There are ongoing studies I am unaware of and writers whose opinions I have not yet seen. Although updated and contemporary literature and evaluations are valuable and included, past writings and views closer to the events described are also considered pertinent. I use original sources where available, but many are those more accessible to readers, and most of them come from my own library. My extensive end notes are to remind me where my information comes from.

We will re-examine studies that some scholars dismissed long ago, and students of this and related topics may already be familiar with much of the material. Most readers will not. It is hoped that selections from both recent and ancient sources will give a clearer and more balanced picture of the endless array of perplexing questions surrounding the fair culture-hero, and a greater understanding of possible but sometimes contradictory solutions. Let the reader who desires more pursue the vast material and add it to this study. There is far more to this ancient story than a host of researchers could ever hope to discover, for a topic as complex as this can never be finished.

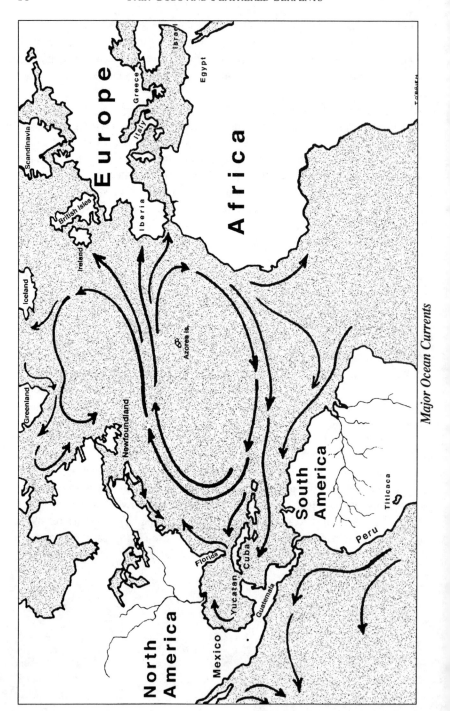

Major Ocean Currents

1

FAIR GODS AND FALLEN EMPIRES

Columbus Discovers a Mystery

The most famous ocean voyage in history encountered one of the world's most baffling riddles. Five-hundred years later, this riddle has yet to be solved. In his journals, Christopher Columbus relates that upon arrival at what he thought were the Indies, only forty-five days after leaving European shores, he did not meet the king of Japan, as he had anticipated, but a few hundred natives. Living in palm-thatched huts on an unimpressive island of the Bahamas which Columbus renamed San Salvador (Holy Savior), and "naked as their mothers gave them birth, with very handsome bodies, and very good faces," the natives rushed out to observe who might occupy such "strange, winged ships" and were startled at what they saw.

Columbus describes the natives' total amazement and fright at seeing Spanish beards, white skin, and strange clothing—all foreign to them. Even more surprising, "they asked us if we came from heaven," and they entered the boats and called, "Come and see the men who came from heaven."[1]

One might wonder how Columbus knew what they were saying, but he states that the Indians kissed the explorers' hands and feet with great solemnity and, raising their hands skyward, made it clear that they believed the white men had come from heaven. It didn't stop there.

Such a show would have been remarkable enough if it had been enacted at that one island alone, but Columbus' writings reveal that this strange, idolatrous reception was commonly repeated by the natives at each of the islands the white men visited. In a letter to Ferdinand and Isabella, Columbus says the natives "were very firmly convinced that I, with these ships and men, came from the heavens, and in this belief they everywhere received me after they had mastered their fear."[2] Even more puzzling, later explorers and missionaries noted similar receptions from native cultures throughout both American continents.

Why the curious association between white men and heaven? Why would such travel-worn Europeans be mistaken for gods? Columbus was unaware that Indian amazement over his light skin and beard and their belief that he had come from heaven were the result of very powerful ancient native traditions held throughout the New World. Those traditions maintained that in the distant past a mysterious, bearded white visitor had come to this land from across the sea. That he was white and bearded is remarkable since Indians are generally copper-skinned and beardless. He had brought with him a more advanced culture than their own and a higher, more spiritual way of life. Thus he is often referred to as a "culture hero." So revered was he that natives placed him among their gods. Then, after he travelled across the country for some time, he departed, leaving the people with a promise that one day he would return. Who was this fair-skinned visitor, and where did he come from?

Five centuries after Columbus, the identity of the legendary visitor to the Americas, where he came from, and why natives expected him to return still baffles historians. He could not know it, but native anticipation of the return of that mystery man was the secret to the riches Columbus sought. Not only in the North, but in South America as well, legends of an ancient visitor proved to be the key to open doors to the countries' wealth, and to the Spanish conquest.

Columbus, as the first honored visitor, never understood nor used that valuable key to the country. Since he never unlocked the door to the new world, he missed the magnificence and fortunes that awaited within. His eyes never beheld the impressive displays of native artistry and other manifestations of intellectual heights attained by ancient civilizations still flourishing in the land. Desperate to obtain rich treasures, he was greatly disappointed and returned home unaware how close he had come. But he left the key in the door for others to open.

Had he ventured inland, Columbus would have discovered the magnificence of the ancient visitor's influence—more than his mind or his caravels could hold: palaces with elaborate courtyards, ornately crafted temples, large caches of gold and silver, pyramids of staggering heights, exquisite works of art, and foods and trade goods never imagined by fifteenth-century Europeans. In spite of their prodigious efforts to amass these treasures over previous centuries, the natives were now strangely eager to hand them over to some bearded white god they expected would return from across the sea. Columbus lost out, but later visitors to these lands took full advantage of the white god legend—and everything else they could.

How to Host a Returning God

Unaware that he had found new continents, Columbus returned to Europe to report his discoveries and to arrange three more visits. Other Spaniards followed him back to the New World and settled in Cuba. For a time, they contented themselves with occasional explorations along the mainland coast. Although contact with natives at first was rare, and though these initial ventures were for the most part uneventful, the power of the legend of the mysterious white god would soon unlock the door to conquest and the unbelievable riches of the inland empire.

While Columbus was making his fourth and last voyage home, unfulfilled and deluded that he had reached Asia, activity was fermenting inland at the Aztec capital of Tenochtitlan (Ten-OSH-teet-LAHN). There the stage was being set for the next act of this remarkable drama. The formidable Aztec empire had been growing for several hundred years at an astonishing rate. Like the Romans, who conquered their Greek neighbors, these "nomads from the mythical land of Aztlan" had overpowered the highly cultured Toltec nation, a mighty people whose historic reign in the Valley of Mexico around 1,000 A.D. preceded them. The Aztecs adopted the Toltec religion, used their science, borrowed their history, and even fabri-

Model of Tenochtitlan (Aztec Capital)
(National Museum of Mexico City)

cated a royal lineage to connect them to the Toltec's so-called "great builders and artisans." Toltecs claimed that these revered men were led by a hero-god who was white and bearded. Fiercely-won borders now encompassed nearly all of Mexico, and few natives remained who did not serve or fear the Aztecs.

Except for unsettling rumors of white men off the coast, the Aztec life of the 1490's was as yet unaffected by the arrival of Europeans. It would be nearly three decades more before Cortez would arrive and bring dramatic changes to the inland kingdom. In the meantime, a new ruler had begun to preside over that vast empire, and the greatest cities on the continent came under the reign of Montezuma II, called by the Indians, Moctecusomatsin (Mohc-teh-cuh-soh-maht-SEEN), Supreme Monarch of the Mexicas. Although Montezuma enjoyed unquestioned power over his people, it was later recorded that with increasing news of the white man's activities the mighty ruler was distressed and confused.[3]

Early Spanish and Indian records show that perhaps more than any other people on the earth, the Aztecs steeped their lives in ancient tradition. Even the most mundane activity had religious significance. While the common native gave unquestioned allegiance to powerful leaders, the priests and kings were in turn subject to whims of the almighty gods. One of the functions of the hierarchy was to discern the will of the gods who presided throughout the empire and to find ways to avert the inevitable calamities that would befall any nation that failed to please those capricious beings.

For some time the appointed royal sages observed omens in nature which they nervously called to the attention of their lord Montezuma: three comets had emblazoned the eastern sky, followed by a strange light resembling a star-studded sheet of fire, and unidentified, low wailing voices seemed to announce some menacing event. Moreover, unexplainedly, without any sign of earthquake or storms, the great lake surrounding the Aztec island, Texcoco (Tes-COH-coh), had violently overflowed its banks, washing away many homes. Strangest of all were reports that four days after her burial, Montezuma's sister returned from the grave[4] to warn her famous brother of the approaching ruin of his empire.

Such unusual occurrences were undoubtedly exaggerated, and of no great consequence taken one at a time, but in the tormented mind of Montezuma they grew into prophetic warnings. This revered sovereign, called the "speaker" of the Aztec world, was so exalted that his subjects and priests dared not look upon his face. Yet, despite his seemingly secure position as King and Warrior, with the power of life and death over millions of his people, he felt uncertain and afraid, in the face of such ominous signs. In order to comprehend how weakness could overcome such a powerful ruler and make him easy prey to a small band of Spaniards, one must first understand something of the Aztec religion and of the white, bearded mystery man who unwittingly aided the Spanish cause.

Daily Blood Baths

Many spectacular temples to the numerous gods of ancient Mexico pierced the skies of Tenochtitlan. One of them was dedicated to a singular god called Quetzalcoatl (Keht-sahl-KWAHT), the ancient fair-skinned culture hero the Aztecs inherited along with other religious beliefs from the Toltecs, who had worshiped him as a prophet and teacher of the arts of civilization and healing. This bearded Toltec deity now resided in the sacred memory of the Aztecs as well, and both cultures represented him with the strange but easily-recognized symbol of a feathered-serpent. Like the coiled serpent, the temple of Quetzalcoatl was also circular in form. The entrance resembled a giant serpent's mouth, bristling with sharp fangs and teeth "diabolically painted"[5]—probably red to represent fresh blood. Although his temple sounds threatening, Quetzalcoatl was a peacemaker, and no god was held in higher esteem.

Sacred manuscripts, guarded since Toltec times, insisted that although Quetzalcoatl had left the land centuries before the Aztec emergence, he promised to return some day and resume possession of his empire which had been passed on to the Aztecs from the Toltecs. Each succeeding generation looked forward confidently to his arrival. But in the long silent absence, the Aztecs had replaced him with their own earlier tribal war god. This one, unlike Quetzalcoatl, hungered daily for sacrificial blood and human lives.[6]

Montezuma painfully remembered the promised return of the fair god, a return awaited by the Aztecs with as much assurance as the Messiah by the Jews or Jesus by the Christians. Rumors of bearded white men along the shores of his domain and of the increasing occurrence in nature of strange signs convinced the disturbed King that the appointed day for Quetzalcoatl's return was finally at hand. He also knew that the revered Lord, Quetzalcoatl, forbade human sacrifices. Yet, daily, the Aztecs now performed these bloody rites to their ravenous war god and his blood-thirsty companion-gods. Some estimates say these sacrifices reached as high as 50,000 humans for the dedication of the great temple.[7]

These human offerings, so abhorred later by the Spaniards, were not from hate or vengeance. Neither were they a solution to a food shortage, as some would have it (although some ceremonial cannibalism was practiced), for food was plentiful in Tenochtitlan. They were, rather, an ancient tradition based in symbolism and self-preservation. Sacrifices to the gods assured the Aztec that the forces of the universe, as they understood them, would continue. Sacrifice of the "few" was essential for the ultimate good of the many.

Priests studied very carefully the Book of Days, which contained celestial observations and prophecies. And, in order to assure that the sun would rise each morning, they thought it necessary to spill a great amount of life-giving blood. This "nectar of the Gods," procured from living human hearts, was believed to strengthen the sun as it turned red each night and fought its way through the threatening underworld.

There was also the "tying of the years" each fifty-two years, an Aztec century. Sacrifice assured the superstitious Indian that the world would not come to an end during that time. Victims were well prepared to be sacrificed, and most of them faced it stoically, for from it they expected "a sure passage into paradise." [8]

Montezuma believed in these traditional necessities, but he also knew that if the white god returned, as promised, he would not be pleased with sacrifices to other gods. Now these were strange, haunting specters to deal with, along the coasts. Aztec couriers had watched the distant Spanish ships with concern for over a quarter of a century, and when Cortez finally landed upon their shores, they reported the vessels to be temples with great swan wings borne upon the shoulders of Quetzalcoatl, for he was god of the air.

It would not do to have the return of a god whose worship had diminished in the land, for it had been such a long time since Quetzalcoatl had taught his gospel of peace. Not only would Quetzalcoatl disapprove of the demands by new Aztec gods for his people's blood, but the new gods would certainly disapprove of any demands made by the long-absent Quetzalcoatl. The bearded strangers had now landed on Aztec shores with "thunder and lightning" in their hands.[9] They could not be ignored. If they were supernatural beings, force and deception would have little power over them. If they turned out to be ambassadors from some foreign prince, they should be treated with dignity and honor.

With such conflicts already in the script, it is no wonder Montezuma was deeply troubled. The bizarre scene was irreversibly set, the doomed Aztecs were on stage, and the Spaniards would soon enter as the curtain lifted on one of history's bloodiest and most compelling dramas.

Coincidence Favors Cortez

The introduction of Conquistadores to inland people of the New World reads like a visit to another planet with so many strange sights and events. Furthermore, the Spaniards, as will be seen, had inadvertently, and to their advantage, prepared the natives to receive them in an aura of mystery and intrigue.

In a most remarkable coincidence, Hernando Cortez unwittingly chose to visit the Eastern Aztec shores in the year "one reed" and on the day "nine wind" of the Aztec calendar. For the Spaniards this was Good Friday, April 21, 1519; for the natives this was a new century cycle. Even more amazing, it was a year prophesied for the return of the enduring and bearded culture hero, Quetzalcoatl.[10]

If this were not enough to stir native superstition, the very beaches upon which the Spaniards disembarked were the same from which the revered Quetzalcoatl supposedly had departed centuries ago. These two remarkable coincidences make it obvious why the Indians greeted the Spaniards with mixed feelings of apprehension and good will.

Although they received the Spaniards enthusiastically, the Aztecs discouraged these visitors from moving inland to their great capital. Montezuma sent lavish gifts in hopes the strangers would then go away, but instead, the Spaniards found the treasures irresistible. Cortez sent word that Spaniards suffered from a disease of the heart for which gold was the only cure, and Montezuma's prompt filling of the prescription only intensified their "illness."[11] Gold drew them onward.

This first warm reception by natives belied the numerous trials and setbacks that awaited the ambitious Spaniards as they trekked across the land. The steep climb over foreign and often hostile terrain exhausted some of their enthusiasm. Still, the challenge of reaching Tenochtitlan, facing the mysterious monarch, and discovering more gold was obsessive. Cortez could not be dissuaded, and, in order to maintain the allegiance of his men, and to prevent them from returning out of fear or discouragement, he scuttled his own ships.[12] It would appear that fate had dictated this encounter; there was no turning back now, he would meet this Montezuma.

For three laborious months, interrupted by many fierce battles, Cortez and his band of four-hundred men marched some two-hundred strenuous miles along steeply inclined Mexican terrain. Their struggle to take the imposing capital of Tenochtitlan is one of history's boldest episodes, and the details are fascinating: allying of Aztec enemies, destroying idols and places of worship, the founding of Spanish colonies en route, and the arduous climb to the great city; the desperate battles, the trickery, the ambushes, and terrible massacres along the way. All of these have been adequately told by Gómara, Cortez's secretary; Castillo, a fellow-soldier with Cortez; and by Cortez himself. For the more complete story, one can refer to the masterful retelling of these engrossing events published in the nineteenth century by William Prescott in his *Conquest of Mexico*, and more recently by Hugh Thomas in *Conquest*.

In company with six-thousand native soldiers acquired from non-Aztec tribes along the way, and a hard-won reputation for being fierce warriors, the Spaniards arrived in Tenochtitlan to be hesitantly welcomed as returning gods and heroes.

The greeting party was a gala pageantry of royal native dignitaries and wide-eyed citizens crowding the avenues and canals to obtain a glimpse of these bearded men from across the sea. The "god-like" appearance of the Spaniards was likely enhanced by the early morning sun radiating as halos off their metal helmets. No doubt the degree of admiration felt by the Aztecs was matched by a similar amount of apprehension.

Spanish Gratitude

Following a royal reception, Cortez and his men settled comfortably into the sumptuous palace of Montezuma's father where each man had a canopied mat bed.[13] Next morning, following a peaceful night's rest, Cortez was led to the lavish quarters of Montezuma where he sat down with the Aztec leader in the world's first conference between Eastern and Western Hemispheres. Their words were translated by a bi-lingual Indian slave girl and a shipwrecked Spaniard. The girl, La Malinche, later called Doña Marina, had been born into a wealthy Aztec family, but was sold by her mother to the Maya whose language she learned fluently.[14] The Spaniard, following his shipwreck, lived among the Maya long enough to master their tongue. Joint facility with the Maya and Aztec tongues made these two invaluable to Cortez, who acquired them on an earlier exploring voyage from his Cuban island base to the Yucatan coast. Marina willingly became Cortez's cohort and quickly learned Spanish, which aided Cortez further with the Aztec king.

Tenochtitlan (Painting by Terry O'Brien)

In welcoming Cortez to his capital city, the courteous Montezuma provided some background to the mysterious reception of near-adulation given Columbus by the natives at so many landings. Prescott relates that Montezuma claimed that his own distant ancestors were not natives to this land either, but newcomers. They were led here by a great being, who, "after giving them laws and ruling over the nation for a time, had withdrawn to the regions where the sun rises. This great lord had declared on his departure that he or his descendants would again visit them to "resume his empire. This valuable insight to the now-familiar white god legend was recorded by Cortez in a document sent to Spain in 1520."[15]

The monarch further explained that the marvelous acts of the Spaniards (i.e., winged ships, rifle and cannon power, horses, and success in battle), coupled with their fair complexions, beards, and the direction of their coming, had led him to believe that these were the men prophesied to return and rule over these lands. Then, in a similar association made by the Indians to Columbus, he added his belief that since the Spaniards *had come from heaven* they "could call down the lightning and thunder, making the earth to tremble."[16]

The ancient "Indian" belief in a returning fair god was so implanted in the mind of Montezuma that, even when he finally realized that Cortez and the Spaniards were mere mortals, he still pledged allegiance to their sovereign, the King of Spain. Although the Aztec ruler was the highest of high priests, with absolute power over millions of subjects, a power steeped in centuries of unchanging traditions, he was willing to concede to a foreign ruler as the rightful Lord of all and to continue his own rule in the name of the Spanish King.[17]

It is hard to imagine a similar situation occurring in Europe with the arrival of a few Indians upon those shores. Clearly, the legends of a mysterious white visitor who would one day return had made the impossible a reality. This hero/god of Mexico had prepared the way for the Conquest.

To prove his stated loyalty to the Spanish crown, Montezuma bestowed rich gifts upon all of the visitors. In return, to show their delight at his generous hospitality, the ravenous Spaniards sacked the royal treasury and took the king hostage in his own palace. The gripping events of total conquest by a few Spaniards in the face of overwhelming numerical odds, the ultimate demise of the Aztec empire under Spanish rule, and the part played by a mysterious visitor from ancient times, grow more fascinating with time.

Pizarro and the Peruvian Prophecy

The incredible experience of Cortez in Mexico found a parallel ten years later in South America. Reports reached an illiterate Spanish Conquistador, Francisco Pizarro, of a powerful monarch who ruled the land of Peru from his court in the interior of the highest Andes. These intriguing accounts claimed the capital was made of solid gold and silver—rumor enough to motivate the ruthless, treasure-hungry Pizarro. In another of history's strange coincidences, the Inca ruler, Atahualpa (Ah-tah-WAHL-pah), had just emerged victor in a power struggle with his brother, and in 1532 he was at the city of Cajamarca (Cah-hah-MAHR-cah), dangerously far from the Inca capital, Cuzco, and directly in the path of the Conquistadores.[18]

Historians still puzzle how a small, ill-equipped band of one hundred eighty Spaniards could completely overpower the highly organized 2500-mile-long Inca empire and dethrone its ruler. The bloody details of the conquest are vividly recorded and will not be detailed here, but the curious reasons for its occurrence are of great interest.

When he first learned of the white men's arrival, the Inca Lord was about to return to his capital. Hearing of huge ships, unusual clothing, fair skin and beards, he reportedly assumed Pisarro and the Spaniards were the legendary supreme white god of the Inca, Tiki Viracocha (Wee-rah-COH-chah) and his vassals. Hauntingly similar to the Aztec/Toltec Quetzalcoatl, the Inca tradition said this ancient Peruvian culture hero once travelled the country, instructed his people, and then set off across the sea with a promise to return some day.[19]

Such a remarkable parallel to Aztec beliefs almost guaranteed that the Inca, like the Aztecs, would also mistake the Spaniards for their early white god, and to their disadvantage, they did. Unlike the conforming Aztec king Montezuma, however, Atahualpa was more interested in personal aggrandizement than fulfillment of prophecy. What a triumph it would be to return to the great capital of his ancestors in the company of the envoys of their ancient god, Viracocha! Especially for the man who had just wrested the throne from his brother.

With less hesitation than that shown by the Aztec monarch, the Inca ruler quickly discerned that these lustful and avaricious Spaniards were not gods. Still, he allowed their advance, hoping to discover what sort of men they were, and, perhaps, believing that in conquering them he would add further victories to his credits.

Unfortunately for him, in a mocking replay of Montezuma's dilemma, Atahualpa also became a prisoner of the Spaniards. They promised him freedom if he would fill his huge prison room with gold, and he condescended. The collecting of beautifully crafted gold objects from all over the kingdom took months. It is the world's loss that the priceless treasures were later melted into gold bars by the Spaniards who saw in them not irreplaceable art, but only precious metal. In Peru, as in Mexico, the Spaniards massacred the people, toppled the beautiful buildings, destroyed the fine crafts, and eventually confiscated the whole empire.

The Inca king was rewarded for his ransom—not with freedom promised him, but with death by garrote. Although his death was violent, this man, in his short life time, had ruthlessly decreed many similar fates.

Legend Topples Two Great Civilizations

It remains one of history's puzzles how two great leaders and two powerful nations were destroyed by a few bearded Spaniards from across the sea. Separated by some three-thousand land miles, and unaware of each other's existence, as far as we know, both Aztec and Inca held similar beliefs in a bearded white man. Both believed this powerful figure had come in the distant past, brought them a great message and promised to return one day to his rightful place with gifts of peace and prosperity for his people.

In a misguided interpretation of their legends' fulfillment, both the Aztec and Inca nations opened their doors to bearded white men who brought destruction instead of the anticipated glory. Rather than being fair gods, the Spaniards turned out to be men hungry for gold and conquest. Instead of peace, they brought terror. Instead of prosperity, they destroyed ways of life that had gone unchallenged for several thousand years.

In Mexico and South America the final results were the same: the Spaniards dethroned the rulers, plundered the cities, slaughtered the inhabitants, and leveled the magnificent structures that had survived the centuries. Less than half a century after the arrival of Columbus, and within ten years of each other, the once-powerful Aztec and Inca Kingdoms were no more—both became victims of an ancient legend and of unquestioned allegiance to their rulers who perpetuated it.

Following the destruction, it would seem that the compelling belief in a great, foreign lord, recognized by native Americans in both Northern and Southern continents, was over. But when the baffling legends of a fair, bearded visitor had endured so long, could the tenacious culture hero still hold true to his promise to return? And if so, how? We will see in the next chapter.

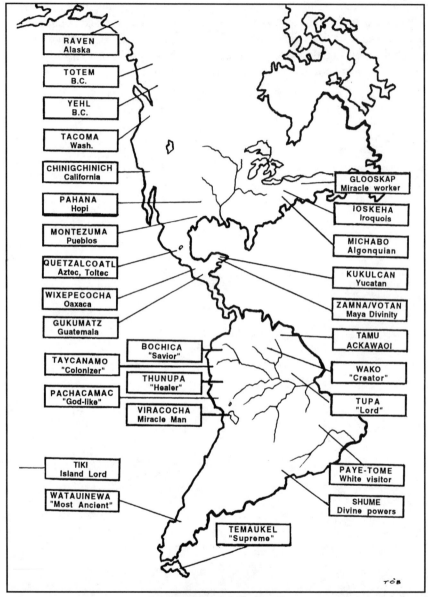

Locations Visited
by the
Bearded, White Mystery Man

2

A LINGERING LEGEND

Intriguing as we today might find the legends of a mysterious white visitor to in the Americas in ancient times, most early Spaniards arriving here were too immersed in subjugation and plunder to give them continued attention. The Conquistadores had used the American native belief in the return of a god-like hero to their advantage for the overthrow of the Indian empires; now they set out to build a new world over the devastation they had caused. Within a few years the Spaniards levelled pre-Conquest structures and left little to remind anyone of the past brilliance achieved in these countries during previous centuries from enlightenment reportedly brought by a bearded lord long before anyone could remember.

Years after the destruction, Bernal Díaz, a fellow soldier with Cortez, who was just out of his teens when the great centers were overthrown, recalled the past beauty of the Aztec capital:

> ... for there is so much to think over that I do not know how to describe it, seeing things as we did that had never been heard of or seen before, not even dreamed of ... How spacious and how well built ... of beautiful stone work and cedar wood ... with great rooms and courts, wonderful to behold, covered with awnings of cotton cloth. I was never tired of looking at the diversity of trees, and noting the scent which each one had, and the paths full of roses and flowers, and the many fruit trees and native roses, and the pond of fresh water ... great canoes were able to pass into the garden from the lake ... and all was cemented and very splendid with many kinds of stone [monuments] with pictures on them. Then the pond. I stood looking at it and thought that never in the world would there be discovered other lands such as these. Of all these wonders that I then beheld, today all is overthrown and lost, nothing left standing.[1]

"Nothing left standing." One of the saddest and too often recurring lines in history. But we can't be too harsh on the Spaniards for the destruction. In plundering and rebuilding they unknowingly echoed a similar Indian practice of creating the new over the old. Like the Aztecs and Incas before them, the Conquistadores constructed their own cities over the levelled monuments of previously conquered centers. Labor and material were readily available, for they simply used native skill and previously carved stones from the huge structures they had just brought down.

Because of the devastation, waves of European immigrants and colonizers who followed witnessed little of the splendor which had so astonished the Conquistadores. These later immigrants never met the well-bred and brilliant native leaders who had died defending their cities, so to them the Indian was merely a barbarian incapable of any of the refinements of civilization. They little suspected that had they arrived earlier they would have seen an advanced level of culture seldom attained even in their own countries. The misleading myth about the "ignorant" savage became a textbook "fact" for the next few centuries. As Europeans went about transporting their own culture into the new land, the glorious native past seemed totally forgotten.

Over the following centuries, the uniqueness of the Aztec and Inca capitals became, like their languages, transformed into Spanish forms. Where magnificent pyramids and temples had once swelled native pride, Spanish cathedrals and, more

Tenochtitlan in Ruins (Downtown Mexico City)

recently, sky-scrapers, now emerged—shrines of a new civilization. Other imposing cities of the Indians, both within and without these central areas, simply fell into desolation and often merged with jungle growth. It would seem that this "cultural fair" of the Western World's ancient marvels and legends was over, and the demanding gods who hosted the event had disappeared with it. These powerful traditions and the intrigue of an ancient bearded, white visitor had survived so long, would they now simply die out?

Contrary to appearance, and fortunate for history, the past was not totally erased. Traditions of early America lived not only in the hearts of the people, but in the land. Like tenacious jungle vines that, upon being cleared, eventually grow back, the heritage of these ancient peoples defied obliteration. Occasional historians would record Indian lore, and following a long dormant season, visual remains of ancient culture would again appear, perhaps not as pervasive nor as brilliant as before, but with roots that extended deeper than anyone could imagine. And besides, had not the bearded white man promised that he and his civilization would return and restore his people to a golden age?[2]

Tlatelolco "Plaza of Three Cultures"—Aztec, Spanish, and Modern
(Mexico City)

Ancient America Rediscovered

Following the sixteenth-century conquest of Mexico and South America, traditional native cultures were successfully subjugated, dispersed, and forgotten. Then, in the middle of the 1700's, buried relics of ancient American cultures began to surface. Objects that emerged would reveal much about the previous cultures and their ancient bearded white visitor. In 1746, a young Spanish family named Solis was seeking firewood in the nearly impenetrable jungle on a mountainside above the village of Palenque in Chiapas, Mexico. Their search led them several miles from home and produced an unanticipated and dramatic sight. Before them, shrouded in vines and dwarfed by towering Chico-Zapote trees, stood ancient buildings. Abandoned long ago to wild beasts and reptiles, their sudden appearance was startling. Who had built these ornate stone structures and when? No one knew.

Word of the discovery spread, and the Guatemalan government sent several scouting parties to investigate. One of these, ordered by the Spanish crown in 1786, was led by Don Antonio del Río, who hired seventy-nine Indians to literally hack their way through the jungle and into the ruins. With pick axes and shovels they laboriously cleared the site of all jungle growth, then proceeded to attack the ancient structures. Unfortunately, their methods were crude: they chopped through walls, knocked down closed entrances, scraped off elaborate stucco designs, and left gaping holes in temple floors.

Del Río was seeking information about a culture no living person had ever seen, and the sight overwhelmed him. In spite of his seeming callousness—judging by the devastation—his report glows with the beauty of workmanship in the ruins around him. The quality of life that produced such marvels, he concluded, must have been a higher civilization than his own.[3] Although no one could know it then, this ancient city would eventually provide penetrating insights to the Maya civilization and to ancient culture heroes.

Del Río's ruinous system of investigation was a far cry from today's sophisticated methods, but it began an archaeological movement that eventually probed the entire Western Hemisphere. In Mexico and North and South America, archaeologists would unearth structures that, in many instances, equal those of the Old World.

In succeeding searches, explorers uncovered towering buildings, statues, paintings, ceramics, and crafts paralleling in technique and esthetic quality those of Asia and Europe. Each discovery bore witness to the past grandeur of the lost cultures of the Americas, and each treasured object promised no end to the amount of material waiting to be found.

Even today, in the heart of Mexico City, the very foundations of Montezuma's ill-fated city have once more emerged. In a daring effort to reveal the past, several city blocks of structures built since the conquest—modern headstones to the buried ruins—have been removed. Where twin-temples to Tenochtitlan's principal gods once towered over the ancient city, archaeologists have unearthed in the ruins many relics hastily buried by the defeated Aztec nation. More important, knowledge of the Aztec people and the fascinating traditions that inspired them expands with each new find.

Documents Preserve Ancient Legends

In spite of the wealth of new discoveries, stone and adobe cannot convey the heart and mind of a culture; only the word can do that. To their advantage, modern scholars can now read much of what the Maya recorded on stone. Scholars have also rescued from obscure libraries Indian and Spanish documents written soon after the Conquest but hidden for centuries. Modern-day reemergence of this information is helping scholars to learn more about the ancient people and their mysterious visitor from across the sea. The origin of these documents is a story in itself.

In the wake of the conquest, while most colonists zealously sought to destroy the visible remains of Aztec life, a few others felt an urgency to gather knowledge of the ancient traditions. The Spaniards began their new capital directly over the old Aztec city of Tlatelolco (Tlah-teh-LOHL-coh), sister city to Tenochtitlán, and the last center to succumb. A new colonial monastery was erected upon Aztec ruins. One of its monks, a young scholar, named Fray Bernardino de Sahagún, would spend his lifetime seeking out the Aztec past.

Sahagún realized that if the Spaniards were to convert pagans to Christianity, they would first have to understand the religion and culture they were trying to erase. He interviewed ten or twelve of the principal Aztecs who experienced life before the conquest and had them record in pictures what they could recall. Then other Indians, trained to write the Latin alphabet, transcribed the pictures into writing.

The work of Sahagún moved slowly, and against much opposition from the church, for some officials felt that to preserve the ancient rites would encourage the Indians in them. He persisted, however, and his efforts resulted in the Florentine Codex, some twelve volumes of invaluable information about pre-Conquest times.[4]

In Yucatán another priest, Fray Diego de Landa, paralleled Sahagún's efforts. At first, anxious to purge the natives of their paganism, De Landa fanatically smashed hundreds of thousands of clay gods which the Indians reluctantly brought him from miles around. He then committed an act for which anthropologists and historians can never forgive him . . . he burned the precious books of the Maya, volumes which held valuable information, including, perhaps, insights to the ancient culture hero. Distraught at having to turn over the sacred manuscripts entrusted to them from many generations past, the Mayan priests cried; some even committed suicide.[5] Later, in an ironic twist of conscience and a classic example of poor timing, De Landa began to seek information about the aborigines.

Like Sahagún, De Landa sent interrogators to the natives to collect ancient customs, traditions, and beliefs. Only a portion of these writings can be found today, but that portion still provides startling insights into the old ways of the Mayas, as will be seen in following chapters.

Sahagún and De Landa were not the only ones to record surviving native traditions. While conquest fires smoldered in some areas, Spanish and Indian writers learned what they could from cultures still intact and from informants who had grown up under the native system before the Spanish invasion. One of these, Ixtlilxochitl (Eesh-tleel-SHOH-sheetl), was a 16th century prince and grandson of the last native king and ally of the Aztecs from the town of Texcoco. Another writer, Diego Durán, was a Dominican missionary who literally grew up in the ruins of Texcoco and wrote from personal experiences with pre-Conquest natives and from early Indian manuscripts and paintings.

King Phillip II of Spain had questionnaires sent all over New Spain to collect information on ancient native life. These, along with writings by numerous historians and natives close to Conquest times, provide great insights into native beliefs, including culture heroes.[6]

In North America, trappers, missionaries, and explorers gathered myths, legends and traditions of Indian tribes in an attempt to preserve the memory of disappearing races there. An excellent summary of early authors up to 1729, and the material they covered, is found in Huddleston's *Origins of the American Indians*. The exciting story and fascinating characters surrounding the deciphering of Maya glyphs, and the colorful players on the historic Maya scene, are delightfully presented in Michael Coe's *Breaking the Maya Code*.

Manuscripts, Myths, and Mysteries

As one might expect, many of these first writings include numerous references to the ancient bearded visitor. However, they so involve this culture hero with supernatural events that it is difficult to discern whether the tales are embellished history, legend, or mythology. These terms are used somewhat loosely, but generally *myth* is considered a sacred story, often dealing with creation at the dawn of time, intended to explain more graphically beliefs and rituals or forces of nature. Gods and heroes are usually the principal characters. Mortals are the basis for *legends*, which usually come from a specific period of history. Although generally assumed to be based in fact, they may not be, and verification is difficult. *Tales* are neither sacred nor historical, and often deal with fantasy and beloved nonsense. *Folklore* is the traditional body of myths, legends, and tales handed down orally by a people.

In searching through these writings, it is tempting to assign the supernatural tales to the realm of myth and the more credible ones to legend or history. To do so would likely be an oversimplification, for there is no myth, however farfetched, that does not have its roots in fact somewhere, and no history is totally devoid of mythical and subjective elements. In the following chapters no hard-line distinctions will be made between these terms.

Since myth and science are different approaches to truth, both contain elements that at one time seem to give satisfactory explanations. These explanations later may be superseded and perhaps even abandoned. Today, when reports of the miracles of Christianity, along with UFO intrigues, ESP, out-of-body experiences, near-death experiences, millennial prophecies, and other mystical phenomena exist beside the more rational and so-called "scientific fact," can the ancient Indians be denied a similar latitude?

Most of the manuscripts containing native lore were never published in their times, but ended up on remote shelves of seldom-used libraries. Some of them, like the Mexican works of Sahagún and Diego Durán, both priests, and Gómara, secretary to Cortez, lay hidden for hundreds of years. Not until the early nineteenth century did they come to light when political revolutions forced restricted libraries open, allowing modern-day scholars access to them. Other volumes, like Las Casas' *Apologética Historia*, went unpublished until the twentieth century.

Nineteenth-century scholars expended great amounts of time and money and even life to include all the newly found manuscripts in their monumental works on the antiquities of the native cultures. Hubert Howe Bancroft hired a committee to assist in his extensive volumes; William H. Prescott, despite blindness, produced lively and timely works on the conquests of Mexico and Peru; and Lord Kingsborough, lacking funds to pay for the printing of his oversized volumes, was sent to die in debtor's prison.

Out of these and other manuscripts have come phenomenal details of Indian life and thought before the changes brought by Europeans. These ancient messages are especially thrilling to students of pre-Columbian cultures for providing insights not previously available, or little understood. None, however, is so intriguing as the mystery which occurs quite regularly—the legend of a bearded white god. Bancroft, in publishing thirty-six volumes of Indian legends and lore in the 1880's, encountered this often-told legend, and, to his surprise, discovered that "Although bearing various names and appearing in different countries, the American culture-heroes all present the same general characteristics. They are all described as white, bearded men, generally clad in long robes; appearing suddenly and mysteriously upon the scene of their labors, they at once set about improving the people by instructing them in useful and ornamental arts, giving them laws, exhorting them to practice brotherly love and other virtues, and introducing a milder and better form of religion; having accomplished their mission, they disappear as mysteriously and unexpectedly as they came." And finally, he says, "They are apotheosized (deified) and held in reverence by a grateful posterity."[7]

The Legend Spreads

A dd to Bancroft the many other collections, and it is extraordinary that these legends of white gods existed in such remote areas and among so many unrelated native peoples of Alaska, Canada, the United States and Mexico, along the Central American bridge, and as far south as Chile. Even in the jungles of South America and the far-off islands of the Pacific, similar stories are told of a culture-hero-god who comes from some distant land to civilize and teach the tribes. Upon departing, he promises he will return. Among the more prominent heroes are:

Yehl, *Totem* and *Raven* along the Alaskan and British Columbia coast,
Tacoma of the Yakima Indians in Washington,
Michabo and *Ioskeha* of the Algonquians and Iroquois in the N.W.,
Montezuma, a savior-god of the Pueblos in the S.W. United States,
Pahana, a wandering white brother to the Hopi,
Chinigchinich in Southern California,
Quetzalcoatl in Tula and Cholula, Mexico,
Kukulcan and *Itzamná* of the Maya in Yucatan,
Votan in Chiapas, Mexico,
Wixepecocha in Oaxaca, Mexico,
Gukumatz of the Quiche in Guatemala,
Theobilahe in Nicaragua,
Bochica in Columbia,
Wako and *Shumé* in the upper Amazon,
Viracocha of the Inca in Peru, and
Tiki of the Polynesian Islands.[8]

(See map, page 30)

These are only a few of the many bringers of culture who appear in Indian legends. They share similar physical descriptions: fair complexions, beards, long robes and sandals. Unlike the natives who revere them, they also share similar missions to enlighten and lift their people. How many more native tribes had hero tales now lost can only be guessed, but considering the ambitious attempts by some early zealots to minimize or obliterate these legends, it is a wonder they exist at all.

From the number of culture-hero legends that survived in Spanish writings, it seems obvious that they thoroughly fascinated the early chroniclers. The church, however, discouraged their preservation, for it early recognized the strong hold these and other legends had on the native allegiance. In order to remove this threat to missionary efforts, the church leaders consequently attempted to suppress knowledge of Indian lore. This disregard for the Indian past tends to negate the idea held by some that Spanish chroniclers created the whole story. It would seem a rather inconsistent approach for the church to deliberately invent a myth and then later forbid its acceptance.

Like De Landa in Yucatan, Zumarraga (Soo-MAH-rah-gah), the infamous Bishop of Mexico, was so convinced that Indian writings were of the Devil, he had all codices (sacred books) of the Mexica burned. He then discouraged any further recording of ancient Indian traditions.[9] This action is not so surprising, when, at the same time, the reading of Christian scriptures by lay-members was also discouraged.[10] Kingsborough suggested that some Spanish historians attempted to obliterate the name of the Mexican hero, Quetzalcoatl, in probable compliance with the wishes of the Catholic clergy to erase the memory of their deity from among the natives. Evidence of obliteration of the name in some Yucatan records would tend to validate his claim.[11]

A most delightfully obvious attempt to erase the hold of Quetzalcoatl upon the Mexican mind is recorded in Book I of Sahagún. In his religious calling as a "mountain unto the Lord" Sahagún rises up more like a "volcano" when his irritation with the native beliefs verbally erupts: *"He* (Quetzalcoatl) *was a man!"* Sahagún demands of his readers. *"He was mortal, for he died; he is no god; he was not to be worshiped as a god."* Sahagún further makes it clear that the miracles of Quetzalcoatl were accomplished " . . . *only through the command of the devil;*" and further insists *". . . he must needs be accursed and abominated."* Disgusted with Indian anticipation that the Lord Quetzalcoatl would return, the learned priest summarily attempts to clear that up too: *"This is not true, it is a falsehood!"*[12] So much for Quetzalcoatl!

It would seem, however, that the ancient Quetzalcoatl was indifferent to Sahagún's pronouncements, for at a great festival held at the town of Maní in Yucatan, the natives insisted that on the last day of the feast this great, bearded leader of antiquity, who Sahagún had assured them was unquestionably dead, "descended from the sky and personally received their sacrifices, the penitences, and the offerings made in his honor."[13] So much for Sahagún!

Ironically, the centuries of suppression when these stories were kept from the public, preserved many of them from further change and destruction. However, their struggle for survival was not yet over. Shortly after their reemergence in the nineteenth century came a rash of skeptics to cast doubt upon their validity. While hesitantly admitting that the story was probably in existence before the European arrival, these writers maintained that the bearded white culture-hero myth was "distorted and manipulated" by the Spanish to facilitate the conquest of Mexico and Peru. They asserted that in Mexico, Cortez cast himself into the role of Quetzalcoatl in order to dramatize his part in the conquest. Less generous critics erroneously asserted that many years after the Spanish conquest, Indian Elders from Tlatelolco, rivals of Tenochtitlan, while helping Sahagún collect Indian lore, invented the story to expose the weakness and irrationality of Montezuma who allowed the destruction of the twin cities.

Considering Sahagún's vehement denunciation of the legend, and its existence among other writers of the time, it is difficult to accept Sahagún as the source of the legend. Cortez, Gómara, Durán, and others all record it independently of each other. Nicholson quotes Mendietta, who, in 1533, makes the first mention of Quetzalcoatl being a white man—long after the Conquest and any political need for Quetzalcoatl. Even the appendix to Sahagún's volumes expresses his conviction that the legend was an Aztec belief which he tried unsuccessfully to suppress.[14] Skeptics do not explain very well how, if Spaniards invented the myth, it was already visible in the art and ceremonies of Indian tradition long before the Conquest. They fail to mention that these compelling tales influenced many cultural areas all over the Americas through various epochs long before the Spanish nation itself emerged.

To validate such a claim against the myth, one would have to ignore the numerous other bearded white gods found on both continents and recorded without Spaniards and long after the conquest. By then the expected arrival of a bearded hero would no longer be to the conquerors' advantage. Many similar tales are told by the French and the English in New World areas to the North, remote from Spanish colonies.

The Enduring Legend

After researching the source of many of the white-god legends, Dr. Daniel G. Brinton, nineteenth-century writer on Indian history and traditions, concluded that: "There is irrefragable evidence that these myths and this ideal of the hero-god, were intimately and widely current in America long before anyone of its millions of inhabitants had ever seen a [fifteenth or sixteenth century] white man." In addition he affirms, "it is, I repeat, the fundamental myth in the religious lore of American Nations."[15]

An early German scholar, Paul Hermann, rejects any argument that the native white god was an invention of the European mind: ". . . the Light God Quetzalcoatl was a real person, . . . he was neither an invention of Spanish propaganda nor a legendary figment of Indian imagination . . . ."[16]

Another recognized authority on American Indians, Dr. Herbert J. Spinden, declared at an international conference of archaeologists in Paris in 1947 that not only was Quetzalcoatl of Indian origin, but that he was "the greatest figure in the ancient history of the New World, with a code of ethics and love for the sciences and the arts."[17]

Such conviction carries heavier weight when multiplied by that of other more recent scholars prominent in their field. One of these, Laurette Sejourné, an archaeologist who excavated much of the grandest of pre-conquest cities, Teotihuacan, with its impressive array of ancient symbols of Quetzalcoatl, agrees with Spinden, clearly assuring us that Quetzalcoatl was the central figure in Mesoamerican history.[18] Nigel Davies, who goes to great lengths to prove European manipulation and distortion of the legends in his *Voyages to the New World*, at least concedes that the deities themselves and the bearded heroes who personified them were "no mere latter-day invention."[19]

Aztec authority Dr. Henry B. Nicholson of the University of California at Los Angeles, after reviewing every possible source for the legend, concluded that although he felt the later seventeenth-century "missionary" versions of the story were largely "unreliable," still Quetzalcoatl was "a very human figure; perhaps the most remarkable figure in ancient American history, the first individual in Mexican history; a genuine historical figure."[20] David Carrasco, a scholar and writer about Quetzalcoatl, states that "These references strongly suggest that the belief in Quetzalcoatl's return was a pre-Columbian attitude and not, as some have suggested, invented by the Spaniards." He is emphatic that "It is not just a rumor started by others."[21] And finally, Michael Coe, prominent anthropologist and author, states that Quetzalcoatl is "the most famous figure in all Mexican history, a very real person." A decade later, he wasn't so sure, and revised the statement to say, "a possibly real person."[22]

In the face of evidence provided by these scholars and archaeological discoveries (including many early images on stone and native manuscripts of the feathered serpent god, so closely identified with the culture hero), it is difficult to assume any position other than that the legends of the bearded hero already were well established when the Spaniards first landed on Western shores. Not only in the Mexico, Peru, and North America of Conquest times were these legends significant, they appear fundamental to many of the Americas' past civilizations. So interwoven with native culture and devotion was the legend in its various forms that, according to Dr. Brinton, "On its recognition and interpretation depends the correct understanding of most of [the early American] mythology and religious life."[23] With such impressive scholarly support, it is not an exaggeration to state that no legend on these continents is so extensive and appears so consistently; no legend is more intriguing, and no legend has had a greater impact upon native life than that of the fair, bearded culture hero of the Americas.

Even with such assurance, the persistence of the legend today still is threatened. Some scholars, who are content to regard the traditions of bearded visitors as either fantastic myth or Spanish invention, feel that these stories have been sufficiently exploited, and should now be shelved alongside the myths of Rome and Greece as mere fables. They would suggest that the hero has had his day and will not be back. Hero myths, they seem to contend, have served their purpose and need no more attention.[24]

But even if the stories were merely mythological, there are, fortunately, those who see current value in these ancient beliefs. Among them is J. Alden Mason, esteemed writer and historian of the civilizations of ancient Peru. He believes that "In these days, when anthropologists are giving more credence than formerly to the probability of pre-Columbian trans-Pacific influence and voyages, these old American traditions of culture heroes might well be accorded new appraisals."[25] Mythologist, Mircea Eliade, contends that the effort to understand peoples other than ourselves "has the effect . . . of enriching the Western-consciousness." He suggests that Western dialogue with other cultures "widens its horizons...and helps Western man to better understand himself." If neglected, our culture "will be in danger of a decline into a sterilizing provincialism."[26] Joseph Campbell, seen in the television series, "The Power of Myth," affirms that "symbols of mythology . . . cannot be . . permanently suppressed."[27] With attitudes like these, the legend's chance of survival improves.

Today we live in an age that once again respects ancient lore and searches for meanings in its stirring messages. Modern archaeologists now give as much attention to analysis and meanings of these discoveries as they previously did to exploration.[28] In so doing, it might be well to reconsider more fully these stories held so dear by the people whose cultural remnants we are studying. Deeper insights into the workings of the ancient mind, and a re-analysis of the objects they left behind, will undoubtedly lead to a greater understanding of the significance of their folklore and, at the same time, might provide answers that have eluded us.

The following chapters will present these fascinating white, bearded culture heroes in numerous, and often startling, native legends. Their messages will be examined and attempts will be made to discover their origins. Solutions will be offered to help identify the elusive and mysterious visitor from across the sea reported so often and in such diverse locations. Many surprises await. The next chapter examines intriguing tales of the most famous and best documented of all native heroes, Quetzalcoatl.

3

MYSTERY MEN IN MEXICO

Much of the information concerning the mysterious, bearded visitor to the ancient Americas, comes from native legends. Although Columbus was mistaken for a white god, he recorded little of the native stories, so the first fully recorded legends of fair gods were those told by the Aztecs to Spaniards about Quetzalcoatl. For that reason, and because much of what is known about Quetzalcoatl will help in understanding other similar legends, it seems logical to start with him.

These colorful stories recount a distant time during the golden age of the splendid Toltec city of Tula when animals and men lived in peace and the land produced abundant harvest without cultivation. Cotton grew in all colors, and fruits of all kinds were available. The palaces of the great Toltec lord, Topiltzin Quetzalcoatl, appeared sumptuous with all manner of finery in their setting above the great river which passed through the city. The people of Tula shared in the great wealth, and out of esteem, dedicated an imposing temple to their priest-king, Quetzalcoatl, placing his statue on the top. Toltec legends declare that wherever Quetzalcoatl walked, he was surrounded by the melodies of elegant birds, "the likes of which have not been heard in the land since." And pleasant aromas filled the air of Tula from the abundant flowers and flowering trees in the area. [1]

Who was this legendary lord of Tula, bearded and saintly, who walked the land some five-hundred years before Columbus? Who was this revered king who built great cities and brought a higher way of life, then departed leaving a promise to some day return and reign? Where did he come from, and where did he go?

Early Spanish chroniclers found the diverse tales about Quetzalcoatl irresistible, and it is no wonder, for even modern-day readers would be lured by superheroes pitted against evil, violence, power struggles, seductive temptations, and sexual intrigues. In spite of attempts by the Catholic Church to suppress these lurid stories, many survived. From them we obtain valuable insights to the identity and origins of the most powerful culture hero in all the legends of Mesoamerica. In becoming acquainted with him we can more easily recognize similarities in other native culture heroes.

Besides the many tales which reveal him, additional help in locating him comes from a conspicuous symbol often identified with the bearded hero—a feathered serpent. This strange and wonderful combination of serpent and feathers pervades the art of ancient Mesoamerica just as the white, bearded figure it represents dominates the mythology. The human face of the esteemed god rarely appears on the countless statues dedicated to him, but his symbol, the combination of bird and serpent, often does. Wherever one finds the feathered serpent, there too, one often discovers Quetzalcoatl.

Quetzalcoatl—Legend in His Own Time and Beyond

L egends about Quetzalcoatl that appear throughout ancient Mexico always portray him as the grandest and most remarkable figure in all Middle American history. His fame today, however, may be due not so much to his position among the pantheon of Mexican gods as to the publicity later accorded him in his fateful role of dethroning the luckless Montezuma and preparing the way for the conquest.

The name Quetzalcoatl was apparently well known even to soldiers of Cortez's army, for an Italian account published in 1556 by one of the conquistadors clearly identifies the god of the Aztec city, Cholula, as "Quecadquaal."[2] (At that time no spelling was standardized, and writing any Indian name was pure phonetic guesswork.) In spite of all the purported attempts by the Catholic Church to suppress stories about the feathered serpent, they failed. More is written on Quetzalcoatl than perhaps on all the other Mexican gods. In fact, to discover no such figure in Mexican mythology when there are so many similar culture heroes everywhere else in the Americas would indeed be remarkable.

It is lamentable that in spite of various picturesque and compelling accounts on this enigmatic figure, some details are complex and conflicting, with many deleted. Church editing and suppression undoubtedly created some of the confusion, but much information was lost as the legends passed from Indian mind to Spanish pen. It has also been suggested, by Burland, that native memories about Quetzalcoatl, even thirty years after the conquest, were still so intermixed and holy that the informants refused (or feared) to speak of him more than necessary.[3] It is apparent from the first meeting of Spaniard and Indian that further mystery and controversy were added to the already strange legend of Quetzalcoatl.

A Super Hero

R etelling the story of Quetzalcoatl is a challenge. Where material on other culture heroes of the Americas is often scant and difficult to find, in the case of Mexico's hero, there is too much: there are countless letters, histories, journals, codices, commentaries, and pictorial accounts by Indians as well as Spaniards. Nicholson, who, for his Doctoral thesis, perused all known original Spanish sources on this complex subject, concluded: "The documentary material is a rich, fascinating, confused, contradictory corpus, a complex melange of intricately blended historical, legendary, and frankly mythological elements."[4] The many faces of Quetzalcoatl that emerge from his studies are apparent in Nicholson's quotation from Thompson that "Quetzalcoatl has been identified with everything under and including the sun."[5]

Descriptions from various Spanish writers portray Quetzalcoatl as tall, of fair complexion, and of majestic stature with a large forehead and large eyes. Spanish writers, Ixtlilxóchitl, Torquemada, Las Casas and Mendieta all say he was fair, wore a long tunic, and was bearded—at times black or red or yellow.[6] The tunic is white, and he wears a cloak decorated with crosses, sometimes red, sometimes black. In his hand he sometimes carries a staff and leaves behind a book.[7] (Other descriptions will be discussed in Chapter 15.) Various Spanish sources reveal that he was, at the same time, god and man, saint and sinner, subject to the earth, yet Lord of the Universe. He was canonized as the highest god of the land, but later ignored in favor of lesser gods. His virtues were wisdom, chastity, a temperate nature, and a love of peace. He despised theft, murder, human sacrifices, and war. He delighted in music and beautiful flowers.

His undisputed leadership over the Toltecs, forerunners of the Aztecs, led them to new heights of achievement, and they called him their patron of the arts, teacher of letters, crafts, and metallurgy. He educated his people in science, morality, agriculture, and in the rearing of the young. Legends say he introduced the life-giving staple maize and invented, or reorganized, the 365 year calendar—both of which date back thousands of years.[8]

To Mexican and Central American natives he was indeed a super-hero. Said to have been miraculously born of a virgin, with full knowledge and immediate use of all his faculties, it was he who created the earth and formed the first man upon it. He placed moisture in the skies and caused the water to fall upon the earth to give life to all things. He set up a religion and laws for the Toltec people to follow. Penance was required of the priests, and they in turn built round temples to him and brought sacrifices of fruits and flowers to the many images dedicated to him. Quetzalcoatl controlled the whirling winds (an act which inspired the circular nature of his temples), and he was considered the very source of life and light in the world.[9]

Such marvelous acts convincingly demonstrate that we are dealing with no ordinary figure. To make him even more complex, in Mexican history there is more than one figure who takes the name Quetzalcoatl. Followers of this impressive lord, in order to enhance their influence, borrowed his name and identified closely with him and his many attributes in much the same way as did the followers of the Pharaohs and Caesars of the Old World. What information remains of this royal line is not only at times fragmentary, but also confusing. The history of others who borrow the sacred name is at best hazy, and even Topiltzin borrows his title and characteristics from an even more ancient Quetzalcoatl. A Nahua document states, ". . . Quecalcoatle [sic] of Tula . . . is he who took the name of the first Quecalcoatle [sic]."[10] (That one will be pursued in the next chapter.) For now only the best-known of these Quetzalcoatls, Topiltzin (Toh-PEELT-seen), will be examined. He was a historic person about whom much is written, and the only one about whom extensive information is available.

Topiltzin Quetzalcoatl or His Priest
(Tula, Mexico)

Known as the Quetzalcoatl who left the land, and whose prophesied return was awaited by Montezuma some four-hundred years later, Topiltzin ruled over the mighty Toltec nation long before the emergence of the Aztecs in the thirteenth century. So sacred was the memory of Topiltzin-Quetzalcoatl that images of dead rulers were dressed in his costume.[11] Following his departure from the land, the later royal Aztec families proudly claimed descent from the great Toltec leader, and they felt responsible to maintain the throne until he returned to claim it. An extreme example of this devotion was the reigning Montezuma who explained to Cortez that he anticipated one day giving up his throne to Quetzalcoatl, or to his returning descendants.[12]

The historic leader of the Toltecs, Topiltzin was ruler and high priest of their magnificent capital, Tollan (Tula) in its golden age somewhere around the end of the 10th century A.D. The earliest Spanish writings offer varying details, but agree on certain basic particulars of his colorful story.

Most of the histories say that Topiltzin was born on the Aztec calendar year, Ce Acatl, "one reed." His earthly father, Mixcoatl (Meesh-KWAT), "cloud serpent" (a comet?), a demi-god, founded the Toltec empire somewhere to the north of the Valley of Mexico, but later met death at the hands of his own brothers. The mother of Topiltzin, according to some writings, was an earth fertility goddess named Chimalma who died giving him birth.

Subsequently, the young Topiltzin, whose name means "our son," or "our Lord," was reared by his grandparents. Little is known of his childhood, but some scholars believe he attended school at Xochicalco (So-shee-CAHL-co), south of today's Mexico City, where the cult of the feathered-serpent dominated. When the boy grew up he hunted down the uncles who had murdered his father, and killed them. Then, recovering his father's bones, he reinterred them on today's Cerro de la Estrella, "Hill of the Star," east of Mexico City, where he built a shrine to his earthly parent's honor.

Native poetry, alluding perhaps to the earlier Quetzalcoatl from whom Topiltzin borrows many characteristics, attributes to him a more celestial parentage:

> Oh precious stone, oh rich feather . . . thou wert made in the place where are the great God and Goddess which are above the heavens. . . Thy mother and thy father, celestial woman and celestial man, made and reared thee . . . Thou hast come to this world from afar, poor and weary . . . Our Lord Quetzalcoatl, who is the creator, has put into this dust a precious stone and a rich feather.[13]

Topiltzin eventually becomes leader of his people and leads them to Tollan (Tula), north west of Mexico City. (Whether he founds the city or merely moves his people into an already existing one is not clear.) There he establishes the worship of Quetzalcoatl, which he may have encountered while at Xochicalco. It is at this time that Topiltzin, like many leaders after him, takes upon himself the name of the previously revered and more ancient Quetzalcoatl so that he might benefit from already established traditions and esteem accorded that figure. Fortified with the magic name, legendary qualities, and his own birthright as earthly king, Topiltzin now becomes supreme high-priest of the cult and political leader of Tula.

Under his tutelage the newly founded kingdom of Tula grows and prospers greatly, for it is reported that he taught the people agriculture, metallurgy, stone cutting, and the art of government. The laws issued by Topiltzin-Quetzalcoatl are proclaimed, either by him or others appointed by him, from a nearby volcano from where it was reported his word "could be heard for some three hundred miles."[14] Life under his rule is superior to anything known before.

The Golden Age is Tarnished

Overburdened with the growing administrative responsibilities of a new city, Topiltzin puts the kingship into the hands of another, and keeps his role as great high priest. But things are going too well at Tula, and darkness begins to descend upon the regal son of Cloud-Serpent. One day an evil god, in the disguise of a beautiful young man, appears in the market place, naked, without a loin cloth. The princess of Tula, upon passing through the market and seeing his elegant manhood, grows ill from desire for him. A marriage is arranged, and soon this intruder, whose name was Tezcatlipoca (Tehz-caht-lee-POH-cah), gains the power necessary to become the arch rival of

Warriors of Quetzalcoatl (Tula)

Topiltzin Quetzalcoatl. The new prince proceeds to lead the people on a path of immorality and teaches them a total disregard for the laws of the high priest.

The battle between Quetzalcoatl and Tezcatlipoca is many faceted, but basically seems to be a conflict between old religious ideas and new ones, forces of good and evil. Fierce combat pits the blood-thirsty practice of human sacrifice and the worship of idols, which Quetzalcoatl opposes, against the offerings of flowers and fruits, which are too tame for the diabolical Tezcatlipoca.

After a series of humiliating upsets at the hands of Tezcatlilpoca, Topiltzin faces defeat. He has the palaces destroyed and buries his rich treasures of silver and gold and precious stones in the near-by mountains. Resolved to leave nothing of value behind, he transforms the flowering fruit trees into withered old trunks. Then he leaves Tula in the company of multicolored songbirds.

Seeing their beloved leader depart, the people come from the farms and villages to play flutes and lift his spirits. Tears pour down his cheeks as he turns back to see the destroyed city which once was so beautiful. His tears pierce the rocks which, believers point out, also bear the marks of his hands and feet where he rested. As a remembrance, he leaves behind his symbol, the cross.[15]

Topiltzin Quetzalcoatl and his followers now travel east, eventually working their way to the Gulf Coast. But, before reaching the sea, they stop for some time at Cholula, where Topiltzin reenacts the Tula situation by accepting the people's pleas for his leadership. There, over a period of twenty years, he reportedly colonizes and governs, as he had done in Tula.[16] At nearby Cacaxtla, a Toltec-Maya city, recently discovered remains of colorful murals depict a feathered priest, believed by scholars like Gillett Griffin to be a portrait of Topiltzin.[17]

Again his fame spreads, and temples are erected to him at Cholula on an even grander scale than at Tula. People come from all over to worship at the new shrines, and nobility arrive from as far away as Yucatan where, in later years, they too claim descent from this remarkable leader from Tollan.

The Serpent Sails Away

The story of Topiltzin Quetzalcoatl ends on the shores of the Gulf Coast somewhere near the mouth of a river called today Coatzacoalcos (Kwah-tsah-KWAHL-cohs) "hiding place of the serpent," just south of Veracruz. Before a gathering of his followers, and in a dramatic conclusion, Topiltzin Quetzalcoatl does one of two things: In one version of the tale he takes leave of his companions, sending them back to their city. With them he sends a prophetic message of a day when he would return with other white men, his brothers, from across the sea where the sun rises. They would be recognized by their beards like his, and together they would rule the lands.[18] In some variations of this version, only Quetzalcoatl promises to return. He then commands a raft of serpents to be constructed, after which he enters, sits upon it, and sets forth alone across the sea, promising again he will one day return.

The second version has him donning his regal attire and then setting himself on fire. Immediately his ashes become birds of beautiful plumage, and he descends into the dreaded underworld. Four days later, he is resurrected and the smoke from his cremated body rises into heaven to become Venus, the Morning Star, and he is enthroned as Lord of the house of dawn, the night habitation of the sun.[19] In some accounts the two versions combine and the ship is his funeral pyre.

These traditions were so imbedded in the Indian mind that, although Quetzalcoatl reportedly left the land some four hundred years before the coming of the Spaniards, the natives still anticipated the return of this remarkable character as late as the time of the Spanish historian Sahagún.

One naturally wonders, "Was Topiltzin Quetzalcoatl in fact a real, flesh-and-blood person, the first historic character of the land? Did he really lead a group of people on an upward path of accomplishment, or was he merely the invention of the Aztec or Toltec mind seeking personification for the higher attributes of life?"

In answer, some scholars like Bancroft, Coe, Carrasco, Nicholson, and Carroll believe he was a real person. This question will receive more attention in following chapters, but one scholar, Daniel Brinton, writing in the nineteenth century, maintained that the great achievements witnessed among such people as the Toltecs and Mayas came "by the influence of great men who cultivated within themselves a purer faith, lived it in their lives, preached it successfully to their fellows, and, at their death, still survived in the memory of their nation (as) unforgotten models of noble qualities." Among the great, he lists Quetzalcoatl.[20]

A Bearded Visitor in Yucatan

Where exactly Topiltzin Quetzalcoatl went on his raft ride and whether he arrived at his destination are not told specifically in the Toltec version of the story. But, other Indian legends provide other insights. Directly across the gulf waters to the east of Coatzacoalcos, another tale washes up on Yucatan shores, announcing the arrival to the Mayas of a visitor from the west.

In many ways, the shadows surrounding this visitor are even deeper than those cast by Quetzalcoatl. Bearded, and dressed in a long robe, the Mayan culture hero appears on the Yucatan coast about the same time as the mysterious disappearance of the Toltec-Cholula leader, Topiltzin Quetzalcoatl. The Mayas called him Kukulcan (Coo-cool-CAHN), which not surprisingly translates, "feathered serpent." Torquemada says, "The people of Yucatan venerated and reverenced this god, Quetzalcoatl, and called him Kukulcan, and said he arrived there from the west."[21]

Yucatan Indian sources say that the foreigner appeared with nineteen follow-ers, all wearing full beards, long robes and sandals.[22] Among the collectors of the tales, around 1573, was Fray Diego de Landa, Bishop of Yucatan (introduced in chapter 2). His attempt to recover the information lost in his earlier attack on the natives' religion in which he burned twenty-seven Maya codices and smashed some 5,000 idols will, sadly, never make up for what he destroyed.[23]

Still, what he did preserve shows that Kukulcan was an astronomer, priest, leg-islator, statesman, architect, conqueror and missionary for his religious views. Veneration and reverence came to him from devotees all over Yucatan, and from as far away as Mexico, for he ruled in peace, setting up laws and justice to which the people of his realm obviously responded. One of these laws was unique to Yucatecans, the practice of confession to the priest and a form of baptism, "zihil, " meaning "to be born again."[24]

After ten years with the Maya, Kukulcan suddenly, and with no explanation, left this orderly kingdom for his homeland in Mexico where he was known as Quetzalcoatl. This move from Yucatan to Mexico is supported by Montezuma's words to Cortez in an intriguing addition to the old tale. He says that after many years Quetzalcoatl did come back to get his people but they refused to accompa-ny him across the sea. So, the Aztec king related, "he departed in great annoyance, telling them he would send his sons to govern them . . . within the ancient laws and religion of their fathers."[25] Not all versions agree, and some would have Quetzalcoatl/Kukulcan begin his regal life in Yucatan and later sail up the coast north-west to Panuco. From there he treks across the land to Tula where he reigns as Lord for several years before moving on to Cholula and back to Yucatan. A complete review of conflicting legends surrounding this enigmatic figure can be found in Nicholson's Doctoral Thesis, *Topiltzin Quetzalcoatl of Tollan* (1957), and Carroll's, *A Search for Quetzalcoatl* (1994).

The Dark Side of Kukulcan

No recounting of the deeds of Quetzalcoatl, or Kukulcan, leaves one satisfied that the whole tale has been told. In the various accounts a perplexing inconsistency arises. Like the Toltec Quetzalcoatl, Kukulcan was a man of peace, a despiser of idols and human sacrifice. But a disquieting element disrupts the drama when another Mexican, also named Kukulcan, enters the Maya "provinces" teaching idolatry, which was unknown there before.[26]

What little is known of this intruder comes from an ancient Yucatecan manuscript of the town of Motul which reads, "Originally a god had been worshiped here who was the creator of all things, and who had his dwelling in heaven, but that a great prince named Kukulcan with a multitude of people had come from a foreign country, that he and his people were idolaters, and from that time the inhabitants of this land also began to practice idolatry, to perform bloody sacrificial rites, to burn copal, and the like."[27]

Nothing more is known about this prince, only his familiar name, Kukulcan, and the general area (Mexico) he came from. It is difficult to equate him with either the virtuous Quetzalcoatl or the peaceful Kukulcan because of the bizarre sacrificial ceremonies enacted in his name at the well of the magnificent city of Chichen Itzá. There it is reported that young virgins were thrown sixty-five feet down into murky waters to drown so that they might take messages to the gods of the underworld.

In the twentieth century, bones from those dark religious ceremonies have been dredged up from the thick mud at the bottom of the huge circular cavern, revealing that along with maidens, young men and children were also sacrificed.[28] Bas-relief carvings on gold plaques found in the well add to the mystery of the usually non-violent Quetzalcoatl/Kukulcan, for they portray not only the figure of an elaborate feathered serpent suspended in the air, but, stretched out below and with the heart removed—the unfortunate victim.

Part of the solution to the mystery lies in the confusing array of Kukulcans. Like the abundant harvest of Quetzalcoatls from Mexican soil, Kukulcans are also a persistent crop in the fields of Maya history. Disciples in both Tula and Yucatan borrowed freely the name of their high leader. On occasion these priests of the same name seem to have wandered into one another's territory. One account by the Spanish chronicler, Torquemada, tells that a leader of Tula left for the east in search of his enemy, Quetzalcoatl, and failing to find him, devastated the country where he went. Out of hatred this deceiver made himself god in order to blot out the memory of the great lord.[29] Because no precise time periods are given, it can only be speculated that some vassal of Tezcatlipoca, the god who usurped the place of Quetzalcoatl in Tula, or the evil lord himself, after several years, followed Quetzalcoatl to Yucatan, where he hoped to reenact the Tula defeat. If Tezcatlipoca was of Maya origin, as Coe suggests, then in arriving at Yucatan, this dreaded foreign visitor to the Toltecs may have been merely returning to his original home.[30]

After the departure of Kukulcan from Yucatan, no more is heard from him except that the people built great temples to his memory and performed rituals in his honor. Similarities to Toltec art appear not only in the architecture, but in pictorial symbols and in the many bearded figures carved in bas-relief on the stone monuments. In addition, the Toltec symbol of a plumed serpent, was carved on pillars and tem-

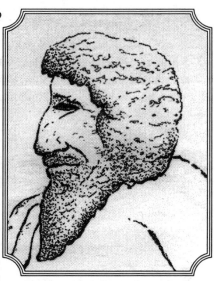

Bearded Face
(drawing from Chichen Itzá ball court)

ples all over Chichen Itzá and in a newer center, Mayapan. Anyone visiting those grand archaeological sites today is overwhelmed by the richness and number of the serpent deities visible everywhere. Before continuing the search for Quetzalcoatl, it might be well to examine the significance of this pervading symbol.

An Unlikely Metaphor

N o one knows when, in the distant past of Mexico and other parts of the Americas, the serpent acquired feathers and the magical power of flight, but this unlikely combination found nowhere today in nature (though Nicholson [1957: 84] says one rare snake grows a head feather), had a remote beginning and remained in use up through Conquest times. Even today the Mexican flag displays a serpent caught up in the talons of an eagle as it flies over Mexico City, once the island capital of the Aztecs. Thus, even the flag of a modern nation preserves an ancient riddle and salutes the haunting and mysterious visitor from across the sea.

In Mexico, as was observed in chapter I, feathered-serpent translates into "Quetzalcoatl," the name by which this highly revered god/man was known. The meaning behind that title is basic to comprehending the mission and place accorded the hero.

The *Quetzal* is one of the most beautiful birds living in the Western Hemisphere. Inhabiting the tops of trees in the highlands of Guatemala and

Chiapas, Mexico, it is seldom seen by humans and is difficult to maintain in captivity. Its iridescent emerald-green plumage, scarlet breast, and unusually long tail feathers are prized for their decorative qualities. In ancient times, the bird's feathers were worn only by royalty, and killing it was considered a crime.

The *Coatl* is the ever-present and ever-threatening serpent, usually the rattlesnake. Mexico, the land of the Mexica, could also be called the land of the serpent. This ominous reptile is not only abundant in nature, it appears in every art form all over Mesoamerica: picture writing, ceramic decoration, painted murals, and carvings on temple walls. Large stone monuments were erected to this fearsome, but highly regarded creature, and religious ceremonies were seldom complete without it. The Aztecs were even reported to have kept living rattlers in their great temples as sacred objects. Housed in earthen vessels, these creatures literally bore their writhing offspring on beds of feathers provided by their keepers.[31]

Although the serpent as a decorative and religious symbol is also found outside the Western Hemisphere, throughout Middle America the serpent motif is so common that depicting it must have engaged Indian artists full time. Literally thousands of serpent forms have been unearthed in a variety of coiled, spiralled, meandering or entwined positions. They also come in many shapes and sizes, and in a variety of materials: wood, basalt, jade, limestone, plaster, clay, and even gold. Some, although beautifully sculpted, are merely serpents, while others arrogantly display elaborate ornamentation with crowns of plumes or scales of feathers.

Forever bound to the earth, and inhabitant of the underground, the serpent (coatl) is considered by many primitive cultures to be supernatural. Its enviable ability to shed an old skin for a healthy new one gave the serpent, in native minds, an association with new life and rejuvenation which also connect the serpent symbol with another symbol for life and regeneration, the sun.[32]

Although the idea of worshipping a snake is repulsive to most people, the worship of birds is not. Birds are of a lofty spirit, free to ride the winds, pierce the clouds, and to soar heavenward toward the gods. Thus they have come to symbolize heaven and the reach for things of a higher nature. The Aztecs assigned a different bird to each of their thirteen heavens.[33] Wings give the birds the same mobility as that possessed by the gods. Birds were considered sacred messengers from heaven. Among many tribes they were seldom killed, and their songs were carefully studied for important omens from the world above.

As different as a soaring bird might seem from a coiled serpent, they do share certain characteristics: the long, flowing feathers of some birds can recall the similarly sinuous movements of a serpent. Both could resemble the winding path of water—another giver of life.[34] Lightning was believed to come from the "flashing eyes of a thunderbird as it pierces the clouds," and the bird's flapping wings caused the thunder. In addition, the quick striking movements of a serpent also represent lightning to the native mind. Tlaloc, the Toltec thunder god, held in his hand a serpent of gold to represent the lightning.[35]

Both bird and serpent are believed to have supernatural powers—those of the bird come from above; those of the serpent reside in the mysterious underworld. Serpents and birds both lay eggs, which are a universal symbol of fertility and birth. Both serpents and birds are associated in the Indian mind with other elements of fertility and new growth: water, rain, and vegetation.[36]

So what has all of this to do with a bearded visitor? In identifying with a feathered-serpent, the culture hero advantageously assumes all the amazing qualities attributed to both bird and serpent. The symbolic transformation of earthly scales into more lofty feathers allows the feathered-serpent of mythology to soar. Represented by this symbol, the bearded culture hero is also believed to ascend into heaven and, through a ritualistic process, generously offers his followers a similar privilege. In accepting Quetzalcoatl, the weary native hopes for a release from his limited, serpent-like, earthbound sphere, and expects to eventually become like serpent-bird and god, able to rise toward heaven.

The combined figure of serpent and bird together unites the saving elements of earth and sky. What at first seemed hardly compatible now becomes a fitting metaphor and symbol for the Mexican hero/god, Quetzalcoatl, whose chief mission, claims Séjourne, was to "lift his people out of their carnal element and make them divine."[37]

Prophesied Return

Like prophecies about Quetzalcoatl who leaves Mexico, native prophecies assure the people of Yucatan that Kukulcan will return: "The Quetzal shall come/The green bird shall come."[38] The old sages of Yucatan believed it and repeated this remarkable ancient prophecy recalled by one of their prophets, Chilam Balam, shortly before the arrival of the Spaniards, that a white, bearded race was to come from the east, from where the sun rises. He told them that the foreigners would rule the lands and that the Indians would pay tribute to them.[39]

The Spaniards, upon hearing the prophecy, according to the historian, Tozzer, carefully deleted any mention of the name Quetzalcoatl/Kukulcan, to make the prophecy appear to refer to the coming not of the native god, but of the conquerors. Tozzer insists that "an examination of the Maya text leads us to the conclusion that the prophecy was in reality speaking of the return of Quetzalcoatl and his white-robed priests."[40]

A Maya song from around the year 1450 demonstrates this strong expectation:

At the close of the thirteenth Age of the world,
While the cities of Itza and Tancah still flourish,

The sign of the Lord of the sky will appear,
The light of the dawn will illumine the land
And the cross will be seen by the nations of men.
A father to you, ye natives of Tancah;
Receive well the bearded guests who are coming,
Bringing the sign of the Lord from the daybreak,
Of the Lord of the Sky, so clement yet powerful.[41]

Whether Kukulcan returned to the Maya from his Mexican visit, is not told. The Indians of his time insist that he ascended into heaven with the gods and was awarded the major position in the Maya pantheon. Others insist he died in 1208 at the Puuc site of Uxmal, south of today's Mérida, where he was buried in the recently restored pyramid of the dwarf.[42]

Over the years, as the fame of Kukulcan spread, kings and rulers of Yucatan, (called Cocomes—"judges," or "hearers") and the noble families prided themselves on having descended from him. Since he was said to have been celibate, the claim to descendency possibly refers to ecclesiastic authority, or else reverts back to a descent from his priests or followers. Feasts were held in honor of Kukulcan even up to the conquest times, reassuring the faithful he would not forget them. As was seen in chapter 2, natives of Yucatan in Spanish times fully believed that he appeared to them from the sky during one of their great festivals, when, they said, he received their sacrifices in person.

One might ask the same question about Kukulcan that was asked about Quetzalcoatl: was he historic? The accounts by the Maya and Spanish historians are admittedly replete with confusion and contradictions, but there is enough similarity to assume that the two culture heroes are indeed the *same individual*. Many scholars argue that if Quetzalcoatl is flesh and blood, so also is Kukulcan.

Winding up his lengthy study of the original sources for the legend, Nicholson concludes that in viewing the events in the lives of Quetzalcoatl and Kukulcan, "it is likely there was only one outstanding figure and that lesser figures were amalgamated to him." Nicholson feels certain that "we are in the presence of a genuine historic tradition in the process of transformation into a myth."[43] Before leaving these two mysterious heroes, one more among a neighboring branch of the Mayas must be briefly considered.

Gukumatz of the Maya

To the south of Yucatan, in the highlands of Guatemala, the invading Spaniards discovered in 1524 another segment of the flourishing Maya civilization. Among this dense population they found evidence of early Toltec influence. Here, too, there were culture heroes, including a "marvelous king," whose story was carefully recorded by natives in a book, the *Popol*

Vuh, written shortly after the conquest. Like Quetzalcoatl and Kukulcan, the Guatemalan hero, Gukumatz "Feathered Serpent" is the creator of all things, knows all, visits heaven and hell, brings a higher culture to his people, and offers salvation.[44] Among the Quiche-Maya of Copan he is known as Nahua Quinak, a divine miracle-worker who comes in ancient times to bless and heal his people and teach them to live in peace. Promising to return, he leaves a book (now lost) with details of his life.[45]

The Guatemalan tribes maintained their loyalty to the great leader who, they said, established himself "in the east" by the sea, and later "at Chichen Itzá." The Lords of the highlands even made pilgrimages to the coast to honor him and to receive religious favors from him.[46] One wonders if this Guatemalan hero was Kukulcan en route to Chichen, or was he just another successor and usurper of titles who had once served in the great Lord's court.

So now there are Quetzalcoatl, Kukulcan, and Gukumatz, each with a title meaning "feathered serpent." This proliferation of Middle-American culture heroes makes it difficult to discern if it is the same hero in various legends or various heroes using the same legend. These varying legends, with their perplexing questions of identities, precise dating and geographical distributions, have puzzled scholars for centuries and will no doubt continue to do so. This all points out the difficulties involved with sorting out the details of a story told hundreds of years after the event.

And Still Another Feathered Serpent

Although it appears most likely that Quetzalcoatl, Kukulcan and Gukumatz are the same individual, there is no certainty on the matter. And, not only does the confusion of Mexican and Mayan culture heroes grow from Toltec times to the Spanish conquest, but it gets even more complicated from the Toltecs back. If, as Nicholson suggests, these characters were becoming myths, it is more likely they were turning back into the very myths from which they had borrowed so heavily—myths about a more ancient hero, an earlier visitor to the land.

This previous "feathered serpent" hero/god, who inspired the later historic Quetzalcoatl/Kululcan/Gukumatz, existed long *before* there was a Toltec nation. This more ancient deity, according to Spanish records, was even greater than the Toltec Topiltzin Quetzalcoatl, or the Mayan Kukulcan, who along with using the title "Feathered Serpent," also adopted many legends, attributes, and symbols from the more ancient, highly revered and long-remembered visitor. This act of borrowing and adopting identities set a pattern for later priests, or merely continued an already well-established tradition that had been in practice since remote times.

In the thick jungle of Indian legends, the exotic Mesoamerican deities—Quetzalcoatl/Kukulcan/Gukumatz, and the more ancient feathered-serpent god—

are so intertwined there is little hope for completely separating them, but the challenge to do so will always remain. One learns a great deal about ancient jungles by
studying existing ones. Similarly, by observing the historic Quetzalcoatl and his
contemporaries in Yucatan and Guatemala, and then, working backward from
them to the earlier deity/hero, it is possible to discover much about the even more
mysterious predecessor. Knowledge learned about his followers should help the
pursuit of this earlier visitor in the next chapter.

4

THE SERPENT SHEDS
AN ANCIENT SKIN

The search for a bearded white visitor to the ancient Americas has led to Topiltzin Quetzalcoatl of the Toltecs and Kukulcan and Gukumatz of the Maya, who, if accepted as real persons, allegedly lived around the ninth through the eleventh centuries, depending upon the source. Now they lead to still-earlier visitors from across the sea—serpents with more ancient feathers, or gods before the gods. Although history grows thin before the great lord, Topiltzin, there is no question that natives had for centuries before been giving homage to similar mysterious figures.

Evidence for the existence of a much earlier culture hero can be seen at Xochicalco (so-she-CAHL-coh), south of Mexico City, where an elaborate feathered serpent carved on the main temple wall indicates the cult of Quetzalcoatl was already ancient and strongly established when young Topiltzin reportedly began his schooling there. No doubt the ambitious student, Topiltzin, studied it and many other similar monuments carefully, along with their accompanying legends, before he advantageously assumed the name and attributes of the older deity, claiming already established authority and symbols of power useful in leading his people. Unfortunately, this practice of borrowing previous titles is quite common in the early Americas, and it makes historical research and identification extremely difficult.

This more mysterious and more ancient figure from whom Topiltzin took his name and strength was also called Quetzalcoatl—Ehécatl Quetzalcoatl (Eh-HEH-cahtl), "the eye of the serpent," or as Dr. Nicholson refers to him, the "old, creator-wind-god."[1] According to Spanish records, he was much greater than Topiltzin Quetzalcoatl. Known as the creator Quetzalcoatl, or "god of our flesh," this previous mystery man was the only member of the old native pantheon said to ever possess a human body—suggesting he was once a real person of high esteem. It was this "first," this most "ancient god" who seemingly had such a profound effect upon later cultures and the impressionable young Topiltzin.

A haunting shadow of a figure about whom very little is written, Ehécatl-Quetzalcoatl goes back, according to Nicholson, to classic times or even before, (near the beginning of the Christian era).[2] Any trail going back that far becomes thin with age, and following the faint tracks of Ehécatl-Quetzalcoatl would be similar to assigning the name "Washington" to all U.S. Presidents and then a thousand years later trying to determine just who was the original Washington and where he really slept.

Fortunately, some tantalizing clues still exist to help locate the ancient "wind god," but available information is, at best, sketchy. And as Carrasco observes, in his *Irony of Empire* (p. 8), "We must be careful not to drive the understood messages of one time period back into the obscurer puzzles of another." Advisedly, one treads lightly upon very old foundations.

Ancestors in Ships

A curious lead to discovering the foreign visitor or culture hero more ancient than Topiltzin or Kukulcan comes from the Aztec King, Montezuma, who told Cortez that his ancestors were not native to this land but were led here by a great being of fair complexion. This personage had later withdrawn to where the sun rises, after declaring that he or his descendents would return again.[3] The difficulty here is in determining whether he was referring to the tenth-century Topiltzin, or to the more ancient Quetzalcoatl, or to still some other being.

Sahagún records further details of this intriguing story from native sources: "Behold the story which the old people told. In the distant past, . . . which no one can still remember, . . . the ones who came (first), . . .came over the water in boats; in many divisions. And they drew along the coast, the coast to the north. . . . They arrived . . . at a place named Tamoanchan, which is to say, 'We seek our home.'"

But these "wise men" of the people, according to the record, did not remain long. "Once again they embarked and carried off the writings, the books, the paintings; they carried away all the crafts, the casting of metals." As the leader departed, his followers promised those who stayed, "He will come, he will come to do his duty, he will come to acknowledge you." The promised return would be at a time "When the world is become oppressed." Then, "they traveled to the east. They carried . . . the knowledge; they carried all."[4]

Who was this lord, the master of all, who was to return, and when did he arrive on American shores? No date is given, but the Aztecs claimed that following this early landing, their ancestors wandered for years before entering the valley of Mexico (sometime around 1200) and settling their deserted island, Tenochtitlán. To compound the confusion, the historians Torquemada and Bernal Díaz insisted that the great Aztec temple of Mexico was erected upon the foundations of a more ancient temple dating 1000 years before the Spanish arrival.[5] If correct, and that is debatable, such estimates would put the builders and their "fair leader into the sixth century—some seven hundred years before the emergence of the Aztecs and five-hundred before the Toltecs and Topiltzin.

Further intrigue comes from the Toltecs who referred to their ancestors as the ancient ones or "giants" who came to the American shores after crossing large islands and seas in seven ships. The Abbé Domenech, quoted in Bancroft, estimates this event to have occurred about the third century B.C.[6]

The same Toltec historians record the arrival in primitive times of an obscure person at the eastern coast on the river Panuco. He was tall, well formed, with broad forehead and large eyes. In addition to a fair complexion he had long black hair and a full beard. He wore a long white robe ornamented with flowers, or, in some accounts, crosses, and he carried a staff. Although his demeanor was austere, his character was good and gentle and chaste; he disapproved of violence. Because there were artists and scientists in his company, many writers considered this group a colony from some foreign land. Bancroft assumes it is Quetzalcoatl.[7]

Possible influence from this colony still exists in the circular temples and altars (often identified with the god Quetzalcoatl) at the ancient site of Tamuin (Tah-MWEEN) on the east coast. Further south at El Tajín (Tah-HEEN), the east coast's most imposing site, a serpent motif meanders up the seven-tiered pyramid of 365 niches. The name Tajín is said by natives to refer to the thunder and lightning, symbols of the local rain-wind god and his robed followers. Since Aztecs habitually borrowed much of their history from the Toltecs, it is possible that both Aztec and Toltec tales of great lords from across the sea originate from the same source and refer to the same personage.

Further clues to the wanderings of this mysterious lord may be found at Cholula, where Topiltzin Quetzalcoatl ruled for a time. In passing through Cholula, one of Cortez's captains recorded local legends from the town elders. They claimed that ancient Cholula was so holy that pilgrimages from all over the country brought worshippers to the hundreds of its pyramids and temples. Without question, the greatest pyramid of Cholula was a massive structure that still dominates the otherwise flat area, a mountain-like edifice that once had a temple with a statue inside dedicated to the patron god, Quetzalcoatl.[8]

Legends say that after Quetzalcoatl founded Cholula, a great earthquake destroyed his temple, which was later rebuilt to that great "god of the air."[9] Many scholars believe that since Cholula was already ancient when Topiltzin arrived, these events must refer to the Quetzalcoatl of more primitive times. Today the air around Cholula is filled with the sounds of bells from the great number of churches which have replaced each of the pyramids. However, the massive adobe shrine to Quetzalcoatl still looms high above the town, now topped by a Catholic cathedral and covering forty-five acres, making it larger in area, although less tall, than the largest pyramids of Egypt (See page 80).

Deep in the bowels of the massive structure, visitors are shown five previous buildings, the earliest of which pre-dates the Christian era. Painted murals on the inner walls, along with other art objects found there, indicate that the plumed serpent was represented here long before the time of Topiltzin.

Ancient Secrets

If Topiltzin left Cholula for Yucatan, as legends indicate, he may have followed the legendary trail of the older Ehécatl, since archaeological remains along with native tales of the prophet, Chilam Balam, strongly indicate his more ancient presence there as well. While this last and greatest of the Maya prophets before the conquest lay in a visionary trance, his utterances were recorded in Mayan hieroglyphs by a local priest. The old man repeated the prophecies given by the gods, who, he claimed, "perched above him on the lodge pole of his house."[10]

Later translated into the Maya tongue using the Latin script, a surprising one-fourth of the manuscripts contain prophesies of the return of Kukulcan, as well as the coming of bearded strangers from the east who would establish a new religion. This last prophecy, and its apparent fulfillment by the arrival of the Spaniards, provided Balam with immense credence among his supporters. Discovered in the town of Chumayel, the book of Chilam Balam reads, "Kukulcan shall come with the Itzá—[founders of Chichen Itzá], for the *second* time."[11] This statement strongly indicates that there was at least one earlier Kukulcan who, like his later counterpart, promised to return.

Another ancient manuscript preserved in the village of Motul reads similarly: "Originally a god had been worshiped here who was the creator of all things, and who had his dwelling in heaven." The manuscript is clear that this occurred *before* the arrival of Kukulcan/Topiltzin Quetzalcoatl. How long before, is not told. Another manuscript, from the Maya village of Quinacama, places this earlier personage in Yucatan about the year 780.[12] A still more ancient date is given by Ixtlilxochitl, who places the first Quetzalcoatl, or Kukulcan around 299.[13] The same reference calls him a "half-hero, half-divinity who came at the head of the first Nahuas (Toltec/Aztec) to America from across the sea."

As if each record is trying to outdistance the other, still another account says that the city of Kukulcan was first built "after the flood."[14] (What flood is not explained.) Other writers insist the hero existed before The Creation. Any attempt to answer these thorny problems of dating drives one to agree with de Landa, who exclaims that "These are secrets which God only knows."[15]

Records indicate that over the centuries numerous culture heroes invaded Yucatan and, like Topiltzin, each borrowed the name of a previously revered deity. Some scholars believe it the other way around, with the Maya influence and Toltec-like buildings invading distant Tula.[16] No wonder native historians disagreed about who arrived when or before or after whom. De Landa reports that his informants were also confused about the identities of the various visitors and the times of their arrivals.

Stones Leave Few Fingerprints

With scanty records, archaeological evidences for an earlier visitor are difficult to establish. In spite of countless symbols, there is no assurance that those associated with Topiltzin Quetzalcoatl belong as well to the older Ehécatl Quetzalcoatl, or that all serpent gods relate to either. Still, Topiltzin set up a remarkable display of feathered serpents carved in stone and an occasional round temple, to identify himself with the old "wind god," as did his successors. Thus it can be safely assumed that any pre-Toltec symbols closely identified with Topiltzin also represented, at least some of the time, the more ancient wind-deity, Ehécatl. With few clues to go on, the characteristics of the more recent Quetzalcoatl/Kukulcan must be followed to lead to the more ancient one.

Works of art seen at Chichen Itzá point to the existence of an ancient Maya hero. Under the great temple to Kukulcan, with its highly decorated plumed serpents, lies an earlier pyramid containing architectural and symbolic differences that may point to the older deity. Deep inside, supposedly hidden, the builders left a bejeweled jaguar throne to the sun-god and a circular stone box—both believed to be remotely identified with Ehécatl, the ancient "wind-god." On the facade of the smaller temple, directly under the floor of the larger one, artists created more of his symbols: a writhing snake and two jaguars usually associated with Venus, who is also identified with Ehécatl.[17] Nearby, the Temple of the Warriors displays bearded Toltec warriors carved on the columns of the outer room—were they priests of Topiltzin or Kukulcan? Those on the inner chamber are for the most part Mayans—were they priests of Ehécatl?

Near the Temple of Warriors, a Maya road leads to the famous cenote (seh-NOH-teh), or well of the Itzá, with its ruins of a small stone temple. Devotees of Kukulcan used this sacred water hole for various religious sacrifices, explained in chapter 3. Being a circular shrine, this may have served the more ancient wind/rain god, Ehécatl, as well.

It's Raining Chacs and Gods

Cross through the scrub jungle that divides "modern" Chichen from the "old" and one finds earlier Maya buildings that visibly pre-date the alleged Toltec invasion. Among them is a familiar symbol for Ehécatl, later borrowed by Quetzalcoatl—a circular temple. Probably used in ancient times as an astronomical observatory for divining the seasons, this circular shrine represented the hero/god who controlled the elements and especially the whirling winds that swept the land and brought life-giving rain. Spinden believes that Quetzalcoatl, to whom this round, snail-shaped (caracol) temple is dedicated, was ". . . the greatest figure in the ancient history of the New World, with a code of ethics and love for the sciences and the arts."[18]

Here, too, one finds numerous stone carvings of the Chacs, avatars of the rain-wind god. Chacs can be found literally all over Yucatan in the form of monstrous, stone-carved faces with long noses. At Kabah over one hundred of these abstract deities decorate one facade alone. Other sites, like Labná, Yaxchilán, and the "nunnery" of Uxmal show these figures with carved human faces emerging from the mouths of stone serpents. Could these be portraits of the elusive Ehécatl? In the Mayan pantheon there were no less than four wind gods and four rain gods.[19] And yet another of the great Maya heroes, Itzamná, also identifies with the rain gods.

A Stranger Called Itzamná

The Itzá, a people said to have preceded even the Maya into Yucatan, derive their name from Itzamná, a mysterious being who anciently founded the great city which bore his name. Later called "Zamná," his name literally means "lizard house," but it can also signify "he who receives the grace, or dew of heaven." He appears first in the Maya tradition as son of the chief deity, Hunab Ku, the great Lord of the Universe, and he arrives, as do most good American culture heroes, from the east, across the water.

The Maya credited this High priest and law-giver with inventing hieroglyphics, and they accepted him as their patron of the arts, science, and agriculture. He was also looked upon as a sort of creator-god, the god of healing and light—a sun god. Itzamná resembles closely the later Kukulcan, who may have borrowed attributes from him. According to Maya legend, Itzamná brought great gifts to the people, divided up the land among them and gave names to all the rivers, mountains and localities.

In Maya, "chan," or "can" means both serpent and sky. One of Itzamná's titles, "Lakin-Chan," means serpent of the east, and "lizard house" refers to his symbol, the double-headed serpent which arches over the sky. Seen in the arms of sculpted Maya rulers, it is a symbol of their authority and descent from this great lord who, natives claimed, disappeared without undergoing death.[20] At the time of the Conquest, Itzamná was the most important Maya god in Yucatan. The people prayed to him, and the Chacs identified with him for the growth of their corn. The city of Izamal became the site of a famous pilgrimage and received devoted visitors from all over Yucatan.

And Yet Another Stranger Called Votan

The traditions of Itzamná and followers from across the sea are very old and vague. Still, what exists closely parallels that of yet another intriguing culture hero of the Yucatan area, Votan, the most prominent deity of the Tzendal Indians, a branch of the Maya living in Chiapas and Tabasco. Written down by a native in the Tzendal tongue from a tradition supposedly recorded in a remote period by Votan himself, the unusual and often wildly speculative story came to Fray Francisco Nuñez de la Vega and was published in Rome in 1690.[21]

Said to be a man of great wisdom and culture, and born in a distant land, Votan was sent to the Americas from across the Eastern seas by "Divine Command." Finding the people in a barbarous state he laid out the foundations for civilization and the various languages. He built the great cities and gave the people civil laws, religious ceremonies, and the calendar. From his native home he brought (or was later followed by) disciples wearing long, flowing robes who assisted him in his work. An unpublished work by Fuentes, a Guatemalan historian, declares that Votan kept a record of the origin of the native races which he passed on to guardians who deposited them underground for safe keeping. He was one of four brothers who were originally the common ancestors of the southwestern branch of the Maya family. This story parallels somewhat the account given Sahagún that not all of the wise men left the shores, "But four remained of the old men, the wise men."[22]

Worshiped as a god, or mediator between man and god, his name means "heart," and he was called the "heart of the people," who honored him with sacrifices and continually blazing fires. The first to be identified with the serpent, he ruled for many years, during which time he made four journeys back across the sea to visit his native land. On one of these trips, the story says, he saw the ruins of an ancient tower men had built to "climb to the sky" in a time when the languages were confounded. The obvious parallel between this and the Tower of Babel did not escape early Spanish writers.[23] Votan's last journey was into the underworld where he found his way to the "root of heaven," by which he returns to his celestial home where he is deified.[24]

Close neighbors to the Tzendal and apparently influenced by them, the Zoques (SO-kehs) believed in a similar kindly culture-god who left the underworld only to reappear in some other part of the world where he continues imparting his divine favors. These two tribes and others nearby shared prophetic expectations that at some future time men from the east, "fair of hue and mighty in power, masters of lightning . . . would occupy the land."[25]

Professor J. G. Müller, quoted in Bancroft in the nineteenth century, completed an exhaustive review of the culture heroes of Yucatan and concluded there were only two, Quetzalcoatl (leader of the tenth-century Toltecs and conqueror of Yucatan), and Votan (whom Brinton places somewhere near or before the birth of Christ). The rest, then, if this line of thinking is accepted, were devoted followers who borrowed their traits from those two leaders, or were especially "deserving men" who were attributed those traits by local devotees. Müller believes Votan and

Quetzalcoatl/Kukulcan produced a great effect upon the people of Yucatan, and that "from them, whether heroes, priests, rulers, or warriors, Central America received the culture which their successors brought to such perfection."[26]

Kings Who Would Be Gods

A common characteristic of all the culture heroes seen thus far is that although they may once have been humans, they were later revered as gods. Rulers and would-be successors, like Topiltzin, eager to assume royal and priestly rights, commissioned powerful works of art to establish identity with these superhumans. Over the centuries these works reached obsessive proportions in thousands of complex monumental structures, carvings, statues, paintings and crafted objects, which proclaimed energetically, if not arrogantly, the rulers' rights of succession from these divine beings. This prodigious effort to establish inheritance speaks eloquently and unmistakably of the powerful impact of the culture heroes who appear in great mystery and then return to their obscure homelands, or retreat into the dark realms of the underworld from which they rise to the heavens to receive anticipated rights and glory of godhood. Small wonder subsequent rulers and priests wished to identify with them.

The Many Faces of a God

It would seem one could easily identify heroes in the art, but there are elaborate representations of each. (There is no limit to what native imagination can do with a serpent.) In addition, the Maya filled up every available space with bewildering figures, making it even harder to pick out the heroes.

Maya artists may picture Itzamná or Votan abstractly as a serpent with a cavernous mouth at each end of an elaborate ceremonial bar representing the powerful Maya "sky god" or "Celestial Dragon." Usually held horizontally against the breast in the arms of an ornately dressed individual, the bar is a symbol of the highest order of religion or authority.[27] But it doesn't stop there.

When depicted realistically, the hero's "human face" emerges from the gaping jaws of a "vision serpent" seen ascending like smoke. In *Blood of Kings*, Schele explains this as a royal ceremony where the ruler pierces a part of the body (usually the tongue or genitals) to draw royal blood which falls into a ceremonial bowl of copal. When lighted, the smoke brings forth a vision of the ancestor or god, thus validating the royal blood line and claim to power.[28] Francis Robiscek, a respected writer on the ancient Maya, suggests this depiction could possibly represent birth from the throat of the divine.[29] Thus, like the "Emperor's New Clothes," native subjects were conditioned to see the appearance of the well-known bearded ser-

The Hero Emerges from the Mouth of a Vision Serpent
(Yaxchilan Lintel 15. Courtesy Ian Graham)

pent rising from the smoking basket with the hero emerging to validate the new ruler.

Other representations of Itzamná, god of light and knowledge, might be the sun, represented by the macaw which can be seen flying past the sun daily. Or a jaguar, the sun in the underworld, whose spots represent stars of the night sky. Votan went into the underworld, and examples of the Maya sun god portrayed as a man, according to Norman Hammond, appear in the Maya area as early as 400 B.C.. Irene Nicholson, who writes on native mythology, asserts that "the more we study the Maya gods the more we find the kaleidoscopic central figure [be it Votan, Itzamná, Kukulcan, or Quetzalcoatl] proliferated in a multitude of patterns."[30]

In trying to identify the array of native deities, it is tempting to suggest that this lintel in Tikal with a feathered headdress is Kukulcan, and that one at Copan with a two-headed serpent sky bar in its arms, or a serpent in its mouth, is Itzamná. A Campeche vase depicting a ruler in the underworld might be Votan, and thus it seems easy to identify the bearded visitors. But although traditions clearly exist of a culture hero or heroes from across the sea who bring knowledge and religious practices, other tribal gods were already here, and archaeologists prefer to assign numerical titles to these complex figures, like god "A," god "B," and god "C." Perhaps, it is best to leave these gods "with titles that are without prejudice," as Spinden observed.

Whoever the visiting heroes (or hero) were, their impact upon the natives was enduring. In identifying closely with Kukulcan, Quetzalcoatl, Itzamná, Votan, or other heroes, the rulers expected to receive similar acclaim and to follow them into the underworld and into the heavens for an anticipated enthronement as gods and objects of veneration to their people. Some Maya lords even went so far as to wear masks of the heroes, thus assuming their attributes and proclaiming their own divinity while they were still alive.

Masks of the Gods

People in all ages have used masks to identify closer with the gods—whoever wears the mask becomes the god.[31] Not always worn, masks appear as rituals, ceremonies, paintings, statues, costumes and even buildings. It would aid in the quest for an ancient culture hero to know when native leaders began to establish identity with images of the powerful visitor from across the sea. Time has eroded much of the answer, but by looking beneath the surface of remaining works of art (the mask) clues which remain can be uncovered.

One among many dramatic examples of a king and city assuming the mask and divine characteristics of ancient hero figures is found at the Maya site of Palenque. Considered by many visitors to be the most beautiful of all Maya sites, instead of a gallery of gigantic and repetitious feathered serpents so prominent at Tula and Chichen Itza, the living priest or ruler was depicted inside the temples on door panels, roof combs, tombs and palace walls. Of course, the serpent is still present, but in a subtler and more refined role.

Probably abandoned long before the Spaniards, (and Cortez missed it by a mere twenty miles), Palenque remained hidden until 1746 when local villagers searching the rain forest for firewood discovered with amazement the growth-covered buildings. Over the next two centuries temples and limestone carvings emerged, but Palenque was slow to give up her greatest treasure, which remained sealed until half way through the twentieth century.

An Archaeological Oversight

Visitors to Palenque had frequently explored the impressive Temple of Inscriptions, but nobody envisioned the existence of an opulent tomb deeply imbedded inside this one. One U.S. archaeologist, Frans Blom, visited the temple in 1925 and, upon seeing a huge stone slab with rows of perforations, could not imagine what they were for.[32] This misjudgment proved one of the greatest oversights in archaeological history when in 1949, Alberto Ruz Lhuillier, a Mexican archaeologist with a grant from the Rockefeller Foundation, raised the floor slab and discovered a steep, limestone stairwell underneath, and a fifteen-ton carved limestone tablet seated over a sarcophagus at the bottom. Such a resplendent crypt had not been known outside of Egypt.

As word got out, people asked who the great lord was buried inside. Wild speculation called him a foreigner or a king from some other Mayan site, and at least one writer declared him a visiting astronaut from outer space. Others proclaimed that here lay the great Quetzalcoatl/Itzamná himself!

For years the world's leading Maya scholars joined forces in probing the expanding pieces of the Palenque puzzle. Then, at a remarkable series of conferences beginning in 1973 called the "Mesa Redonda," under the inspiration and leadership of a dynamic lady, Merle Greene Robertson, the collective findings of Mayanists confirmed that the remains were those of Palenque's greatest ruler, Lord Pacal, a Mayan name for the "shield" found on his name glyph. Ascending to the throne at age twelve and ruling for sixty-eight years until his death in 683, he built the pyramid during his reign.[33]

Over the large stone sarcophagus of the great lord rests a huge limestone slab carved with the likeness of the deceased ruler, depicted seated or falling backward. This is not an astronaut in his capsule ready to blast off into outer space; this is an earthling, highly esteemed, and unquestionably Maya. Crowded into the space surrounding the king are numerous complex symbols including a bizarre creature with a strange crown upon its head, and a large tree of life, or serpent tree above which is perched an extraordinary bird. Around the stuccoed wall are nine imposing figures.

This impressive display is a metaphor, or death mask of a king who brings together in one place all that the Maya considered sacred. These complex symbols contain evidence of the presence of the powerful culture heroes Quetzalcoatl, Kukulcan and Votan, who descend into the dreaded underworld to face the gods, then climb the sacred tree to escape (the hero twins of the *Popol Vuh* follow a similar course), and Itzamná, with his symbol of power and authority—the double-headed serpent bar of the day and the night sun. Based on what has been learned of the visitors from across the sea, there also are indications of power and ruler-

The Sarcophagus Cover—Pacal, Lord of Palenque
(Drawing by Merle Greene Robertson)

ship passed on from an ancient ancestor, or culture hero, and evidence of ultimate apotheosis and union with the divine.

Maya scholars today interpret the figure of the dead or dying king as falling into the gaping jaws of the Maya earth monster at the instant of death. His long and dangerous passage through the underworld, called by Merle Greene Robertson a "very complicated place," will not last forever, for the tomb and all of its intricate symbols represent a prayer for the king's eventual rebirth and emergence into a "state of eternal divinity."[34]

The huge tree, often described as a cross, is most likely the giant ceiba, common to this area. Symbolically growing at the center of the Maya world, the roots of this sacred tree extend into the underworld where they provide a means for the dead to climb upwards into the heavens. Pacal, in making the ascent, becomes to his people the Tree of Life personified, or as Schele & Friedel identify him, "the Tree of Life who raised the sky that arched over his entire realm."[35]

Halfway up the tree, is the now familiar symbol of power and authority, the double-headed serpent bar associated in the minds of many scholars with Itzamná. The serpents, if not feathered, are bearded. From the gaping jaws of one of them emerges a strange figure, God "K," recognized by a cigar protruding from his hair—smoke being a symbol of prayers and visionary experiences. A principle Maya deity, God "K," is identified with the serpent, bloodletting rites, royalty and mythological ancestors who may ultimately be the culture heroes. Like culture heroes, it is believed there were both a more ancient God "K" and a more recent one.[36]

J. Eric Thompson and other scholars have identified God "K" with the hundreds of Chacs, the "rain gods," and with Kukulcan. These endless deities can be seen wearing their long-nosed masks on temple ruins all over Yucatan. Other writers, including Robiscek, are certain that God "K" is the personification of the rain-sending Sky Monster believed to be the omnipotent Yucatec God Itzamná, who is closely related to the Chacs.

God "K" is also identified with another God, "B," who represents Kukulcan. At times God "B" is depicted wearing God "K" and even Quetzal feathers on his head.[37] Maya scholar Michael Coe believes God "K" is Tezcatlipoca, who in Toltec times was the enemy of Quetzalcoatl, and in Aztec times was a brother or even father to the feathered-serpent God.[38] Confusing as it may be, most Mayanists agree that the metamorphic God "K" is the protector of noble lineage and royal ancestry, the deity from whom Classic Maya rulers claim descent.[39]

Near the top of the tree are three stylized jade serpents emerging from bloodletting bowls used to legitimize Pacal's ancestry from the sacred family of the distant ancestor. At the top is perched a fabulous bird with the head of God "K" and serpent-like features in its feathers. The bird and serpent together are symbols of resurrection.

In Maya mythology, the sun is said to emerge from the underworld through the serpent's mouth, as if it were a cave. The ruler, by associating himself with the serpent, and bird, reassures his subjects, and probably himself too, that like the sun, he has risen, thus succeeding in his transformation from the underworld to final celestial deification and life eternal. Linda Schele, a colorful contributor to the Palenque puzzle, tells the story in *Blood of Kings*, (268-9). Pacal may have gone beyond the claim of merely descending from God "K" by actually donning his characteristics (wearing his mask). The identifying cigar/torch in his headdress indicates that in death he believes he has become that God. Of this impersonation, Schele continues that the Palencanos wanted to record that at death Pacal was a divine being, "a living incarnation of God "K," a living divinity on earth. Or as Merle Greene Robertson puts it, "The king dies, a god is born."[40] In carving the image of the king, as explained by Carrasco in his *The Irony Of Empire* (174), the Mayans were merely following an old, established tradition of legitimizing the throne. They claimed divine authority from an ancient source that assured new life or resurrection would follow death—the same message left elsewhere by visiting culture heroes.[41]

To make it even more sure, they continued the same tale nearby in three smaller temples with similar earth monsters, a cross of bejeweled serpents, double-headed serpent bars, the serpent bird, sky bands, sun symbols, and, oh, yes, God K. The two standing figures in the temples are thought to be the new ruler, Chan Bahlum, receiving the implements of rulership and lineal authority from his deceased father of the great tomb, who has now become a god.

An Impatient Royal Son

It was still not enough for Pacal's son to proclaim his authority in three elaborate temples, but high above his father's tomb on the piers of the Temple of the Inscriptions, stucco figures show the infant king-to-be in the arms of some royal attendant. Robertson suggests this is the boy's grandmother, for a small, stone duct, possibly representing the umbilical cord, runs from her down the stairs to the tomb of her son, the infant's father. Others have suggested the duct is a symbolic serpent, which would again indicate the boy's genealogy and connection to his forebears. Schele calls it the "founder of the lineage."

The child's royal and divine lineage through his father, grandmother, and other ancestors, dating back to A.D. 465, is further established in stucco portraiture surrounding his father's tomb. To assure his association with the serpent figures so often identified with culture heroes, his arms and legs grow serpent scales transforming him into the very body of a serpent. Even the face of the child is that of God K, the snake-footed god. Chan Bahlum has outdone his celebrated father, and the message is clear: he not only descends from some ancient serpent king, but announces that from childhood he was divine, the living incarnation of God "K." He is not to become a god, Robertson suggests, he *is* God![42]

Such monumental efforts provide a valuable insight to the importance given ancient culture heroes, for Schele believes all this elaborate art provides a means for these theocratic rulers to prove they are divine descendants of Kukulcan. Palenque thus becomes the masking of a city to convey a message of power and authority from a distant source, and it demonstrates the great lengths to which rulers of a new power will go to secure and validate their own dynasty.

With such obvious effort to relate to some ancient personage, where does one find this patron god of Palenque? Where does one find an authority figure with such divine powers of rulership and promise of new life that nearly all Maya rulers laid claim to kinship with him? One cannot be sure, but found deposited with Pacal in the tomb was a strange object —a tiny, bearded figure—an icon of a more ancient hero. It would seem that Pacal, like his "brother kings," also claimed descent from an earlier, undisputed bearded figure of great power, and the search for that source must continue.

A Familiar Figure

A llegedly dating back to the time of Christ or before, and possibly the source of Maya devotion, comes a familiar story and hero, Votan. Ancient legends claim that with his followers, centuries before the time of Pacal, Votan ascended the nearby Usumacinta, Mexico's largest river, and founded his capital at Palenque on one of its tributaries.

The original name of the city was probably not Palenque, which may come from the Spanish, palancada, "planked fortress," or as David Kelley suggests, a corruption of the name "Xbalanque," one of the twins found in the Mayan book, *Popol Vuh*.[43] Other scholars have suggested the name was Na-chan or Gho-chan, which in the sixteenth century Tzeltal vocabulary book translates "City of Serpents," or "Capital of the Snake People."

Natives believe that others of Votan's distant nation of "serpent people" came to Na-chan where they received the local daughters in marriage. Votan's great wisdom and power earned for him recognition as the supreme prince and legislator of what eventually became the center of a mighty kingdom and, according to the Tzendals, the reputed cradle of American civilization.

Like Quetzalcoatl, Votan records the origins of his people in a book in which he declares himself a serpent of the race of Chan. As late as from conquest times up to the 1880's some Yucatan Indians and Lacandones near Palenque still bore the name "Chan" or Serpent, and claimed descent from Votan. Robiscek, in *The Smoking Gods* (107) reports that several Yucatec pueblos today still honor the serpent-footed god K, their wind-god, in special celebrations.

Since Votan's fame survived the centuries, his power and control on the people would surely not have escaped the attention of the king now in the tomb, Pacal. And, apparently, they did not, for both journeyed down into the lower realms of the earth. Votan, as "son of the Serpent," enters that bizarre domain through a gaping snake hole, while Pacal's port of entry was through the jaws of the earth monster. Both terminate their descent at the "roots of the sky," the sacred ceiba tree whose roots and branches provide eventual ascent into the heavenly realm where both Pacal and Votan become gods. The implication is that Pacal, like the Toltec Topiltzin three centuries later, identified closely with an already established tradition that would add further to his credibility.

It is a historic tragedy that so little was preserved about Votan, his serpent origins, or verifying his American visit. Further difficulties lie in connecting Votan directly to the Maya lineal authority, although Müller believed he was either the original Quetzalcoatl, related to him, or a disciple. Others believe that as there were many Quetzalcoatls, there were also numerous Votans. Until these questions are answered, this puzzling and intricate story must remain in the realm of pure legend. Possibly here may be the missing key to the whole Maya mystery of the serpent hero for, according to Spinden, "The uniqueness of Maya art derives from the treatment of the serpent,"[44] and its connection to the ancient hero.

So at Palenque is ample evidence of what was going on all over Middle America, rulers seeking credibility by wearing the mask of an already-established authority. Aztec and Toltec nobility claim descent from Quetzalcoatl, Yucatecan royalty affirm kinship from Kukulcan, and other Mayans declare their divine and royal powers from Itzamná and Votan, who ultimately may be the source for the ubiquitous God "K" of royal lineage.

Such claims to divine authority through ancient traditions seem remote to us today, yet the Japanese, leaders in the modern world, still believe their emperor to be a living god whose successor must go through a long enthronement ritual in which he communes with his ancestor, the Sun Goddess, to receive a mystical transmission to his body. Like the Maya, the Japanese at the death of Emperor Hirohito in 1989, spent a fortune ($80 million) on the royal tomb. Such traditions date back 2600 years to a legendary "first emperor."[45]

During the Renaissance, Pope Julius II brought together all the greatest artists to make Rome, and especially his Sistine Chapel, a masterpiece of cultural and spiritual expression to himself, the high priest and ecclesiastical representative of Christ, a powerful and revered divinity from the past.

Similarly, as has been seen, Pacal and his sons engage artists to produce some of the finest Mayan art to connect them with not just one culture hero, but with all four: Votan, Itzamná, Kukulcan, and Quetzalcoatl. Even the very buildings at Palenque were adorned with elaborate stucco masks to proclaim royal power from an ancient source. Surely this site deserves the title "Cross-roads of Western Culture Heroes." But The Maya were not the only people to cloak their cities in masks of power. Before leaving Mesoamerica, two more important areas even more ancient than Palenque, must be considered: the valleys of Mexico and Oaxaca.

Where Men Became Gods

Palenque displayed refinement, Tula had culture, Tenochtitlan imposed imperialism, Chichen Itza evolved a theocracy, and Cholula was holy. They all claimed culture-heroes, but one place alone was grandiose enough to be called the "City of Quetzalcoatl." That city was ancient America's first, the Rome of the New World, Mexico's largest archaeological site—Teotihuacan, "The City where Men Became Gods." What few legends remain from this ancient city come from their successors, the Toltecs, as recorded in turn by their successors, the Aztecs. An Aztec poem recalls:

> Even though it was night,
> Even though it was not day,
> Even though there was no light,
> They gathered,
> The gods convened
> There in Teotihuacan.[46]

While the Mediterranean was still under rule by a Rome that was stagnating in prosperity and edging toward its fall, the North American Continent was dominated by a progressive Teotihuacan of an estimated two hundred thousand persons. Massive pyramids, myriad craft shops, schools, market places, and temples complete with courtyards and sumptuous living quarters, witness to the skill of Teotihuacan's architects and artisans. From all over Mexico, craftsmen came to create the sprawling metropolis under the direction of the highly inspired and organized leadership which pervaded most of Middle America, including the Maya, for the first six centuries after Christ.

Along the ascending three-mile axis to the city rise the towering pyramids of the Sun and the Moon, surrounded by prodigious works of architecture. At the heart of the great city, directly across the avenue from the ancient and current market place, lies a vast complex of severely horizontal edifices where the faithful worshiped before the pyramid of Quetzalcoatl.

Many centuries later, Aztecs, as much in awe of the place as the world is today, recalled that the "Lords of Teotihuacan" were wise men, knowers of occult things, possessors of the traditions." Although this situation existed long before the Aztec nation, oral traditions maintained that when the Teotihuacan Lords died, great pyramids were built above them.

Today, archaeologists are finding this statement to be true, for under the elaborate pyramid dedicated to Quetzalcoatl, covered with great stone depictions of feathered serpents, remains of some 200 individuals have been found. Buried at the construction of the temple around 200 AD, with a cache of impressive art objects of obsidian, shell, slate and wood, they are believed by archaeologist John B. Carlson to have been sacrificed as eternal guardians to the tomb of a "great charismatic leader" who was to be buried inside.[47] As of yet, the anticipated tomb has not been found, and who he might have been is still a mystery

A clue to the possible origin of this mysterious being opened up in 1971 when an unexpected stairway cut out of bedrock was discovered at the foot of the great pyramid of the sun, whose base is as large as the pyramids of Egypt. A three-hundred foot long tunnel led to a natural cave and chambers directly under the center of the massive pile of adobe. Scholars felt these might be the legendary "Chicomoztoc" (Chee-coh-MOHZ-tohk), or "seven caves," identified with the original seven groups from Toltec legends and the great lord from across the sea who brought them.

Some of Mexico's most impressive images of the plumed serpent existed at Teotihuacan four-hundred years before Palenque, and nearly a thousand years before they appeared at Tula or Chichen. Did the mysterious visitor make his first appearance at Teotihuacan? Was the worship of this powerful god taken into the Maya region early in the Christian era by Teotihuacan missionaries anxious to spread their beliefs, or was it brought back from Mayan traditions? At such a remote distance in time answers are difficult to find, but Teotihuacan's strong influence upon other areas is evidenced in the art at Mayan sites like Kaminaljuyu and Tikal in Guatemala. And images of Quetzalcoatl appear at the Mayan site of Acanceh, south of Merida, Yucatán, at the same time as Teotihuacan. How much the Teotihuacanos brought back from the Maya area is not known, but it is curious that the very title *Quetzalcoatl* includes the name of the very shy Quetzal bird found only in the Maya area and nowhere near the Valley of Mexico.

At the Teotihuacan temple huge, grotesquely fanged serpent heads protrude from a crown of feathers, while large-scaled bodies undulate up the stairs and along the sides of the temple. Accompanying them are other symbols identified with both Ehecatl-Quetzalcoatl, the ancient wind/rain-god, and Tlaloc, another rain god, who share the space and complicate any attempt to separate them. As in the Palenque tomb, these symbols of feathered serpent, shells and water can represent birth, death and new life. Since many of these once highly painted figures are aquatic in nature, they are thought to be of possible Caribbean origin. Perhaps

Feathered Serpent (Teotihuacan, c. 200 A.D.)

they suggest, as do the legends, that Quetzalcoatl, like the sweeping wind and rain, had originally come here from the sea.

Like the Maya cities, Teotihuacan may bear a close kinship to the ancient and mysterious Olmecs, another well-advanced coastal native culture that entered the Valley of Mexico perhaps as early as 1,000 BC. Although no legends exist from that period, they left numerous identifying objects at the mountain site of Chalcatzingo, and also at the cave of Juxtlahuaca where art historian Gillett Griffin discovered and identified a feathered serpent.[48] Another is seen on a stone at the Olmec site of La Venta. Powerful as the Olmecs were, it would be strange indeed if something of their culture did not leave its mark on Teotihuacan. And perhaps it did, at Cuicuilco (kwee-KWEEL-coh), an ancient ceremonial center immediately south of Mexico City which was destroyed by the volcano Xitle (SHEET-leh) around 200 B.C. Still imbedded in thick lava can be seen a large circular stone pyramid often identified with Quetzalcoatl and the ancient wind/rain-god. It is believed that refugees from Cuicuilco drifted over to Teotihuacan and helped build that city.

Sacked, burned and left in ruins around 600 A.D, the severe, naked buildings left today at Teotihuacan, according Laurette Sejourné, display enough colorful symbolism and decoration to indicate that the city was once draped in splendor, which gave visual reinforcement to the teachings of the Great Lord and Patron of Teotihuacan, Ehécatl Quetzalcoatl. Teotihuacan was the city where men became Gods, and, perhaps the first to immortalize in grand scale the haunting feathered-serpent god whose mission was to prepare the way. Again, in the words of Sejourné, Teotihuacan was where the great god of Mexico, Quetzalcoatl, "learned miraculously to fly."[49]

Bearded Men in Oaxaca

Around the time the Greeks were levelling the Acropolis in Athens to prepare for the building of their beautiful temple to Athena (4th C. B.C.), the Zapotecs of Mexico were clearing their land for a similar religious shrine on a rocky hill above the valley of Oaxaca. With tremendous effort, they hauled water, earth, and stone from the valley to create pyramids, temples, an "astronomical observatory," and other large stone structures.

But these were not the first monuments on the sacred mountain top. At the far corner of the sanctuary are stone slabs from a much earlier period. On each of the 130 slabs were carved strange, sometimes bearded, figures looking unlike the Indians of the area today. One can only conjecture who they were or what they represent—Coe believes they were ancient chiefs or kings slain by early rulers of Monte Alban. There is evidence that they, and a form of hieroglyphic writing, may have been brought here by the early Olmecs. Whether these bearded Olmec-like figures relate to our search or not, one thing is certain, Quetzalcoatl was there!

Fifteen centuries after the Olmecs, came Toltecs,who brought images of their revered god found at nearby Mitla (MEET-lah), the great Zapotec/Mixtec center, on fragmented wall paintings in no less than nine representations of Ehécatl-Quetzalcoatl. Still another local god in the form of a bird and serpent was depicted on a large emerald found locally.

The few native codex writings in existence from this area (i.e. Nuttall, Vienna, Bodley, Seldon Roll, Borgia) give a graphic record of bearded lords travelling over the water on some kind of raft. In the Nuttall pictures, under the rafts of one party, the familiar symbols for Quetzalcoatl are seen—the bird, the serpent, and the aquatic shell also seen at Teotihuacan. Other codices contain graphic examples of the feathered serpent.

These illustrations are a fusion of the then-current Toltec legends of Quetzalcoatl and the more ancient stories of Ehécatl-Quetzalcoatl. It would be inconsistent if later dynasties, called Mixtec (MEESH-tek), did not trace their descent directly back to this ancient figure also, and apparently, if the pictorial representations are correctly interpreted, they did. Carrasco points out that Ehécatl Quetzalcoatl is the figure from whom Mixtec rulers claim their descent.[50]

Again the question is asked, who might this ancient culture hero of the Oaxacan area be and when did he arrive? No one knows. But these are intriguing possibilities. The first Catholic padres recorded from native sources that in very remote times, about the time of the Apostolic missions in the Old World, there appeared in this area an old man with fair skin, long hair and bearded. He arrived from the south-west by sea, and preached to the natives of the town of Huatulco (Wah-TOOL-coh) in their own tongue. His life was strict, and he spent most of his nights in a kneeling position.

When many of the unbelieving natives received his word poorly, he disappeared as mysteriously as he had arrived. But, before departing he left a memento of his visit with them—a cross. The stranger admonished the people to keep the cross sacred, and assured them that one day they would be taught its significance.[51]

The natives called the foreigner Wixepecocha (Wee-sheh-peh-COH-chah), meaning "heart of the kingdom," and they erected a statue to him in the village of Magdalena near Tehuantepec. The statue could still be seen during conquest times. It depicted the old man seated before a kneeling woman in the attitude of confession. In addition to the white beard, Wixepecocha wore a long, hooded robe tied around the waist with a rope.

Many years following this remarkable visit, and long before the conquest, the Zapotecs made sacrifices to the statue, hoping to learn its secrets. Their priest reportedly received a message from the idol admonishing the people that soon white strangers from the east would appear and take away their freedom, leaving them powerless. The famous cross, a beautiful object left by the mysterious Wixepecocha, was reportedly still in position fifteen hundred years later. In 1587 an English Corsair, Thomas Cavendish, tried unsuccessfully to destroy it, according to Spanish records, and in 1613 a portion of the ancient cross was sent to Pope Paul V. Although the people of the Oaxacan area did not understand the cross's significance, they worshiped it as a divine object and called upon it to cure their infirmities.

Examples of the ancient use of a cross symbol among Oaxacans can still be seen today at Monte Alban in the form of great cruciform-shaped tombs carved out of living rock and decorated with "mosaics, frets and frescoes." Mexican scholar/artist Miguel Covarrubias believes "these point to the cult of Quetzalcoatl."[52]

Adios to Mexican Heroes

In these two chapters several Mexican/Mayan culture heroes have been observed who had a great influence upon their posterity. At the same time, they received great strength and influence from earlier heroes who, in turn, claimed their powers from still more ancient, mysterious white bearded foreigners. Great works of art were dedicated to these heroes and to the rulers who donned their masks in order to assume the heroes' characteristics, thus strengthening their own positions. Amazingly, this occurred among Indians who were, for the most part, beardless and bronzed. Presumably, none of them had previously seen a white person.

For now these tales about men and cities wearing masks of gods are but a few of the countless witnesses to the importance and wide-spread presence of the most powerful figures in all the mythology of Mexico and Central America. In pursuit of these elusive beings, we have looked at the Valley of Oaxaca, the Valley of Mexico, and the jungle habitation of the Maya. We will next probe the plains, jungles and mountain heights of the vast continent of South America for legends and myths about visiting culture heroes there.

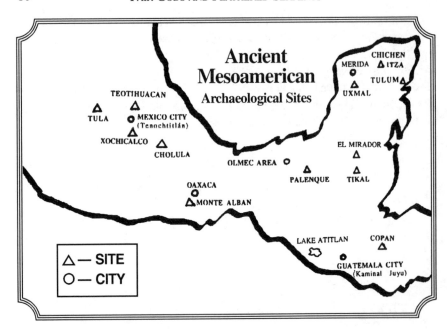

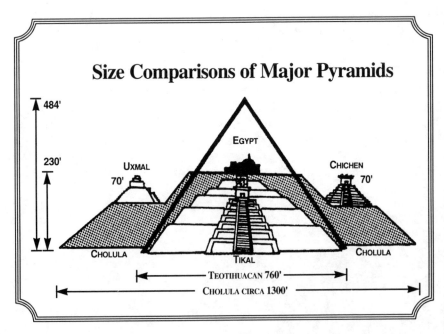

5

BEARDED VISITORS TO SOUTH AMERICA

From Columbus's first encounter with New World inhabitants, to later exposures by Cortez and the Conquistadores, intriguing legends came to light about the earlier arrival of a bearded white man long before them. We have observed that everywhere Europeans went in Mexico and Yucatan, puzzling questions arose about the origin and identity of this haunting figure. But, stories about the ancient visitor were not limited to those areas, for as we observed in chapter one, similar tales awaited Pizarro in Peru.

Few of the world's continents are as isolated as South America, and none invites less hope for influence from the outside. The interior is home to a sizeable variety of cultures, but extreme contrasts in the environment create some of the world's most difficult barriers for social contact. Vast, impenetrable rain forests cover much of the land. The backbone of the continent, the Andes, is one of the earth's major mountain chains, so high the air is rarified and snow caps never melt. Conversely, the western desert lands are so perpetually dry that in some areas rain never falls. All this makes any anticipated visit of a bearded foreigner and spreading the word of his appearance seem much less likely than in the North.

Still, despite these seeming obstacles, what begins as a trickle of hero tales in Nicaragua eventually becomes a river of legends: a favored "son" comes down to earth. Below Nicaragua, the growing stream picks up a mother goddess and a promised paradise. Worship of the sun, moon and morning star with a Lord of all creation add volume along the narrow straits of Darien. There the river of myths swells as the Cuna Indians of Panama recall a great personage who appeared following a devastating flood, then left his disciples behind to spread his teachings. The story rapidly builds momentum through the narrow mountain chain linking Panama with Columbia until it bursts forth fully-developed upon the sprawling continent of South America and floods its fascinating details into the far-flung reaches of that vast land.

In spite of the remoteness of South American peoples from one another and from the Northern Continent, they share similar legends, fragmentary or whole, with the now-familiar sequence of a "world creator" followed by the mysterious appearance of a gentle, bearded white teacher who leads his people into a golden age of civilization and then departs, leaving them with his promise to return. Several of these fascinating stories, in their basic details, bear curious similarities to the visitor in Mexico and Yucatan.

The large pre-conquest population of South America fits conveniently into three groups or races: the highly civilized people along the west coast and mountain ridges; those who survived in the jungle forests throughout the upper and central portions of the continent, and the less-advanced cultures of the east coast. Most of the surviving myths and traditions about foreign visitors come from the first two groups.

Among the South American peoples, the art of writing was either lost or not known, and what mythology has been preserved was chronicled by the early Spanish. Writing in the first decades after the conquest, they received their information orally from Indian amautas, "wise men" who had been chosen by the tribal leaders. These native informants were highly valued for their unique ability to accurately perpetuate the legend and history of the tribes in song and recitations from generation to generation.[1]

As in Mexico, Spanish writers in South America unfortunately often ignored valuable materials. Not highly educated in their own tongue, let alone any other, they often shunned legends as being trivial or "of the devil." In many cases, only details which paralleled their Christian doctrines were preserved.

Pursuit of the white bearded culture hero in South America is unaided, for the most part, by archaeology, which proved so useful in the Mexican search. Although it exists on a very impressive scale—even the familiar feathered-serpent and staff god of the Mexican/Mayan hero appear in some form—too often there are no recorded local legends to accompany the ancient pictorial representations. What was preserved comes mainly from surviving cultures who, unfortunately, knew little or nothing of their illustrious predecessors who created the enduring monuments.

Still, something of ancient history may have survived, for scholars are examining the well-preserved ancient South American textiles to discover a system of pictorial and hieroglyphic writing as they did on Maya pots. If their theory proves true, there is hope that some day decipherment will enrich the mythology.

Even before the Spaniards began the arduous struggle up the formidable Andes to meet the Inca, the grandest empire on the continent, nervous Indians spread the word of the coming of bearded white men in shining attire, armed with fire. As was observed in chapter one, they mistook the Spaniards for a returning ancient visitor who wore a long robe and who, like the Spaniards, was fair and bearded. As in Mexico, they accepted the stranger as a revered culture hero.[2]

In a strange parallel to the European reception in Mexico, the Inca (often spelled 'Inka') showed the Spaniards structures which they attributed to the efforts of a bearded white race they claimed had possessed the country long before the founding of the current Inca dynasty. They also recalled prophesies foretelling the coming from the direction of the sun of men of fair complexions and flowing beards who would someday conquer and rule their empire.[3]

Natives called the Spaniards by the name of the ancient hero and his followers, Viracocha. Although the meaning of the term was actually lost in antiquity, it has been argued by some to signify the foam of the sea which brought Viracocha, then took him away, and will one day return him.

Viracocha was adored as a loving god, the creator of all things and the bringer of the arts of civilization. When the Conquistadors took over the highly advanced empire, they greedily absorbed the rich results of Viracocha's cultural influence in the form of statues and wonderfully crafted objects of gold reportedly worth $200 million. These they took from the sacred temple of Viracocha and from the temples to the Sun God closely identified with him.

There are other compelling heroes closely identified with him. Other areas of South America will be examined. As in Mexico, since the visitor is occasionally elevated to the status of a deity, it is often difficult to separate the legends of the mysterious visitor/hero from myths of the native gods.

A Visitor to Columbia

In Columbia, below the narrow land bridge that connects the southern continent to the northern, live the Muyscas (MwEES-cahs), in highly organized villages ruled by powerful chiefs. Like the followers of Quetzalcoatl, these chiefs were said to be divinely chosen, and traced their dynastic line of authority far back to a great High Priest and law-giver, Bochica (Boh-CHEE-cah), who they claimed was the earthly manifestation of the Great Father. Another name for him, Sua (SOO-ah), means the "White One," a name natives gave the Europeans upon their arrival.[4]

Bochica appears in ancient times just as the people were disputing over who would be their king. Establishing a civil government among them, he also founds a new religion, sets up sacrifices, and regulates the ecclesiastical order of the priesthood. He also bestows the art of weaving, the cultivation of fruits, the building of houses, and the painting of textiles. He introduces the calendar and regulates the local festivals. Natives said he taught a form of writing, but that it was later lost.

Like Quetzalcoatl, his Toltec counterpart to the North, Bochica appears mysteriously from the east, according to native calculations, around the time of Christ. He is white and bearded, and wears a long, flowing robe. In his hands he carries a magic staff. Speaking in the various tribal dialects, he teaches the natives to follow just laws and to practice chastity, soberness, and a better way of life. So moved were the followers of this great man that he has to be protected from the pressing crowds that come to hear his words, and that worship him as a god.

The Muyscas claimed that Bochica lived among them for some 2,000 years. (Such dating is somewhat curious, considering they estimated he arrived sometime after the birth of Christ, but departed long before the Spanish in the 1500's).[5] Great pilgrimages were made to his sanctuary following his deification.

When at last he departs, it is in reverse direction from which he had come— toward the eastern coast from across the sea. Some recalled that he rose to the heavens after appointing a successor and recommending that he follow the paths of justice. It is recorded by Fray Pedro Simon, a Spanish chronicler, that as a remembrance of his visit and mission, Bochica left the symbols with which he was identified, "designs of crosses and serpents."[6]

More Visitors on the Continent

Alexander Humboldt, famous nineteenth-century naturalist and explorer, reports that in Venezuela among the numerous tribes of the Carib along the upper Orinoco river there existed a tradition of an ancient teacher called Amalivaca who was the "Father of Mankind." He arrives in a canoe at the time of the deluge. After regulating all things, he embarks for another shore.[7]

Patron of these Caribs was Tamu, the "Old Man of the Sky," a fair-complex-ioned man who came from the east in olden times. Tamu gives the people agri-culture and the arts, and an assurance that they could rely on him in the future. Before disappearing in the east, he leaves a promise that upon death he would meet their souls at the top of a sacred tree and accompany them safely to his celestial home.[8]

Other Orinoco tribes had a similar hero, Ackawaoi (Ah-KAH-wah-OH-wee), "the creator," whose son, Sigu, rules over the people and brings a golden age. Following death and resurrection, Ackawaoi disappears into the sky. It is highly possible that Carib legends of Tamu are variations of this same personage.[9]

To the inhabitants along the upper Amazon river there suddenly appeared a fully grown man, Wako, the creator of the earth, sun and moon. He stays with the people a year, giving them instructions on how to treat one another, and then ascends into the heavens where he resides today.[10]

Making a memorable appearance in the Brazilian and Paraguayan jungles was Shumé (Shoo-MEH), a white man wearing a thick beard, who crosses the ocean from the direction of the rising sun. He commands the elements, sometimes walk-ing upon the treacherous waters, and at other times parting them with his divine powers so that he can cross on dry land.

Ferocious animals crouch submissively before him, and he teaches the people agriculture. Not everyone reveres the great Shumé, however, and, because of per-secution from unbelievers, he finally leaves the land, crossing back over the ocean toward the east. His parting promise, that at some future time he would come back to them, is well remembered. He also prophesies that a race of men would some day come to organize and rule over them peacefully. Bancroft writes of Paye-Tome, another white "apostle," whose history is so similar to that of Shumé they are probably the same person.[11]

Brinton mentions the Tupis of Brazil, named after Tupa who alone survives "the flood." He is one of four brothers, and is described as "an old man of fair complexion." They make him their "highest divinity," believing he is the "maker of all things, ruler of the lightning and the storm, whose voice is the thunder, and who is the guardian of [their] nation." Tupa in Quechua means "Lord."[12]

At the far southern tip of the Andean chain where Charles Darwin made his well-publicized scientific explorations, native traditions closely resembled aspects of Christianity. Belief in a Supreme Being, Watauinewa (Wah-tah-wee-NEH-wah), "The Most Ancient One, the Powerful, The Most High." Inspired prayers to him began with the words, "My Father." He lives above the heavens and is the "giver and sustainer of life, protector of the social and moral code."[13] He also controls animals and food plants.

Magellan, in discovering the Straits, named the southern area Patagonia after some big-footed giant he reported seeing there. The man's tremendous size was probably exaggerated, and he is not a culture hero, but like the natives greeting Columbus, this "Big Foot" thought the Europeans had come from the sky.[14]

In the same region of Tierra del Fuego, the Ona, or Selk' nam believed in Temaukel, (Teh-MA-ooh-KEL) "The one above in the heaven," a Supreme Being, who sent the first man to bring civilization and culture to mankind. They make sacrifices to him, and the dead return to his presence. In addition, they practice a form of baptism, believe in resurrection, and insist that upon his death, their hero was transformed into a star. Especially remarkable was their belief that formerly a race of "bearded white men" inhabited the land.[15]

Knowledge of the traditions of the Patagonian pampas of Chile is as sparse as the land, but the Tehuelcho (Teh-WEL-cho) tribe mention several deities who may belong to the same family. There was a Supreme Being, a "good spirit," and a Son of the Sun named Ellal, who creates all men at a hill called "god's hill." He also brings them civilization and is considered lord of the dead.[16]

The Chileans recalled a "wonderful man" who came to their country wearing shoes, an Indian-style mantle, and a long beard. Although his name is not recorded, he performs many miracles, heals the sick, gives sight to the blind, causes the rains to come, and makes their crops grow. A worker of great marvels, he can kindle fire with his breath.[17]

In Peru the story is told of Thunupa (Too-NOO-pah), also spelled "Tonapa," who appears in ancient times on the altiplano, "high plane," with five disciples. Of large stature, he is blue-eyed and bearded, wears a long tunic, and has no head covering. Although he is a sober man who teaches peace and brotherhood, he is also capable of action: he can change the hills into valleys and valleys into hills. Once he curses a town so that a lake appears, drowning all the inhabitants. At his command water flows from the stones.

Travelling the land and working his miracles among the people, whom he calls his sons and daughters, he banishes their idols and practices of human sacrifice, teaching them to love one another. He institutes the practice of baptism, and carries a large wooden cross which men tried unsuccessfully to destroy. The cross was reportedly discovered and unearthed by Augustine Fathers in 1569; and was supposedly seen at the village of Carabuco on Lake Titicaca as late as 1897.[18]

Tunupa preaches in a loud voice from the top of a mountain. As he speaks, tears fill his eyes. His words against "drunkenness, polygamy and war" annoy some of the people, who drag him down from the high mountain to the seashore. There they place him in a boat and try to kill him, but his holy body is miraculously spared as it departs for the sea. The Inca Lord, Pachacuti (Pah-cha-CUH-tee), heard from other Inca sages that Thunupa passed by what is known today as the Panama strait into the other ocean. (This recalls the story of the white, bearded Wixepecocha in the Oaxacan area who comes up from the southwest area— chapter 4.) Although many of the details of Tunupa's story seem intertwined with those of the creator-god Viracocha, many early Inca monarchs praised and identified with Tunupa as a separate individual.

Colonizers From the Western Sea

Not all visitors to American shores arrive from the east. A number land along the western coast. Many of these are often credited with founding great civilizations and establishing cities or kingdoms. Mason suggests these kingdoms would be similar to Medieval kingdoms of Europe. In Peru their efforts range from small colonies to vast empires.[19]

Neither beards nor color of skin are mentioned in one startling account of a race of giants landing anciently on the Pacific coast south of the equator. As recorded by Cieza de Leon, a sixteenth-century Spanish soldier and explorer in Peru, these "naked strangers" had arrived in reed boats, large as ships, about the time of the Christian era. Their wanton acts of sodomy make them unlike any visitors yet encountered.[20] Inca Garcilaso de la Vega, son of an Inca princess, tells what may be the same tradition of giant men arriving by the sea, so tall that a normal person hardly reached their knees. His giants, unlike the previous ones, have long hair and are bearded. Juan de Velasco, another Spanish writer, claims that six or seven centuries following the above landing, another boat load of men disembarked upon the same Pacific shores where they dwelt until 980 A.D. They then travelled up into Quito where they established a rulership that lasted until they were ultimately overpowered by the Inca.[21]

Another mysterious landing of ancient seamen initiates one of the largest of the South American kingdoms before the Inca absorbed it along with so many others. This kingdom, called "Chimu," eventually stretched six hundred miles along the coast of northern Peru. Its capital city, Chan Chan, was once the largest pre-Columbian city on the whole continent.

Covering some ten square miles with adobe walls towering up to thirty feet, the city included royal enclosures, individual houses, broad streets running parallel and crossing at right angles, sophisticated reservoirs, mammoth pyramids, craft centers, extensive burial mounds, and great wealth. (One door discovered by the Spaniards was covered with silver worth half a million in today's currency.) In many ways, excluding its bleak setting, this grandiose city could be called the "Teotihuacan of South America."

The mysterious origins of Chan Chan occur sometime around 1200 with another culture hero, Taycanamo (Tay-cahn-AH-moh), who arrives on a raft of logs. He proclaims that he has been sent to govern this land by a great lord from across the sea. Within a year he learns the local language, builds a palace, and becomes the ruler of the valley—no small accomplishment, especially for a foreigner. Taycanamo's god-like nature and rulership qualities so impress his followers that subsequent kings, who already claimed to have been born with celestialized bodies, also insist that they have descended directly from the ancient colonizer.

Following Taycanamo, each successive monarch built a huge compound for his royal family, servants and armies. In all there were twelve kings, but only ten royal compounds have been identified. The still-impressive but desolate remains of the city today, called by its excavators, Michael Moseley and Carol Mackey, "the adobe monster," loom like a great canyon of dry and crumbling cliff-like adobe walls dominated by the ten bastions. Walking through these lifeless ruins, one feels a mixture of awe and despair: awe at such a prodigious effort, and despair that it could eventually succumb to this desolation.[22]

Beautifully carved clay figures, once painted, adorn the massive mud walls, but it is difficult to assign any specific meaning to these mythical representations. Feline figures, snakes, birds, and marine life, probably religious in nature, are prominent among the various symbols.

One palace, known as the Huaca del Dragon, "Sacred Shrine of the Dragon," is dominated by dragon or serpent-like monsters with heads at each end of their bodies. These figures also appear in the Moche culture which earlier inhabited the same valley. Like the similar Maya staff god, examined in chapter 4, these symbols, too, may represent divine authority and the day and nighttime sun. Following four intense years of unearthing its secrets, Mosley and Mackey said of Chan Chan, "This was a place of sacredness, wealth and military power centered upon

Bearded Moche vase
(Museum Anthropology,
Lima, Peru)

each celestial king in his turn, that he might, with the blessing of the gods, build, expand, and rule a desert empire."[23]

The kings of Chimu were not the first royalty in the area. Balboa, the Spanish explorer and discoverer of the Pacific, heard legends of a remote hero named Naymlap (NIME-lahp), a brave chieftain who founded a dynasty long before the Chimu. He arrives in style from the south, on a fleet of balsa rafts in company with his wife, a harem, and a large entourage of colorful officers, each with a specific service to be rendered to the great chief. His followers must have believed him divine, for they build a temple to him and place inside a statue of green stone to his memory. Upon his death he allegedly acquires wings and flies to the heavens. Years after, successive kings imagine themselves to be the incarnation of their great leader and, like him, leave a reputation for immortality.[24]

A Congregation of Gods

It would appear that the visitor from across the sea was received in a number of locations. It is unfortunate that so little information remains, but in Peru, the local myths have been recorded with more detail than elsewhere in South America. At the same time, they contain more confusion. Here culture heroes proliferate and seem to have invented the very process of cloning as they assume one another's characteristics and even, on occasion, time periods. This is not, of course, uncommon to the vast pantheon of American culture heroes taken as a whole, but in such a confined area as Peru, it compounds greatly any attempt to separate and identify them. In collecting the sparse threads of information about each hero, however, it is hoped enough material can be obtained to weave a clearer picture.

Gomara reports that "at the beginning of the world there came from the north a man called Con . . . ." Lacking human form, this deity becomes the "child of the sun" and fills the land with men and women whom he created. He also provides them with maize and fruits. He creates the sky, the sun, the moon, the earth, and the animals.[25]

Next on the scene comes an even more powerful god, Pachacamac (Pah-chah-CAH-mahk), the Supreme Being, whose name means literally, "earth maker" or "maker and giver of life, and sustainer of the universe." He was also called "the teacher of the universe." He sacrifices the body of a divinity into food plants for his people. As a Son of the Sun and the Moon, he is a brother to Con, whom he drives from the land. Con, irritated at this defeat, takes the life-giving rains with him and leaves the land parched.[26] Pachacamac has also been identified by some writers with Viracocha, although others disagree strongly. His great gift to the people is life, after which he gives them everything they possess and teaches them how to live. Out of their deep respect for all he did, they make him chief over all their gods.

The worship of Pachacamac was very old in Peru, extending back long before the emergence of the Inca as a power. Many remains of temples along the Peruvian coast have a local tradition as shrines to Pachacamac, but by far the most prestigious of all, and according to Garcilaso de la Vega, the only real pre-Inca shrine to Pachacamac was the great fortress-like temple built of stones and adobe on a hill overlooking the sea just south of present-day Lima. A powerful priesthood grew up around the cult to this Supreme Being, which included rituals, sacrifices, and a much celebrated oracle. So renowned was the oracle that the town of Pachacamac became a large center of pilgrimage, which Prescott notes resembled the "oracles of Delphi of the Greeks, Mecca of the 'Mahometans,' or Cholula of the Anahuacs."[27]

These religious treks from remote areas continued from before the time of the Inca up to the time of the Conquest when Pizarro's brother, Hernando, forced his way into the most sacred shrine of the oracle and, angry at not finding the reported gold, demolished their sacred idol. At that very moment, and in a strange quirk of timing, a great earthquake hit the area convincing the natives of Pachacamac's anger. In defiance, the Spaniards set up a cross on the temple and proceeded to sack the area of all remaining gold and silver. (It was rumored that the Priests, having received word of the coming plunderers, had already carted off four hundred loads of gold.)

Culture heroes do not die easily, or sometimes not at all, and long after the conquest people of the fading city of Pachacamac still revered their ancient divinity. Today, as a result of Spanish destruction, little remains of that great shrine but a vast expanse of crumbled ruins, leaving any visitor with a feeling of melancholy for the lost magnificence one can only imagine was once there.

City in the Clouds

B y now, the sheer number of stories about visitors and heroes in South America leaves one bewildered wondering where they all come from, and asking why the haunting similarities? Could they have originated from a common source at a very early time, and what might that source be? The search for answers to these questions requires travel even farther back in time to seek evidence for early sources of the visiting culture hero.

In Mexico the hero was a builder of cities, and examining those remains gave insight to the nature of the builder. One of the the the most mystifying of all cities connected with a South American visitor or culture hero is Tiwanacu (Tee-wah-NAH-coo), also spelled Tiahuanaco, sequestered in the Andes at a staggering height of nearly thirteen-thousand feet, and forty miles from today's La Paz, Bolivia. Not far from the colossal wind-swept ruins lies Lake Titicaca, the highest navigable lake in the world, whose shores are said to have once lapped the very edge of the desolation where Tiwanacu now stands. Perhaps no pre-Columbian city has inspired more fantastic speculations and, at the same time, revealed fewer answers than this one.

So little grows on the altiplano "high plane" to sustain life: only corn, potatoes, a few roots and the hardy cameloid family of llamas and alpacas. Yet the monumentality of the remaining ruins, with chiseled stone blocks weighing up to a hundred tons, and the intricate carvings and sophisticated crafts from the area, witness that a tremendous, highly skilled and hungry work force was there.

Nothing is known precisely of the creators of this astonishingly advanced civilization—not their names, not their language, not even their exact place in history. One tradition insists that the real Tiwanacu is actually a subterranean city far greater than the one visible today. Archaeologists have, in fact, partially unearthed several previous cities beneath this one.

Wild speculation has the earliest ruins here as the cradle of American culture anywhere from 10,000 to 200,000 years ago.[28] Rarified air, and the assumption that at that height it would be humanly impossible to create such prodigious monuments, has suggested to some people that the structures were built back before the recent geological era (no matter that natives in near-by La Paz today perform equally demanding tasks). Many claim that earth forces in ancient times actually lifted the plateau up to its present height from several thousand feet lower. Less romantic estimates would place Tiwanacu at 250 B.C., with its peak around A.D. 400-700.

But "less romantic" is not usually the case at this perplexing site. Natives recall ancestral stories that the huge structures still visible appeared overnight in ancient times. One of the first Spaniards to the area, a Jesuit, wrote that "the great stones one sees at Tiwanacu were carried through the air to the sound of a trumpet." These two extravagant explanations, if believed, would conveniently eliminate the problem of getting a work force and of feeding it. The Incas were convinced the ruins had been erected by giants who were later turned into huge monoliths by Viracocha, whom the giants had displeased. As proof, one is referred to the great carved stone figures still standing visibly in the area, or others removed to La Paz.

Archaeologists today have at last discovered quarries some sixty to one hundred miles away from which the ancient builders chiseled their stones. It is still somewhat of a mystery and a matter for speculation how huge slabs twenty-six feet long and weighing up to one hundred tons were transported so far.[29]

The first Spaniards to the area proposed many questions about Tiwanacu, but because the Inca had obliterated much of the remembered history, most questions will probably never be fully answered. Although the ruins were still majestic when the first Europeans saw them, since the nineteenth century thousands of the finely cut stones and statues have been removed, dynamited and wantonly ruined for the construction of roads, bridges, railroads, churches, houses and even for tourist souvenirs. It is fortunate that much of the site still remains to be excavated.

For all of its devastation, Tiwanacu is still the city of culture heroes. Much of its fascination, aside from displaying the most spectacular ruins on the continent, some of which were apparently left unfinished when the site was mysteriously and abruptly abandoned long ago, is the distinctive art. That, and mere fragments of mythology about its origins, defy us to extract its hidden story.

Earliest references to Tiwanacu by Spanish chroniclers speak of the unexplained existence of two separate races of white people—some with beards—in this area long before Spanish times. The first appeared in remote times on an island of Lake Titicaca just fourteen miles from Tiwanacu. They were later killed by a group of native Lords who left stories, but no traces of the whites having been there.[30]

The second group of white people came to the plateau long before the Inca. They set up an unusual style of architecture which one can observe in the stone blocks held together with copper rivets. Bearded statues at the ruins are said by local natives to represent these ancient foreign builders.

Carved stone heads of rulers or Gods tenoned into the sides of the buildings proudly proclaim that this city once boasted an illustrious leadership. None, however, was so pretentious as the great Creator and Father of mankind, Viracocha, who made Tiwanacu his principal abode while he created the sun and moon and stars at the beginning of time.

Tiwanacu is loaded with mysteries, but the most remarkable and puzzling object there, and perhaps in the world, is a huge monolithic slab ten feet high weighing some ten tons, called the "Gateway of the Sun." Directly above its doorway is a broad band of carved figures in low relief. On each side of the band are three rows of winged figures clutching staffs and wearing crowns. They are either kneeling or running toward the central figure, a curious divinity who wears a similar radiating headdress and carries a staff in each hand.

The meaning of the figures is lost, but limited experience with the somewhat similar native mind and pictorial symbols of Mexico, supported by similar hero myths, suggests that this monument somehow depicts the origins of the people.

The central figure is apparently a deity and may be the Supreme Being, the Creator-God, an early Sun-God, or a colonizer of the people of the plateau. Some writers have, of course, suggested that this is the mysterious Viracocha himself.

The strange attendants to the Deity might be lesser deities, his priests, or the children of his creation. Posnansky, who studied the ruins for 50 years, suggested they were calendrical figures representing the months running towards the sun.[31] It is unlikely they are ancestors, since the culture heroes are creators of people, or the first of their line, but it is highly possible they may be descendants of the divine lineage.

Staffs and figures upon which the Deity stands appear to be Condors with serpentine bodies—recalling again the bird-serpents or two-headed sky gods, similar to authority symbols identified with Itzamná of the Maya. In Peruvian mythology, the Condor god carries the sun across the sky. One tiny figure blows a trumpet and, like the Palenque ruler, Chan Bahlum, has a serpent foot representing, perhaps, the lineage from a serpent-god.

Still Earlier Symbols

A similar "staff god," and possibly the inspiration for this one at Tiwanacu, can be found at Chavín, another elaborate and perplexing temple site near the northern Peruvian coast. Here may be the earliest examples of South American culture heroes, and of the white bearded elusive visitor, for Chavín dates back before 1,000 B.C., and bears striking similarities to the Olmec culture of Mexico of approximately the same date. Like the Olmec in Mexico, Chavín may be the "Mother Culture" of South America, since its art appears in most later cultures.

Here, in underground stone galleries constructed in the form of a cross, what must have been important Chavín gods decorate the walls. Hair and eyebrows on the figures are made up of writhing serpents, attesting to the importance of that figure in the Chavín mind. Hidden deep in the deserted chambers where few would ever see it stands the Raimonde stone, a great monumental shaft with "serpent hair" and serpent belt. Serpents also form the staffs which the grotesque figure holds. The elaborate headdress is made up of more serpents whose tongues connect with one another, as if communicating mouth to mouth. Like Maya serpents, this may be an effective depiction of lineal descent.

Along with the serpent, other figures depicted at Chavín, the Jaguar, the Caiman, and the Harpy Eagle or Condor, represent the most powerful of South American creatures. For this reason Donald Lathrop, who has extensively studied Chavín, suggests one gets the idea that the message has something to do with power and authority from some mythological deity.[32]

The people of Chavín must have had a strong religious fervor, for archaeology indicates their beliefs, expressed in art, were spread in a great missionary effort all over Peru. Whatever the message, its profound influence is evident in the art of all the Central Andean people after them.[33]

Is it possible that at Chavín we are looking at the very beginnings of the feathered-serpent cult and the graphic representations of the culture hero, from whom descent and authority are deemed so important all over the Americas? Whoever the central figure of Chavín de Huantar is, he is powerful, and he is pervasive. He is reflected in every major deity of the central Andes from Chavín times through the Inca period.

Again, Lathrop, who has studied the Chavín culture for years, believes the influence of these people and their indelible god may have reached Mexico and the Olmecs. If so, it did not stop there, for Olmec themes are seen up to conquest times. Lathrop is adamant that this very ancient civilization originated inland, perhaps in the tropical jungles of Peru. If that proves true then, not only the culture heroes, but even the aborigines came from the east.[34]

Gods on Loan

The final culture heroes, and perhaps the greatest in South America, come from the varying histories of the Inca, also known as the Empire of Tahuantinsuyu "World of the Four Quarters." This was the last empire upon the South American scene before the arrival of the Spaniards, and certainly one of the world's most extraordinary. From their myths, which are much more recent and complete than those of the rest of the continent, valuable insights may be obtained about the ancient visitor.

The term "Inca" actually refers not to the people of the kingdom, but to the nobility. They were a proud, imperialistic-minded race said to differ from their non-Inca subjects who submitted passively to their rule. This elite body of aristocrats claimed to be no less than a race of gods, "God's chosen people." Inca monarchs, selected from these ranks, were believed to be living representatives of God.

Upon what basis could the Inca claim to be so unique and separate from their subjects? Inca legends go to great lengths to verify it. They assert that following the destruction of the world by a flood, a new race of men was established by the Creator-Father, who then sent a culture hero to earth to bestow the arts of civilization upon his primitive children. Several legendary founders of the Inca civilization can be discovered among the diverse traditions, and all of these "colonizers" assume the divine characteristics of a culture hero.

The Inca were at the end of a long line of Peruvian cultures, each cherishing its founders and heroes. Like the Aztecs of Mexico, they suppressed former tales that would elevate other races, and rewrote history to favor their own divine acceptance and authority. In so doing, they undoubtedly borrowed from older traditions which would be accepted by the conquered peoples and then simply added them to their own. Thus they were able to convince their subjects as well as themselves that their authority was divine.

This process of compounding and adapting, however advantageous to the Inca, makes it almost impossible to disentangle the ancient tales from the more recent, or to discern those peculiar to the Inca from those borrowed from earlier neighbors.

Inca traditions, as reported by Herrera, speak of a bearded white race in the country long before the Inca dynasty.[35] One of these traditions, widely dispersed in song among the people of the Inca Kingdom, tells of the ancient appearance of four brothers in the land (some say six) who were quite different in their bearing and manner of dress from the local inhabitants. Their fine, skillfully-made robes were long and flowing, and they possessed much gold. One of the brothers was sent back to their place of origin to recover golden objects left behind. Proud and powerful, these brothers gained ascendancy over the local natives.

A terrible argument ensued among the four, and the most valiant of the brothers, Ayar Cachi (Ah-yahr-CAH-chi), was rejected by the others for his supposed "feats of strength and boastfulness." Enraged by envy, his brothers accused him of trying to obtain power and wealth over them. The argument was apparently settled, for the other three eventually bowed before Ayar Cachi in recognition of his holy nature. Legends say that two of the brothers separated themselves and established colonies apart from the others. From the colonies, established by the four brothers and their sisters, came the Inca race, leaders of the indigenous inhabitants. The name of the country itself, "Tawantinsuyu," derives from the title of the founders, "Lords of the four quarters of the earth." This family, and especially their more saintly brother, Ayar Cachi, are closely identified in the native mind with the white god, Viracocha.[36]

Another story of the origin of a separate Inca race was recorded by the post-Conquest Peruvian historian and a Prince, Garcilaso de la Vega, who said he received it as a boy from his uncles of the Inca aristocracy. "Following the creation of the races of men at Lake Titicaca," he recalls, "Our Father the Sun" sent down to earth his son, accompanied by a sister, to instruct the rude natives in higher laws and civilization which would raise them above the level of the animals. They were also to teach his loving children to worship him and to obey the race of Lords and kings who would proceed from his two divine children.

These two, Manco Capac, and his sister/wife Mama Coya, travelled away from their first home at Lake Titicaca. With them they carried a magical golden staff once belonging to the culture hero. When these two "children of the Sun" reached the area now known as Cuzco, they planted the sacred staff in the earth and began to teach the people to dwell in houses and towns. They instructed the people in the breeding of animals and the cultivation of various crops, including maize and fruit, so they could live in a more civilized state above the animals. This was the beginning of the great Inca Capital. And what of the heroes? Of Mama Coya nothing more is known, but the son, Manco Capac, did not die, but instead ascended to the heavens and to his father. The golden staff stayed with the people as a sign of sovereignty, the royal wand of the kings who succeeded from this divine couple.[37]

The precocious youth, Garcilaso de la Vega, who recorded this last tale, later wrote the *Royal Commentaries* and was given by his Indian uncles the names of the official line of Inca rulers—thirteen in all. Earliest on the list was Manco Capac.

It is interesting that number eight of the rulers was listed by the name "Viracocha Inca." Although there is no question that he was not the original Lord Viracocha, he encouraged the worship of that ancient deity whose remembrance, like that of Quetzalcoatl of the Aztec, had faded in later years among the common people now favoring lesser gods, including the Sun.

Viracocha Inca built two temples to his earlier namesake; one of them over three hundred feet long and fifty feet high. The very use of the name Viracocha demonstrates convincingly the royal practice of borrowing titles of a previous Lord or Deity, as Topiltzin had borrowed the name "Quetzalcoatl" from the Toltecs. Like the Toltec leader, Topiltzin, Viracocha Inca had chosen the most powerful and revered name in the history of his people, a name appearing frequently and over a wide area of the Andean region.

A God of Gods

In South America, the most compelling legends of an ancient visitor who becomes a hero-god were unquestionably those about Viracocha, the principal figure of Inca mythology. He is the "enigmatic one" mentioned by all early recorders of Inca civilization, the Supreme Deity, said to be the Creator of the Earth, and the Revered Father of Mankind. More is written about him than about all the others combined.

These varying legends, with similar details of tradition, are recorded in the early 1600's by Francisco Herrera, a Spanish chronicler, Christoval de Molina, a priest who lived among the Indians, and two Catholic Indians, Don Juan Salcamayhua, and Cieza de Leon, whose stories, received from great-great-grandparents, Indian chiefs of the conquest, are considered reliable.

Viracocha and Thunupa are often interchangeable, with one confused for the other. But unlike other culture heroes, Viracocha did not come from the east across the great ocean. Yet, like the others, he comes from where the sun rises, and under quite unusual circumstances. Early legends and songs about him tell of a very remote time when there was great turmoil in the land followed by a long period of darkness. Out of this darkness appeared the great Lord Viracocha. Molina records it in these words, "They say it was dark, and that . . . he (the Creator) ordered the sun, moon and stars to go to the island of Lake Titicaca, . . . and thence to rise to heaven. They also declare that when the sun, in the form of a man, was ascending into heaven, very brilliant, it called to the Incas and to Manco Capac, as their chief, and said: 'Thou and thy descendants are to be Lords, and are to subjugate many nations. Look upon me as thy father, and thou shalt be my children, and thou shalt worship me as thy father.'[38]

Following his miraculous appearance, he walks among them for a time, calling them his sons and daughters, and works miracles, healing their sick by his touch and bringing sight to the blind. The fields were often his bed. The people erect many temples to him (Viracocha/Thunupa) in which they place statues in his likeness and make sacrifices (most likely of llamas, as did later cultures).[39]

His last act among the people is a memorable departure. In one version he is accompanied by a host of attendants, messengers and soldiers, who like himself are also white and bearded. They arrive at the coast, and spreading his mantle over the waters, Viracocha and his followers enter upon the waves as if they were dry land, and depart out of sight toward the west.[40] After he is gone, all that remains is the foam of the restless sea, from which it is reported the natives gave him the name Viracocha. He also leaves in the minds of his subjects a clear memory of his accomplishments, and an unforgettable prophecy that one day there would appear other white, bearded "Viracochas" in the land, his messengers who would rule the land until the great Viracocha himself returns to bring a golden age to his people.[41]

So implanted in the minds and traditions of the people were these great events that as years passed the details of the occasion were preserved carefully by men trained to remember with faithful accuracy, and they were still being recalled even as late as Conquest times. Prayers recognized him as "merciful" and "mighty," and without equal among the gods. Brinton, summing them up, says: "Thus Viracocha was placed above and beyond all other gods, the essential First Cause, infinite, incorporeal, invisible, above the sun, older than the beginning, but omnipresent, accessible, beneficent."[42]

Whatever the role or title of Viracocha, and whoever records it, the description of him is almost always the same: he is a tall, imposing figure of great authority, white and bearded, and he wears his hair long. He dresses in flowing white robes, belted at the waist, and wears sandals or goes without shoes altogether. He carries a staff in his hand. (One Spanish writer insisted he carried a prayer book.) Salcamayhua claims he was older, greyed, and lean.[43] His identity with the feathered serpent is unsure, but de la Vega describes him with serpents twined about his arms, and Brinton mentions that in Peru, the god of riches, a golden serpent identified with the hero, descends from the heavens in sight of all the people. Marcos writes of feathered serpents in the designs of the Northern Andes.[44]

The temples to Viracocha had his image carved in marble. A statue to him was placed on the temple altar in Cuzco where the Cathedral now stands. At Urcos the statue was at the entrance to the temple. Both statues are described as representing a white man with a floor-length robe. At his feet were birds—the eagle and falcon.

Some Spaniards overenthusiastically saw this as a represention of a visiting Christian saint.

Although inconclusive, many ancient Peruvian symbols are said to be pictorial representations of the god Viracocha. Included among them are the sun-god mask with its bolts of lightning, the double-headed dragon masks, feathered serpents, serpent staffs, jaguars, and pieces of crystal representing prophetic gazing and personal revelation. Even among remnants of the Chavín culture, the fifteen-foot monolithic carving hidden within the deepest recesses of the temple, far from public view, is believed by some to be an earlier representation of "Wira-Kocha" the sun god of Tiwanacu. In spite of most of the detail coming from the more recent Inca, the nature of the legends and age of the artistic depictions indicate that Viracocha was a very old tradition, a culture hero to many other nations preceding the Inca.

Whoever Viracocha might have been, he was impressive, and he was enduring, for similar to native customs in Mexico, the subsequent kings of Peru would add great stature and authority to their images by identifying themselves with the reverence given Viracocha and his divine power. A list of over one hundred kings of the Peruvian Dynasty from the time of Viracocha was compiled by Fernando Montesinos in 1650. If authentic (it was never corroborated by other historians), the list shows the first eighteen rulers claiming to be direct descendants of the great, white god. The next forty-six maintain a strong religious connection to him in their roles as priest-kings.

Thus sixty-four rulers preserved a close spiritual tie with their revered predecessor. The rest did not stray far, because ninety-four kings later, Inca Viracocha was still teaching his people reverence for the earlier Viracocha. Even the last of the Inca kings, the father of Atahualpa, immediately preceding the conquest, encouraged his sons in the worship of the white god who was soon to come.[45] It proved their undoing, for in reinforcing the powerful hold of the legend upon the Inca people, they unwittingly welcomed in the bearded Spaniards as the returning Viracocha who they believed would usher in a golden era, and instead, ironically sealed their doom.

From what has been seen thus far, it would seem some mysterious, bearded stranger made his way from Mesoamerica down through Central America and into the vast reaches of the South American continent. It would also appear that he could have equally begun his visits in South America and then worked his way northward. Everywhere he went he reportedly had a great cultural and spiritual effect upon the native peoples who revered him as a deity, and like the Mexican heroes, anticipated his eventual return.

That any one man could cover such a widespread area as Central and South America on foot or in legend is remarkable enough. Yet, the following chapter will report the effects and extensive distribution of similar bearded, white culture hero legends upon the diverse tribes of North America as well.

6

FAIR GODS
IN NORTH AMERICA

Early Legends Ignored

He came to the native people from across the sea, he who was a god, yet appeared as a man. He wandered the earth, possessing great power and loving all things, teaching men to live happily, bringing them the arts and civilization. Yet, his hearers misunderstood and abused him. When his mission was over, he entered into a birch-bark canoe and drifted slowly away toward the sunrise, his beautiful song fading softly behind him. He promised he would return one day.

Such stories of a revered visitor to North America awaited the first Europeans who penetrated the vast sixteenth-century wilderness of Canada and the United States. English and French colonizers, trappers and missionaries sailed up the coast, worked their way along winding rivers, crossed extensive lakes, plodded through heavy forests, and eventually encountered some 2,000 fascinating Indian tribes with wonderful tales. They tell of animals who speak with men, voices in the wind, symbols in the sky, spirits in the mountains and rivers, and, as expected, they include mysterious heroes from across the sea.

That any of these legends survived is a wonder, for early European explorers and settlers of North American colonies brought along fewer scholars to record native life than had Spaniards to the south. French Jesuits collected first-hand observations of Algonquian and Iroquoian religious customs, but most missionaries to the Indians considered the native stories naïve and not worth preserving. Later, many anthropologists dismissed much of this rich feast of folklore as a more recent mixture of Indian and Christian beliefs. A typical example of this disdaining attitude was that of the Reverend John Campanius, pastor of the Swedish-American churches along the Delaware river in 1642. Acquainted with the local Indian language, the learned Reverend judged the numerous Indian traditions "all alike foolish and ridiculous" and would therefore "say no more about them."[1] Even the great "liberal" of religious toleration, Roger Williams, refused to be present at Indian ceremonies out of fear of "Satan's inventions and worships."[2]

Because of this kind of narrow judgment, perhaps only one in a thousand of the ancient North American legends survived years of change and destruction. With the formation of a new Republic, some Washington scholars, like Thomas Jefferson, encouraged the preservation of Indian lore. Indians were, at first, willing to share their stories with writers like Adair and Schoolcraft who lived among them, but when they later felt European scorn, they learned to avoid the subject of sacred myths and legends, keeping them to themselves. Fortunately, as Christians encouraged the Indians to put aside old ways, conquest and colonization did not fully destroy native folklore; it merely went underground.

By the early 1800's, when scholars finally awoke to the urgency of preserving the Indians traditions, a large number of the tribal guardians had died, and an unfortunate amount of past knowledge and oral tradition had died with them. In spite of the cavalier handling of these traditions, however, some enchanting and compelling tales managed to hold on.

Strange Legend Survives

Among the surviving North American stories, one stands out as distinct from the rest. It occurs frequently and with similarity of detail, even in areas far apart, as it recounts the mysterious arrival of a foreign, bearded white hero who often becomes the chief god of a tribe. Like the visitor to Mexico and South America, he wanders the land and visits the various tribes. He displays creative powers and, at times, is said to have assisted the Creator with his work, bringing cultural traditions and religious ceremonies. When his work is done, he disappears or becomes the morning or evening star. His haunting story was told wherever Indians were found, including places previously untouched by Christianity.

The first Europeans to North America, unlike those in Mexico, found no written records among the Indians. What fragments of tales which are available today are preserved because of the curiosity of those few missionaries and scholars who, on rare occasions, were allowed to sit in special native gatherings and listen to the narratives. Important tribal myths and legends were carefully preserved over the centuries by older members who rehearsed the stories to the youngsters. Constant repetition guaranteed each generation would remember them accurately. Later, some of the Indians themselves recorded ancient folklore using the newly acquired alphabets from the English and French.

Tales From the East Coast

In the long, dark, winter months by the evening fire of a snow-blanketed dwelling, impressionable young men often sat cross-legged while their grandfather, perhaps the old chief, recited the hero legends. He would stress that the stories were sacred, handed down for many generations by their grandfathers, the prophets. Tales from the east told of a world of nature where spirit powers and men dwelt side by side. They whispered of the Algonquin origins from the Abnakis, their distant white ancestors. They told of a great and eloquent man with a long beard who came to them in the past, the gentle Michabo "Great Hare," god of winds and storms and the rains, the great god of light who so long ago brought fire and agriculture and made the world inhabitable.[3] The old man would impress upon the young minds the inventions and miracles of the wise Michabo—creator and protector of their people, who, when he left, ascended into the sky.[4]

European awareness of tales of a mysterious white visitor to the Northeastern United States began with the Algonquins, who were the first Indian tribes to be in contact with the recently arrived white men. From them the earliest travellers recorded stories about the ancient hero who was called by various titles: Manabozho, Missabo, Manitou, Gluskap, or Michabo. Although the names appear at first to be different, they all refer to the great light of dawn, for the ancient white visitor was identified with the warmth of the sun, because he was a bringer of light and knowledge. It was believed he would one day return.[5]

With slight variations from tribe to tribe, and from the same sources, these tales basically agree that the great Michabo was born of a virgin and was sent to earth in human form with all knowledge to fulfill a special mission to enlighten and to civilize the people through his teachings. In the complexities of myth, he can be a twin (having an evil brother), or he is one of four brothers (a story prominent among all American natives) As brother from the east, he has power over his other brothers. As Gluskap he falls dead, but by his great magic he comes to life again.[6]

Because legends say he returned to the sky, natives worshiped the morning star as his sacred star. His dwelling place, they claimed, was his medicine lodge in the east, where the earth is cut off. Among the tribes it was strongly expected that when he returns he will bring a golden age to the Indians.[7]

Similar stories by the Pawnee, along the eastern Platte River of Missouri, expressed a similar feeling about the Morning Star, which they identified with a man sent by the Great Spirit to give life and strength. Their sacred ceremony to the deified star included this song:

> Oh Morning Star, for thee we watch! Dimly
> comes thy light from distant skies: We see
> thee, then lost art thou.
> Morning Star, thou bringest life to us.
> Oh Morning Star, thy form we see!
> Clad in shining garments dost thou come,
> Thy plume touched with rosy light.
> Morning Star, thou now art vanished.[8]

In one of the few Indian tales he condescended to record, the skeptical Reverend John Campanius added an intrigue to this ancient Michabo legend. The Reverend had befriended the Algonquin Indians along the Delaware River and understood their language. They, in turn, entrusted him with guarded information they had received by tradition from their ancestors, which usually was revealed only to tribal leaders. They claimed that their knowledge was taught them long ago by a venerable and eloquent man who wore a long beard like the "Big Mouths" the whites called preachers.

Their great teacher had a miraculous birth, and he performed many miracles. His speech excited much wonder, and when he departed for heaven, he promised to come back. In sadness, the Indians told the Reverend Campanius, "But, he has not come back."[9]

Neighbors to the south of the Algonquins were the mighty Iroquois, who at one time dominated some of the most beautiful portions of Northeast America. Wise legislators, orators of eloquence and fierce warriors, they could be called the "Romans of the North American Indians." In spite of being bitter enemies to the Algonquins with a totally different language, their culture hero was almost identical to the Algonquin Michabo.[10] (This strange sharing of a similar hero among dissimilar tribes suggests that such traditions go back to very remote times.) These heroes became so well known, even among non-Indians, that they appear in a famous modern-day poem, "Legend of Hiawatha," by the American poet Longfellow, who blended the hero's exploits with those of later Iroquois chiefs.[11]

Although an actual Hiawatha lived in the late sixteenth century (some claim 1350) some of his nobler attributes are borrowed from a fellow-traveller named 'The Peacemaker,' who was said to have been sent by the creator in a white canoe. Other traits come from the earlier demi-god predecessor, Michabo.

The powerful influence of Hiawatha/Michabo extends far beyond the Iroquois and Algonquin nations, for just fifty years before the Dutch colonized New York, Hiawatha's prophetic dream of peace among his people was realized in a famous Five-Nation-Confederacy of the most powerful Indian tribes in the east. It didn't stop there, for it is reported that the Indian Democratic organization was studied by the founding fathers before they wrote the United States Constitution. Benjamin Franklin, in observing the Iroquois Confederacy, received inspiration for a Federal Union of the Colonies.[12] This curious, latter-day infiltration by a native culture hero into our very foundations extends the ancient visitor's influence into the daily lives of even modern society.

When the Algonquin Michabo became the principal deity of the Iroquois, they called him Ioskeha. Like Michabo, Ioskeha had a lodge far away in the east. Considered the father of mankind, he taught the Indians how to grow crops, make fires, and perform the arts of life. Much of the Iroquois religion centered around this bringer of life and light.

In the fall when the hunt was over, thoughts turned to matters of the spirit, and the Indians gathered at the long house to perform ceremonies of thanksgiving at the festival of the harvest. They brought out strings of wampum beads which helped them recall marvelous tales they had rehearsed for centuries. Although the Iroquois were fierce with the enemy on the battlefield, they were mild and good-natured with their own people. A highly developed belief in a loving and great spirit closely identified with their culture hero, Ioskeha, made their religion similar to Christianity "in its simple, gentle, and warmly human aspects."

Ioskeha, like the Algonquin hero, was half man, half god, and born of a virgin. He formed the plants and animals. He created men and gave them the arts. This great ruler was said to be white, the Iroquois symbol of purity and faith, and his name, Ioskeha, meant literally, "about to grow white." This apparently refers to his role as bringer of the dawn and light, since it was believed he originally came from far away where the dawn begins.

Whoever this mysterious visitor was, he eventually achieved a high status among the natives, for after the Iroquois gave thanks for all things: the earth, crops, animals, the sun, the moon, the rain, the stars, each other, they gave special thanks to their revered hero. This they did by placing tobacco leaves upon the ceremonial fire. The smoke and incense from this sacred plant rose slowly upward, creating a path to carry their prayers to the culture hero/creator, who now resides in the heavens holding up the sky as he watches over them. He received their offerings of gratitude and in turn, it was anticipated, would bestow blessings upon them.

Iroquois and Algonquin legends of a tribal hero were not unique to North America: as in the countries to the south, he apparently moved around. Wherever Europeans went, Indians identified them with a remarkable prophecy about the return of a fair-skinned, bearded, god-like being who wore a long tunic and in the clouded past brought the scattered Indian tribes knowledge and prosperity. He had founded their institutions and established their religion. His final departure, in most tales, was as mysterious as was his arrival, including the promise to return one day to his beloved people.[13]

On the shores of Lake Michigan another tribe, the Winnebago, had a divine culture hero, born of a virgin, who roamed the world which he had created, and showed love toward all things.[14] Similarly, the Penobscot, in the Northeast, spoke of Glooskap, previously identified with Michabo, a great teacher and miracle worker who died and was then resurrected. Reminiscent of Quetzalcoatl in the Mexican area, he was a son of the sun who came to earth to enlighten and to civilize. On the shore they held a great feast in his honor before he departed, singing, in a great canoe toward the sunset. As he left, he promised that some day he would return to restore the golden age of the Indian nations.[15]

West Coast Legends

The ancient stranger, or hero, did not confine his visits to eastern North American tribes. Incomplete but familiar forms of the story emerge from cloudy narratives of other areas. Far to the west, along the rugged coastline of the Pacific, Europeans encountered the Northwest Indians a mere thirty-five years before the American revolution. There, over twenty-eight Indian tribes fished the icy waters from Alaska to northern California. Many lived in sophisticated villages where several families inhabited cedar plank houses. On chilly nights, the youngsters would gather at the firepits and hear the house chief exhort them to self-discipline and restraint. As was done in other tribes, he also filled their fertile imaginations with tales of the clan heroes.

Among these tribes were the Tlingit, fourteen independent clans who inhabited the Northwest gulf coast from Alaska to British Columbia. Foremost among their supernatural beings was Raven, or Yehl, a white creator and culture hero. Yehl's offspring were beautiful white-skinned boys, and it was said that Yehl lived before the world was and that he was born of a virgin. Clothed in a bird skin, this honored visitor could soar and do miraculous things. It was he who provided light with his gifts of fire and the heavenly bodies. Before returning to his habitation in the east, into which no man could enter, he promised to return and reward those who obeyed his teachings. So imbedded into the Tlingit mind was the life of Yehl that his people vowed "as Yehl acted and lived so also will we live and do."[16]

Further on down the coast, on Vancouver Island, the Nootkas carved huge wooden images to recall the visit of an ageless and supernatural benefactor who came up the Nootka Sound long ago in a copper canoe. His instructions to the people included prophecies about their eventual destruction. But he left them a marvellous promise that they could one day rise and live with him in the sky, for that was where he said he came from. Stories about him spread, and many Indian people still mention "the Old Man above."[17]

Fine wooden images to these heroes, who are often the creators of their people, were sculpted on ceremonial masks and on totem poles of the native villages. Once they stood in front of the dwelling of the chiefs, but now these rare works of art are found only in museums.

Light-skinned heroes played dominant roles in many of the California legends. Because of the fragmentary nature of the legends, all the basic details of beards, the coming from across the sea, and promising to return, do not always appear in each story as they have been preserved, but every tale has elements so much in common with other white-god tales that it is tempting to assume the basics are there, or that there is a commonality among them.

The Carocs along the California Russian River were favored with the appearance of a great deity called Chareya, who wore a close tunic and had long, white hair.[18] The Olchones, a coastal tribe near Monterey, identified the sun with a "big man" who made the earth and who rules in the sky. The Pericues of lower California worshiped a great Lord in heaven whose son was born on earth to become their hero and teacher. The Mojaves tell of a creator named Matevil who lived among them before departing eastward. They expected his later return to bring about a condition of prosperity forever.[19]

Near San Juan Capistrano, the Acagchemem (ah-HAH-shay-mem) tell of their hero, Chinigchinich, in several conflicting versions. Basically, he came from the north and grew old among them. Like the hero/gods to the south, Quetzalcoatl and Viracocha, he left his people at the seashore, but promised to return to them soon. Some of his attributes were the power to create "rain and men and all things." Upon dying, he miraculously changes into a bird that resurrects. His ways were recognized as not being the ways of men.[20]

Stories of the Southwest

Evidence places the visitor in the Southwest as well. By 700 A.D. the people of the Four Corners area of Utah, Colorado, Arizona and New Mexico had created a highly sophisticated cultural and social organization that later produced one of the richest sources of archaeological studies in the United States. Europeans encountered impressive remains of buildings and fascinating legends of the Southwest people as early as 1539, just eighteen years after the conquest of Mexico. The Spaniards had invaded that area in a search for the legendary seven cities of gold. Knowledge of building great cities and casting objects in gold were considered to have been brought by the hero, and were therefore signs of his presence. Even though the gold was never found in this area, rumors of its existence have persisted. As recently as 1990 newspapers carried articles about the discovery of a cache of gold in a cave on Victorio peak near White Sands, New Mexico. Details of the contents of the possible legendary treasure were not given, only the legal disputes over possession.[21]

There were no follow-up articles, but a short time later, the author met a young man, Terry Delona, who claimed his ancestors owned the land and that years ago his great grandfather had brought some of the ingots out of the cave to relocate them. With the treasure, he said, were papers, but since his grandfather was unable to read them, and fearing they might be ancient deeds or claims to the treasure, he burned them. This story appeared on television's "Unsolved Mysteries," and Delona expresses hopes of still reclaiming the prize.

Other reports include gold hidden in caves protected by the Yaqui Indians of Chihuahua, and others in Utah and Michigan. If these caches actually exist, and if the gold emerges, could they be remnants of the treasure Montezuma was guarding so carefully for the returning Quetzalcoatl—the treasure that disappeared after the Spaniards left it behind in their hasty departure from Tenochtitlan? The final outcome of these reports is yet unknown, but a sure treasure exists in the legends of the people.

Stories from the Indian people of the Southwest report fair gods among the Pueblos, the Hopi, the Navajos, and other neighboring tribes—wherever the ancient legends were not totally destroyed or altered by the Europeans. Each tribe called the visitor by a different name, but the meaning and many details were similar.

One of the more fascinating of ancient visitors to this area was the great leader, teacher and god, Montezuma, who, except for the obvious name, has no known direct connection with the supreme monarch to the south. This divine priest or prophet made his sudden appearance among the Pueblos long before they built their present communal dwellings in the Four Corners region. He had "created" his people somewhere else, and then led them to this desert area in "Moses" fashion. Here he taught them to build cities and shrines. He was said to have been born of a beautiful virgin, and possessed supernatural powers received from the sun; his hair was golden. The various Pueblo tribes looked forward with assurance to the day when the revered Montezuma would return with a race of white people to save the Pueblos from their enemies.[22] Other Southwest Indian tribes seem to have borrowed from the Pueblo legends, for they too misguidedly anticipated the eventual coming of a white race that would bring a sublime condition to the races. One cannot but reflect upon the irony in the many expectations of the white race bringing a "sublime condition."

Fair Gods in Numbers

While some stories strongly support the belief in an ancient white visitor from afar, others raise perplexing questions about additional visitors—sometimes a whole company of them. The granddaughter of the chief of the Piute nation in the Nevada desert reported that when her grandfather was told of the coming of the white man in the 1800's, he jumped up, clasped his hands together, and cried aloud, "My white brothers, my long-looked for white brothers have come at last!" Up to that time, it is believed, the nineteenth-century Piutes had never seen a modern-day white man, and it is strange that, although they inhabited most of the desert land of Nevada, far from any large waters, they expected the legendary whites to return from across the mighty ocean where they had reportedly gone a long time ago in a move which separated them from their darker Indian brothers.[23]

The Piutes were not alone in their expectation of visitors from across the sea. The Hopis, who have lived in the landlocked Arizona area for over a thousand years, also believed that one day another race of people would claim their land.

They saw in the coming of European explorers the return of their long lost wandering white brother, the mythical Pahana.[24] Pahana, one of the sons of a Bow Clan Chief, was separated from his younger brother in ancient times. With him went one of the tribal stone tablets containing the Hopi laws given them by the Great Spirit. Pahana had travelled east toward the rising sun, and, it was believed, he would one day return with the tablet and wisdom to reestablish balance in the world. In a strange coincidence, the expected time of his return coincided with that of Quetzalcoatl of the Aztecs. This legend is beautifully told by Robert Boissiere in *The Return of Pahana.*

The Shawanoes, an Algonquian tribe, recalled that their ancestors crossed the sea. Although they had no memory of when that occurred, they believed they had then migrated from Florida where it was said that the first inhabitants were a white, sea-faring people who used iron tools.[25] Most Indian tribes and nations, including the Cherokees and Algonquins, had similar traditions that the Abnakis "white ancestors," and the gods who bring arts and religion came from the east, over the sea.[26] The Hopis recalled a sea crossing of their great ancestors, arriving somewhere along the coast of Mexico and gradually working their way up to the four corners area of the present continental United States.[27] And the Okanagans, in the Northwest, claimed they descended from a race of white giants who eventually lost their whiteness after arriving here from an island of the sea.[28] Traditions among the Seneca tribe in the same area recalled a whole fleet of foreigners who not only landed on these shores centuries ago, but also intermarried with the natives. In time their descendents lost some whiteness, but were still reported to have pale skin and eyes.[29]

Apparently not all lost their alleged whiteness, however, for in the grasslands of the midwest and along the Missouri River roamed a race of Indians reported to be quite different from their neighbors. Described as "polite and friendly," the Mandan Indians of North Dakota were also said by George Catlin, an early nineteenth-century artist who painted them in accurate detail, to have "fair skin." He noticed some of them were almost white with blond hair "soft as silk" and blue and brown eyes in place of the usual black eyes of other tribes, who called the Mandans "Half White."[30] It was reported that they carried ancient skin-wrapped parchments which no one in the tribe could read. They also remembered a remote time when their ancestors had come a long way over a great water to reach this country.[31] To add to the intrigue, they spoke of a tribe of people, now dead, whose faces were white. In addition, they spoke of a great flood where only one man was saved—a white man. A major religious ceremony involved the tradition of this white man who they believed came to them at a "very ancient period" from the West.[32] This intrigue will be pursued in chapter 8.

Evidence for Higher Civilization

The impressive body of North American myths and legends reveals many examples of a mysterious visitor from across the sea. He was usually described as being white and bearded. He wore a long, white tunic, was considered god-like, and travelled extensively. In addition, the hero stories had two other important features in common: he was reported to have come in remote times, and he was a bringer of a high level of civilization. Later chapters will deal with the time of his coming, but remains of a high level of civilization, although not as grandiose as those seen in Mesoamerica and Peru, are still evident in impressive structures and refined art objects.

Although it was said the hero-god was a builder of great cities, to an Indian living in primitive circumstances it would not take much of a building complex to fit the definition of a "great city." But there is evidence that North American Indians had impressive "cities" even under today's concept.

One of these, Pueblo Bonito "Beautiful City," in Chaco Canyon, New Mexico, near the four corners area, was once a magnificent five-story commune of 800 rooms housing over 1200 people. Built between A.D. 850 and 1125, this monumental masonry structure covered more than three acres around a great central plaza. Along with the surrounding area of some 150 communities within a 35,000 square-mile area, it is believed to be the largest ceremonial center in North America. Further witness to the high level of technology and organization achieved by these people are the two-hundred miles of well-constructed highways only recently discovered through the process of aerial photography. These marvelously engineered roads were perfectly straight, up to thirty feet wide, one-hundred miles long, and connected over eighty Indian towns, for which Chaco Canyon was apparently the spiritual hub.[33]

Add Mesa Verde, an imposing cliff dwelling containing a palace with over two-hundred rooms, and these amazing monuments witness solidly to a period of prosperity and cultural development among a people who, after but a short time of living in them, like the culture hero, strangely just disappear.

Other impressive buildings were constructed outside the Southwest area by Indian architects using wood and earth. Sadly, the eroding nature of the material has left little to observe today. A prime example of that achievement was the impressive collection of Mandan lodges, along the great bend of the Missouri river, which once were grouped like honeycombs to protect a highly complex village life. Today, unfortunately, they exist only in early paintings.

Reports of a high culture, which the white visitor allegedly brought, were made by the first English explorers. Early in the seventeenth century, five British sailors journeyed through the lower Mississippi area of the Natchez, Creek and Choctaw Indians. They told a somewhat incredible story of having seen splendid palaces of timber and stone built upon imposing mounds of earth and decorated with pearls and diamonds. The inhabitants, according to the reports, wore fine clothing and adorned themselves with jewels and gold. A similar description was made of a temple in Savannah, Georgia, fifty years earlier by the Spanish explorer Garcilaso de la Vega.

Whether or not these early reports were exaggerated cannot be determined, but, a century later, the French, who took over the sacred city of Natchez, found only a poor wooden village built upon earthen ramps. Even at that time, however, the Natchez were highly organized into a complex social system of aristocrats, priests and commoners whose various towns had close social contacts. Some validation might exist in the pearls and copper reportedly found in Natchez burials, but little remains of the oral history and legends.

Great Mound Builders

If the visitor, or visitors, brought a highly organized and advanced culture, then nowhere in the continental United States is the evidence more apparent than among the mysterious mound builders centered in the Mississippi and Ohio regions. Flourishing about 2,000 years ago, these impressive centers were the result of two waves of culture called the Adena, from 500 B.C., and the somewhat later Hopewell, from around the time of Christ, ending about the same time as the Adena around A.D. 700.[34] Both groups raised imposing earthen mounds in geometric shapes whose size often rivaled the pyramids of Mexico, although lacking their elegance and refinement. These centers were eventually established along the Mississippi from the Great Lakes to the Gulf Coast, and reached into Georgia, Alabama, North Carolina and as far east as Florida.

Today very little remains of these ancient structures, for they have deteriorated from weather or have been replaced by modern buildings. But early settlers came upon the mounds by the thousands, and created almost as many theories about who had built them. Heated discussions ensued in the early eighteen hundreds about the mound builders, and it was supposed they were some foreign race of high civilization that existed before the present Indians had arrived. Modern archaeologists are reversing that idea by providing evidence that the newer race was the more advanced, and that they moved in over the previous simpler Indian cultures.[35]

Who were these newer people, and were did they come from? No one knows for certain. Artifacts from the area show striking similarities to those of Mexico and South America. With rich goods of finely-worked copper, mica, obsidian, meteor iron, shell, animal teeth and ceramics, Adena graves in the Ohio valley compound the mystery by producing remains of women said to be six feet tall and men who were nearly seven. Whoever they were, if this is the case, they were impressive and they were majestic.[36] Fine craftsmen, engineers and artists, they apparently traded goods extensively. The surviving symbols indicate these people were steeped in ceremony and religion. They were also prodigious builders of a complex civilization that included a great trading network passed on to later Indians who attributed it to a legendary white visitor out of the dim past.

If this mystery man introduced architecture, by far the greatest existing evidence for advanced city planning among the ancient North Americans can still be seen east of St. Louis, in what is now Cahokia Mounds State Park. There stand the remains of what was once North America's finest metropolis. A magnificent Indian settlement of over one-hundred man-made earthen mounds, it contained burials and supported residences and temples. Largest of all these earthen monuments is Monk's Mound, a massive structure rising some one-hundred feet into the air. On the top once stood a temple about the size of a modern-day football field. The colossal base of the mound covered some sixteen acres, an area larger than the greatest pyramid of Egypt.[37]

Seven hundred years ago, the plazas of Cahokia swarmed with as many as forty thousand people gathered together on feast days from the corn fields which still surround the area today. They watched the mysterious rituals being performed by revered priests who dressed ornately in feathered headdresses and glittering jewelry of copper and pearls. The society also had its elite, for one male burial reportedly had 20,000 shell beads, 800 arrowheads, and numerous sheets of mica and copper.

Information about the traditions behind these activities would no doubt cast light upon the nature of the foreign visitor, but little remains. What is known about the rites and ceremonies performed on these large mounds comes mainly from the Natchez of the lower Mississippi, a tribal remnant of more brilliant days. When discovered by the French, the Natchez were still practicing ceremonial rites on temple mounds. Like the Cahokians to the north before them, the Natchez were ruled by a living deity called the Great Sun, aided by his mother, a white woman. This despotic chief claimed to be a descendant of a great being who mysteriously appeared long ago among the people during a time of hardship. The ancient hero had become their ruler, and set up a benevolent system of laws by which the people were to live. He had instructed them to build a temple to the Great Spirit, and gave them directions to continually burn the sacred fire sent from the sun.[38]

Temple-topped mounds were not unique to the Cahokians and Natchez, for one of the most-often-mentioned accomplishments of the fair visitor was that of teaching the people how to worship and how to build great houses for that purpose. For thousands of years Indians had been going to the hills and mountains, home of the Gods, to burn perpetual fires of prayer to summon their deities. Where no hills and mountains existed, they were simulated on a smaller scale in the shape of earthen cones or pyramids, the common meeting place between heaven and earth.

There man might rise above the earth to communicate with God, and divinity could find a home near the earth at the sacred altar.

Under the inspiration of the fair god, these ancient altars of worship became sophisticated mounds topped by small, wooden or adobe temple structures. Here great light and knowledge could go forth to the people: for instruction, according to many of the legends, was the greatest mission of the hero-god.

The temples have long since disappeared, but some of the great mounds can still be seen: Rock Eagle Effigy Mound in Georgia, Town Creek Mound in North Carolina, seventy-foot-high Grave Creek Mound in downtown Moundsville, West Virginia, are only a few of the impressive structures that demonstrate the considerable skill, labor, and time required of those devoted people.

Symbols of a Fair God

In the absence of ancient records, some of the best guides to identifying the tracks of visitors and culture heroes are the symbols identified with them. Teachings among the various tribes often included colorful ceremonies performed on mounds or in village plazas using animals or other symbols connected with the mysterious hero who had brought culture and civilization. A great bird sometimes represented the hero-god: "The sweep of his wings is thunder/ the lightnings are the glances of his eyes."[39] The mighty eagle and its prized feathers were objects of worship for nearly all the tribes in North America. Dances simulated the graceful movements of the great bird that soars heavenward, as represented in paintings and songs.

More often than the graceful bird, the favored symbol of the hero was the more mysterious and fearsome serpent—especially the rattlesnake. Subtle, sinuous, rhythmic motions of the feared snake resemble water and the winding rivers over which the fair god presided. The glittering, sinister intrigue of its eyes recall the supernatural qualities of the ancient visitor who had wisdom and magic power. And the quick spring and rapid recoil typify the lightning which came from the sky home of the powerful hero.

As in Mexico and South America, many legends about the Northern culture hero attach a special importance to the ominous serpent. The Dakota spoke of the serpent as a "man of god," and Algonquins and Iroquois wore garments of serpent skins and worshiped a great serpent deity.[40] Pueblo tribes in northern Arizona identified their hero myths with the serpent, believing that all their people were once serpents and that snakes were their brothers.

These customs are not merely a thing of the past, for even today, each year in August, the Hopi priests of New Mexico dance around the village plaza with the poisonous reptiles in their mouths, believing that these creatures whose zigzag movements symbolize lightning will bring the rains. Snake handling is reported today in churches in the Appalachian mountains as well.[41]

Kachina dances are performed in the southwest to insure the rains, over which the white hero presided. Dancers wear masks which represent the presence of ancestors and the gods. These Pueblo people recall their great leader, prophet and teacher, mentioned earlier, Montezuma, who commanded his people to pray to the great serpent for rain and life. To the Indian mind, the serpent had immortal life, for did it not each springtime cast off its old skin in a manner more dramatic than any other animal, and become a new creature? Like the serpents to the south with feathers, this creature could lift its people from an earth-bound life heavenward (the feathered serpent does appear among the Hopi and Zuni).[42]

On the North American Continent, serpent symbols reach even greater proportions than in Mexico and South America (some over 1,000 feet in length). The most impressive is found in a wooded area outside Cincinnati, Ohio, where an uncoiling, earthen serpent dominates the summit of a high, crescent-shaped hill. A quarter of a mile in length, thirty feet wide, and five feet high, this colossal reptile demonstrates the engineering genius, the dedication, and the devotion of a people who began building mounds for ritualistic purposes long before the time of Christ. These amazing serpent figures, carved so laboriously upon the hills, raise many unanswered questions concerning their builders and purposes and whether these puzzling serpent-mounds are the beginnings of ancient religious rites dedicated to a culture hero, as elsewhere, or the end results of long-established ones. Future findings may tell.

The Hero Departs

Although the mysterious visitor is gone from sight for a time, he leaves behind the enigmatic serpent figure dedicated to him in some symbolic form, either present or represented, in large earthen mounds, sacred ceremonies, carved statues, and embedded in the architecture, in colorful picture writing, painted on pottery, woven into basketry and textiles, and used as body decorations. Other visual tributes to the mysterious hero are eagles, jaguars, trophy heads, two-headed serpents, and especially feathered serpents. Wherever the use of these symbols have been discovered, researchers often have discovered, at the same time, that the fair god was there.

The last six chapters have followed extensive myths and legends about the elusive visitor. Beginning with Columbus and tracking the stories back through time in Central, South and North America, a host of fascinating and puzzling figures have been presented. Considering the number of tales that were lost and left out (perhaps several for each of the thousands of native languages and dialects spoken), the sheer number of legends remaining about the inscrutable traveller, along with geographic remoteness and varying times of arrival make one wonder whether he is dealing with only one mystery man, or with legions. It is now time to investigate this question as well as the questions of origin and identity.

The search for the identity of the fair god, will lead to some of history's most prominent candidates, beginning with Leif Ericsson and the Vikings, then moving back through time to examine the Irish, the Celts, the Asiatics, Romans, Greeks, Egyptians, and Phoenicians, as well as some unexpected possibilities. By then, we should be ready to draw some final conclusions about this baffling intrigue of fair gods and feathered serpents.

7

CULTURE HEROES
AND COLONIES

Northern Immigrants

So far in this book, the mysterious bearded visitor has been pursued through seemingly unlimited accounts from all over the Americas and throughout various ages. Now the obvious questions must be faced: What is the source of so many similar myths? Was the hero a real-life person? Was there more than one? If so, who?

Over the centuries the many answers have resulted in a bewildering clash of ideas and theories: "They were Asiatics," "They must have been Phoenicians, Greeks or Romans adrift." "Perhaps the Lost Tribes of Israel!" "They were from Atlantis, or outer space." "One of the Twelve Apostles." Each explosive suggestion has been raised, bantered about, discarded and raised again.

The outcome of this ideological battle is a division into two opposing camps of thought called *transocean culture diffusionists* (*diffusionists*), and *independent inventionists*, (*isolationists*).

Diffusionists hold strongly that following the ice age, visitors continually entered the Americas from other lands, bringing and influencing native culture. Caught up in the stimulation of gathering evidence, diffusionists are sometimes accused of romantically seeing the oceans as early means of travel for pre-Columbian tourists from all over the world. Many of the earliest diffusionists were sixteenth-century Europeans who had just barely stepped onto American shores after crossing the ocean themselves.

Fierce opponents in this ideological battle, *isolationists* are generally scientifically-oriented persons who dogmatically subscribe to a kind of scientific "Monroe Doctrine" of their own making. It denies significant foreign intervention in, or contribution to the cultural development of native America after the last separation of the American land bridge from Asia over the Bering Straits around 10,000 years ago. Isolationists believe that all of the man-made wonders found on the American Continents were created by natives who invented their own civilization independently of or in isolation from later Asian or European influence. Thus, tales of the culture hero would also be native. This unwavering attitude is often denounced by diffusionists as blind to contrary evidence.

Both sides of this unresolved conflict have impressive evidence to give, as scanning the literature from their conferences and endless lists of bibliographical references easily demonstrates. The strength of this ongoing skirmish has intermittently favored one side and then the other, but just as soon as one flag-waver declares a clear victory, new arguments arise which shift the balance again.

The irony is that when one side offers pyramids or wheels in both lands as proof of contact, the other side uses the same evidence to maintain that pyramids and wheels clearly demonstrate man's independent ability to create similar objects from similar needs. After all, they argue, who taught the Egyptians to build pyramids, or the Romans to build wheels? This is an unfortunate situation in which both sides suffer. But at the same time, undue agreement would take some fun out of the whole affair.

A highly entertaining and sardonic isolationist appraisal of this fascinating battleground of theories and the steadfast warriors involved can be found in Robert Wauchope's *Lost Tribes and Sunken Continents*. Another is found in Stephen Williams' *Fantastic Archaeology*. A convincing attempt at an impartial overview of both sides of the issues, which provides bibliographical references from the last 50 years, can be found in Fingerhut's *Who First Discovered America*, and *Explorers of Pre-Columbian America*? Also well-researched, but less successful at fair mindedness, is Davies' *Voyagers To The New World*. On the other side, diffusionist arguments abound, as will be seen.

The next chapters will consider both diffusionist and isolationist points of view in order to present evidence for both sides. Although it is not the intent of this book to take sides, it is impossible to deal with culture heroes and not stir up some arguments. One cannot hope to cover all the issues to the satisfaction of everyone. Readers might be swayed at times to one side or the other, but, hopefully, will emerge with some understanding of both positions. Three questions will be kept in mind: Were American culture heroes born on native soil? Were they transplanted from some other country? Or is there some other solution? Eventually, some conclusions must be drawn.

Both diffusionists and isolationists agree on early immigrations from Asia crossing the Bering Straits millenniums ago. What specific traditions these migrations might have brought concerning a culture hero is still debatable. No doubt these people brought into the new land seeds of culture, and their descendants evolved later traditions. The big questions are: how much of the tales were brought by those early migrants, how much filtered down through the centuries, how widespread were the original stories, how much was altered by later cultures or visitors, and how this was all accomplished. Finding answers is no small project. Modern-day archaeologists have discovered promising new doors, and in the next few chapters many of them will be opened.

Wonder Leads to Wander

From the beginning, people have wandered the earth in search of food and shelter. In addition, they have always been curious to know what mysteries await them beyond the next hill, on a distant island, or over the far horizon. This kind of curiosity is responsible for various migrations from ancient times through the Bering Straits and down the Pacific side of the Americas. It also led at least one other group of wanderers to the Atlantic shores five hundred years before the arrival of Columbus—the group most people think of when they hear of white visitors arriving from across the sea—Vikings. So the obvious question to be posed is, "What influence have the Vikings contributed to the stories about the white bearded visitor?"

Visitors From Across the Atlantic

Grade-school children often take delight in advising their less informed friends that Columbus was not the first to discover America. It was, they gloat, Leif Ericsson, the Viking. What they do not know is that up until recently, there had been no proof of Viking arrival.

Early Norse legends from Iceland recorded in the 1300's in a book called the *Flateyjarbók*, now in the Royal Library of Copenhagen, told of several voyages from Greenland to a land beyond the west sea called "Vinland." An even earlier reference to "another island in the sea," beyond Greenland, was recorded by a German priest, Adam of Bremen, who in 1075 received the information from the Royal courts of Denmark.[1]

Although the various accounts of these legends contain some discrepancies about who did what when, they are consistent enough for today's scholars to believe actual locations were somewhere on the American east coast. Claims of Nordic origin have often been attached to numerous artifacts, inscriptions on stones, maps, and even ancient buildings and sites on the North American soil. These have then been held as proof of Viking arrival sometime around the early eleventh century. Unfortunately, some scholars who have carefully scrutinized these impressive "evidences" consider them to be either fakes or created by Scandinavian settlers who arrived after the sixteenth century.

Aside from the authentic sagas which pre-date the sixteenth century but are not totally free from controversy, no tangible, indisputable remains of any Viking visit had ever been produced. Still, the conviction persisted that the Norse colonized some five centuries before other Europeans, although no one knew exactly where they had landed.

In Roman times the so-called Vikings reportedly fled northward through Russia from their first home near the Black Sea to the lands of Denmark, Sweden and Norway. Led by their first King, Odin (Wodin), who much later was worshiped as a hero and god, the purpose for their peregrination was to escape Roman sieges.[2]

For centuries they developed peaceful communities in their new Scandinavian homelands where they became farmers, merchants, craftsmen and fishermen. Their cities grew into large centers of trade with a high level of culture in the arts, literature and government. Having lived by the Baltic and North seas, these Norsemen (or north men) were born sailors and became the medieval world's greatest navigators. Master shipbuilders, they created a unique style of vessel with up-swinging prows and square sails that were fast, large, and sufficiently sturdy to defy the most threatening of seas.

Setting their course by the sun and stars, the Vikings were able to move farther out to sea with this distinct navigational advantage over other sailors of the time who seldom ventured very far from the sight of land. Viking sailors could sail as far as they chose in any direction on the seas or rivers. They used the waters to take them wherever they wished. Beginning in the ninth century, these northern warriors spread their terror all over Europe, the British Isles and Ireland, France, Spain, and well into the Mediterranean and North Africa.

Not all Norsemen, however, were harassing, blood-thirsty conquerors. Many hard-working citizens stayed home while others, rejecting the increasing violence and disruptive efforts to unify the kingdom, left their homes and followed the route of Viking conquests to distant islands where they built peaceful settlements and colonized them. The Norman (Norseman) role in England and French history is quite familiar, and in the tenth century these wandering adventurers could be found practically all over the known world.

This restless and inquisitive nature in the blood of a people accustomed to unrestricted travel would inevitably lead them to undiscovered lands. With remarkable navigational skills, they followed the setting sun to several islands of the icy Atlantic until they finally discovered Iceland. There, in Scandinavian tradition, they established large colonies of emigrants from Norway, Northern Scotland and Ireland. By the year 930, Iceland had become an independent state.[3] Predictably, the Norse age of discovery in the west did not stop there.

One of the most colorful characters of Viking sagas was born in Norway around 950. This nomadic rebel, Eric the Red, sailed to Iceland with his parents and was later exiled for three years from that country for too freely wielding a deadly sword against fellow-Icelanders. In order to make good use of his banishment time, he acquired a ship and sailed southwest in the year 982 to search for a land he had heard about from exploring sailors.

One could hardly sail due west from Iceland and not come upon the world's largest island stretching some1600 miles and only 250 miles away. Eric, along with his men, explored the huge land, mostly a frozen wilderness except for a coastline that was much warmer and greener than today. In the spirit of a true modern-day land developer, Eric assigned the compelling but misleading name of "Greenland" to this oversized ice box, hoping to later attract colonists.

Eric's transgressions were apparently forgiven when he returned to Iceland in 985, for he managed to sell his remarkable story of a wonderful new land to some 400 men, women and children. With livestock and goods filling twenty-five ships, they sailed off to colonize Eric's deceptive "Greenland" and established two colonies on the west side of the cold land facing the Americas a little over two hundred miles distance.[4] No doubt Eric got a handsome fee for his trouble.

Life there was not as easy as Eric had promised, but the immigrants managed to build farms and eventually reach a peak population of some 3,000-4,000 persons. To augment their meager crops they traded furs, fish, walrus tusks and even live polar bears to the occasional visitors from Iceland and Norway.

Following acceptance of Christianity in the year 1,000, the Greenlanders maintained communication as far away as the British Isles and the seat of their new faith, Rome. This contact, according to reliable records kept by the Vatican, continued for several hundred years more.

With the continual coming and going of ships to these remote colonies, it would have been strangely inconsistent had the intrepid Norse curiosity not led them a few days further west across the Davis Strait to add the American coasts to their 1500-mile-chain of discoveries. Clearly, they did so.

Vikings to North America

The first European to see the North American coastline, according to one version of the "Sagas of Eric the Red" which was compiled some three-hundred and fifty years after his death, was a young man named Bjarni Heriulfsson, who sailed from Norway in 986 to spend the Christmas season with his father in Iceland. Learning that his father had sailed with Eric to the west, Bjarni convinced his crew to continue onward to the new land called Greenland.

The waters were unfamiliar, and in a dense fog they missed the cape and ended up several days later at a level, wooded coastline very unlike the icy mountains of Greenland they had been told to look for. Continuing south for a time they observed from the ship the varied coastline of the new land, but, unlike most Viking explorers, because of harsh weather and limited time, never went ashore. For this they were later ridiculed by their countrymen. Turning out to sea again, they sailed north until at last they kept their Christmas appointment in Greenland with friends and family for a festive Yule.[5]

Naturally, the sighting of lands to the west would be no small topic of conversation in colonies filled with explorers eager for adventure but short on excitement. Bjarni's moving story undoubtedly influenced Eric's adventuresome young son,

Leif, who, a skilled sailor himself, had just voyaged over 3,000 miles to Norway and back.

Leif bought the ship from Bjarni and equipped it with thirty-five men, many of whom had probably just returned on the same ship from the new land. Sailing off, they seem to have had no difficulty discovering three new western lands. These they called Helluland (rockland), Markland (wooded land), and Vinland (wine, vine or grass land), a bay by a lush meadow with a mild climate.

The sagas say they built a large house at Vinland on the northern tip of a large island and settled there for a season. Part of their time was used scavenging for food, but there was also time for exploring the area. Following Leif's directions, however, they went no farther than they could return in a day's journey. Upon his return to Greenland the following summer, Leif's recounting of the adventure must have stirred his family, for in subsequent years both of his brothers and a sister set out for the same area in separate voyages, carrying large numbers of people who spent considerable time and encountered numerous adventures in the pleasant new land.

Romantic as these legends of discovery might seem, the truth of them was never really doubted by scholars, for it would be harder to believe the restless and adventuresome Norse lived for five centuries within a few days' voyage of the North American Continent and never found it. No doubt they landed there, but where?

Many searchers over the years had championed one location or another, but had failed to turn up remains of any Viking settlement along the Canadian or United States coastlines. It was fitting that a Viking descendant should at last accomplish the task.

A Norwegian explorer, Helge Ingstad, using the Norse Sagas for direction had been following the trail of Leif Ericsson for some time. Finally, in 1961, with his wife, Anne, he began to excavate the now-famous site on the northern tip of Newfoundland called L'Anse aux Meadows, "Bay of the Meadows." The site was sparsely populated, but had changed little over the centuries, and fit the description in the Sagas.

In the process of digging, they unearthed signs of Norse occupation—iron nails, iron slag, an iron smithy, a spindle whorl typical of European flywheels for weaving found at other Norse sites in Iceland and Greenland, and house foundations. One of the larger foundations was 70 by 55 feet with various rooms and foundations for several fireplaces. It would appear a sizeable group of people had lived there for a while. Carbon dating established the correct time period for Viking settlement.[6]

Notable authorities from Canada and the United States were called in to visit the site, and agreed that this was without any doubt a Norse settlement. Some felt it might well be Leif Ericsson's Vinland. Others held that this was Markland and that Vinland was to be found farther south, perhaps in the New England area. At any rate, it now looks certain that the Vikings were in America before Columbus. Further sites and artifacts will undoubtedly be found.

A Viking Culture Hero

With scholastic assurance that the Vikings did actually land on American shores around the year 1,000, it is natural to wonder whether or not these Nordic visitors had any bearing upon the hero stories. Could the Vikings be the source for the white, bearded bringers of culture and religion from across the seas? Certainly they fit the physical description with long fair hair, beards, tunics, and arrival in large sailing ships. And could the native hero from the sea be Leif Ericsson?

Certainly culture-hero material, Leif Ericsson was described by Sagas as a "large and powerful man, and of a most imposing bearing, a man of sagacity, and a very just man in all things." Of his spiritual qualities, one of the sagas relates that while in Norway, Leif had received the Catholic faith and returned to Greenland with a priest and a mission of conversion about the year 1,000. The mission was a total success except for one colonist who resisted baptism—Leif's father, Eric. It is not known if Leif was an aggressive evangelist for the new faith, but when he later stepped upon American shores any show of zealousness for the new-found faith, as fanatically displayed by later Spaniards, would have had a memorable effect upon natives there.

It has already been shown that in Yucatan and Coatzacoalcos, Mexico, the hero landed on native shores in company with nineteen men. The books of Chilam Balam mention three arrivals of foreigners in Yucatan, and with the third group came Kukulcán, who ended the turmoil between Mayas and Itzas.[7] According to native legends, this occurred about the time Leif sailed off from Greenland.

This neat solution to the problem of North American culture heroes would answer many unresolved questions. Leif and his recently-converted Christian followers can easily be pictured piously instructing the natives in a less primitive way of life and demonstrating cultural and technical skills previously unknown to them. The natives could have passed on this new knowledge and religious fervor to their fellow tribes until it filtered throughout the land and down into South America.

But such answers are already suspect in their simplicity, and Leif's timing was actually off. Aside from the obvious overwhelming problems involved in making such a solution work, the Vikings were too late to spread into all the distant corners visited by the fair god, and Newfoundland was too far north to influence the already well-established stories of Kukulcan and Viracocha so far to the south. The Olmec settlements and Teotihuacan of Mexico, with their hero images of feathered serpents, were geographically closer, but had peaked and disappeared centuries before the Viking era of conquest in Europe.

Itzamná and Votan, culture-gods of the Maya, were performing their memorable feats long before Viking exploration. They were already legendary in Yucatan before or about the time the first Viking leader Odin urged his Nordic band up through Russia to begin the settling of Scandinavian countries somewhere around the time of the early Christian era.

It is true that according to some estimates, Topiltzin Quetzalcoatl, bearded leader of the Toltecs, and Leif Ericsson were actually contemporaries, and there are striking similarities between the two. Both were large and imposing individuals, fair and bearded, descended from ancient migrations and from a leader who had crossed the sea. Both were instrumental in struggling with old gods and in championing a new faith. Each worshiped and received ecclesiastical authority from a more ancient deity—Quetzlacoatl from an older Quetzalcoatl and Leif from ancient Christianity. Ericsson and Topiltzin had each left their homelands to colonize new lands, and both were regarded highly in the literature of their people.

Except for the distance of approximately 4,000 sea miles, there might have been a direct meeting of the two, for about the time Topiltzin was leaving his beautiful cities of Tula and Cholula and crossing the ocean to the east on his "raft of serpents," Leif was heading west on the same ocean toward the new land. If Leif had been sailing a Viking warship, he too, like Quetzalcoatl, would have displayed a serpent or dragon on the prow of his ship, for Vikings also called their ships "feathered serpents."[8]

Similar as the two might seem, Lief was born in Norway, while Topiltzin was born in the Americas. The ancient deity from whom Topiltzin claimed authority, Ehécatl Quetzalcoatl, was said to have crossed the waters for the Americas centuries before Leif or Topiltzin. Some writers have tried to equate the earlier Odin with Votan, but Norse Sagas would surely have stressed any contact between their culture and that of the natives, but they are silent. The only cultural activity attributed to Leif during his brief stay in the New World is that he built a house. It is interesting to note that Leif and Topiltzin had one other very important thing in common: after leaving their homelands, both anticipated returning.

Leif did return—to Greenland. Nordic records do not relate that he ever again visited his winter home in Vinland, although records indicate his intention to. Had he ventured farther south into the waters of the Gulf of Mexico, he might have been hailed as the returning god Quetzalcoatl—or killed, for, according to a warning given one Viking on native shores, ". . . this is a large country . . . and people everywhere are hostile to foreigners."[9] If Leif got into Mexico, he would have beheld civilizations so grand no European in the Middle Ages could have imagined them; and if he got out, the Vinland Sagas would have become a best seller.

Still, history was good to "Leif the Lucky," for Norse sagas say that in Greenland Leif now had a goodly store of property and honor. A culture hero to his own people and a memorable character in the annals, his place was secure.

John Spencer Carroll, in the epilogue of his *Quetzalcoatl*, proposes another Icelander, Bjorn Ásbrandsson, who lived about the same time as Eric, and is believed to have come to American shores before Leif. There is, however, no real evidence for such a proposal, and the same arguments used against Leif apply to Bjorn.

Other Viking Candidates

Although Leif Ericsson does not qualify as a possible Quetzalcoatl and culture hero to the North American Indians, what of other Norsemen? Could they have worked their way along the land, carrying with them the seeds of tradition about fair gods from where the sun rises?

Chapter 6 examined various legends held among native tribes who dwelt along the rivers and coasts of America's northeastern lands. They spoke of a loving, white bearded god who came to them in the distant past bringing knowledge of the arts, agriculture, and a better, more-prosperous way of life. Some tribes believed he had come in a large canoe—possibly the native term for a ship. Some said he came alone, while others insisted he was in the company of peers. Always he came from the same direction—across the sea.

A chance landing on the North American coast of bearded, long-robed Vikings, recently Christianized and versed in the arts and agriculture, would have no influence in earlier Mexico or South America, but might have gotten a stronghold upon the later mythology of the local native North American tribes.

The Norse Sagas, a main source for investigation, tell that while in Vinland, Leif and his men explored the rivers and coast around them. From lack of any documentation, it is assumed no native inhabitants were encountered at that time. (John Cabot encountered no Indians when he re-discovered Newfoundland in 1497.)[10] However, in a later exploratory visit, Leif's brother Thorvald came across natives, whom he called "skraelings" or "wretches."[11] Instead of revering him, the natives killed him and ran his entourage out of the land in a very unViking-like manner. Since this is not the stuff culture heroes are made from, Thorvald can also be dismissed as the white bearded culture hero.

In an attempt at colonization, another Norseman from the Greenland colonies, Thorfinn Karlsefne, sailed three ships to Vinland with 160 men and women and their livestock. There they enjoyed good grazing, fish and game and lumber for their homes. During those three years, many voyages of discovery might have taken them southward along the Canadian and American coasts, or even far inland to more distant native contacts. Again, they fail to record any such explorations.

While in Vinland they traded with a few local inhabitants who at first seemed friendly. But the over-ambitious Vikings ruined the alliance when they exchanged milk and strips of cloth with the Indians for more precious pelts and furs. The "Skraelings" got wise to this exploitation and made life difficult for the foreigners with constant threats of attack.

After three years of this disruptive life, Karlsefne had had enough. He sailed away. No sooner did he arrive at his homeland, however, than Leif's sister, Freydis, set out for Vinland with several ships. It was a bizarre journey, during which she allegedly bared her breasts and gave a shriek that terrorized the natives. She then performed a very unsociable act of hatcheting the women in the party. (It's a wonder that story didn't make it into the living legends of the American Indians—what a tale to tell around the campfires.) On the return trip she was accompanied by "all of the products of the land which they could obtain, and which the ship would carry."[12]

These few native contacts obviously do not lend themselves to the story of a fair god, but there must have been other contacts of a more heroic nature, and possibly colonies whose influence may have persisted. In 1121 it is recorded that Erik Gnupson, bishop of Greenland, sailed to Vinland. Why, it has been argued, would he go to Vinland if not to administer to an existing colony of the faithful there? A robed priest might have impressed some of the natives, but, after their experience with Freydis one cannot say how much. No more is said of him.

Annals record later voyages for timber, and other Norse ships may have landed on American shores by miscalculation. The Sagas say that only fourteen of Eric's twenty-five ships made it to Greenland. A few returned to Iceland, but the others, with their cargoes of colonists, were never heard from. Few clues exist, but upon his return from Vinland, Leif encountered a floundering boat of fifteen men lost at sea.[13] Surely there must have been other Norse sailors who, like these men and Bjarni, allowed human error to lead them through the icy waters and fog past Greenland's cape and on to American shores a few days distant. Norse records say that "many of the ships headed for the colonies were lost."[14] Were they sunk, did they continue on to North America, or did they sail south only to capsize there? It seems there is always some intrigue to elicit fantastic speculation: eleventh-century murals on the lower Temple of the Warriors at Chichen Itza, Yucatan—now lost, but copied in 1928 by Jean Charlot—depict a long boat with shields along its side. The boat is sinking, and with it, wearing only blue-beaded necklaces, are nude, blond, fair-skinned sailors.[15] Vikings adrift?

To add to the mystery, not only Norse ships, but eventually all of the communities of Greenland vanished. One of the last visiting ships from Iceland to the colonies in the late fourteenth century found some 300 farms and seventeen churches—but no people remaining: no Christians and no Skraelings. What had happened to the Greenlanders after so many successful years? No one knows.[16]

Reports indicate the climate had grown increasingly colder, making agriculture more difficult. The Vatican received reports of attacks from British pirates and Northern Eskimos, which compounded the difficulties of the already oppressive life in Greenland. Possibly the people grew bored and weary of it all and migrated to more desirable lands in Iceland or along the American coast. If they arrived in Iceland, there should be a record of it, but none exists. Had they reached the Americas, they may have found an already established colony. There they might have died of disease or starvation or at the hands of unsympathetic natives. They may have travelled along the coast to the north or south or even further inland, where they eventually colonized and gradually intermixed with the inhabitants.

Renowned writer and admiral, Samuel Eliot Morison draws upon Norse sagas to tell of a voyager, Gudlief Gunnlangson, from Dublin, who in 1025 or 30, missed Iceland and drifted into an unknown harbor, possibly in the Americas. There, hundreds of natives threatened his life and that of the crew with death, but their leader, a tall, old, white-haired man riding on horseback under a banner, called them off. Speaking in Norse, the grand old man asked about "his people" in Iceland, mentioning several of the most prominent citizens. He then told the visitors to leave or face death by the natives, for they were not to be trusted, and were hard to deal with. They claimed to recognize this old leader, the man previously mentioned as Carroll's proposed Quetzalcoatl, Bjorn Asbrandsson, who years before had sailed westward from Iceland and had not been heard of since.[17] That some Norse intermixed with natives is believable enough, but Morison wonders where Bjorn would get the horse—a good question. Carroll says the legend uses the word, "reida," which can be translated, "upon a horse." But, he adds, it can also mean to be carried on the shoulders or on the cushioned chair of a litter.[18]

Norse and Natives

Hjalmar Holland reports a possible intermixture of natives and Norsemen reported in 1656 when a ship from "Fluching" (Flushing, Netherlands?) visited the shores of Baffinland, a Canadian island directly west of the old Norse settlements. The ship's commander, Nicholas Tunes, reported seeing among the common Eskimo of that region another type of people, distinctly taller, well-built, and of fair complexion.[19]

He also reports that farther south along the Labrador coast lived various other Eskimo tribes. Among them was a tribe called the Tunnit. They were visited in 1921 by G. M. Gathorne Hardy, who gave an inconclusive and puzzling report to the London Geographical Society, saying that they were not just another Eskimo tribe. He wrote that the Tunnit were treated all along the Labrador coast "as something not Eskimo, but contrasted with that race."[20] Was he suggesting they were Europeans?

Halfway across the upper continent in the Coronation Gulf and on nearby Victoria Island, Dr. Vilhjalmur Stefansson discovered in 1910 a pleasant people he called "blond Eskimos." In contrast to the more Asiatic Eskimo, he observed a strong resemblance to white men. Some, he reported, had blue eyes and curly hair. The few beards among them were light brown. These people were taller than the typical Eskimo and their customs, language and features, Dr. Stefansson determined, pointed to an Eastern contact.[21]

After living among them for a time, Dr. Stefansson wrote about widespread European characteristics among these tribes indicating that a mixture involving both European men and women had taken place in very remote times. Using some unexplained formula, he determined that "no intercourse between Eskimo and European [seemed] to have appeared in post-Columbian times." At the same time, however, he also noticed that "recent mixtures of whites and Eskimos produces Eskimo-looking children. His unhesitating conclusion to the matter was that blond Eskimos were related to Norse Greenlanders."[22]

If one allows for some mixture of Scandinavian and native Eskimo, not an unreasonable assumption, it would then seem likely that existing Eskimo legends would be replete with stories of white men who came from across the waters. But, strangely enough, here, where contact is most probable, the anticipated tales are apparently missing. Perhaps future research will suggest some.

Eskimos have no lack of mythology, for their collection is rich and goes back over a thousand years. But the closest they seem to come to any white hero is in tales of white spirits shaped like men who live in the underworld, and of the Inugpait, a race of giants who inhabit a country beyond the sea where the one-eyed people live."[23]

Eskimo hamlets are widely scattered, making inter-communication difficult. Yet many of the legends recorded by visitors to tribes living at great distances from one another are identical. The many ancient tales the natives held of animals, ancestors and supernatural beings were considered important enough to pass on and preserve in accurate detail, but any they might have once had about white, bearded bringers of culture were apparently not. Although white men unquestionably arrived, either they were forgotten or the stories were never recorded.

When John Davis rediscovered the near-deserted island of Greenland in 1585, he found Eskimos in the southern area whose features would indicate a possible mixture with Scandinavians. However there was not the slightest evidence for any European influence on the native culture. If there were once traditions about white settlers, they were no more.[24]

Judging from these Greenland Eskimos, it would appear that Scandinavians who were reported by the Vatican to have left their Christian faith, then in a weakened physical condition from lack of proper nourishment and living in the extremes of a country growing colder each year, became desperate to survive and simply moved north and intermixed with the Eskimo who had long ago learned well how to exist there. Cut off from their own people and customs, these people eventually absorbed the native traditions instead of the reverse. Any traces of culture heroes there faded long ago.

Vikings Inland?

For many years Diffusionists have been convinced that Scandinavians of the late Middle Ages had contact with native Americans all along the Canadian-American shores and as far as 2,000 miles inland. They point out that had early Norsemen explored the St. Lawrence river, they would have eventually entered the Great Lakes areas and perhaps the lands beyond.

Undaunted by scholars like George Bancroft, who in the nineteenth century wrote off the Norse stories as merely "mythological," they continued to look for clues. A real boost came in 1837 when Scandinavian scholar Carl C. Rafn brought the Vinland Sagas to the attention of the public. His timing was right, for it was the Romantic era of exploration when historical societies everywhere were searching for antiquities of any kind. Rafn's challenge to every historical society in the United States to find Norse antiquities was quickly taken up and suspiciously produced immediate results. Within a short time Norse relics turned up everywhere where none had been previously known.

Morison points out, in his scholarly and somewhat jocular coverage of the phenomenon, that "Local antiquarians found inscriptions carved in the runic letters of Scandinavia on rocky ledges facing the sea, on boulders in their pastures, and almost anywhere."[25] The surprising quantity of claims to Norse artifacts grew for over a century until, Morison quips, "few local histories of seaport towns between Newfoundland and the Virginia Capes [did] not open with a chapter asserting, 'Leif Ericsson was here!'"[26]

Eventually some two-dozen "Norse Inscriptions," three times that number of artifacts, and nearly as many sites— all on American soil—were attributed to the supposed Norse-Vinland voyages. Many of the "finds" were in Rhode Island and Massachusetts where Vikings admittedly might easily have sailed. Others were found as far away as Minnesota, during an 1893 revival of Norse searches, where later Scandinavians actually did settle in the Nineteenth Century. There, it was argued, the ancient Viking predecessors would also have likely settled had they sailed the Great Lakes.

Controversial "Norse" discoveries like Dighton Rock, Newport Stone Tower, copper discs from the Great Lakes, a skeleton in armor, a Norse axe, the Kensington stone, etc., have received much publicity and thorough examination written up in numerous books, including Williams' scathing *Fantastic Archaeology* (Chapter 9). In spite of favorable first appearances and some hesitant confirmations, none of these "finds" has ever been proven Norse to archaeologists.

In many cases, as with the Kensington stone, purportedly discovered under the roots of a large tree and bearing impressive Runic writing, inventionist scholars call them ambitious but obvious forgeries. On the reverse side, however, those who believe these objects authentic have a strong presentation in Cyrus Gordon's *Riddles of History* .

Since these finds offer little to the search for a culture hero, it is not the purpose of this book to determine the authenticity of such controversies. But one wonders why so many of the runic writings and some artifacts supposedly from Norse colonists have turned up where no Norse settlements existed. But at L'Anse aux Meadows, the one site definitely known to have been inhabited by the Norse, among the hundreds of artifacts, no runes at all were discovered.

Vanishing Vikings

Viking colonization in the Americas appears to have been short-lived. From what has been seen thus far—and the facts are not all in—it must be concluded that Viking influence upon the traditions of the Americas, and especially concerning the fair hero gods, appears negligible, and if at all, only in the North.

But while American Indians were busy enriching their own mythology without Viking help, later Europeans in America became fully occupied in assisting them. In many cases they far outdid the natives by providing obscure details of unauthenticated voyages, names and origins of passengers, ports of departure, size of ships, and even landing sites. What can one believe?

In the next chapter, startling reports of blond, blue-eyed natives in a genteel native setting stir the early American rivers of controversy as compelling claims of early Welsh movements across the sea and into native American life are considered.

8

Fair-Skinned Natives and the Welsh

The discovery of an eleventh century Norse colony at L'Anse aux Meadows on the northern tip of Newfoundland not only establishes firmly that Europeans were in the Americas before Columbus, it also resurrects questions previously dismissed as pure fantasy about the possible sea arrival of other early colonists. A more probing question is: If any, what influence would these foreigners have had upon the development of native cultures and upon stories about the culture hero?

Purported Norse influence along the Northeast coasts was examined in the preceding chapter and was found to be lacking or obscure. Now what of earlier European peoples reported to have come here even earlier: the Welsh, the Irish, the Celts? Considering their known history of extensive oceanic travels, is a North American visit possible? And if so, what, if any, influence remains from their arrival? This chapter will consider the intriguing possibility of Welsh colonies in the Americas.

One of the most dramatic cases raised for supposing foreign influence among ancient Indians involves the controversial Mandan tribes (introduced in chapter 6), who once lived on river bluffs of the great bend of the Missouri river in North Dakota. The Mandans had welcomed European arrivals long before Lewis and Clark's historic trek in 1804, and several writers observed these natives were the personification of the ideal Indian found in romantic nineteenth-century novels.

A reportedly peaceful people, the Mandans had settled into these plains about the same time Vikings were supposedly exploring the Great Lakes areas. Nine-thousand strong at one time, their numbers shrank considerably in the 1780's from a smallpox epidemic, and again reached near extinction shortly after 1837 from another. Thanks to the writings of early adventurers and trappers in that area, however, much that was intriguing about the Mandans still exists.

Prominent and last among these early recorders of Mandan life was George Catlin, a lawyer and portrait artist who abandoned civilization and a new bride to pursue an obsession with Indian cultures. On his canvases he sought to preserve from oblivion "the looks and customs of the vanishing races of native man in

America." He travelled thousands of miles through Indian territory from 1830 to 1836, painting a prodigious number of colorful, lifelike portraits. Many of these masterworks now hang in the Smithsonian Institute as illustrations of an extinct era of American heritage.

Although Catlin visited some fifty different tribes, he was most intrigued by the "hospitable and gentlemanly" Mandans who allowed his candid brush to capture them in detail and spirit. Living with them for many years, learning all aspects of their lives while painting their leaders, and engaging them in conversation for hours at a time, he found their origins to be especially mysterious and obscure. Of all the Indian tribes, he felt strongly that they were a most "peculiar and distinct race" and that they were "different in looks and customs from all other tribes he had seen." Any stranger among them, he insisted, would agree that "these are not Indians."[1]

He described Mandans as "light as half-breeds." Some of the women, he observed, had nearly white skin, hazel, grey and blue eyes, a sweetness of expression and great modesty of demeanor. He was amazed to find among them "every shade and color of hair," with the exception of red or auburn, existing among his own people, including bright silvery grey to white. In contrast to the coarse hair observed in other tribes, he found Mandan's hair to be "fine and soft as silk."

Their elegant appearance, diversity of complexions, various colors of hair and eyes, and the "singularity of their language" along with their peculiar European-like customs, which he could not account for, convinced Catlin they had sprung "from some other origin than that of the other North American tribes." He imagined them to be "an amalgam of natives with some civilized race."[2]

Familiar Stories

Although the great Mandan villages with their fascinating traditions are now gone, some results of those traditions still remain. In a reconstructed Mandan village above the river at Lincoln State Park, near today's city of Bismark, one can observe the Mandan "Ark" which was always displayed in their communal areas. Made of nine-foot wooden planks, it is reminiscent of a tower said to have been built anciently by their ancestors to save them from a great flood.[3]

The Mandan legend of that great event, as recorded by Catlin, somewhat parallels the Biblical account: a boat on a high mountain, a sole survivor, and a bird returning with a twig in its beak. Special religious ceremonies witnessed by Catlin were related to this flood, and began each year when the willow bough put out its leaves, for the natives believed "the twig which the bird brought in was a willow bough with fully grown leaves on it."[4]

A lively ceremony prepared the people for the coming drama with the shrieking of women and the howling of dogs (one understandably followed by the other).

At the peak of fervor, a "solitary individual could be seen, about a mile away, descending a prairie bluff, and making his way in a direct line towards the village!" All eyes watched, and no one objected when he entered the village. The chiefs then received the visitor graciously, shaking his hand and calling him "Nu-mohk-muck-a-nah" (the first or only man).

Catlin describes the body of this strange person as "chiefly naked, . . . painted with white clay, so as to resemble at a distance a white man." The color white seemed important to the ceremony, for it represented a real person said to have come to them in ancient times. In addition to the white man, the people also held in reverence a white robe, somehow identified with the Great Spirit, "Who lives in the sun and commands the thunder of heaven."[5]

In order to impress the event upon the minds of all Mandans, according to Catlin, the haunting figure stopped at each lodge of the village and related the terrible occurrence of the overflowing waters, telling them that he was the only person who survived the universal calamity, and that he in his big canoe landed on a high mountain in the west, where he now dwells.

Although other Indian tribes of that area had a similar story of a flood and a large canoe landing on a high mountain, Catlin points out that the Mandans were unique in insisting that it was not merely a local flood, but a universal one, covering all the land of the four corners of the world. Throughout the deluge the ancient Mandan people had managed to remain safe by staying deep underground. They were assured that as long as they continued to make sacrifices and perform the ceremonies taught them by the Almighty, they would be His favored people.

As Indian trust in him grew, Catlin was privileged to witness many sacred ceremonies and to hear legends and secrets kept from other white men. Among these he mentions the peculiar Mandan traditions recalling the appearance and death of a "Savior" and of an "evil spirit." He heard of the transgressions of the "mother" of these people, who claimed they were the first people of creation.

Another early nineteenth-century visitor to the Mandans, the German Prince Maximillian, in his rather detailed description of the Indians shortly before Catlin, mentions other Bible-like traditions among them such as belief in a future life and worship of a Lord of Life, most exalted and powerful, who created earth and man and all things. He also mentions their belief in some divine being who was the mediator between the creator and the human race.[6]

It would be very tempting to explain these unusual "European-like" characteristics of physical appearance, demeanor and religious beliefs in a tribe surrounded by other more typical Indians, with early visits from European explorers before Columbus. If newly Christianized Norsemen got into the Minnesota area from the Great Lakes, as an accumulation of supposed "Norse artifacts" there would seem to indicate the distance from there to the Mandans was the same as from Greenland to Vinland, only this time by more hospitable land.

Opponents to such an idea point out that in addition to the lack of any recognizable and conclusive Norse artifact ever having been found in this region, the Norse, in all their explorations, travelled exclusively by water and never by land.

Welsh up the Mississippi

A more romantic proposal to this perplexing conflict was offered by Catlin himself, whose imagination was excited by the then-common belief, that Mandans were actually a remnant of a lost Welsh colony that had settled along the Mississippi and Ohio river banks in the twelfth century. On a journey up the river, Catlin had seen what he describes as ancient remnants of Mandan lodges all along the banks as far as the Ohio river where he believed earlier tribes once resided and intermingled with the newly-arrived Welsh. Later, under hostile attacks from other tribes, they had moved gradually north to the present sites.

In support of this migration theory, he mentions the name they had previously called themselves, See-pohs-ka-nu-mah-ka-kee (the people of the pheasants). Locating them near known groupings of pheasants could place them in the forests of Indiana and Ohio, hundreds of miles to the southeast.7 Maximillian adds credence to this idea by also mentioning a Mandan tradition that in the distant past they "separated from the rest of their nation and went higher up the Missouri."[8]

So convinced was Catlin that these were remnants of the Welsh race that he compiled a list of Indian words he found similar to those of the Welsh language. After conferring with Welsh scholars upon the matter, he willfully wrote that modern Mandan was basically different from Welsh, but that the existing similarities were so pronounced that he felt there "must be a link between the two languages."[9] He felt it a tragedy someone did not study their language a century earlier, for, he lamented, the Mandans' use of Welsh-sounding words had by the 1830's almost gone out of practice.

Not outdone by early Norse and Spanish discoveries of the Americas, the Welsh in the 1580's had indeed come up with an intriguing legend about a prince named Madoc whose god was a bird-serpent seeking to escape from family contentions, he sailed out into the ocean in 1170 (some claim 562). There he supposedly discovered a wonderful new land and immediately returned to Wales to report it. He then equipped ten ships with eager colonists who sailed to the pleasant country, never to be heard of again.[10] In support of this theory, Deacon tells of Catlin hearing the words "Madoc Maho" in their prayers to the Great Spirit, although, he puzzles, the natives could not explain the reason. Della Armstrong, in *Who Discovered America?*, reports that the Mandan recalled their ancestors had come a long way over a great water to reach their present location. With them they had carried skin-wrapped parchments, mostly religious, which they believed told of their origins, but that present natives could not read.[11]

So could our visiting culture hero have been Welsh, not Norse? A large colony of highly cultured Welsh immigrants in ten sailing ships proudly parading up the Mississippi with a tall, handsome, valiant prince at the fore would have an indelible affect upon the aboriginal spectators. If the foreigners were to colonize, the Indian "neighborhood" would never be the same, and neither would their traditions.

The seemingly extravagant idea of Welsh colonization is not without some foundation. Stories of chance encounters with Welsh-speaking Indians and tribes were quite common in the late eighteenth and early nineteenth centuries. Some of these can be shown to be products of pure imagination, and some are exaggerated and enlarged versions of earlier stories; but many convincingly come from otherwise reliable people with alleged firsthand experiences.

Daniel Boone, for one, explored the early American scene until his death in 1820 and knew of the Welsh traditions. Because of his experiences with blue-eyed Indians in Kentucky and Tennessee, he believed the stories, although he lacked any Welsh background to enable him to verify such claims.[12]

In many of the tales, the narrator is far from the protection of civilization and in immediate peril from white-looking men in Indian dress. Although his unfortunate comrades often perish brutally, the teller of the story is spared for his ability to communicate with these fair natives in the Welsh tongue. Just a few of these fortunate adventurers who were spared because of their reported facility with the Welsh tongue were the Reverend Morgan Jones in 1666, Maurice Griffith and Captain Isaac Stewart around 1764, and Benjamin Sutton in 1775.[13]

Other less dramatic but equally compelling stories are similar to one Williams extracts from the 1806 "Greal" of Louisville, Kentucky, of a Lieutenant Joseph Roberts who reportedly encountered a Welsh-speaking Indian chief in full native dress in Washington D.C. eighteen years earlier. The Chief claimed that his forefathers had come from a "far distant country, very far in the east and from over the great waters." He explained that his tribe taught the Welsh tongue to the children until they were twelve, after which they could learn other languages. Roberts was amazed that the Indian spoke Welsh better than he did.

Another story stretches the mind even further. Deacon tells of a a charlatan known as "Chief" or "General" William Bowles who in 1791 posed as a Red Indian Chief. A known white man of probable Welsh descent, but armed with red Indian headgear and colorful tales of his alleged adventures, his stories did financially well in the pubs of London. And his efforts went far to advance the Welsh-Indian frenzy.[14]

The abundance of incidents like these readily feed the fires of diffusionistic thinking, but at the same time, they usually are poorly documented, if at all. Written so many years after the event, and often coming from persons of questionable reliability, they are rejected without consideration by the cautious isolationist.

Another Side of the Coin

Such romantic stories make fascinating reading, and there seems to be no end to them, but even Norse and Welsh coins have two sides. To accept perfunctory explanations without delving further would be short sighted and would certainly be unfair to the origin of Americas' pursuit of the culture hero.

George Catlin scrupulously recorded in word and painting minute details of Indian life as he saw it. He took a few liberties, like placing summer costumes on the natives in a winter scene, but for the most part, according to those who saw his works, he portrayed them faithfully. If, as he relates, the Mandan were so strikingly different from their neighbors, it would seem an easy task to verify the fact in similar accounts by other visitors to the tribes. Surely, they too would have noticed the obvious contrasts.

The Mandan lodges were a long way from colonial settlements and a difficult three-months journey up river from St. Louis. Although the French discovered the Missouri in 1673, it was over a half century before they reached the Mandans. The first French visit on record was that of fifty-two Frenchmen, in the company of a missionary, seeking a route to the western sea in 1738. Before moving on, the leader, Sieur Verendrye, left two men among the Mandan villagers to learn the native language. These men seemed to have enjoyed themselves considerably, and a year later reported that they had been well treated and that the natives regretted to see them leave. Verendrye found the Mandans different in customs from other Indians, and observed that their villages were laid out in streets and squares. He called them "white beards" and believed they might have had some trace of European ancestry because of their light skin and fair hair. One of the chiefs told him that his people once lived far to the south before being driven north by their enemies.[15]

In spite of these suggestions of fair-skinned natives, however, a search through the early journals and reports of the many explorers and fur traders to the Mandan, both before and concurrent with Catlin, reveals, oddly enough, that although a few writers hint at differences, most did not.

Following another visit by the Verendryes in 1742, British traders from the north followed the trail, commencing a long history of trade with the Hudson Bay and Northwest companies. As much as the British trafficked with the Mandans, their records show they seemed not to have found any special reason to idealize them.[16]

James Mackay, who visited the tribes for the Missouri Company in 1797, shortly after the first small-pox epidemic cut the number of their villages from nine to two, said he found them "as good as they are mild," but made no mention of any unique appearance. At the same time, his notes recorded in the Missouri Historical Society show he was intrigued by the Welsh-Indian concept. He surprisingly painted a glowing picture—not of the Mandans, but of another tribe instead, the Paduacas, in whom he noted a fair skin and civilized manner resembling that of white people.[17]

Another explorer, Trudeau, visited many tribes between 1804 and 1834. He mentioned reddish hair and fairness among the Canabiches and Padaucas, but described the Mandans only as "gentle and peaceful."[18]

Some early visitors to the Mandan villages recorded an actual disdain for them. Chardon, a colorful and usually cheerful character in the early scenes, and a friend of Catlin, lived at the nearby Mandan fort for years and knew the Indians "intimately." To him the idea of Mandan superiority was absurd. He described them sweepingly as the "meanest, dirtiest, worthless, cowardly set of dogs on the Missouri."[19] This was hardly the view of his friend Catlin. The fact that he was in fierce competition with them for the fur trade may have had some influence upon his attitude.

Two more foreign residents among the Mandans between 1784 and 1812, David Thompson and Alexander Henry, seem to have experienced some unpleasantries with the natives. Their vivid descriptions made the Indians out as "stupid, superstitious, gluttonous, lewd, cowardly, ungrateful and barbarous, cruel, lying and thieving."[20] Thompson and Henry were apparently not prepared to see the Indians favorably in any condition.

Thompson's life was one of strictest austerity, and he found all Indians "repulsive and barbarous." When he saw an Indian woman dance she became, in his eyes, a lowly "courtesan." Henry was disgusted with the Indian practice of eating Buffalo entrails. He might have found the European custom of eating "escargot" snails equally disgusting, and entrails are not uncommon in the American diet today. Both writers undoubtedly projected the inhibitions of their own backgrounds, and one wonders why they stuck it out so long.

Not everyone, however, was so demeaning. Truteau, a schoolmaster sent to Indian country by the Missouri Company ten years before Lewis and Clark, called the Mandans "good savages."[21] Lewis and Clark, on their historic trek of 1804-1805, found these people, newly added to the United States with the Louisiana Purchase, peaceful and seldom aggressors.[22] With a specific assignment from President Jefferson to keep their eyes open for the Madogwys "Welsh Indians," these famous explorers too had a keen interest in locating Welsh descendants among native tribes, but say little except that the Mandan chief was called "Big White," and mention a "half-white breed" Indian boy said to be preserved from a fire by the great medicine spirit "because he was white."[23] It is interesting that none of these writers seems to have seen what Catlin describes with glowing conviction.

So what has been learned? The Mandans were unique or they were not. They were wretched or they were wonderful. They borrowed their traditions from earlier visitors from the east or they did not. It's a perplexing situation filled with many paradoxes. Perhaps what has been witnessed is that writers express the same things in divergent ways, or that Indians in the same hunting party will have different tales to tell.

Conflicting Reports

The Mandans were not the only Indians to suffer contradictions from white observers. Lewis said of the Teton Sioux that they were the "Vilest miscreants of the savage race," while Caleb Atwater thought them a "fine race." George Kennedy studied them up close and saw them as "proud samples of men in a savage state," while others insisted the Sioux were the "greatest villains in this part of the world."[24]

It is likely that these ambiguities reflect more of the personalities and literary abilities of the writers, and the particular times of their exposure to the native races and to individuals in that race, than they reflect the inherent characteristics of the tribes. Many early writers agree that the "barbaric and deteriorating nature" of Indian tribes was largely due to their exposure to unscrupulous whites who exploited them mercilessly, then passed on their vices instead of their virtues. Such experiences rapidly changed the white man's image in the mind of the natives who, according to Nasitir (297), had previously regarded them as divinities.

Practices previously unfamiliar to the Indians, like being sold as slaves, receiving easy credit and then later having to pay heavy, unexpected debts—along with broken treaties and epidemics brought in by whites—are a few of the irritations that could easily vary the Indian temperament from one visit to the next. Depending upon the tribe's most-recent experience with these unpredictable white intruders, the attitude toward them might be favorable one year and hostile the next, a fact which Chardon witnessed and wrote of in his experiences with them. Truteau also reported that his experience with the Sioux was at first pleasant and friendly, but as soon as the Teton Sioux joined up with them they became traditional and hostile.

Undoubtedly the Indian character was no more uniform than that of the whites. Maximillian reported that some of the Mandan tribe members were rude and savage, and some addicted to thieving, while on the whole the rest were well disposed toward the whites. Dealing with the wrong Indian on a bad day might establish distasteful attitudes, which would account for at least some of the discrepancies in the early writings.[25]

Still, it is singular that George Catlin stands practically alone with his insistence that the Mandans' unique look and traditions might have resulted from a mixture with a lighter race. It is perplexing that the purported fairness of the Mandans was already a legend by Catlin's time, but he alone elaborated upon it. Maximillian provided a mixed review. He stated as unfounded the notion that the Mandan's had a fairer complexion than other Indians, but then remarked that upon removing the paint from their faces they appeared almost white, with some color in their cheeks.[26]

At one point, some of Catlin's writings were disregarded by other fellow travellers when he published a description of a unique viewing of the tortuous and excruciating Okeepa Ceremony enacted to bring young men to full manhood. Other visitors to the Mandans claimed they had never heard of or witnessed the self-inflicted hanging of young Indian men by rawhide straps until their flesh tore. Later on, when the Indians allowed others to view the lurid ceremony, it was reported that Catlin's description of it could not be improved upon. Perhaps one day his statements about fair skin and hair will be vindicated as well.

If there were among the Mandans people of a "half-breed" appearance, as Catlin and Lewis and Clark suggest, it should not be surprising, for every writer except Catlin mentioned the "promiscuous nature" of the Mandan women and the indifferent-to-enthusiastic attitude of their men toward sharing them. Truteau remarked in his journal of 1794 that the favors of wives, daughters and sisters could "be bought with a little vermillion or blue ribbon." Lewis and Clark's report of the Ricaras, neighbors to the Mandans, and perhaps applicable to them as well, said, "These women are . . . disposed to be amorous, and our men found no difficulty in procuring companions for the night . . . ." Lewis later added, discretely, "The fair sex received our men with more than hospitality."[27]

Apparently nothing had changed by Maximillian's time some forty years later, for he says the conquest of the Mandan maids was the "chief business of the young [white] men among these tribes" and in fact "filled up the greater part of their time." Each women often had two, three or more white lovers.[28]

Lonely, indulgent trappers and traders would not be slow to advantage themselves of this inviting situation. Truteau confessed that "our young Canadians and Creoles who come here are seen everywhere running at full speed like escaped horses, into Venus' country." [29] These young, amorous mavericks often paid for their indulgence with painful diseases but it did not slow them down, for, according to many writers of the time, the Indians had amazing cures.

Whites living among the Mandans over a one hundred year period would tend to increase the incidence of fair appearance of the Indian. The Verendreyes mentioned in 1738 that a Frenchman had been living among the Mandans for years before their arrival, and one of the neighboring tribes already had Spanish-speaking members among them, indicating a long contact with outsiders. One of the men left among the Mandans from the Verendrey party observed more than language, for he admitted that the erotic rites of the Mandans attracted many visitors from European traders. These situations would extend the period of possible intermixture of whites and Indians considerably.

In the American wilds, after years of separation from their families and white settlements, it was not uncommon for traders to have several native families as well. Chardon married more than one Indian woman, and most of his white associates had several Indian families, leaving half-breed children. The first offspring from such a union would likely be Indian in appearance, but each successive breeding with whites and with each other would increase the possibility of lighter characteristics.

The large number of trading posts along the rivers attracted groups of traders, trappers, scholars, scientists, artists, and writers—sometimes 50 to 100 at a time. With an abundance of inviting native women whose good looks and light appearance no doubt increased in proportion to the number of years the solitary white man had lived in the wilderness, it would appear that America's native land was not the only object of early exploration. What a curious oversight if one hundred years and several generations later Catlin had not recognized in the Mandans some fair hair, light skin, and blue eyes.

This is not to suggest that a few passers-by, however promiscuous, could within a century alter the characteristics of a whole nation of Indians, but a great number of them could leave a considerable mark. Also, the smallpox epidemics would have less effect upon the half-breeds whose resistance to the disease would be higher than that of the full-blooded native. Catlin did not make it clear just how many of the tribe members appeared unique.

Contact From the Past, But Whose?

It was not just the physical appearance that made the Mandans different. They had many traditions that closely parallel those of Christian teachings. A Savior, a white Noah, an ark, Mother Eve, the great Creator God, and hope for life eternal can all be read into the tales without the slightest stretch of imagination. Could these be attributed to mere coincidence? It would appear there is a clear-cut case of foreign influence upon the Mandan tribes from somewhere out of the past. But whose past, and how far past?

If historians, by some remote bit of luck, should someday discover pre-Columbian Welsh settlements where Mandan tribes once resided, and which modern-day developers have not obliterated, the answer will be clear. But until then, no settlement has been discovered, and many scholars on the issue are more than content to dismiss it at that.

One of them, Admiral Morison, argues convincingly against any Welsh influence by bringing forth a strong witness from the past, John Evans, a "pious" young Welshman from a family of Methodist clergy. (Some would have Evans himself in the clergy). At age twenty-one this Welsh venturer set out for America on a mission to discover Welsh Indians and to reconvert them to Christianity. Sailing up the long Missouri in 1796, he finally reached the Mandan country and spent a winter with them and their neighbors.

Upon his return, Evans reported that "the Indians differ but little one from the other in manners and customs."[30] As for the supposed Welsh Indians, which Evans was admittedly well qualified to discover, Morison reports that Evans had met no Welsh-speaking Indians, and said, "By my Communications with the Indians. . . I am able to inform you that there is no such people as the Welsh Indians."[31]

Morison is adamant that Evans' firm testimony should have spiked the "venerable myth," which was still being passed on by Catlin and others. But, in order to erase any lingering doubts, and to make his case conclusive, Morison further dismisses the idea of Welsh influence with the "authoritative words" of the Bureau of American Ethnology: *There is not a provable trace of Welsh, Gaelic or any other European language in any native American language.*"[32]

One might reasonably assume that such a conclusive argument should close the Welsh-Indian case once and for all, and to do so at this point would seem justifiable. But in research, as in a good mystery, there is always one more intriguing point of view to consider, and conclusions are seldom so final.

Unalterable as Morison's arguments may appear, there is still the unaccountable existence of over seventy individual reports of Welsh language among Indians collected during the Madoc wave of the seventeenth and eighteenth centuries. Could they all be lies, misunderstandings or accidental similarities? To suggest Welsh influence *never* existed, based on the Bureau's statement that there is not even a *trace* of the language raises some doubt, for all languages bear an occasional resemblance to other languages, however remote. One can't help admiring the Bureau's incredible resourcefulness in being able to check out every last tribe, word and report, but had the Welsh arrived in the twelfth century, as some claim, most remnants of the Welsh language, six hundred years later, would surely have faded from use or been absorbed altogether by Indian dialects, making detection difficult at best. Lewis and Clark report that the dialect of the Mandans differed from other tribes around them, but "their long residence together blended their manners, and . . . language."[33]

Certainly no Welsh exists among the "pure-blooded" Mandans today, for the simple reason that there are no more "pure-blooded" Mandans. But who would suggest that proves there never were such people? For that matter, many historical records which reject the idea of Welsh among the Mandans also authoritatively state that the Mandans were totally obliterated by the smallpox epidemic of 1837. However, the many living descendants of the Mandans today invalidate that belief (as calling Fort Lincoln State Park can quickly verify). Modern-day Mandans explain that when most of the tribe was destroyed by the dreadful disease, the surviving 125 or so merely moved in with neighboring Ricara and Hidatsa tribes. Although the last "pure-blooded" Mandan reportedly died in 1974, many "half-blooded" Mandans still live in North Dakota near Ft. Lincoln State Park and the Knife River villages.

The Remarkable John Evans

Of course there is John Evans, who, as a Welshman living among the Indians in 1796, was in a much better position than Catlin to determine the whole Welsh/Indian matter. The likelihood of his finding any Welsh "traces" among the Mandans a quarter of a century before Catlin was somewhat better. Also, Evans was reared in Wales and spoke the language, which Catlin did not. He was reported to have come specifically in search of Welsh Indians, and yet living among the various tribes, flatly denied their existence. There would appear to be little room for dispute.

Critics of the John Evans argument have stubbornly suggested that like other whites to the area, he was too busy while there to notice his own language among the Indians. But anyone who has ever travelled far from home knows that a single word or two in one's own tongue among foreigners literally shouts out and is most welcomed, however preoccupied one might be. No, Evan's testimony is too strong to ignore, and opponents of the Welsh theory have leaned heavily upon it for a reliable and accurate evaluation. What more qualified witness than a Welsh-speaking missionary to settle the matter! But, even here, there are some surprising elements to the story that invite reconsideration. Those who have built on Evan's authority are either unaware of or have conveniently neglected to mention some lingering inconsistencies surrounding this complex young man. His story, briefly reviewed here, is aptly told in Williams (1979), Deacon (1966), Morison (1971), and Nasitir (1927, 1952).

The assumedly "pious" Evans, according to his journals and to those who knew him, came to America with less interest in religion than in adventure and liquor. He worked in Baltimore for a while when he learned that the Church back home would not provide for him adequately, and in fact, discouraged his going because of the difficulties and dangers involved in such a trip. With youthful determination he chose to ignore their caution, and instead worked his way to St. Louis, Missouri, which at the time was under Spanish control.

His arrival there was ill timed, for the Spanish had been battling the French, the British and the Americans for control of the Missouri territories, and they looked upon the Welsh as British agents. They also believed Evans to be a spy and threw the luckless newcomer into prison. Embittered and discouraged by his confinement and the lack of support from the homeland, he was soon freed by turning his back on his countrymen and joining up with his captors, who were on the verge of war with Britain.

The Spaniards must have recognized some value in the spirited youth, for they hired him as second in command to James Mckay, a Canadian fur trader who also gave up allegiance to his country for the Spanish camp. Together they were to sail up the Missouri, build forts, and protect the Spanish interests there. The close friends, Evans and Mckay, were temporarily separated when "Don Juan" was sent ahead in 1796. Evans' mission to discover long-lost ancestors among the Mandans had at last materialized, and he was one of the first white men to reach them from the southern route, although whites from the north had been in that area for some time.

At the Mandan camp, Evans showed his loyalty to his new company by lowering the British flag and hoisting the Spanish banner over the fort in the name of "their great father the Spaniard," thus becoming the first white man to establish Spanish authority on the upper Missouri. The ties with his homeland were now completely severed, and he had found new acceptance. By what means he was able to communicate with the Indians we are not told, but he seems to have obtained an unusually strong hold on them, for he records that they heard what he had to say and vowed that hereafter they would follow his counsels on all occasions.

For the short duration of a harsh, lonely winter, Evans was busily occupied maintaining Spanish claims against the protesting British and French. The following spring when he returned to St. Louis, he did not return to his country, but remained with the Spanish as a land surveyor. It was from there he made his statement about the absence of Welsh among the Indians.

Those who question the validity of Evan's testimony point out that he refused to return to his Welsh home, or even to Philadelphia, because in joining with the Spanish he became a traitor to America and to Britain. They claim that Spaniards had seen in Evans an opportunity to communicate with the "Madogwys" and to have any report of their existence convincingly denied through a young Welshman out to discover his lost ancestors. Why else, it is argued, would they want Evans? He was no seasoned traveller and had no experience among northern Indians.

There is no doubt the Spaniards feared the British might attempt to claim possession of Mandan lands if they could prove an early Welsh colonization. They make this clear through a declaration by the Spanish Governor of New Orleans: "It is in the interest of His Catholic Majesty that the reports of British Indians in Mandan country be denied once and for all."[34] Again, some writers insist that in Evans they apparently found the man to do it. They believed that Evans reported only what the Spaniards told him to report. In his orders from the Missouri Company he was instructed to reveal his findings only to his superior officers, and to no one else.

That Evans would deliberately misrepresent the Welsh issue is somewhat difficult to accept and even more difficult to prove. But curious information comes from Arthur T. Halliday of Baltimore, who said his great-grandfather, Jabez Halliday, knew Evans personally. In a letter he wrote to the author, Richard Deacon, Halliday claimed his great-grandfather believed that when financial aid did not come from his countrymen, Evans kept what he found out about the Indians to himself, hoping to sell his discovery to someone else. Halliday's grandfather also believed Evans failed to return to Philadelphia because he had lied to his friends about the Indians. He stated in 1803 that Evans boasted he knew more about the Welsh Indians than anyone, but that "when heavily in strong liquor he bragged to his friends in St. Louis that the Welsh Indians would keep their secret to the grave because he had been handsomely paid to keep quiet on the subject." Although rumors reached Wales that Evans had in fact discovered the Madogwys, Evans purportedly contended that ". . . in a few more years there would be no trace of any Welsh ancestry or language, as time and disease would eventually remove all traces."[35]

The explorer Maximillian was perhaps referring to Evan's negation of Welsh involvement when he wrote of the Mandans some thirty years later, "Some have affirmed that they have found in North America Indians who spoke the Gaelic tongue . . . but it has long been ascertained that this notion is unfounded . . . ."[36]

Evidence demeaning Evans is thin and difficult to corroborate, especially since it existed only in one unavailable letter, and it is uncertain how reliable Mr. Halliday's great grandfather is as a witness against Evans, or if he might have perhaps had a grudge against him. In Evan's favor are his own journals which demonstrate an apparently strong and honest character, although self-professed. His orders from the Spanish-owned Missouri Company were to record all that might be remarkable and interesting, especially customs, religion and language. He was told to "prove the truth of everything."[37]

Something of Evan's character is revealed in a letter by him to the Company, in which he pleads with them to keep promises with the Indians sacred rather than fall into the same discredit as the traders who were there before them. Concern for his own character appears in his journal where he says he would be happy and satisfied if his actions served some day to attest to the purity of his zeal and the integrity of his principles.

Again, on Evan's behalf, it is often mentioned that he was well educated and highly capable. He provided a fine map of the upper Missouri which, along with his notes, later benefitted the Louis and Clark expedition; Williams calls him the last of the great Conquistadors for Spain. Following his stay with the Mandans, he returned to St. Louis a hero and took a job settling newly arrived Americans in Jackson, Missouri. Unfortunately, little more is known about the elusive John

Evans, or upon his intentions, for he reportedly died of alcohol before he was thirty. At the time he was living in the home of the Spanish governor.

The Evans story shows the difficulty of determining the truth of a matter. By leaving out some information, or by favoring some other, a strong case may be made for either side of a question. Most followers of the Welsh theory seem not to be indifferent to the outcome and, in fact, take sides quite vehemently.

Until new and substantial evidence surfaces, the Welsh question remains unsolved. This fascinating controversy, contrary to Morison's and others' dogmatic pronouncements, is far from over and may never be resolved with satisfaction to everyone.

Gwyn Williams in her extensive coverage and dismissal of the myth in *Madoc, The Making of a Myth*, quotes her rival and champion of Madoc, Zella Armstrong, who in *Who Discovered America?* avoids any hint of denial, but hesitantly confesses: "If the Amazing Story of Madoc is a myth, it is a *good* myth."[38]

Still, determined to keep the Welsh issue alive, the Virginia Cavalier Chapter of the D.A.R. in 1953 erected a memorial at Fort Morgan, Alabama, with this statement:

> In Memory of Prince Madoc, a Welsh Explorer,
> Who landed on the Shores of Mobile Bay in 1170
> and Left Behind, With the Indians, the Welsh Language.[39]

Some Thorny Questions

Unresolved questions still hover: How much of Mandan traditions that closely parallel the tenets of Christianity were native and how much did the Mandans absorb from the teachings of various Christian missionaries who visited there? And did those teachings endure to Catlin's time? What Christian teachings may have been imparted by the Minister's son, John Evans, in his conversations during the long winter months among the Mandans? At that time, Evans' only active missionary effort was apparently in the Spanish cause. But what person, raised in an active Christian family, could resist sharing some Bible stories with a people who delighted in telling tales and who were curious about the ways of the white man?

The earliest recorded contacts with the Mandans were the French, who, in 1738, expressed surprise in discovering that one of the Mandans wore a cross and spoke of Mary and Jesus. Barring any previous modern-day contact, one would be forced to accept the existence of pre-Conquest visits from European Christians, however remote the period. A careful reading of the French account, however, sheds some needed light on this remarkable incident.

While the Verendrey party was with the Mandans, they recorded that the Mandan tribes were visited by another tribe from some distance away. This tribe knew of a white people to the west who "wore beards and prayed to the Grand

Master of Life." In addition, they prayed to "Mary and Jesus and used a cross " in their worship. It is also within reason that the same tribe introduced the Mandans to stories of The Flood of and Mother Eve, though there is no record that such a circumstance occurred.[40]

The Frenchmen were sufficiently intrigued to follow the stories in an attempt to discover the identity of these mysterious white men, but were unsuccessful in locating them. However, they assumed them to be Spaniards, who at the time inhabited lower California. It is highly possible that the Mandans experienced early contact with the Spaniards, for Spanish horses were reported up the Missouri as early as 1706, and Mandans had horses, bridles, and guns by 1750.

The Verendrey contact with the Mandans in 1738 may also have contributed something of Christian teachings, for that was the main purpose of taking along a missionary and of learning the language. Whatever all of this means, it is certain that the Mandans were at least exposed quite early to Christian doctrines similar to the religious traditions Catlin found so unusual among them. What of all this may have predated the eighteenth century arrivals cannot now be determined.

Now several centuries after these occurrences, it is easy for one to reflect upon them because they were written down by trappers, traders and missionaries. But how much of it was absorbed, retained or even registered by the Indians of the early 1800's who had no writings to refer to? The first smallpox epidemic, shortly after their initial contacts with the whites, undoubtedly took many of their historians and preservers of tradition. With them may have gone some of the memorized legends. The newer generation, in attempting to recall the past, might have included some of the recently received Christian teachings. But how much of an occasional encounter with Christian doctrines would become a part of the permanent traditions of the Mandan nation, or how much was similar to what was already there cannot be determined, but a later event may provide some insight.

An example of mixing traditions occurred in the 1890's when Christian and Indian beliefs fused and blazed across the plains into much of North America. The newly-founded Native American Church mixed Christian doctrines—such as God, Mary, the angels, and Jesus—with strong doses of Indian symbolism, which the various tribes readily absorbed.[41] With so little recorded about the earlier Mandans, perhaps a similar absorption of Christian ideas occurred with them as well. The full Mandan story, one that promises the elucidation of many intrigues, has yet to be written.

Some people in search of authentic Indian myths would be content to summarily dismiss any native similarities to Christianity on the assumption that they must have been introduced since Columbus. But to assume that all Indian parallels with European characteristics were direct implants from the early days of American colonization would be as wrong as to deny there were any. Cultural parallels do not always require contact, and, theoretically, what surfaces in one culture can surface independently in another. On the other hand, if Mandan similarities to foreign cultures are eventually shown to have come from European exposures, either in recent or in ancient times, we will have a unique record of syncretism, that fascinating union of divergent religious beliefs and cultural practices.

These pursuits have left some unresolved questions about white, bearded foreigners among the Mandans in ancient times, but they have also given insights to the complex nature of the fascinating traditions of the elusive white bearded culture hero. Reviewing this period provides one with a better perspective of the confusion resulting from the intermixture of post-Conquest European and native cultures which occurred all over the Americas. The quest gets even more challenging as one moves farther back in history.

The next chapter enters the so-called "Dark Ages" to examine fascinating candidates far across the Atlantic and Pacific Oceans who offer more intriguing possibilities in the search for the identity of the Americas' culture heroes.

9

MIDDLE AGE CONTACTS FROM EAST AND WEST

Of the perplexing questions that obsessed the first European visitors to the Americas before the devastation of conquest, the most asked was, "Where did these advanced civilizations come from?" And the answer natives gave was that their civilization came in ancient times with a white, bearded visitor from across the sea. If this mystery man is indeed a foreigner, the search must be for a candidate whose native culture included a highly developed civilization—one who, no doubt, would have been as revered in his own land as in the Americas.

Most legends about the hero are not specific about the time of his arrival, so every age needs to be scanned in search of him. But, in scanning highly developed periods of Old World history, it would at first seem natural to bypass the seemingly "dark" period in Europe called the Middle Ages—between the fall of Greece and Rome around the fifth century, and the renewal of enlightenment brought on by the Renaissance in the fifteenth. During this stretch, according to tradition, classical knowledge was all but lost. Yet a closer examination of this overlooked era demonstrates a surprising intellectual expansion in Europe and Asia, providing some promising candidates for heroes in ancient America where cultural achievements at that time reached an even higher level than in countries across the sea.

It has been suggested that the only thing "dark" about the "Dark Ages" is present-day man's knowledge of them. Certainly the people who lived through them did not consider them dark; too much was going on. Menacing tribes like the Huns, the Goths, the Franks, and the Vandals fiercely conquered and redefined their territories. European kingdoms dramatically shifted and expanded. Cities grew and trade flourished. Expressions of faith in art, music and architecture, blossomed, and Christianity, which had vigorously penetrated the known world, faced an explosive new challenge—Islam.

At the same time, great advances also followed the decline of old powers in the Orient. Political upheavals in China forced new dynasties to actively protect and expand their territories, and eventual unification led to an unprecedented imperial glory, with growth in the arts and sciences. Awareness of other lands and people was growing, and missionaries of the recently arrived Buddhist faith infiltrated extensive areas, perhaps far beyond areas history has previously considered. In reality, the fourth through the eighth centuries A.D. burst upon the world with explosive activities and dramatic contrasts.

If ignorance of a culture and its accomplishments constitutes a "dark age," then all of Europe at that period, and for centuries following the Conquest, were "certainly in the dark" about ancient America. Only in the twentieth century has man come to realize that in many ways Old-World activity in the Middle Ages was matched or surpassed by the New-World cultures which reached unprecedented heights in both the Northern and Southern hemispheres.

This extraordinary period of accelerated achievement in Mesoamerica, referred to as the "Classic Period," is marked by a burgeoning population, the spread of wealthy kingdoms, and the building and expansion of great cities such as Teotihuacan, Tikal, Caracol, Copan, Palenque, and Cholula with their ornate and imposing structures. In addition, American natives employed complex art forms and advanced sciences, invented the use of zero, evolved strong dynastic lineages and, among the Maya, developed the art of writing and one of the world's most complex calendars. Similar, but less dramatic, events were happening in North and South America as well.

The driving force behind many of these remarkable accomplishments in the Americas was the white, bearded culture hero. Since Indian legends insist that he came from across the seas, candidates from both Atlantic and Pacific sides of the Old World of the "Dark" and Middle Ages will be considered for possible candidates.

Prospects from Old Ireland

Sixth-century Europe provides a consideration for an American culture hero from an obscure, but nonetheless historic group of Irish monks. Four-hundred years before the advent of the Vikings, these religious enthusiasts discovered the best way to minimize their exposure to life's evils and temptations was to practice religious penitence out on the Atlantic. The most famous of these wandering ascetics, Saint Brendan, has survived obscurity through the preservation of his journeys in the Irish Sagas, called "Imrama," recorded in the *Navigatio S. Brendani*, popular about the time of Greenland's discovery by the Norse.[1]

Typical of the times, St. Brendan allegedly sailed from Ireland into the inhospitable ocean with seventeen fellow Monks. Their aquatic odyssey took them to the Faroe and Shetland Islands, to Iceland, perhaps to the Azores and, according to surviving legends, to several other undetermined lands including the Terra Repromissionis Sanctorum, a mysterious "Land Promised to the Saints." This land was said to be on the far side of the Atlantic somewhere between Europe and the Orient.

Their humble means of travel was the curragh, a small, wicker-framed, leather-covered boat invented by the earlier Celts and still in use today by Celtic-Irish fishermen. The seaworthiness of this type of vessel has been reconfirmed in modern-times by the British author and explorer Timothy Severin, who revived the old Brendan legend and made it even more plausible by following the legendary route in a similar curragh. (His rigorous modern-day 3,500-mile voyage is dramatically recorded in *The Brendan Voyage* and in *National Geographic*, December, 1977.)

Following Brendan's ambitious trail for over a year, Severin eventually landed at Newfoundland. Although he could not prove that the American shores were Brendan's legendary island, Severin concluded that such a trip was possible even in the small basket-like boats.

Brendan's colorful voyage involves sea monsters, birds that sing words of praise, miraculous appearances of food, fire on the back of a whale so large it was thought to be an island, and even visits by other monks who were marooned on islands of the sea. In spite of the fantastic nature of the tales, many writers, including the usually skeptical veteran seaman and naval historian himself, Samuel Morison, believe that Brendan was a real person. They also believe that his seven-year journey was just as real, although considerably embellished by Brendan or later copyists.

Most interpreters of the saga deny emphatically that Brendan ever reached the Americas, but a few romantics, like Boland (1961), would have him not only in the Americas but all the way south to Florida, where they speculate he settled in a supposedly already-established colony of fellow-Irish monks. This ungrounded contention he bases mainly on native traditions recorded centuries later that white men actually once lived in Florida and used iron. Such compelling legends are a sure foundation for imagination, but not sufficient to support the spectral walls of a monastery no one has ever found.

The sagas do say that following years of adventuresome island-hopping, Brendan at last found a "great island" whose trees bore ripe apples, and whose river of clear water sustained his life. While Brendan explored the area, a youth suddenly appeared and announced to his party that this was the land God had promised them. Shortly after that, Brendan left for his home in Ireland where, just before his death, he recounted the marvellous experiences of his past seven years.

What then can be made of Brendan? Did he reach the American coast? Was there a colony of monks basking in the Florida sun? (At one time the whole Eastern coast of America was called Florida.) Could Irish visits there be the beginnings of stories about white, bearded gods from across the sea? Is there any evidence to support such a premise?

Clearly, Irish monks with their long robes, pale skin, beards and saintly demeanor, fit the hero descriptions, and there can be no question they braved the formidable north seas in their courageous little boats capable of reaching the Americas—especially within the seven years they were away from home. The Irish boats had square sails, which provide an intriguing parallel to the Mexican legends which say their revered leader, Quetzalcoatl, came from the eastern sea in the company of robed, bearded, priest-like followers in square-sailed ships. Tantalizing but sparse remnants of legends along the Florida coast, however, fail to attribute to their fair visitor the grandeur and cultural influence possessed by Mexican heroes.

That the Irish had a migratory nature was discovered by the Vikings who, upon settling Iceland in the ninth century, found colonies of monks, perhaps up to 1,000 individuals, already there. What happened to them? They left. There was just no living in spiritual peace with the pre-Christian Vikings.

And where did they go? Some of these Icelandic Irish may have returned to Old Erin, but others could have sailed on to the west past Greenland. And it is not unreasonable, since they had made it to Iceland, to imagine them settling upon Northern American shores. Future discoveries may yet demand reevaluation of such an arrival and its subsequent influence upon native tales.

In the absence of actually existing foundations of Irish Monastic orders in America, and the lack of even one lingering artifact from such supposed colonies, one can make no legitimate claim to monks or Brendan ever having visited the New World lands or having had any influence upon North American Indian traditions, however attractive that might seem.

Brendan's voyage, like that of the other navigating Monks before him, was not to seek dramatic conversions, but to such isolation for the purpose of spiritual contemplation and to avoid the temptations of the flesh in all their inviting forms. One chance encounter with free-loving Indians the French and British found so irresistible along the Missouri, or exposure to the wanton ways of Mexico's Tezcatlipoca, adversary of Quetzalcoatl, would have shattered the poor monks' spiritual austerity to the point of their seeking absolution out on the ocean for the rest of their troubled lives.

Although he was away from his homeland for seven years, the *Navigatio* says Brendan's short visit to the "Promised Land" only lasted a mere 40 days—hardly enough time, it would seem, to learn the various local languages and establish himself as a culture hero to native Americans in Mexico, and among natives in South and North America. Ninth-century Christian monks were not successful at converting the Norse, who were not Christianized until much later—what chance with human-sacrificing Toltecs? Besides, Irish sagas mention no contact between Brendan and native Americans.

The old travel-worn priest must have had some experiences worth recording, but it is likely many of them were added centuries later from other clerical adventurers. One author, Ashe, calls him "a hero summing up a whole epoch of Irish exploration."[2] Besides, Brendan was doubtlessly far from possessing the zest and energy necessary to convert a continent of "barbarians" to a new way of life, for these carefully recorded events occurred in his ninety-third year. Still, Brendan, like Leif Ericsson after him, became a culture hero to his own people who canonized the adventuresome old monk and placed him on a highly prestigious list along with another great Irishman of the Middle Ages—Saint Patrick.

Celtic Intrusion

The next investigation of purported Northern-European intrusions into the early American scene spans the Celtic period, from which no sagas nor legends of any oceanic voyages have survived from either side. Still, recent New World explorers claim to have unearthed clues to that silent era of America's cloudy past from perplexing inscriptions carved on stone tablets. Modern discoverers of these mysterious markings claim they are alphabets dating back as early as 2500 years ago, making them America's oldest writings. They are also convinced these cryptic messages represent evidence of colonies of immigrants from early Celts, Basques, Romans, Greeks, Lybians, Phoenicians, Asians and even Egyptians. Many of these claims will be examined in following chapters.

Diffusionists believe that these scripts were laboriously carved on stone and deposited in underground tombs and shrines all over North America. With the greatest number found in the New England area, it is claimed they duplicate similar writings found in a similar environment of the Celtic regions of Europe and North Africa. Only recently has it even been possible to decipher many of these strange markings.

Of the various scholars who discern in these stones evidence for Atlantic crossings from the ancient world, the most vocal is Barry Fell, an undauntable New Zealander with an impressive list of credits: marine biologist; linguist; epigrapher; explorer; archaeologist; decipherer of ancient writing systems of Africa, Asia and America; author; and professor at Harvard. His provocative books have had an embroiling effect upon the scholastic world.

Fell had spent years developing his epigraphic skills by studying Old World and Far Eastern inscriptions left on stones and cave walls by mariners on remote islands. When archaeologists presented him with inscriptions found in America, he recognized they were not unlike those he had seen in the Old World. This came as a surprise, for he asserts he was previously unaware they existed. Archaeological journals had largely ignored them.

Highly motivated by a growing and insatiable curiosity, he spent a summer scrambling over the hillsides and pushing through the woodlands of New England. His intense search managed to unearth marked stones all over the Northeast where no one else had seen them. What he believed were traces of ancient civilizations turned up virtually everywhere—a sore point for Inventionists.

Fell readily identified dolmens—large boulders supported by vertical stones erected in memory of a ruler or event—used to create Druid's circles, astronomical observatories, underground shrines and tombs, and foundations for religious centers and temples. Many of these dolmens, he claimed, displayed the identifying markings of Ogam, an ancient Celtic writing which appears as vertical grooves on both sides of a center line.

Discovery of these monuments and markings was not entirely new; settlers in these areas had unwittingly encountered them for centuries. However, it was the newly developed ability to recognize them and to decipher their slumbering messages that caught the imagination. The more Fell and his colleagues witnessed, the more convinced they were that these objects projected back to America's forgotten ages of discovery and colonization.

Similar ancient monuments and inscriptions, still visible on the west coast of Europe although largely destroyed as pagan by later Christian priests, convinced Fell that here in America were remnants of settlers brought by roving Celtic mariners from Portugal and Spain to establish colonies in New England and Oklahoma. Other early colonists, he believed, followed from North Africa and other areas of Europe.

A colleague of Fell's, Gloria Farley, scrutinized the cliffs and caves of the Cimarron River of Arkansas, Oklahoma, and Colorado and boldly determined, from the markings she found, that the Celts did not stop on the coast but braved the rivers inland, leaving a trail easily followed by later waves of Libyans and Punic-speaking Iberians. With growing self-confidence at her ability to authenticate these markings, she even hazarded identifying the presence of at least one Basque king in the Americas sometime B.C.[3]

In the east, after he had viewed numerous underground rock structures, Barry Fell pronounced them Celtic shrines. He believed that nineteenth-century Scotch and Irish Celts who came to the Americas to escape famine had unknowingly used these rock temples of their ancient ancestors to build "root cellars." They also could have disassembled many shrines to construct stone bridges and churches or walls around their fields, just as their medieval ancestors had done with similar Celtic structures in Europe. In this respect, he concludes, the Americas turned out "far more like Ireland than they could dream."[4]

Root Cellars or Shrines

Fell survived the scathing furor of the highly critical forces of the scholastic world with his first hurried book, *America B.C.*. Encouraged, he gathered new ammunition and fired off two more barrages of controversy against the skeptics, *Saga America* and *Bronze Age America*. In the ensuing skirmish many sympathetic diffusionist followers rallied, thus highly increasing the pitch of battle against inventionists.

At first Fell and his co-workers were accused of creating their own inscriptions. "Why is it," critics maligned, "Barry Fell comes into an area that has been thoroughly combed by other archaeologists and immediately discovers artifacts no one else had?" Fell's quick response was that the archaeologists are not looking for inscriptions, nor are they prepared to recognize them if they see them. Therefore, they find none.

Fell claims these "Celtic texts" have been found as far south as Iberia, and that some pre-date the time of Christ. Archaeologists maintain that Ogam writing is found only in Ireland, and was not even invented until the Fourth Century A.D. Fell insists their dating is off and produces Celtic coins found in America with the same ogam script dating to the second century B.C.. Modern linguists, he asserts, confirm his findings.

Critics attest that the "shrines, altars, and temples" Fell assigns to the Celtic architects are merely "root cellars" constructed by eighteenth-century colonizers. Fell retorts by producing charcoal from the structures that carbon dates to A.D. 1200, or earlier. He demands of his opponents reasons why colonial farmers took the time to systematically orient the cellars "with respect to the ancient rites of the Celtic solar year"—and then further bothered to inscribe them with "Ogam and Phoenician dedications?"[5]

Doubters wonder how Fell can be so confident these markings are Celtic or Phoenician when similar markings can theoretically be made by accident, or by the plow or roots of a tree. Fell answers with another twist, if one attributes the invention of writing to the plow, why do plows in Pennsylvania "usually write in Basque or Iberian Punic, whereas those of New England are apt to ascend the walls of stone buildings to write Celtic Ogam upside down on the ceiling?"[6] Critics argue that Celts in Europe built more than potato cellars, and demand to know where are the tangible, ground remains of such settlements.

Fell, like the erascible Celts he studies, has been described as having an undeniable "barbaric brilliance," but scholars who praise his "tenacious endurance" at the same time shudder at his wild statements, such as those found in *Saga*,[7] and find irresistible pleasure in countering them: "Libyans found themselves landing on the opposite sides of America." (They had a map showing both sides of the continents?) "They liked what they saw, and stayed." (Their enraptured remarks are recorded in some ancient hotel roster?) "Some of them established schools of learning here where mathematics, astronomy, navigation, and geography (Old, or New World?) were taught." (Fell has come across a copy of their curriculum catalog?) Undaunted, Fell, and another distinguished colleague, George Carter, believe that all the major races of the world eventually found their way to the Americas.

The inventionists' battle with Fell and Carter and other diffusionists is not that they are probing new territory—If that were not done modern man would have no knowledge of Troy, Herculeneum, or even America, for that matter. No, it is not the newness of the territory that grates, but the somewhat exaggerated claims that often precede and exceed evidence. In the overly cautious, scholarly circles, the reverse is the accepted (although not always practiced) norm. Conclusions usually come painfully slowly, following years of careful, collaborative research.

While promoting these new finds, Fell freely admits that it is all "exploratory" and that he is "surely making many errors that only time will reveal and correct." He recognizes that much of his material is "not understood at all" and that he is still "fumbling with details." Critics, and even many diffusionists, will agree with him on that point. Despite the criticism, he believes that what he is doing is basically correct.[8]

Fell and Carter fit an old tradition that the unfettered enthusiast, with no particular allegiance, will pioneer new territory that the cautious "fear to tread." In history there are far too many civilizations and relics from the ancient past where the wary have assured there would be none.

Celtic Culture Heroes

Should Fell eventually prove his case for Celtic arrival in the Americas, what about the Celts would make them candidates for the Americas' fair visitor? Described by Julius Caesar and others of his time as tall, fair-haired and blue-eyed, with long moustaches and sometimes bearded (although many did not fit that description), Celts are among the most interesting and enduring people in European history. With a passion for fine clothing and jewelry and a propensity for drinking and quarreling, they inhabited most of the continent before the armies of Rome, who called them the "Gauls," drove them into the far corners of Spain, Brittany, Ireland, and Wales in the centuries before and after Christ. Linked by similar languages and culture, they have endured through following centuries, and their influence has been strong even into modern times.

Rapidly growing Celtic populations habitually expanded toward the west. Their young aristocrats would often cluster and move off to colonize distant lands. Just how far distant is the unanswered question. They had strong beliefs in a life after death which transported their minds, if not their bodies, to a land "beyond the horizon" where the sun set, a land rich in food and nature's delights. The dead

Celtic kings, heroes, and gods were thought to luxuriate on this mystical land of youth, feasting and love-making.[9]

Whether or not curiosity lured the Celtic youth out onto the ocean in an attempt to verify the existence of such pleasant lands is not known, but their navigational abilities were equal to it. Fell (1977, 112) mentions the *De Bello Gallico* where Caesar recounts his greatest naval battles against the Brittany Celts and expresses amazement at the soundness of their several hundred ships and their remarkable ability to handle the vast open seas.

Notable parallels between the Celts and early American cultures could easily reinforce beliefs in Celtic arrivals upon these shores and cultural influence among the natives: both lived in fortress towns with large earthen mounds, both loved war, and both displayed fierce, rash courage; Celts and American natives decorated their bodies with elaborate tatooes and war paint, and both ornamented their war equipment. Captives of battle were often beheaded and their skulls displayed on stakes, or carved in stone on building walls. In times of peace they both proudly sported fine clothing and jewelry.

Indians and Celts both used art in the abstract, displaying their favorite themes: birds and serpents, as well as the cross and swastika. Religious ceremonies of both have close parallels: all fires were put out at the beginning of the new year and rekindled again in special ceremonies, both counted by twenties, rites were celebrated to good and evil spirits, and altars were stained with the blood of human sacrifices. Fasting and vigils were practiced along with self-inflicted punishment.

Both had a similar pantheon of gods including a mother figure and an earth goddess, twin brothers of light and darkness, gods of thunder and lightning and rain, animal deities and goddesses of fertility. Fires and sacrifices were employed to rejuvenate the sun, and both cultures sought constant communion with their deities through perpetual sacrifices and offerings. Important people were given elaborate burials in shaft tombs accompanied by objects of a sacred nature. These objects were often adorned with sacrificial and religious scenes. Graves were considered the entrance to the underworld.

Both Celtic and Indian worlds depicted two and three-headed deities and erected circular stone shrines and stelae to their gods or rulers. Both societies were layered, with priests, warriors and merchants positioned above the craftsmen and farmers. Both had medicine men, or Shamans, to predict the future, fix times and seasons, and instruct the youth in preserving oral traditions by committing them to memory.

Celtic traditions included stories of a universal flood and legends of fair creator gods arriving from over the seas (the Celts do not specify which seas). Sons of god, they were healers and bringers of salvation.[10] Both Celts and Indians speak of white leaders among darker inhabitants, and both were called by their neighbors the "Noble Savages."

Taken as a whole, the list of similarities between Celts and American Indians is quite impressive. One can almost envision many of the American Indian practices being introduced by the early Celts anxious to establish themselves in a new homeland providing unlimited space for expansion. But caution must be used so these striking similarities do not lead into premature or unwarranted conclusions. No one of the American tribes possesses an abundance of these traits, as would seem the case had they fused with Celtic immigrants. Neither do all of these characteristics exist in any one of the Celtic or Indian tribes. One must collect traditions from many separate Indian nations, some quite removed from one another, to come up with such parallels. Also, similar practices have been found among other peoples of the earth who never came into contact with either Celts or American Indians, as far as anyone has determined. All of this would tend to weaken the case for Celtic arrival in the Americas.

Skeptics point out that no Celtic skeletons (which at times measured up to 6'5") have been identified in so-called America-Celtic shrines, and no conclusive Celtic artifacts have turned up either. Theoretically, although it is unlikely, even the supposed Ogam writing could be forged, mistranslated, or by some remote possibility, planted here by later immigrants.

Before it can ever be concluded satisfactorily that the Celts actually arrived upon the early American soil, many of the characteristics uniquely identified with them, but which so far remain missing, must still be explained or unearthed. For one, elaborate Celtic burials contained large amounts of gold and precious offerings. (Such a custom was practiced in Oaxaca and Peru where no ogam is found, but is missing from the New England area). For another, the Celts also buried their kings in an upright position, sword in hand, alongside their wheeled carts left to speed them into the next world.[11] These have so far gone undetected at the "shrines" of New England.

Masters of the wheel and plow, these progressive people also mined and knew how to find iron ore. With the plow came horses, which the Celts loved, and which they rode to war and depicted in bronze. It is difficult to imagine a colony of Celts sailing to colonize distant lands without these beautiful creatures, either real or sculpted, complete with trappings, harnesses and bits. Examples of the widely-spread horse goddess and the oft-depicted bull of the European Celts, except for some lost stuccos and murals reported by Robert Marx in Yucatan,[12] are so far missing in the Americas.

The Celtic Genius

Wherever there were Celts, one would expect to unearth at least some of their amazing inventions and exquisite art objects that spread all over Europe: pointed bronze helmets and war trumpets, statues to various gods, serpent icons with ram's heads, iron works and hammers, anvils, tongs, handsaws, chisels, tweezers, shears, files, needles, picks, sickles, knives and the fishing trident.[13]

Because they exist at European Celtic sites, one might expect to find at an "American Celtic site" something of roasting spits, two-wheeled chariots with iron rims, tall shields with metal adornments, chain mail, daggers, axes, gold and silver coins, jewelry and wheel-made pottery. And where, around monumental fortresses, are the huge concentric ramparts and urban centers possessing shrines, workshops, flour mills, and mine shafts? Fell claims to have discovered some of these, but to verify them to the satisfaction of all scholastic disciplines is no easy task.

In Europe, Celtic groups survived the Roman armies and other difficulties, resisting separation. Modern-day Celts do not comprise a single community, but in Ireland, Wales, and Brittany they are still a strong, united people clinging to their cultural past. That past is known today mainly through their ancient legends of King Arthur and the Round Table. Because they maintained a fairly strong identity in those countries, in spite of mingling with other races and nations, one wonders that if they had come to North America, would they not also retain their individuality here? If, indeed, they crossed the ocean, where in the Americas today are remnants of the same unbeatable, tenacious, recognizable Celts? Many pieces have yet to be assembled in this disturbing puzzle.

If the announcement is ever dispatched from hallowed ivy halls that controversial North American stone markings are in fact Celtic inscriptions—and a growing number of professionals, according to Fell, are beginning to seriously investigate the possibility—the fact that Celts carved them will have to be accepted, and also that they came here from Europe to do it. That would open another exciting chapter on bearded visitors.

Prospects from the Pacific

Up to this point this book has considered only Europeans as possible candidates for the elusive immigrant hero. The reason for this is clear: most native-American legends say that he came from across the sea from where the sun rises—from the east. However, an occasional myth insists the mysterious visitors came across the Western sea. In chapter 6 a visitor from the Pacific Ocean among the Nootkas of Vancouver was discussed; and in chapter 4, another, Wixepecocha, in Oaxaca. Others were Taycanamo, Naymlap and the bearded giants of Peru in chapter 5. Naymlap, you will recall, arrived at the Western coast with his attendants on a fleet of large rafts, and Taycanamo was said to have been sent by a great Lord from across the Western sea.

Although these cases are rare and demand less attention than the abundant reports of gods from the Eastern sea, still they are part of the mystery, and along with increasing evidences for Asiatic contacts, may help in determining the origins of stories about the bearded visitors and culture hero.

The earliest intimations of trans-oceanic contact with Asia comes from some of the oldest pottery known in the New World, along the coast of Ecuador. It appeared about five-thousand years ago: a sophisticated style of ceramics strikingly similar to and at the same period as Jomon ware of Kyushu, Japan. Including depictions of similar human physical types, the parallels have led highly qualified scholars like Meggars, Evans, and Estrada to suggest possibilities of Asiatic arrivals by current, or by fishing boats blown off course down the Western coasts as early as 3,000 B.C..[14]

Even if such voyages occurred, it seems more likely they would have landed on closer, North American shores. In support of that, relics from the Jomon period have been found in Alaska, and other ceramic objects of alleged Japanese origin have surfaced in Washington State.[15] Still, chances of fishermen bringing with them Oriental sages of great culture possessing advanced skill in pottery and culture are definitely slim. Since there are among the remnants of Valdivia and the north no bearded figures, or remaining legends of feathered-serpents, those cultures will not be pursued further. But if contact from Asia at that time is ever proven, it would lend credibility to later arrivals.

And what are the chances for later sea arrivals? Of course, Eskimos have been making the twenty-five-mile journey between the continents of Asia and America for millenniums, but there is no evidence that they are responsible for the Classic Age expansion of cultural and intellectual levels. Since initial immigrations came overland from Asia in ancient times, scholars are more willing to consider possibilities of subsequent contacts from the Pacific as more likely than from the East.

According to Elizabeth Benson, director of pre-Columbian studies at Dumbarton Oaks, Washington D.C., one migration through the Bering Straits in ancient times "does not begin to answer all the questions." Could later migrations by boat across the Pacific, she asks, have brought "cultures more developed than those of the people who had wandered down the Pacific coast from Alaska to Mexico and Peru?"[16]

Certainly ancient boats sailing down the Pacific coast bypassing ice-bound land would explain why the earliest Amerindians are found not in the north but in South America. Overwhelmingly complex voyages of Polynesians over vast areas of the Pacific prove such feats were being done. Answers to questions of other oceanic migrations may ride on Pacific currents which flow northward past Japan and Asia before sweeping the cold Alaskan waters down the American coast south to Mexico. Modern DNA studies, and a high incidence of type B blood reported among the Zuni Indians, common in Asiatics but not in Caucasians, definitely indicate an eastern migration from lands across the Pacific.[17]

Following an examination of the seaworthiness and excellence of ancient Asiatic crafts and the famous Hyerdahl raft conquest of the Pacific in recent times, Edwin Doran Jr., professor of Geosciences at Texas A. & M. concludes,"There appears to be no question that rafts could have crossed the Pacific, repeatedly and in appreciable numbers."[18] To further support his argument for possible early transpacific crossings, he produces dozens of instances of historic drift voyages from Pacific currents and storms which deposited oriental survivors along North American and Mexican coasts—many in the eighteenth and nineteenth centuries. It seems logical to assume similar occurrences in ancient times.

Robert Wauchope, in his thoroughly entertaining survey of the Asiatic controversy, *Lost Tribes and Sunken Continents* (1962, 97), presents evidence from the scholars Estrada and Meggars that by the third century A.D., Asiatic ships were "capable of carrying six hundred men and one thousand metric tons of cargo." Although it is still not known how such ships would return against prevailing winds and currents, it is often conceded, even by skeptics, that ships of Asia, which were considerably larger than those that carried Columbus and the later Spaniards, could certainly handle a Pacific crossing.

Again, Benson believes that it would be difficult to construct a "reasonable theory" for the origins of New World cultures based upon transoceanic influences, but at the same time concedes that the many similar traits between the Americans and Asians make it hard to argue against at least occasional contact. She recognizes that definite proof is "hard to come by."

"The Wrestler"
Oriental-looking Olmec
(National Museum Mexico City)

It would be even harder to deny the numerous visual similarities that exist between the New World and Asian objects. A leading American archaeologist, Gordon Willey, once skeptical of such influences, now admits to disturbing similarities between objects of the Shang Dynasty of China and those of the Chavin of Peru—both around 1,000 B.C..[19] Going beyond that claim, Betty Meggars, a highly respected scholar, sees evidence for social contact between the Olmec and Shang dynasties. Similarities between the Western and Asian worlds noted by other scholars, including anthropologists Dr. Gordon Ekholm and Dr. Robert Heine-Geldern, make an impressive list: oriental-looking clay figures, with implied hand and body movements recalling oriental dances; depictions of oriental-like houses in pottery, complex bark cloth, and folded books; the use of the parasol, the litter and the fan; cylindrical pottery vessels with tripod feet and conical lids, pottery molds, rocker stamps, shaft-holed star maces, and parallel metallurgical techniques; similar pottery motifs; figures emerging from the mouths of monsters, double-headed monsters, the use of feline deities and dragons, and warriors standing upon the vanquished.

This extensive list continues with corbelled arches, mansard roofs, decorations from the lotus plant with stylized fish, sun discs and diving gods, a game like the Hindu game of Parcheesi, nearly identical calendars and zodiacal signs with the association of animals and days of the week; possible ele-

Oriental-looking Dancer
(Veracruz)

phant headdresses, stacked figures and totemic heads, the use of the zero long before Europe discovered it, jade beads painted with cinnabar placed in the mouth of the deceased, and stairways guarded by serpent balustrades. Added to these are stone neck rests, graduated pan pipes, the coolie yoke worn across the shoulders, and a sail driven raft with a center board.[20]

At the Veracruz site of El Tajin (on the east coast) one sees a double-edged scroll design unique in Mesoamerica. Its closest affinities, Michael Coe admits, "seem to lie, for no apparent reason, across the Pacific with the bronze and iron age cultures of China."[21] Many scholars feel these mounting parallels (considerably shortened here) are too numerous to be mere coincidences, and suggest that contact may have occurred, although art objects alone do not prove the case. Evidence for similar writing, language, and religious and political influence would add weight. Even better would be Asiatic records of such visits, and some writers claim to have come up with them.

Oriental Monks in a Distant Land

The past two centuries have spawned multiple theories about Asiatic arrivals to the Americas—many of them fantastically imaginative. Among the colorful treatments on either side of this issue are Davies' *Voyagers to the New World*, Gladwin's *Men Out of Asia*, Mertz's *Pale Ink*, Shao's *Origin of Ancient American Cultures*, and Thompson's highly illustrated *Nu Sun* and *American Discovery*. Wauchope playfully resurrects a proposal by the author John Ranking in 1827 that South American civilizations were founded by "the crews of a few of Kublai Khan's ships driven eastward across the Pacific" by a storm which destroyed most of the fleet sent against Japan by the emperor in the thirteenth century. He then treats a similar proposal by Gladwin from *Men Out of Asia*, suggesting that Greek sailors numbering up to six hundred from the fleet of Alexander the Great sailed eastward across the Pacific from the Red Sea after picking up "artisans in India and southeastern Asia."[22]

He adds still another claim proposed by MacKintosh in 1836 that would have the Koreans leaving their oppressed land in search of a distant land to colonize during the Tsin dynasty. After nine weeks of sailing northeast "through several islands," they "arrived in a country, whose bounds they could not discover." This land is declared by some to be the Americas. Such theories are highly questioned by scholars like Bancroft and Lothrop, who cannot imagine 10,000-mile crossings without the compass, and doubt that any substantial cultural inroads would be made by an occasional ship cast ashore by accident. Extending his views, Wauchope quotes Helland that of all the individuals cast upon a deserted shore "Never have these [Robinson] Crusoes served the cause of civilization."

One, however, who may have served the cause and whose impressive story is often repeated by advocates of Asiatic crossings is a Buddhist priest named Hwui Shan. He purportedly came to explore the Americas from China around 500 A.D. during an expansion of Buddhist missionary activity. The extensive sources for the narrative come from France and Germany and were published by Eward Vining in *An Inglorious Columbus* (1885). Much of the Hwui Shan information, along with compelling evidence for another obscure Chinese expedition in the twenty-third century B.C., was republished more recently by Henriette Mertz in *Pale Ink* and *Gods From the Far East*.

The Hwui Shan story resurges often and much earlier. Published in 1321 by the Chinese historian, Ma Twan-lin in his "Antiquarian Researches," it came from an earlier seventh-century historian Li Yen, who recounts the still-earlier, fifth-century journey of the priest Hwui Shan to a country he calls Fusang, far to the east of China. The innocent Chinese classic became a heated controversy when in 1761 the Frenchman, de Guignes, published his opinion that the Fusang tree after which the country was named was the aloe cactus, or century plant, and that the country of Fusang was Mexico. The distance from middle China to Fusang was given as 40,000 LI, or 13,000 miles. Depending upon where one begins measuring from that vast country, the foreign land could be as far as the Americas or as near as Japan.[23]

Again, the question arises, how would this priest have crossed the Pacific Ocean? Since he does not mention how he got here or back, one is left to speculate. Charles Boland, in his sweeping concession, *They All Discovered America*, describes a Chinese junk out of Calcutta in the 1330's that not only had private baths and class cabins, but sailed with up to 1200 passengers and 1000 more in crew and guards. One voyage cut through the South China Sea, endured severe gales, and lasted 82 days. He suggests that with such boats Hwui Shan would have been able to reach the American shores. But impressive arguments are still not a substitute for tangible proof.

In the mid-1970's, just off the California coast at Palos Verdes, professional divers discovered a suspicious assemblage of eleven stone rings in seventy feet of water. Weighing up to four-hundred pounds, and of a sandstone said to be uncommon to the area, the odd stones were well-worn, and appeared to be counter-balancing weights, a rolling mill stone, and weight anchors like those used on ancient Chinese ships. Whaling beaches exist three miles south of there, but modern whalers would not have used such outdated equipment. Besides, here were cliffs, eliminating any possibility of this site being a whale-tethering station. More likely the stone rings were simply discarded at that place.

Marine geo-archaeologists James Moriarity and Larry Pierson were contacted, and they sent out core samples of the stones for testing. Labs in Taiwan and Beijing, China reported back that the stones most likely came from Pothoi quarries on the Northern coast of China—the objects were a type of Chinese anchor no longer in use after the twelfth century. However, Frank J. Frost, in an article for Archaeology, refutes this evidence in favor of immigrant nineteenth-century Chinese-American fishermen. Then again, Fang Zhongpu, a maritime historian, claims that over thirty such stones have been found from California to Ecuador, evidence that the Chinese did arrive anciently. A fuller review of this story is found in Fingerhut.[24] Obviously, further examination of the stones is necessary, but their connection with a pre-Columbian Chinese ship is at least no more questionable than the arrival upon American shores by Hwui Shan.

In spite of admitting to the superior seamanship of the ancient Orientals and to the largeness of their vessels, many scholars still contest the idea that they ever crossed the vast ocean. Others point out that smaller vessels, like those of the Tahitians, were able to sail thousands of miles into the expansive ocean, locate tiny islands, and somehow return. Hwui Shan enthusiasts insist that he needed only to follow the coastline to the Americas. It was the same distance as crossing the ocean, but safer. The Prussian scholar Klaproth believed that although the event may have occurred, the Chinese had no way of measuring the distance accurately.

In opposition to that point, Dr. A. Gordron, President of the Academy of Sciences of Nancy, France, argues that even the ancient Chinese "were no novices in the art of measuring distances and fixing their directions." He points to various articles published by Klaproth himself, showing that even he was aware that as early as 1100 B.C. the Chinese possessed magnetic compasses which enabled them to steer upon the ocean.[25] Nigel Davies, in *Voyages to the New World*, says the Chinese compass was not used for sea travel, but rather for divinatory practices and games of chess. He feels that deliberate travels between China and the Americas "are hard to credit."[26]

Proposals of Asiatic encounters with the Americas have livened up discussions and studies for years. The clash has produced an equal number of impressive evidences and extravagant claims. Among the more interesting claims are the suggestions that the American Indian name "Maya" comes from the identical name, Maya, the mother of Buddha; Guatemala becomes the place of Guatama (the name of Buddha); and the Yucatan city of Chompoton refers to the Cambodian stronghold, Champa, where Buddha walked and meditated. The Zuni word for a person of greatest respect is reported to be, "Bitsitsi," while a similar Japanese word, "Butsu," means Buddha.[27]

Great learning and refinement from the world's oldest continuing culture would certainly leave its mark on any civilization it encountered. Some culture was no doubt brought by the first Asiatics across the Bering Straits in unrecorded times, but whether it came more abundantly at a later time to further influence the flourishing cultures of the Americas, and in the process to contribute to the legends of visitors from across the sea, is still an issue. Opponents believe that had the number of foreign visitors claimed to have arrived actually landed, the evidence for their presence would be undeniable. They also point out the absence of any identifiable objects transported directly from the Orient, such as the plow, the potter's wheel, oriental glazed tiles, and Chinese writing, as assurance they did not arrive here.

Controversy over the issue of Asiatic contacts with early America is intense. A fair and extensive review of arguments on either side is found in Fingerhut's *Explorers of pre-Columbian America*. But even if such visits can eventually be supported, and some cultural influence demonstrated, which in the light of mounting evidence seems not unreasonable, it is somewhat difficult to imagine the natives of the Americas identifying a shorter, dark-haired Asiatic as their tall, white, bearded culture hero. For one reason, any faithful Buddhist who came to convert "barbarians" would promote not himself, as did the hero, but rather his revered sixth-century B.C. leader, Buddha, who, at present, is not known to have walked among native Americans. Most of all, there is the persistent and more common native theme that the culture hero came across the sea *from where the sun rises*. Even diffusionists would think twice about proposals of Asiatic arrivals from the Atlantic side.

A Closed Door—Well, Almost

Until the day when less-speculative information is available from Irish, Celtic, and Asiatic sources, and scholars come to some agreement—a day that may prove as illusive as the date of the predicted return of the culture hero—judgment upon these proposed immigrations as foundations for the white bearded visitor legends must be reserved.

Other doors remain to be investigated, and the search for a visiting foreigner will be continued by returning to candidates from the other side of the sea where the sun rises, by moving back in history to the highly advanced civilizations surrounding the Mediterranean area around the time of Christ.

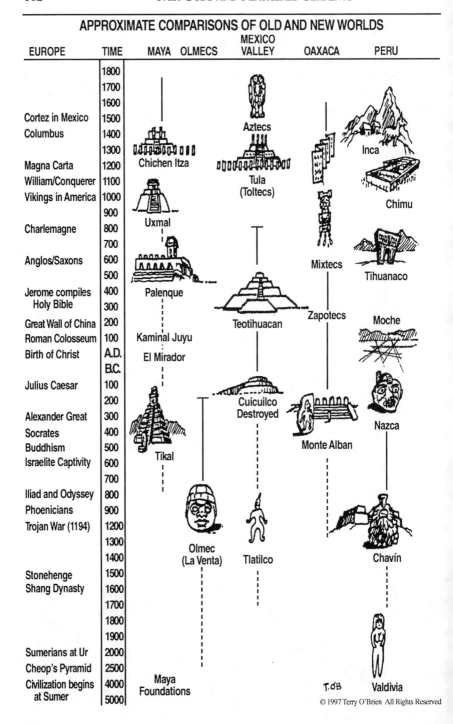

APPROXIMATE COMPARISONS OF OLD AND NEW WORLDS

EUROPE	TIME	MAYA	OLMECS	MEXICO VALLEY	OAXACA	PERU
	1800					
	1700					
	1600					
Cortez in Mexico	1500			Aztecs		
Columbus	1400					
	1300					Inca
Magna Carta	1200	Chichen Itza				
William/Conquerer	1100			Tula		
Vikings in America	1000			(Toltecs)		Chimu
	900					
Charlemagne	800	Uxmal				
	700					
Anglos/Saxons	600				Mixtecs	
	500					Tihuanaco
Jerome compiles Holy Bible	400	Palenque				
	300				Zapotecs	
Great Wall of China	200			Teotihuacan		Moche
Roman Colosseum	100	Kaminal Juyu				
Birth of Christ	A.D.	El Mirador				
	B.C.					
Julius Caesar	100					
	200			Cuicuilco Destroyed		
Alexander Great	300					Nazca
Socrates	400					
Buddhism	500				Monte Alban	
Israelite Captivity	600	Tikal				
	700					
Iliad and Odyssey	800					
Phoenicians	900					
Trojan War (1194)	1200					
	1300					
	1400		Olmec (La Venta)	Tlatilco		Chavín
Stonehenge	1500					
Shang Dynasty	1600					
	1700					
	1800					
	1900					
Sumerians at Ur	2000					
Cheop's Pyramid	2500					
Civilization begins at Sumer	4000	Maya Foundations				Valdivia
	5000					

T.óB

10

VISITING SEAMEN FROM THE MEDITERRANEAN

Scattered throughout the fertile fields of American mythology, the accounts of a bearded, white hero-god and his followers have consistently sprouted forth richer and more abundant than all others. Where do these tales come from? Their possible origins from among Vikings, Welsh, Irish, Celts, and Asiatics have been considered. In this chapter, the search moves southward, to see if these influences could have been from ancient Mediterranean spores borne upon the winds across the Atlantic. The search begins with an incredible story.

Scouting along a rock ledge in Southern Illinois in 1982, a lone caver (cave hunter), Russell Burrows, stepped on a rock slab which flipped and dumped him twelve feet down into a large pit. Luckily, as he fell, the stone shifted so that it did not roll back over the opening creating a death trap, which he later discovered it was designed to do. On the underside of the stone were strange writings, and at the bottom of the pit a sealed door. Leaving the pit, Burrows discovered it was there to protect a nearby cave. Although well experienced with caves, Burrows was totally unprepared for what he saw inside. Confronting him was an army of staring faces—many wearing beards and helmets. They were carved on walls and upon thousands of stones scattered about. An earthquake had previously released water which covered much of the collection with eight to twelve feet of silt, leaving little head room and making exploration difficult. The cave was deep, and he quit scouting at 550 feet. Half buried along the passageways, he says, lay several full-sized statues, bearded and dressed in gold. Even more astounding, he discovered thirteen sealed doorways carved into the stone walls. In successive trips to the cave, Burrows managed to break past three of the doors and discover rectangular, stone-cut rooms with burials. One of the two smaller rooms contained a solitary skeleton with bronze or copper spears, and other weapons. The second revealed sacrificial victims—a woman with two children and repositories with gold coins. The third room held the greatest surprise, which will be discussed later on.

Overwhelmed but cautious, Burrows says he made molds of the gold coins, leaving the originals in the cave. Then he removed several thousand stones (ranging from 1½" to 2') carved with figures and strange writing. He says that what he removed is nothing compared to what is still there. An acquaintance, Virginia Hourigan, photographed most of the objects. Experts in various fields, like Jack Ward, Warren Cook, Cyrus Gordon, Cyclone Covey, Jim Shears, and John White, studied the strange-scripted images. Of those who studied these carvings and photos, some recognized in them a bizarre combination of Lybian, Egyptian, and Persian. Others saw in them Roman, Greek, and even Hebrew. No one could imagine how these objects got to Illinois or why, but the spectacular collection was determined by them to be an

Burrows Cave—Black Stone 10"
(Drawn from a Photo by Wayne May)

ancient treasure either brought to the Americas by North African and European seafarers about 2,000 years ago or created by them after they arrived. A few who studied the figures speculated that they might be remnants from the ancient continent of Atlantis brought to the Americas for preservation. Burrows, who is not an artist, archaeologist or epigrapher, was growing anxious to discover the origin of this unexpected treasure, whatever it might be.[1] After examining some of the challenging possibilities, more information on Burrow's mysterious cave will be presented.

Sunken Dreams

Plato, in his fourth-century B.C. dialogues, the *Timaeus and Critias*, describes a terrible and spectacular event related by his grandfather who heard it in Egypt. He tells of a time more than 9,000 years earlier when the violent forces of nature broke through earth's crust in a fiery outburst of energy that would make today's hydrogen bomb look like a mere campfire. This dramatic display, goes the story, resulted in the total destruction of one of earth's great continents—Atlantis—somewhere in the ocean between Europe and the Americas, and the obliteration of its brilliant and beautiful inhabitants.[2]

Such stories were well known and accepted by many educated Spaniards in Columbus's time, who claimed the lost continent was larger than Europe and the alleged home of Earth's mother culture, the Garden of Eden, the Elysium plains, and that it was the source of all the magnificent creations of mankind in the arts, sciences, and literature. Today, after unsuccessfully searching the ocean floor, most scholars believe the Atlantis story to be mere allegory or a recollection of the lost Minoan city of Thera which was destroyed by volcanic fire and a devastating tidal wave in 1650 B.C..[3]

Advocates of Atlantis claim great ships carried survivors and their marked accomplishments to other shores, both east and west. They point to the ancient cultures of the Americas as proof of brilliant remnants of that great island in the Atlantic ocean. Doubters ask why Atlantean culture doesn't show up in the Americas until 9,000 years later, around 1,200 B.C.? Believers respond that the 9,000 years were Semitic years, which were actually months. Thus, Atlantis would have disappeared sometime near 1250 B.C. Following that reasoning, Methuselah, who in the Bible lived to be 969, and Noah, who lived to be 950, would have really been about 80. Accordingly, then, Moses, who in Bible years died at 120, would have been ten, and a mere toddler when he led Israel across the Red Sea. If one accepts all the details later added to Plato's thin story, all the Gods of men originated in that wonderful land of Atlantis: Yahweh of Israel, the Sun Gods of Egypt and Peru, and the Greek God Atlas. Some writers even assert that Quetzalcoatl, the Toltec feathered-serpent, had his beginnings there.[4]

If that were the case, this mystery could be resolved with the knowledge that the white, bearded visitor crossed the seas eons ago, bringing cultural remnants from a putative paradise and highly developed people which are no more.

Many New-Age writers predict the world today is going through dramatic changes that soon will turn the planet on its side, allowing the great Atlantis to emerge once more. But, until nature provides that encore to her alleged disappearing act of the past with a magical reappearance of the vanished continent from its watery chamber—complete with ancient wonders for everyone to behold, judgment will have to be reserved. In the meantime, however, ancient Atlantis can be envisioned as a magnificent land and people like none other on earth.

Roaming Romans

The disappearance of Atlantis, mythological or otherwise, did not seem to discourage beliefs that early Mediterranean peoples visited native Americans; imaginative writers have brought them here by the book-load. The rarity of recorded or concrete evidence for these visitations has forced proponents to rely mainly upon arguments of cultural similarities in order to sustain their positions. In comparing ancient Old-World cultures with the New, results have been highly creative and impressive. But unfortunately, too often the accounts have been fantastic with little supportive evidence.

Shortly after World War II, the U.S. Military attaché stationed at Caracas Venezuela, Berkley Lewis, was approached by a local peasant who had made a remarkable discovery along the shores where the northern bulge of South America plunges into the Caribbean. Just below high-tide level the receding sands had partially uncovered an 8" ceramic pot containing a hoard of some 6,000 miscellaneous coins. Later, while working at the Smithsonian Institute, Lewis showed the well-worn objects to his friend, Mendel Peterson, then acting Curator. A marine archaeologist and collector of ancient coins, Peterson was well qualified to pronounce the coins authentic, which he did—issued by Roman legionary settlements in Spain sometime before 350 A.D. These coins are reportedly still in the possession of the Lewis family today.[5]

How Roman coins got into Venezuelan sands can only be guessed: buried by Roman merchants, washed ashore from an ancient shipwreck, Roman colonies, or a lost collection? Two of the coins, however, were Arabic—eighth century A.D., which, if they arrived with the other coins, would eliminate any previous date. Strange as it may seem, finding Roman coins on American soil is not uncommon.

In the past one hundred and fifty years a variety of coins from the Roman Mediterranean of the second century A.D. has been dug up and reported in the newspapers of such widely diverse areas as Tennessee, Kentucky, Montana, and New Jersey. Some have turned out to be modern reproductions sold in museums, but others, like the Venezuela cache, have been authenticated. Peterson, who jokes that these coins virtually walk up New Jersey beaches, says he has sorted through many authentic Roman coins in the tourist shops of Hispaniola. Shop owners assure him that similar coins are often found along the shores of that Caribbean island. These amazing discoveries on American soil raise the age-old question of smoke and fire: where there are authentic Roman coins, are there necessarily Romans?

Roman sailors were venturesome in their nautical pursuits. Their easily recognized ceramic grey-ware has been dredged up 150 miles off the coast of Ireland and, for whatever it means, ancient Roman coins have been reported in Iceland.[6] But did Roman seafarers actually brave the Atlantic currents and pioneer the American shores? Peterson, who along with his Smithsonian duties has devoted much of his life to naval history (he served as Chairman of the Armed Forces History Committee) believes they did. "Their ships were certainly large enough, and seaworthy." "Given the wind patterns and sea currents," he insists, "it is more reasonable to believe some of them made it than to believe they didn't."[7]

At the same time, Peterson admits that coins alone don't prove Roman arrival. "Why bring a bunch of worthless coins to the Americas?" Did the foreign visitors anticipate trading with the natives for goods? It's more likely they had not intended to trade with Americans at all, but with Africans. Rome was basically a land empire, but occasionally its slow-moving ships defied the African coast. A careless galley off course could be swept across the Atlantic by natural forces, dashing the ghost-ship upon rocky American shores, spilling out dead sailors and coins.

On the other hand, not all Roman coins had to be brought by Romans: during the early explorations of the Americas the Spanish on occasion used the weight of valueless old coins by the shovelfuls as ballast to steady their ships. Some of these later Spanish vessels were wrecked along the coasts and their goods gradually washed ashore. Morison reports that ballast often became the garbage dump for the ship, and was occasionally unloaded onto a beach for cleansing.[8] The coins, some dating back as far as the first century, didn't all make it back into the ship, and discoverers of these discarded treasures could carry them to far reaches of the continents, depositing them in the ground for safe-keeping—and if forgotten, for later discovery by others.

As a boy of thirteen in Oregon, Richard Dodi, Curator of Imperial Roman coins at the Smithsonian, helped his father dig up a willow tree. In the roots, about a foot down, he discovered, to his delight, an authentic second-century bronze Roman coin. Proof the Romans made it to the west coast? To some it might be; to Richard it was just a lucky day: he had lost that very same coin the previous year. Imagine what marvellous tales might have been spun had someone else found his coin first![9]

Roman Roads Across the Americas

Opponents to the idea of Roman visitations argue that wherever Roman legions went they established colonies, and had they arrived on American shores they would have left some evidence. Proponents point out that Romans were eclectic and did not implant their cultural ideas as much as they absorbed those of the people they conquered. Besides, they insist, sailors were not always colonizers or bearers of culture.

Still, Romans were great builders, and it is difficult to imagine even Roman seamen if they reached New World shores not leaving some physical trace of their country's architectural and engineering genius. Supporters of Roman visitors point to South America, where the Inca built upon ancient roadways to create, in Roman-fashion, the finest roads in the ancient world, crossing rivers, mountains and deserts for some 4,000 miles. Still, attempting to lay a second-century Roman foundation for a fourteenth-century Incan road may take more than mere speculation.

Such a challenge could more easily have been carried out by the Maya who, in the fourth to ninth centuries, performed similar but less ambitious feats in Yucatan. There, cement causeways stretch through scrub jungle in a straight line for up to sixty miles. On a rare occasion, as at the great site of Tikal, they even seem to have produced what appears to be an occasional rounded arch, a trademark of Roman construction.

The wheel, so common in Europe, was for years thought unknown by the American Indians. How could Romans enter a new territory and not bring the wheel? Then in the late 1800's Old-World-looking (Anatolia) wheeled-toys turned up along the Mexican Gulf coast as well as inland—created near Roman times. On Maya causeways were found large, wheel-like stones containing squared centers, which in theory at least, could have functioned as axles. Archaeologists explain these away as ceremonial objects, never used for any practical purpose. If they served no practical purpose, It might be argued, why invent them? That would be a point for their having been brought by outsiders. Others quickly pronounce them children's toys. One wonders at the Maya whose children cleverly devised a use for the wheel when the adults couldn't. Surrounded by the modern wheel, today, however, most Mayan Indians still do not use it.

Evidence for a chance Roman visitation to the New World is one thing, but any serious contention for ancient Roman colonies, judging from those found in Europe, ought to include more than wheels and highways. Who can envision a sister city for Rome in America without something of columned temples, fortresses, aqueducts, domes, domesticated animals, Roman numerals, and classical works of art? And where in all the Americas are the great coliseums, theatres and baths? All of these could be waived for just one Circus Maximus.

But wait, the fires of Rome are not out yet—there is always more fuel. In 1961 a prolific writer and well-known marine archaeologist, Robert Marx, was called to Rio de Janeiro to identify a large accumulation of two-handled clay vessels, discovered at the bottom of Guanabara Bay. Disillusioned from just having proved several previous claims false, he approached the area with great skepticism, but what awaited him in the murky water was astonishing—over 200 large clay vases on the surface alone! Each was over four feet high and encrusted with marine growth. He recognized them as second century B.C. Roman vases, "amphorae" which he had seen many times before on dives in the Mediterranean and off the coast of Spain—but there, in Rio? Dr. Harold Edgerton of the Massachusetts Institute of Technology flew to Rio and also pronounced them authentic.[10]

Could some modern ship have brought them over? Probing directly under the amphorae, deep in the mud, they discovered large wooden planks—remains of a ship? The planks were carbon dated, and proved to be neither modern nor from colonial times, but the same age as the amphorae—200 B.C.. The fires were getting hotter.

As soon as word got out, Marx says, the local government insisted he cover up the find and, from political fear, they blocked further search. It would not do in a Portuguese country to admit to an earlier arrival by Romans. Present Italian immigrants might demand "first arrival" rights. In a move reminiscent of John Evans's denial of the Welsh/Indians (chapter 8), further explorations would be allowed only if Marx would disclaim any Roman origin in favor of something like the earlier arrival be Phoenicians. He refused.

If the Brazilian government changes heart and if the scattered wooden planks below the amphorae prove to be a Roman ship, it would be the first undisputed evidence that even if they didn't make it back to home port, at least some pre-Christian Europeans reached the Americas. It would also open a door some people would prefer to keep shut. Apparently the Brazilian government feels a Roman ship in the bay would have a volatile effect on today's local citizens. How much influence such visits might have had on earlier American natives is another question. The sudden appearance of Romans among native villages would no doubt embellish the stories of bearded, white men from across the seas, but what would it add to the culture hero search? Caesar believed himself a god, and the "ideal Roman" is reported to have been a "good man" of excellent mind who could sway the multitudes with eloquence. But just how far he could sway native Americans with a triumphal "Vini, Vidi, Vici," cannot yet be answered.

Classical Candidates

Incomplete as the case may be for a Roman culture hero in the Americas, it is somewhat stronger for the Greeks: sailing power, cultural and philosophical similarities, religious parallels, and known historical writings about distant lands make arguments for Greek visitations seem somewhat more likely.

Among those who have written convincingly on possible Greek intervention in New World life are some distinguished scholars. One of them, Cyrus Gordon, head of Mediterranean studies at Brandeis University, fears that too often the great cultural offerings of our ancestors are lost. He lets the Greeks tell their own story. Realizing that not everything recorded as history can be accepted at face value, Gordon, in *Before Columbus*, submits these ancient writings as proof of the Greek "awareness of transatlantic contacts."[11] Although these stories have been around for some time, they are worth repeating.

He begins in the fourth century B.C. with a Greek writer named Theopompus, who tells of "an enormous 'continent' outside the Old World, inhabited by exotic people living according to the strangest life-styles." These people live in cities where gold and silver are common.

Next he presents what he calls a "collection of ancient Greek 'Believe-It-or-Not' reports, *Concerning Marvelous Things Heard*, supposedly written by Aristotle. Number 84 on the list concerns the Carthaginian discovery of an "island" with navigable rivers. Gordon explains that "Old Mediterranean people used the term 'island' to mean any land mass that could be reached by sea, even huge continents," since shores—whether continent or island—look the same to approaching sailors. Diodorus Siculus, who lived from 80 to 20 B.C. declares the island to be of considerable size and a number of days (Pliny says 40) to the west of Libya (North Africa). He describes it as having fruit trees of all kinds, mountains, and navigable rivers.

After discovering the "distant island," some of the Carthaginians settled there, but to prevent mass migration from Carthage and to keep that excellent land a secret, further communication was forbidden, and those who knew of its location were silenced by death. Gordon points out that west of Africa there are no navigable rivers to be found until Haiti, Cuba, and the American mainland.

Samuel Eliot Morison, the Admiral who compiled a comprehensive account of all known voyages across the Atlantic prior to 1600, expresses his weariness at these "blown across the Atlantic theories" but at the same time reluctantly allows an occasional "vessel in the trade wind belt—if partially disabled" to be "blown across." His strongest objection with the whole matter is "how would she have got back?"[12] Since they lacked the compass or sextant, and since prevailing winds and currents flowed west, his point is well made.

Outdistanced By Earlier Seamen

It would seem, however, that what the earlier seamen didn't know didn't detain them. The Greek geographer, Strabo (born c. 63 B.C.), in his *Geographika and Diorthosis*, tells that "the ancients" made longer journeys by land and sea than the later Greeks and Romans, whose world seems to have narrowed down as it neared the time of Christ.

The expanded age of navigation, made famous by Homer in his 8th Century B.C. *Odyssey*, included voyages beyond the Mediterranean north to the fogbound Cimmerians (probably England). He does not, however, mention any side trips across the ocean to distant or undiscovered lands.[13] Pytheas, of the Greek colony in Marseilles, also sailed north into the rough Atlantic during Alexander's reign five-hundred years later, passing the coast of Britain to some place he called Thule, "land of the midnight sun," commonly believed to have been Iceland. Morison admits that this "boldest of voyages" only led "other men of enterprise to believe that they could do even better."[14]

If they didn't do better, at least they boasted of doing better, for Greek poets instilled a vision of some distant "islands of the Blest." Hesiod, a Greek poet of the eighth century B.C., provides the hope that "Father Zeus, at the ends of the earth, presented a dwelling place, apart from man and far from the deathless gods. In the Islands of the Blest, bounded by deep-swirling ocean, they live untouched by toil or sorrow." He paints a vivid picture of "Happy fields, surrounded by ocean . . . where the land without tillage produces grain abundantly, the vine bears grapes without pruning. There is no pestilence to hurt the cattle." He speaks of a "gentle, fertile rain, and never is there drought."[15] Without straining the imagination, one could almost identify it as the land "where the skies are not cloudy all day."

The "Happy Isles" may just be allegorical, and equivalent to the "Great Beyond"—both indefinite places of repose for the worthy dead. But such a graphic picture as "Happy Isles" must have presented some hope to the Greeks as a real place, just as living on the edge of the "Great Beyond" today, men have been sent "out there" to explore the moon and space. No doubt some Greeks even dared to dream of going to the "Happy Isles" before death. Living on the edge of the ancient world, they must also have sent men into the watery "out there" to explore it.

Fear of dropping over the edge? From the time of the Pythagoreans in the sixth century B.C., it was known that the ocean covered a sphere. This was taught not only in ancient schools but also into medieval times. Although Greek mythology held that the world was flat, Greek maps—especially those drawn by Ptolemy (c. A.D. 73-151)—show the world as round. The idea was not new with Columbus. The Greek Eratosthanes stated that it was "theoretically possible" to sail from Spain to the Orient and that "certain sailors had tried to do it but gave up their quest for want of provisions."[16] The want of provisions also plagued the voyages of Magellan and other fifteenth-century explorers. Still, Eratosthanes' pronouncement may have later reassured Columbus.

The most controversial discussion about a "New World" comes once more from Plato, who, as the teacher of Aristotle, no doubt implanted in his pupil's mind some ideas of distant lands. Writing about Atlantis, he leaves more to think about than a lost continent when he relates that: "Because of its [Atlantis's] presence, voyagers could cross the Atlantic Ocean—thence westward to other islands and finally to a *real continent*"(emphasis added).[17] Although he treats the continent of Atlantis as somewhat of a myth, he gives full credence to the *real continent* beyond.

Visitors Lost and Found

Believers in the idea that the "real continent" could refer only to the Americas have gone to great lengths to get the Greeks here. Some of these efforts appear somewhat overzealous and unconvincing. An example is found in Harold S. Gladwin, who in *Men Out of Asia* would bring to the Americas the whole navy of no one less than Alexander the Great! And why not? Alexander conquered everywhere else. Alexander's fleet was, in truth, awesome. It consisted of some eight-hundred ships, each carrying crews as large as six hundred of the most experienced seamen of their day, in ships fully equipped and well provisioned.

But just when they were ready to sail from the Gulf of Persia, in one of history's great moments of drama, the curtain came down; Alexander died. He was buried in Egypt, and centuries later, his rich tomb just disappeared—Alexander's gold-encased remains were reportedly last seen by Octavian in 30 B.C., and by

Strabo were reported to be gone by 7 B.C..[18] And what became of the fleet? Gladwin concluded they had nowhere else to go but to the Americas.[19] It sounds far fetched, but wait . . . the belief that Alexander's ships might have sailed to the Americas pales beside the next proposal. Recent archaeological discoveries have led some scholars to believe that not only did later ships arrive in the New World from the Mediterranean with ancient treasure, but that Alexander himself was aboard . . . and is still here!

This wild speculation is inspired by the thousands of objects allegedly removed from Russell Burrows' cave discovery in Southern Illinois. After examining skeletons and objects in two rock-cut rooms of the cave, Burrows broke into a third, and larger room (about 12'x12'). There Burrows discovered carvings and paintings around the walls, along with urns, jars, bronze swords, lances, helmets, spears, and shields. Something even more startling awaited. Dominating the center of the room lay an impressive burial housed in a solid rock-cut sarcophagus. With a metal bar, Burrows inched the heavy stone lid aside and gazed down into the haunting face of a man covered with solid gold, dressed like an Egyptian pharaoh. Who could be buried here? Around the wall were small gold statues.

Burial Crypt—Burrow's Cave, Ill.
(Painting by Charles R. Platt, Midwestern Epigraphic Society)

Information carved on the tablets, (many on a soft, black stone not yet found in the area), and descriptions by Burrows of the crypts, have led Schaffranke and others to provocatively identify occupants of the cave as Alexander Helios and his sister, Selene, the twin children of Mark Anthony and Cleopatra. Interpretations from the scripts, many written in Greek with Latin characters, have led others to believe that not only did these two outcasts from the Roman revolution following Julius Caesar arrive here together, but in company with some of the ruling family, the Ptolemies. Even more incredible, they assert that this party brought with them from Alexandria the missing royal relics and sarcophagus of Alexander the Great.[20] Not everyone agrees. Burrows and others accept the objects as authentically from the Mediterranean, but they debunk the presence of Alexander the Great. The recent discovery of the sunken palace complex at Alexandria may eventually turn up a better answer to the missing tomb.[21] But adding to the intrigue, Pidgeon (1853, 308) reports another catacomb in near-by Kentucky with perfectly embalmed Egyptian-like bodies discovered in 1795.

Some who have studied the thousands of objects and photographs of Burrows' cave, believe this is the most important archaeological discovery ever made in North America. They feel the mystery of this American "Valley of The Kings," located coincidentally (or is it?) near towns named Karnak, Thebes, and Cairo will all clear up when they finally enter the cave. Burrows claims the urns in the smaller room contain rolled-up scrolls of papyrus which may one day help explain this great mystery. But who knows when that will be? To date, only Burrows and few others—three now dead—have ever seen the cave. Skeptics say, "Put up or shut up," and view the whole story with suspicion, awaiting validation of the cave and its contents by a professional scholar.[22] But, concerned with preserving the objects, and with legal complications, Burrows has covered up the entrance, and refuses to disclose the whereabouts to anyone else. This incredible mystery, said to be sealed up for 2,000 years, once again silently waits.

With the Greek issue unresolved, enthusiasts have been, perhaps, too eager to discover cultural clues elsewhere, conveniently finding them strewn all over the rest of the Americas. In Peru, Columbia, and Panama, Hellenes supposedly left the panpipe, an admittedly complicated wind-instrument—which, proponents assume, only the Greek goat-god Pan could invent. Greek helmets with their curved crests were believed to be worn on the Moche pots of northern Peru and later in Hawaii. It seems only fair to admit that these examples work just as well for the inventionist as for the diffusionist. Peruvian and Hawaiian inventiveness could theoretically create such items without the help of Greece.

In Yucatan, cloaks, robes with wide belts, and jewelry, preserved on Maya codices, have been too loosely identified as Greek. The appearance of Cerbus, a three-headed dog, and the placement of coins in the mouth of the dead were Greek customs said to be well-received among the Aztecs (no matter that Aztecs don't appear until 1400 years later).

The Greek Atlas and the Toltec Quetzalcoatl were both said to be twins and magicians. Both hold up the skies. In the Aztec Nahuatl, the "atl" signifies sea or water (*At*lantic immediately comes to mind). Quetzalco*atl* brought the rains, and *At*las was the son of Poseidon, the Greek sea god. To some this unusual combination of letters, A-T-L in both names is an undeniable link.

So was the culture hero a Greek? If a Greek entourage from the Mediterranean actually settled in Illinois, as artifacts from the Burrows cave might someday indicate, natives could have elevated them to a "white god" role for ancient Greeks, according to the poet Hesiod, were a "godlike race of hero-men."[23] American culture heroes were said by natives to have brought civilization, and no one had more of it to bring than the Greeks, who were soft-spoken, bearded, and often wore long robes—excellent qualifications for a culture-hero.

But how would Greeks become associated with the strange native combination of serpents and feathers? American Indian myths, as has been seen, identified this unusual symbol with the great bearded man or men who brought civilization from the east, across the ocean. Among the so-called Greek artifacts found in Burrows's cave, one can see beautifully carved bearded figures, some crossing water in boats accompanied by serpents and birds. Burrows claims at least one stone displays a feathered serpent. Of course that alone does not prove Greeks identified with feathered serpents. But did the Greeks lack anything? On a pediment of the Athenian acropolis, the heart of the Greek world, are carved not one, but three heads of bearded men. On each is the body of a *winged serpent*.[24]

Worship of a bearded white man with the body of a strange, hybrid serpent displaying plumes where scales would normally be is not the thing one generally expects to find. Yet it existed all over the Americas, and its origin was said to be from across the sea. Now it is found carved on stones believed to have been brought to the Americas with Greek culture, and also in Greece on an Athenian temple. Still, fascinating as this may be, one can not yet assume anything. Feathered serpents appear to have flown to Greece from across still another sea.

Feathered Pharaohs

Another bizarre tale about a serpent/ruler from a distant isle comes unexpectedly across the Mediterranean from the Egyptians, whose Pharaoh wore on his crown the feathers of the upper Nile falcon god, Horus, alongside the serpent of the lower Nile. This tale from sailors of the second millennium B.C. has the narrator shipwrecked on a distant island of the sea where the good things of life are abundant. While there he meets the king of the island, a larger-than-life bearded-serpent.[25] This haunting image naturally brings to mind Quetzalcoatl.

When most people first witness the great temple-pyramids of Mexico and Peru, they automatically reflect upon those of Egypt. With no two exactly alike anywhere, pyramids on both continents continue to be rediscovered today, although it is difficult to imagine that anything as large as a pyramid could ever be lost. Over ninety pyramids currently break the Egyptian horizon, and in the Americas there are even more, although it is unlikely that anyone has counted. (At Cholula alone, the Spaniards reported seeing more temple-pyramids than days in the year, and over 400 temples were reported in South America at Cuzco.) Standing upon the massive structures on either side of the Atlantic, or entering the chilling tombs, one naturally reflects upon the similarities and possible influences one culture may have had upon the other.

Egypt's pyramids and her history are ancient. The Old Kingdom of Egypt was as remote to the Romans and the Greeks as those civilizations are to Americans today. The great Egyptian god, Osiris, "the good one," was said to have built Egypt's first temples and to have created the first divine images around 4,000 B.C.. He then set out to spread civilization to the whole world. Possessing characteristics similar to those of Quetzalcoatl, he was a god of vegetation identified with the sun, the rain, and the morning star. Upon his death he was resurrected, and presides over the dead in the land where the sun sets, promising hope for an eternally happy life. [26]

The earliest Egyptian pyramids, being stepped, are the only ones that resemble those of the Americas. The oldest was created by Imhotep at Saqqara in ancient Memphis for the pharaoh Djoser of the third dynasty about 2670 B.C. This great structure and the staggering monuments that followed were not only tombs for the deceased Pharaohs, but pleasant homes for the "living dead." Death was only the beginning of their journey, and pyramids served as stone ladders whereby they could ascend to the heavens. Eventually, stepped pyramids gave way to the smooth-sided "true pyramids," and greatest of them all was that of Khufu, or Cheops, who reigned about 2570 B.C.. [27]

Actually, instead of looking Egyptian, American pyramids more closely resemble the flat-topped ziggurats of ancient Mesopotamia, Babylonia and Assyria with their stepped levels culminating in the temple, a "mountain unto the Lord." Pyramids on both hemispheres became part of complexes resembling small cities. In America, these complexes developed much later and more slowly than in Egypt. The most famous ziggurat in the world was the tower of Babel, said to rise seven stories above the waters of the Euphrates. The eleventh chapter of the Book of Genesis relates:

> Let us make brick . . . and . . . let us build us a city and a tower whose top may reach unto heaven; . . . And the Lord came down to see the city and the tower which the children of men builded . . . and the Lord said: . . . Let us go down, and there confound their language that they may not understand one another's speech. (verses 3-7).

Pre-conquest legends from ancient Cholula echo with familiarity when one of the giants, Xelhua, begins to build an artificial mountain to reach the clouds and heaven itself. But the anger of the Gods was aroused, and they launched their thunderbolts upon the builders and slew many, so that the work stopped. On seeing their work destroyed, the builders "were much frightened, and scattered themselves throughout the earth." [28]

In the same reference, Ixtlilxochitl mentions that seven families speaking the Toltec language wandered for one hundred and four years over land and water before reaching the New World. Although Bancroft records these tales, he casts doubt upon the whole interpretation as a fanciful invention by the Spaniards upon examining a native drawing.

Several notable differences exist between the pyramids of the Old World and those of the Americas. Excepting the missing tower of Babel, whose dimensions are unavailable, the ziggurats were generally smaller than American stepped pyramids. The largest in Sumeria was only seventy feet high, while American pyramids often exceed 200 feet. In contrast, Egyptian pyramids were generally larger than the American counterparts. The width of the great pyramid of Cheops (about 750 feet) is almost identical to that of the Pyramid of the Sun at Teotihuacan, but the height (450 feet today) is nearly double the Teotihuacan structure. The straight sides of the pyramid of Cheops were once smooth and of highly polished stone, while those of Teotihuacan are of adobe, and stepped. (The outer shell, now missing, was of polished stone.)

Remarkably, the mammoth structure at Cholula, Mexico, dedicated to Quetzalcoatl, is almost the width of two Egyptian pyramids, but only half the height. Another marked difference is that the small temples to American deities appeared on the flat-topped pinnacles of massive pyramidal bases, while the more elaborate Egyptian temples remained at ground level as an entrance to the pointed-topped pyramid some distance away (See page 80).

Still, there are haunting similarities. For years it was argued that American pyramids did not serve the same burial purposes as those of Egypt. But that was before the unexpected twentieth-century discovery of the elaborate seventh-century Palenque crypt in Chiapas, Mexico (Chapter 4). Numerous finds since have revealed that perhaps over half the American pyramids contain Royal burials.

Chronology would make any speculation about Egyptian influence upon American pyramids difficult to establish. The most impressive pyramids in Egypt were built during the Old Kingdom (c. 2640-2160 B.C.), after which their significance dwindled, and few appear after 2100 B.C.. It then seemed more in vogue to bury royalty in splendid rock-hewn tombs in the Valley of the Kings. It is difficult to imagine homebound Egyptians sailing all the way to the Americas to teach natives how to build massive pyramids—not to the pharaohs, but to their own gods—a thousand years after pyramids had lost their significance in Egypt.

Dawn Comes Later in America

The dawning of civilization was well over and the sun already casting long shadows on some Old World cultures when American pyramids began to appear. For the advanced cultures of Chavin in Peru, and the Olmecs in Mexico, the mid-day of their cultures was around 1,000 B.C.. Except for the large, once impressive conical Olmec pyramids of adobe resembling "jello-molds," stepped, temple-topped pyramids of any size do not appear in the Americas for centuries more. Large pyramids of the Moche in Peru, the Maya in Yucatan, and others at Cuicuilco, Teotihuacan and Cholula of the Mexican areas may appear as early as a few hundred years before the time of Christ, but by then Egypt's once-brilliant sun had long since set.

America's earliest pyramids were a far cry from the sophisticated structures of Egypt, and didn't achieve stature until Egyptians, and Assyrians, and Babylonians as well, had lost all interest in such projects. In spite of the difficulties in proving any inter-cultural influence, the haunting spectre of these great monuments on both sides of the Atlantic is difficult to dismiss. The sheer size and numbers of pyramids built to royalty on both sides of the Atlantic indicates that their kings had at least one thing in common: greatly enlarged and super-indulged egos.

Cleopatra Down the Amazon?

After a staggering display of pyramids, no other evidence for Egyptians in America seems quite so impressive; still, several intriguing parallels stubbornly appear in any arguments. Similar resins and oils were used for mummies and embalming techniques in both Egypt and Peru. Circumcision and successful trepanation (skull operations) were common practices. Both wove elaborate materials on identical looms (eleven working parts) to create similar cloaks, loin cloths and burial wraps. Both ate with utensils, a practice not common in Europe until the late sixteenth century. And both sailed nearly identical papyrus-reed boats—proved seaworthy by the well-publicized Hyerdahl expeditions when he used Peruvian natives from Lake Titicaca, Peru, to build his Egyptian-like rafts.

Incredible systems of cutting huge stone blocks and great monuments to their kings are impressively demonstrated by both sides; both buried slaves to serve royalty in the afterlife. A flare-base on the Egyptian sarcophagus allowed it to stand upright; America had the same flare-base at Palenque, but, strangely, it lay flat.

Reports of hybridization between cotton strains from both worlds remain unexplained since cotton cannot cross the ocean alone. Wheeled ceramic dogs and a special breed of dogs for mummification appear in both areas. Similar calendars of 360 plus 5 unlucky days date back to 3113 B.C. for the Maya,—and sometime earlier for the Egyptians.

Both Egyptians and New World cultures depict the "flowing vase" symbol of the milky way, or the seed and life-power of the gods. Both depict the "sacred bucket" held by a religious personage. And commonly found on monuments of each is the looped cross, or ankh, the Egyptian symbol for eternal life. Both carved statues to the leaders with dates, genealogies and accounts of their victories. Leaders on both sides wore false beards and elaborate ceremonial head coverings.

Many of these unusual customs could have developed independently without foreign influence, but when they all appear in the same restricted areas of Peru and Mexico along with Priest-Kings, stone-cut temples, tomb embellishment for the afterlife, intermarriage of royal families, sun worship, fitted megalithic masonry, bird-man deities, underworld journeys, and many more unexpected similarities to Egyptian culture, the likelihood of coincidence becomes less. [29] Some people use these striking resemblances as proof of obvious foreign intervention. Others are convinced they merely demonstrate how similar mankind is.

Because of his great antiquity, if the Egyptian Osiris were to be accepted as a real-life world traveller, he would have arrived in the Americas long before the advent of pyramids and temples on either side of the Atlantic, and certainly before the impressive list of Egyptian/American parallels. American Indians would then, like the Egyptians, still have been on their own to invent it all. Later contact with the followers of Osiris might explain some similarities (one writer, Honoré, without reference or explanation, self-assuredly proclaims: "Queen Hatshepsut— launched great expeditions across the sea").[30] Aside from any real evidence of visitations, what would be the attraction? Egyptians didn't travel beyond Egypt; they were comfortable where they were. They had no need to go to other nations; other nations came to them. Still, considering such a possibility is always intriguing.

In the search for bearded visitors, there seems to be no limit to seafaring people who allegedly crossed the oceans. In addition to Egyptians, Romans, and Greeks, many authors would have the natives lined up on American shores to welcome Carthaginians and Blacks from Africa, Etruscans from Italy, Minoans from Crete, and Babylonians, Sumerians, Asiatics, Hebrews—even Christians. One of the best qualified of these authors, Cyrus Gordon, concludes "the main consequence was the mingling of highly civilized people from all over the world."[31] Unpopular as it might be, many writers in their eagerness to place foreign visitors in the Americas, would have Columbus's signature appear far down on the native guest register.

To gain more understanding of such sweeping theories, a few more of these potential culture heroes and bearded men from across the sea will be considered. For now, this chapter will wind up with the most celebrated of all ancient mariners, the Phoenicians.

Vast Influence From a Small Country

Tucked into the upper eastern corner of the Mediterranean is a small country that was destined to wield a powerful influence upon the ancient world. These Semitic people of the land of Canaan, like America today, were made up of many nations. Their ancestors settled before the rise of Egyptian dynasties, and were probably present at the raising of the pyramids.

They became the leading merchants to the Pharaohs of Egypt and the suppliers to the Kings of Israel, Nineveh and Babylon. Giant cedars from their majestic forests provided lumber for most of the great ships and buildings of the Mediterranean cultures (one invoice around 2700 B.C. shows forty shiploads of lumber delivered to the Egyptians alone). Dye from tiny marine snails along Tyrian shores provided the nation's kings with the rare purple for their royal robes, and the country's name, Phoenicia, means "purple dye."

The great king David, and his son, Solomon, employed the advanced carpentry and masonry skills of the Phoenicians to build the famed temple at Jerusalem, and then sent them out to bring back the world's goods. The Old Testament (I Kings 10:22,23) relates how the navy of Tarshish (Phoenicians) every three years brought "gold, and silver, ivory and apes, and peacocks. So King Solomon exceeded all the kings of the earth for riches and for wisdom." The "perfect beauty" of Tyre, one of Phoenicia's great cities, is spoken of by the God of Israel. (Ezekiel 27:3).

Phoenicians have been credited with giving the world a twenty-two letter alphabet by which the Greeks formed modern writing and with which they wrote about the Phoenicians, whose histories either rotted away or went unrecorded by them. Many people are surprised to learn the name "Bible" comes from the Egyptian papyrus marketed at the ancient Phoenician town of Byblos—holy scriptures were written in Greek on papyrus from Byblos.

Phoenician Daring

Phoenician involvement with the seas was in heavy, deep-hulled ships exceeding 100 feet in length, constructed of the finest polished Lebanon cedar, and, according to Ezekiel (27:24), they had large square sails of fine linen. Crews benefited from centuries of training techniques, and Tyrian chefs provided sumptuous meals selected from the best cuisines of the known world along with large clay vessels filled with olive oil and rich wines.

When the Greeks and Philistines subjugated Egypt and Israel, Phoenicia ruled the Mediterranean. Her captains began scouting distant locations for ports and colonies, and many of today's familiar names like Cadiz, Tripoli, and Beirut, were the results of such humble settlements. Around 814 B.C., Carthage was the last great city colonized by Phoenicians. As it became a rich and dominating force in the western Mediterranean, Phoenician ships began to sail beyond the known world, past the Pillars of Hercules (Gibraltar), and into the Atlantic. They picked up silver in Spain and tin in England and Ireland.

Moving continually farther west, they eventually sailed to the distant Azores, some 1500 miles west into the Atlantic where Punic Phoenician coins have reputedly been found. Carthaginian sailors allegedly reached the farthest island of Corvo in the eighth century B.C. where they supposedly left coins and a statue pointing the way to the Americas.[32] Relying solely upon their knowledge of the positions of sun and stars for guidance, sailors eventually mastered wind and sea currents to assist them on their return voyages.

With increased daring, they explored the west African coast where Hanno is said to have moved 60 ships with 30,000 colonists south (some writers find this number somewhat exaggerated) past the tip of Africa. And finally they made the most ambitious of all journeys—a complete circling of that huge continent. Commissioned by the Pharaoh Neccho in the seventh century, this ambitious effort was recorded by the Greek Herodotus. Sailing south from the Red Sea, they took three years to circumnavigate the dark continent and return to the Mediterranean through the Straits of Gibraltar.

Great skill, courage, and aggression pushed these intrepid explorers from effortless cruises of the Mediterranean onward until the scriptures proclaim, "Thy borders are in the midst of the seas." (Ezekiel 27:4). Fearless masters of their borders for over a thousand years, they lost their leadership only when rising forces finally stopped them—the Greeks in the east and Romans in the west.[33] The Phoenician drama had a long run. But before the curtain fell upon their nautical act, did they make the epic thrust across the mysterious ocean to the New World? Of all the ancients who braved that turbulent stage, they were the most likely.

Phoenicians Adrift in America?

The champion doubter of ancient Atlantic crossings is S. E. Morison, whose books on the discovery of America before 1600 reveal his vast and impressive knowledge of the subject. As an Admiral who crossed the oceans several times himself, Morison is not unaware that in the twentieth century many daring navigators have successfully made the threatening journey in "open dories and tiny sailboats." But, he argues, they already knew the territory and had knowledgeable help. In the case of the ancients, he claims, it would be another thing, for they would be "thrust forth into the unknown on a voyage of undetermined length and dubious destination."[34]

His argument is sound, but, it should be noted that Mediterranean cultures all had ships far larger and better equipped than those of Columbus, employing greater numbers of skilled crewmen whose inherited traditions of centuries of experience and expertise Columbus lacked. Some writers have felt this so strongly they have made ungrounded claims of Phoenician colonies in New England and visits to South America by King Solomon. Again, Morison adamantly insists that ancient sea craft were not capable of crossing the Atlantic both ways.

Still, a most compelling, as well as controversial, indication of Phoenician crossings comes from South America, directly across from the eastern bulge of Africa often frequented by the Phoenicians. Constance Irwin, in *Fair Gods and Stone Faces*, argues convincingly that these fantastic seamen did not follow closely the treacherous coasts with their thunderous waves, but chose to stay at a more secure distance. If they were too far out at sea, however, an unexpected Atlantic gale, in company with swift currents, could within weeks carry them to South American shores only 1500 miles away (sailing 100 miles in a full day was not uncommon). Such a situation did occur in 1500 A.D. when the Portuguese navigator, Pedro Alvares Cabral, much against his plans, was blown across the Atlantic from Africa to Brazil. Gordon, who reports the event, also explains that the winds and currents favor an east-to-west crossing at that narrowest portion of the Atlantic.[35] (See p. 18.)

For the less-experienced seaman, a return trip would be near impossible, which might explain why so little information got back. But for highly experienced Phoenician mariners with a total mastery of the 2,200-mile-long Mediterranean, plus a successful record of 13,000 miles around the African Continent and twice the distance to the Americas in one trip from Tunisia to the Azores and back, a return trip does not seem unreasonable.

For many centuries, Gordon relates, explorers were seeking a mythical island in the Atlantic called BRZL, "island of Iron." "No country in the world," Gordon says, " deserves the name BRZL 'Iron' more than Brazil, whose chief resource is still iron."[36] Morison refutes that idea, and he insists "Brazil" is the name for wood coals glowing bright red in a brazier. Still, he condescends to tell the story of a reported discovery on a plantation at Paraiba in 1872 by the slaves of Joaquim Alves da Costa of an inscribed stone—ancient, and broken into four pieces. A copy of the text was sent by da Costa to the Historic and Geographic Institute at Rio de Janeiro. This is Gordon's translation of the text:

> We are Sidonian Canaanites from the city of the Merchant King. We were cast up on this distant island, a land of mountains. We sacrificed a youth to the celestial gods and goddesses in the nineteenth year of our mighty King Hiram and embarked from Eziongeber into the Red Sea. We voyaged with ten ships and were at sea together for two years around Africa. Then we were separated by the hand of Baal and were no longer with our companions. So we have come here, twelve men and three women, into "Islands of Iron." Am I, the Admiral, a man who would flee? Nay! May the celestial gods and goddesses favor us well.[37]

Various scholars have pronounced the inscription in turn authentic, and a hoax. If it was a planned hoax, no one ever benefited, for neither the stones nor da Costa were ever located. Gordon claims that those who have disputed the inscription's authenticity have misread the text since some was unknown in the last century, and therefore could not be forged. Only in this century, he insists, with newly discovered inscriptions, has it been possible to authenticate it, which he feels confident he has done.

If Phoenicians arrived on American shores, it would seem they would colonize or attempt some kind of trade or exchange with the natives. The explorer Gene Savoy believes they did. In 1989 he claimed to have found tablets with Phoenician and Semitic hieroglyphs along the Amazon in the highland jungle of Peru.[38] He ties the discovery in with the lost gold mine of King Solomon. Skeptics doubt the origin of his tablets, and the controversy will likely continue.

The Tyrians Meet the "Rubber People"

In 1858 a native was hacking away at the jungle on the sultry Gulf Coast of Mexico when his machete bounced off a hard object. Clearing the thick growth, he saw what he thought was a huge, overturned kettle. One that size, he envisioned, might hold a fabulous treasure, and he ran for assistance to turn it upright. What emerged was not a kettle of gold at all, but a stone carving of a colossal, bodiless, human head, darkened with age, and helmeted like a football player.[39]

In succeeding years more of these surly faces turned up, weighing some fifteen tons and carrying distinctive negroid characteristics: broad noses and thick lips. Eventually the whole southern Veracruz area was found to be strewn with very ancient and very mysterious ceremonial centers of a people labeled Olmecs, "rubber people." Puzzled, archaeologists began to unearth templed courtyards, pyramids up to 100' high, pillars, drainage systems, exquisite jade carvings, highly crafted stone monuments (in addition to the large heads), elaborate mosaics, and some tombs. These Olmecs had skill at using iron ores, and had even developed, according to Coe, a simple magnetic compass.

At first no one would believe this culture dated before 300 B.C.. But later carbon dating shot a cultural rocket into the Olmec sky that spelled out 1200 B.C.! Archaeologists were shocked; the rest of Mexico was still in its formative stages of development at that time. It was like finding a skyscraper in the middle of sixteenth-century Indian hogans. A thorny question surfaced that still has some scholars bristling: Who came first, the Olmec or the Maya? Other questions were equally stubborn: Why such a highly developed people only here? Why the isolation?

Some onlookers waved it away with a simple wand of cultural evolution. Others resurrected the Greeks, Romans and Egyptians. But the oldest of the centers, San Lorenzo, existed too early (1200 B.C.) for Aegean Greeks who were busy fighting the Trojan war, or Romans, not yet in their infancy. And the main center, La Venta was too late (900-400 B.C.) for the waning Egyptians. Most writers avoided dealing with the precise negroid head shape and features found not only on Olmec statues, but directly across the ocean in living form on the dark continent, and on similar stone carvings as far away as Egypt. A few suggested the majority of the Olmec race was black.

Olmec Head with Negroid Characteristics
(Museum, Mexico City)

It is possible that black sailors crossed the Atlantic in pre-Columbian times, but few scholars have pursued the theory. Some have suggested a black-like race came across the Bering Straits. But for the most part, they have assumed that Africans were land people with limited sailing experience who never crossed the oceans at all. In spite of African Mandingo legends that fleets of rafts braved the Atlantic to land in the west, and tales from the Spaniards that Balboa and Columbus found Blacks on the Atlantic coast of Panama, supposed remnants of shipwrecked black pirates, it seems doubtful that the legendary "white" visitors will be found among them. If blacks ever came, they may have brought the whites, but more likely, as in recent times, whites brought the blacks.

Along the shores of Africa, opportunistic Phoenician merchants often picked up Black slaves for the trade markets in Egypt—one of the reasons for colonies in Africa. If Phoenicians drifted to the Americas, Blacks may well have accompanied them. Irwin points out that in returning to the Mediterranean from around the African continent's lower bulge, and in an effort to avoid the powerful headwinds and currents, ships would head northwest, then swing far out into the ocean and continue between the Madeira and Canary Islands. She admits such an occurrence does not automatically place Phoenicians in the Americas, but asks, "What would happen if at this point a storm arose?" This question is not unrealistic, since Caribbean hurricanes originate in Africa.

The answer to her question comes from an eminent Portuguese geographer, Armando Cortesao, who explains that such winds "come from the northeast," and a ship "would stand every chance of being propelled southwestwards until reaching the belt south of the Saragasso Sea . . . [then] irresistibly toward the Antilles." From there the current could easily carry them to Yucatan and on to the Olmec area.[40]

It has been argued that no society ever created great monuments to slaves, but if perchance Olmec artists saw in the Blacks compelling traits for portraiture, would they not also see in their Phoenician transporters something unique worth preserving? Unearthed alongside the carved stone heads were other carved figurines revealing a distinctively different type—taller and bearded with aqualine noses and thin lips. One of Mexico's great archaeologists, Miguel Covarrubias, called them "some of the most mysterious and exciting sculptures of Middle America." He believed they were foreign visitors.[41]

Carved slabs from the major site of La Venta show priest-like men in long robes (although some are in war dress, or nude), pointed helmets or caps, long false beards, high-bridged noses and up-turned toes—enough like Phoenicians to feel at home on Assyrian bas reliefs. One of these aristocratic figures is so unlike Gulf area inhabitants that archaeologists have labeled him "Uncle Sam." Other carvings suggest a known Phoenician practice—infant sacrifice.

Other Phoenician similarities found at the Olmec sites are: adorned stone altars with a twisted-rope pattern holding a captive slave, a "cat (jaguar) god," deities floating overhead, head deformation, special clay seals, wheeled toys, and oracles to read the future. Von Wuthenau, who collects small terracotta faces from all over Mexico, in his *Unexpected Faces in Ancient America*, shows one he claims is the bearded, phallic God Bes, which accompanied every Phoenician ship.[42] Olmec art includes several phallic figures otherwise rare in Mesoamerican art. Robert Marx's further claims of Phoenician writing and copper discs discovered in the area, recorded in his *Still More Adventures* adds to the intrigue.

If these are indeed Phoenicians, arrived from their homeland to spread advanced skills and learning, is it possible that the Olmec figures are the first depictions of the legendary "White Gods" from the east? An Olmec monument at Chalcatzingo, and perhaps another from la Venta, displays a feathered serpent. Could these be the earliest culture-hero traces? Accounts of these visitors might easily be accepted as occasional additions to the tales of white visitors from across the sea, blown off course and leaving behind an isolated memento. But, if they stayed to colonize, infusing their culture and a higher way of life, even more functional elements of Phoenician life should accompany them: trade ports, large ships, an alphabet, writings on papyrus, the use of native woods; glass beads, necklaces, and vases; gold and silver objects, fine embroidered clothing, ivory ornaments and ornate burial practices. And where is the royal purple? The list is too long to investigate, but gold and silver were never unearthed among the Olmec. On the other hand, Michael Coe reports that Olmecs, like the Phoenicians, did use purple paint.[43]

Unfortunately, much conclusive information is missing, for the Olmec heartland is damp, and organic materials have disappeared. For that matter, so have the Olmecs. Stone sarcophaguses have been found, but few people. Much valuable information was covered up when an air strip was laid at La Venta. However, hundreds of Olmec mounds nearby await excavation, and when they are unearthed, new light will be shed.[44] To discover Phoenicians in America would place a disturbing piece in the American puzzle, for the Olmec were considered the "Mother Culture" of all Mesoamerica, and, as they say, "as the Olmecs go . . . " In the meantime, what do the Phoenicians themselves say of this? Nothing. They remain silent.

Greeks and Phoenicians

But then, Phoenicians were always silent. Secrets were well kept; that is how they survived for so long. If it weren't for Greeks who recorded much about them, people today would have very little, for what records the Phoenicians did keep, over time mildewed and rotted. Aristotle's fourth-century B.C. report of an "island" out in the ocean discovered by the Carthaginians and later hushed up is frustratingly incomplete. One has to wait two hundred years more for Diodorus of Sicily in his *Library of History, Vol III*, to fill in missing details of the Sicilian Phoenicians who had made extensive voyages for trade and colonization beyond Gibraltar.

Diodorus's description of a vast "island" in the ocean "many days" off the coast of Africa includes mountains, beautiful plains, and navigable rivers, which were introduced earlier. He also tells of well-constructed homes surrounded by irrigated groves and gardens. This wonderful land, he explains, was discovered by chance by Phoenicians blown off course by strong winds while exploring the shores of Libya (today's Africa). They were carried to the island, and having "observed its felicity and nature they caused it to be made known to all men." (That would be somewhat unexpected for people who traditionally remained silent.)

Diodorus further reports that the Etruscans (pre-Romans), sufficiently impressed by the descriptions of the excellence of the distant "island," desired to send a colony there, but the Carthaginians prevented it, wishing to keep the place a secret known only to themselves should the need arise for a future retreat to a land unknown to their conquerors.[45] It is believed that in order for Phoenicians to keep their trade monopoly, especially against the Greeks, they spread the myth that the Atlantic was muddy, impassable, and full of sea monsters. That alone would be sufficient to discourage most superstitious navigators.

Enthusiasts of the Phoenician discovery of America present an impressive bit of evidence in a world map painted in 1513 by the Turkish admiral Piri Re'is ("Re'is" means Admiral) which contains one of the earliest renderings of the eastern American coast and surprisingly shows South America and Africa in a correct longitudinal relationship not known by modern cartographers until the mid-eighteenth century. The admiral claims he got the information from several sources, including ancient maps drawn up in the time of Alexander the Great and kept in the great library at Alexandria which was partially burned in 47 B.C. and completely destroyed in the seventh century A.D..

Researchers, like Charles Hapgood, suggest that only Phoenicians, not Greeks, could have provided the Egyptians with such information. It is accepted that early Portuguese navigators contributed something to the controversial map, but whether or not the ancient sources are authentic is still in dispute.[46]

At this point there are too many questions and too few answers. It is possible the whole story is pure allegory. But if so, why try to suppress it? Was it just an island the Phoenicians found, and if so, which one? There are so few in the Atlantic, and the few are insignificant. Besides, all the islands of the Atlantic were by that time commonly visited, and England is not located across from Africa. Did they actually discover South America believing it to be an island?   Continents are often referred to as islands, and four trips to the American continents never convinced Columbus he had seen anything other than large islands.

If after visiting the island/continent Phoenicians were able to return, why is this not common knowledge? Many may not have returned, or if they did, they kept it secret—like telling of UFO visitations today. Who would believe them? Today, archaeologists are finding earlier native beginnings for the Olmecs—perhaps in South America. Arrivals from overseas now seem unnecessary.

Even if the independent development of native cultures without foreign assistance is accepted, the greatness of early Mediterranean cultures in their periods of expansive exploration and achievements makes it seem inconsistent to deny them the use of the same winds and currents and intelligence that later brought Columbus to these shores. Which lends back to Burrows's mystery cave in Illinois that has yet to be examined by archaeologists. Opinions differ, but among the 4,000 artifacts removed from that elusive site were numerous portraits resembling Phoenician merchant princes as well as the Phoenician alphabet. Perhaps the late Sir Eric Thompson, who described the Maya as the "Phoenicians of the New World," was more correct than he knew.[47]

If the cave actually contains ancient Egyptian-like crypts with urns containing written scrolls, as Burrows claims, and he decides to re-open it to archaeological investigation, it may be necessary one day to re-write early American history. Until then, knowing that people of the Mediterranean were capable of such voyages, and that evidence for their arrivals may exist, is still not sufficient in the eyes of most scholars to make such visits a historical fact.

Out of New World cultural ingredients: physical appearances, skills, traditions and possessions, the Romans, Greeks, Egyptians and Phoenicians, have been thrust one at a time upon American soil to test their influence upon the unwary natives. The bigger question is not so much "did Mediterranean civilization get *to* the Americas, for evidence continues to mount, but rather, "did Mediterranean civilization get into the Americas?"

The next chapter will examine an enduring culture that more than any other is believed to have gained that access.

11

LOST TRIBES
IN A PROMISED LAND

As New World natives observed conquest devastation and religious fanaticism, many learned to remain silent about their beliefs in a bearded, white visitor from across the sea. Thus, much valuable information was lost. Yet, today, occasional chance discoveries still give startling insights into his possible origins. A modern-day example comes from a young missionary, Jess Groesbeck, during a tropical downpour in the Indian town of Quetzaltenango, 7,600 feet up in the highlands of Guatemala.

An apologetic knock at the door revealed a barefooted native begging shelter for the night. Usually cheerful, the Indian youth from the nearby village of Totonicapán was not cheerful now, and his reason was somber and as chilling as the night. Hesitant at first to open up, the naturally shy Quiché Indian slowly unfolded a frightful story that his mother had overheard in the marketplace of plans by village leaders to use their machetes on her son that very night. She admonished him to go into hiding.

The boy and his close friend had some time ago been entrusted by town elders with knowledge very sacred to their clan. The old sages had revealed to the boys a weathered pine box bound with rusty locks from another era. They said it could be opened only when all the key holders of the clan were there. Hidden inside the heavy box, they explained, was a very ancient record of the clan's history. So sacred was this record, and their obligation to preserve it so binding, that if they were ever to reveal its location, they would be killed. The boys' association with foreign missionaries had made the town Elders suspicious, and now there was a price on their heads. The young men survived, and the intrigue of a hidden record fired the imagination of the missionary, who made several attempts to see it.[1] But convincing Guatemalan Indians to part with old traditions is like trying to extract jungle vines from ancient walls. Based upon unfortunate experiences with Conquest devastation, Indians justly maintain heavy suspicions of modern civilization and its purposes. The labored search for that record by others, and its eventual appearance spanned several years, and is a tale of amazing dedication which will be examined later.

Because of wanton destruction by the Spanish of so much recorded native history, any addition from newly-discovered manuscripts could add greatly to the pitifully small amount that remains. Shortly after the Conquest, Indians intent on preserving the traditions of their people learned the Spanish alphabet, with which they wrote in their native tongue the legends and practices previously handed down only through word of mouth or by native artists. Unfortunately, many of these valuable records were carelessly destroyed or misplaced, ruined by misuse, or, like this one, secreted away by cautious leaders.

Ancient Records Raise Age-Old Questions

A few of these precious documents, however, did survive, and a previous record had already surfaced in Totonicapán. Named for its origin, *Title of the Lords of Totonicapán*, it was written in 1554 by the Quiché elders, but then the original manuscript disappeared. A copy was entrusted to Catholic priests, who set the record aside, and not until 1834 was it translated into Spanish and French and much later into English. The small but significant manuscript relates the ancient wanderings of a people who settled into Guatemala after coming "from the other part of the sea from where the sun rises." It then makes the surprising declaration that these nations are descendants of the Ten Tribes of Israel, ". . . of the same language and the same customs."[2]

Amazing as this sounds, the story is corroborated by two other records recorded by the Quiché and their nearby cousins, the Cakchiquels. These fascinating books, the *Popol Vuh*, and the lesser-known *Annals of the Cakchiquels*, were written in the middle of the sixteenth century by Indian lords and their families. The *Popol Vuh* was written at the town of Santa Cruz, Quiché, near the colorful market town of Chichicastenango, and the *Annals* were recorded in the picturesque town of Sololá, which clings to the steep shores of one of the world's most beautiful lakes, Atitlán.

The *Popol Vuh*, along with the works of Chilam Balalm, the "Jaguar Priest" of Yucatan, discussed in chapter 3, is the most notable of the surviving works of Maya literature. It is an attempt by the Quiché elders to recreate an "original book" that existed among them anciently but "is no longer." Although the *Popol Vuh* does not make the direct claim of Israelite origins that its companion record in Totonicapán does, it still relates that the ancient people of the Plumed Serpent. . . "came from across the sea" with enlightened writings about their gods. Another title for the *Popol Vuh* is *"The Light That Came from Across the Sea."*[3] In Old Testament tradition, the Maya also believed in a creation, and a flood, and that the end of the world would come by fire.[4]

The *Annals* are very specific that "From the west we came to Tulán, from across the sea." The book also gives an intriguing insight to that crossing which occurred in "Moses fashion" when the leaders thrust forth their staffs so they could cross on dry sand. Similarly, the *Titulo* states that "When they arrived at the edge of the sea, their prophet Balam-Quitzé touched it with his staff and at once a path opened."[5] Upon arrival they must have made some impact upon local natives for the same reference states that they were given a stone of power and majesty by which other people feared and respected them. (Durán, a priest who grew up hearing native legends in Mexico, goes even farther when he relates that Topiltzin Quetzalcoatl touched the sea with his rod and parted the waters, allowing his people through on dry land while the persecutors were drowned.)[6] Native sources complete the obvious parallels with Old Testament stories when they give the startling information that these overseas visitors "were the true descendants of Abraham and Jacob."

So three native records, *Popol Vuh, Annals of the Cakchiquels,* and *Lords of Totonicapán* all contain what not only seem to be strong references to native awareness of Hebrew people and traditions, but also contain affirmations that they are distant ancestors. Two of the records claim ancient Hebrew descent from across the sea, and from the same village where the third record originated come reports of still other mysterious records, whose emergence could possibly shed further light on this tantalizing claim.

These amazing Guatemalan records do not stand alone in their declarations; many early writers about Indian cultures readily believed they could see Hebrew characteristics in the natives. From thin threads of Indian traditions numerous writers attempted to weave an historical blanket of supposed Israelites reaching all the way from North through South America. One of these "weavers," De Landa, collected remembrances of the Indians in his attempt to rectify his unfortunate earlier burning of Indian manuscripts. He tells that "Some of the old people of Yucatan say that they have heard from their ancestors that this land was occupied by a race of people who came from the East and whom God had delivered by opening twelve paths through the sea." He further speculates, "If this were true, it necessarily follows that all the inhabitants of the Indies are descendants of the Jews."[7]

So extensive became this kind of thinking that Bancroft, who pursued all the known writings and published volumes on Indian history himself, states: "The theory that the Americans are of Jewish (Israelite) descent has been discussed more minutely and at greater length than any other."[8]

These volumes of opinions vary from colorful and intriguing to belabored and tedious. To understand the reasons for such extensive beliefs in the arrival of these controversial people, one must first be acquainted with the presumed visitors—the Israelites.

A Lasting Covenant

A people of many names, these "Sons of Abraham," "Israelites," "Hebrews," "Twelve Tribes," and "Jews," begin with a vision—not especially unique, but among the most enduring visions in history. It came to an old man named Abraham, who lived some 2,000 years before Christ. Genesis 12:1-7 records that he was promised by God that if his people would do as commanded they would be especially favored, become a great nation, and bless all the families of the earth. In the bargain, they would also receive the land of Canaan.

It was a fabulous life insurance policy, for in accepting it, Abraham not only provided for the family's future following his death, but also established a system that would keep the family together longer than any other in history. Four thousand years later, this remarkable covenant is still in effect and provides not only material guarantees for his posterity, but a persistent motivation to survive. The bonding ingredient in this contract was the enduring belief that the descendants of Abraham were God's "Chosen People."

In his highly readable *Jews, Gods and History*, Max Dimont points out that the only peoples who have endured as long as the Israelite family are the Chinese, the Hindus and the Egyptians. And only the contributions of Greece and Rome have had as profound an intellectual and spiritual influence upon the culture of the Western world as the Israelite legacy. He underscores the paradox that other civilizations who grew right alongside Israel: Egyptians, Assyrians, Babylonians, Persians, and other Mediterranean peoples, had the stabilizing influence of continually possessing their own countries. Many of them rose to remarkable heights, creating magnificent and enduring monuments to their greatness, but these countries have all vanished, while Israel, which maintained none of those visual supports, has survived solely upon its ideas.[9] Furthermore, those ideas have survived every threat, in every language, and among every culture on earth.

Israel's ability to endure is legendary. Pagan practices tempted Israel away from its monotheistic beliefs with intermittent success—but ultimate failure. The dispersion of this family to distant parts of the world and among foreign cultures would have sounded the death knell for others; it left them resolute. Cultural absorption by Rome and Greece was eventually shed, and they successfully rode out the seven-hundred-year rise and fall of Islam. From the dark threat of the Middle Ages: accept Christianity or be destroyed, their faith emerged even stronger. Modern bouts with anti-Semitism find them scathed and scattered but even more determined. Survival seems assured.

Well known to even non-Bible readers are the prophets Abraham, Isaac, and Jacob—whose name was changed to "Israel" and whose twelve sons became the twelve tribes. School children and a Broadway musical recount the dramatic story of Joseph and his technicolor coat, the favored son of Israel sold into Egypt where he worked his way into the house of Pharaoh and there presided over the distribution of wheat during a seven-year famine. Later, around 1600 B.C., he brought his family to Egypt, where for nearly four-hundred years they were exposed to that nation's alluring ways and culture, while struggling to maintain their own religious identity. Eventually, they ended up in Egyptian bondage.

Widely publicized through modern-day films, if not through teachings, are the miraculous events that led to the release of the house of Israel under the leadership of its greatest prophet, the "son" of Pharaoh's daughter, Moses. Defying the Pharaoh and wielding a staff, he led the twelve tribes through the parting of the Red Sea and into the wilderness for forty years.

While there, Moses was visited upon Mount Sinai by the same God of Abraham, who reconfirmed the sacred covenant and gave further commandments. This new law, the Mosaic Code, was one of the first and most humanitarian in history. The tribes of Israel carried that code with them into their promised land. Sandwiched between Egypt and Phoenicia, they struggled to bring forth a new nation and create their glorious, but short-lived homeland. Ironically, the great man who brought them to it, Moses, was not allowed to enter. To this day, it is not known where he went.

Said by Dimont (1962, 48-9) to be the first constitutional monarchy in the world, and the blueprint for the United States Constitution, the new nation soon spread its fame. Who has not heard of Israel's illustrious kings, David, and his son Solomon, who, for a short time, achieved unity for those bellicose tribes? With the accumulation of wealth at their disposal, they became great not only in the eyes of their people, but to the world. The first-century Jewish historian, Josephus, records that when David died, he left behind "greater wealth than any other king ever did."[10] And, of Solomon, who married the pharaoh's daughter, 2 Chronicles 9:22-3 simply says, "And King Solomon passed all the kings of the earth in riches and wisdom." Further, it says, with this wealth, Solomon built a great temple to God and a magnificent palace for himself. And to hear his wisdom, "all the kings of the earth sought the presence of Solomon."

Alas, this overwhelming opulence soon tarnished. Who else could equal the power of David or match the wisdom of Solomon? Within a year of Solomon's death, the empire split into two independent kingdoms: Israel, with ten tribes to the North, and Judah, with the remaining two tribes, Judah and Benjamin, to the South. Under succeeding aggressive kings, many battles were waged, and peoples of both kingdoms faced eventual conquest, captivity, and deportation out of their beloved land. Northern Israelite tribes and portions of Judah were taken in 722 B.C. by the Assyrians. The rest of Judah succumbed to the Babylonians 136 years later, in 588 B.C..

When Cyrus conquered Babylonia and offered freedom to the kingdom of Judah (now called "Jews") a little over fifty years following their captivity, only an estimated one fourth of the survivors chose to return. The rest remained in Babylonia or moved elsewhere. The Northern Kingdom of Israel had already been broken into segments by the Assyrians and dispersed in order to shatter their unity. So where did the people of these ten tribes go? The disappearance and dispersion of these people created one of history's most intriguing riddles—the whereabouts of the Lost Ten Tribes, and set the stage for the search for the bearded, white traveler among the Israelites.

Tracer of Lost Tribes

No one knows precisely where these tribes went. The historian Josephus simply says the "Ten Tribes were removed . . . and transplanted into Media and Persia," and "Judah was taken captive into Babylon."[11] But not every wolf travels with the pack, and in both cases as they watched their country crumble, no doubt many fled to near-by Phoenicia and to other organized Jewish territories. According to the political leader and historian, Ben Gurion, some even " fled to Egypt."[12] The Biblical prophet, Ezekiel (33:27), records that a few stubbornly remained in their homeland, hiding in the "wastes . . . in the open field . . . in the forts and in the caves."

Of those who were taken, some would gradually blend in with their captors, while others would become slaves in distant countries. Some from the tribes of Israel were carried away to the "north," while many others just disappeared. All of them unwittingly fulfilled the prophecies of God to Amos (9:9) that He would " . . . sift the house of Israel among all nations," and to Zechariah (10:9), that he would "sow them among the people: and they shall remember me in far countries."

Just how far did these backsliding people travel in their dispersion? In addition to the near countries of Egypt and Phoenicia, Israelites are reported to have eventually established cities among the Greeks and Trojans and large settlements in Italy and Carthage. Other reports of migrations have them crossing the plains and mountains of Asia and Europe over many centuries, until they filter into most of those countries, mixing their genes with the local citizens. They apparently reached both ends of the continent, for one authority even reports blond Israelites in China.[13]

The challenge to locate the "Lost Tribes" has stretched many an imagination. Because Bible prophecies say the tribes will come down from the north in the last days (Jeremiah 3:18), some fantastic speculations would have them hidden and doing well in a colony near the North Pole, or, even inside the earth, which some people declare is hollow. The most flamboyant suggestion comes from the Mormon leader, Joseph Smith, who allegedly said the tribes are living comfortably on a distant planet which was separated off from the northern part of earth. On a clear night, he pointed out, it can easily be seen near the North Star (a statement inspired, perhaps, by Deut. 30:4). When the tribes return to earth, he assured, their land will once again be miraculously reunited with the mother planet.[14] Whether he was serious, or this was his droll way of saying, "No one knows,". . . no one knows.

On the more conservative side of the issue, many of the fleeing tribes may have entered the sea along the Palestinian coast where seafaring Israelites used ships for fishing and industry. King Solomon had a navy, and the scriptures (1Kings 9:26, Genesis 49:13, Judges 5:17) say tribes of Dan, Asher and Zebulun were mariners. Undoubtedly, those who could escape in ships, would do so. Information on immediate migrations is sparse, but later history indicates that Spain, which was on the Phoenician trade-route for iron, tin and lead, received some of them. Colonies of Ephraimites are believed the first blond migrants to have entered Ireland and Britain, where they reportedly fought the Celts and eventually became one with the Anglo/Saxons.

Little is written about those areas in early times, but genealogical records claim descent for even the royal house of England from scattered Israelites. Legends indicate they may have continued as far north as Denmark and Scandinavia—the name "Denmark" is said by some people, although without foundation, to have come from the tribe of Dan.

Evidence is scarce, but what fragments of support do exist for such settlements come from legends, genealogies, and numerous burial mounds along the routes. Objects with Hebrew inscriptions occasionally turn up, and some even identify the names of individual tribes. Wherever the various branches may eventually prove to have settled, evidence indicates that the Tribes dispersed to all parts of the known ancient world, true to God's pronouncement to His prophet Zechariah (7:14), "I scattered them with a whirlwind among all the nations whom they knew not."

With migrations perpetually moving out like waves from a stone dropped in water, one wonders if any of these tribal swells continued rolling across the great oceans until they lapped American shores. Reports of people with ruddy complexions, hairy bodies, and Israelite customs come from as far as the Ainu in Japan. Many believe, without verification, that from there they travelled up the coast and over to the Americas. Having lived in close proximity to Phoenicians and Egyptians, Israel learned her maritime trade well. Ezekiel says, "thy rowers have brought thee into great waters" (27:26). Jeremiah speaks of them living "on the coasts of the earth" and "in the isles afar off" (31:8,10). Could part of the tribes have intentionally migrated across the Atlantic? And, if so, what evidence remains?

Identifying Israel

S ituated at the hub of the ancient world, Israel was a literal crossroad for civilization. Into this melting pot came a broad variety of cultural influences from Egypt, Mesopotamia, Syria, Rome, Phoenicia and Greece. From admonishings by Israel's prophets to "come out from the world," it can be assumed they must have absorbed a good deal of it. America's culture hero was said to be a bringer of high culture and civilization. Surely the arrival in the Americas of some of the world's highest cultural achievements, housed in the minds of a large group of Israelites using Phoenician and Egyptian sailing methods and wearing long robes, pointed caps and tapered beards, would not go unnoticed by natives.

But, as many writers have noted, ocean crossings do not make lasting trails or identifying footprints, and Israel did not leave behind great pyramids nor elaborate burial tombs to mark their presence. In the absence of such monuments, or reliable records, the only hope of tracing alleged intrusions into the Americas would be to discover remnants among native cultures of the characteristics that were so distinctly Israel (Judah included).

Israel had many unique practices and characteristics. These traits so deeply believed in and strongly adhered to not only made them seem strange to their neighbors, who for the most part practiced pagan traditions, but are so unique that if discovered outside of Israel, should help to identify them in their wanderings. A thorough review of them can be found in Dimont's *Jews, God and History*, and De Vaux's *Ancient Israel* (two volumes).

Some of these unmistakably identifying traits are worship of one God (identified as YHVH, Yahweh, or Jehovah); the practice of circumcision in all males; prohibition of human sacrifice (although there were periods of backsliding when even infants were offered); disapproval of pagan hierarchies of gods; and abhorrence of graven images (or any images most of the time). Further distinguishing features were strong family ties in the form of twelve individually organized tribes, close adherence to religious and secular laws, requiring that judges and kings be equally responsible to them; and a powerful faith in patriarchs and prophets who spoke on behalf of God. Additional characteristics were their refined manners and grace, and the implacable belief that they were the "Chosen of God."

In any country inhabited for any length of time by remnants of these tenacious preservers of tradition, one would expect to find at least some form of the Hebrew alphabet and writings, a 365-day lunar calendar, bronze musical instruments, use of sacred waters, reverence for holy mountains, feast and fast days with food taboos, animal sacrifices, observance of the sabbath and other specifically Hebrew doctrines. Most assuredly, their descendants would retain a strong sense of their history. Above all, Hebrews travelling to a distant land would carry with them some indication of the preservation (if only in remembrance) of Israel's most recognizable feature—without which there would be no Israel—the temple, with its never-ending rites and ceremonies, ritual clothing and Ark of the Covenant. Here God could come down from his heavenly home, and the priests could represent the people to Him.

Such deeply held concepts can sometimes be more enduring than the stone structures that house them, so that when the temple is gone, the beliefs and rituals still remain. This was demonstrated following A.D. 70 when in spite of the destruction of Jerusalem's temple and further scattering of the Jews by the Romans, Jewish beliefs and practices continued.

Ancient Tribes in a New Land

Early Spaniards were surprised to discover what they considered Israelite characteristics in the practices of New World inhabitants. Among those who wrote about them were Las Casas, Sahagún, García, Torquemada, Gómara, Durán, Diaz, De Landa, and even Cortéz—far more than can be covered even in several volumes. In the nineteenth century, after millenniums of languishing on forgotten shelves, many of these records became available again, and scholars began to pore over them. The most energetic of these, Lord Kingsborough (mentioned in previous chapters), gathered many of these writings between 1831 and 1848 into nine huge, leather-bound volumes. In a fascination that reached near-fanaticism, he attempted to prove that Indians were of the Lost Tribes of Israel. In the overly expensive process of publishing his research, he needlessly lost his own life in debtor's prison—just one year before he would have inherited his father's fortunes.

Later in the century, Bancroft, while writing extensively on Indian cultures, faced the same overwhelming volumes of theories about American Indians being of Jewish descent. And although he did not particularly favor the "Jewish" theories, he still records them impartially.[15]   Seeking a direct way through the "labyrinth" of material, he chose to summarize Garcia and Kingsborough. To keep this part of our search for a culture hero readable, we will summarize them further.

The first parallels most early writers note between American natives and Hebrews are those of native temple structures and ceremonies. Like Israel's only temple, the American ones face east and had fine work in stone. Spaniards found that Peruvian and Toltec temples had similar gold plating. Fine woods adorn the Mayan temples (e.g., Tikal). Both Israelite and American temples were supported by columns (e.g., Sayil, Chichen, Tula), and both sported horns on each of the four altar corners (Monte Alban urn).[16] Both had perpetually burning fires and the pervading fragrance of incense (still observable at Chichicastenango, Guatemala), and both had trumpets and bells to announce religious ceremonies (depicted on the Bonampak walls). Temples in both places were presided over by priests, wearing long robes and turbans, who made blood sacrifices at the altars, gave communion, and took confession. Only high priests were allowed into the holy of holies. American priests, like the Levites, were entitled to their offices by tribal inheritance—families marked for that purpose. Of course one wonders why Israelites in the Americas would place their sacred temples upon pagan pyramids resembling so closely those they had left in Egypt.

Both the Toltecs under Quetzalcoatl, and the Israelites, prohibited human sacrifice, but submitted to it on occasion.[17] Later Aztecs instigated the sacrifice of children, and by conquest times they had allowed human sacrifice to reach unbelievable proportions. More often in earlier times animals were sacrificed—but only unblemished ones. Like the Israelites, American natives were forbidden to eat the flesh of certain animals (like the peccary, or South American swine). Purification rituals for birth were similar, and in both areas boys of eight-days of age were circumcised. According to Sahagún, both cultures brought their first-born young men to the temple to serve.[18]

The most revered possession of the Palestine Jews was their Ark of the Covenant, a symbolic resting place for God. It was an elaborately decorated box kept in the temple and touched only on certain occasions by designated priests. Instances are rare, but Durán reports that the Mexicas had a similar Ark at Huexotzingo, "held in as much reverence as that of the Jews."[19] Kingsborough states that only specific persons could touch the sacred object. James Adair, an eighteenth-century writer who lived for forty years among the North American Indians and thoroughly believed they were of Jewish origins, notes a similar Ark among the Cherokee and tribes along the Mississippi.[20]

Mounting Similarities

Traditions of both Israelites and Indian nations say their origins began with a long journey in the wilderness. They were divided into tribes, unified by strict laws, and led by a prophet who was directed of God. Their homeland was a prophetic gift from God. In the case of the Aztecs, they were led by the priest Mecitli (Meh-SHEET-lee), or "Mexi," with his brother Tecpatzin and sister Malinalli, suggesting to the Spaniards Moses "Moshe," his brother Aaron, and their sister, Miriam. Tozzer and Brinton both record Indian recollections of the opening of twelve paths through the sea, and that the Quiché prophet parted the waters with his staff so they could cross on dry land. Like Israel's prophets Moses and Aaron, the distant Aztec prophets were also denied entrance to the "Promised Land."

Along with historical traditions, many religious beliefs of both peoples appear similar. At times both worshiped one God, while at the same time allowing for angels and subordinated personages of their hierarchies who attended them closely. In some Indian cultures the God's name was YOHEWAH, readily recalling the

Israelite YHVH, YAHWEH, or JEHOVAH. Both believed god created people in his image, and like the Israelites, American Indian tribes insisted they alone were God's "Chosen." The Mexican god, like Israel's, dwelt in obscurity, and no one looked upon his face. He was "Supreme Lord of the Universe," "The Father of Mankind," "Forgiver of Sins," "Omnipresent" and "Omnipotent," "Merciful and Long Suffering." "In short," Kingsborough says, he has "all the attributes and powers which were assigned to Jehovah by the Hebrews."[21]

Discovered among some Indian tribes are other typically Hebrew doctrines such as observance of a Sabbath of the seventh day and a form of ten commandments. More commonly found are beliefs in the fall of mankind, brought on by the sin of man at woman's suggestion, expulsion from paradise, building of a high tower, and the confounding of languages with a subsequent scattering of people. Native mourning ceremonies and burials under the foundation of the house parallel Israel's beliefs, as well as a hope for resurrection of the body—yes, says David Goldstein in *Jewish Folklore and Legend*, Judaism did teach resurrection (p. 34). By far the most common of all similarities to Biblical stories found among the natives of North, Central and South America are the numerous stories of a flood and the preservation of one man, his family, and animals in a boat or hollowed log coming to rest on the highest mountain. As was observed earlier, they believed the end of the world would come by fire.

In an unexpected reversal, some bizarre Indian practices abhorred by the Spaniards and usually thought of as unique to natives of this land are also found in ancient Israel: scalping, eating of sacrificial victims, "Holy Wars," and displaying the heads of sacrificial enemies.[22] Other practices, surprisingly found in both Biblical and Indian cultures, were bows and arrows (1 Chron. 12:2) and smoke signals.[23] Both also employed the more pleasant social customs of washing the feet of strangers and anointing them with oil.

Kingsborough sees great similarities between the Aztecs, Incas and Jews in the traditions of their kings. Although similar practices can be found among other people of the world as well, he is certain that these, found in the Americas, were modeled after the Jews: the presiding of royalty at sacrifices, dancing at religious festivals, royal consecration at the hands of the high priest, the wearing of crowns and bracelets, many royal wives and concubines, removal of royal sandals upon approaching a temple, the practice of not looking the king in the face upon speaking to him, and elegant burials with incense and perfumes.

These seemingly endless similarities also include the use of unleavened bread, reverence for sacred mountain tops, punishing of adultery by stoning, corresponding holy days, frequent bathing even in cold weather, a 52- or 50-year cycle along with a 360-day calendar and five additional unlucky days, flowing water from both sides of a sacred vase, use of the lion and jaguar as symbols of rain and power, belief in Satan (called Mictlantecuhtli in Mexico), the depiction of the five- and six-pointed stars of Israel, and a strong expectation of a coming Messiah.

If the above parallels weren't quite enough, Thomas Stuart Ferguson, in *One Fold and One Shepherd*, provides over 300 additional American similarities to Bible land cultures. His listings, along with those which have been summarized from Kingsborough (Chapters. VI-VII), Bancroft (Vol. V), Huddleston (1967), De Vaux (1965) and Dimont (1962), taken as a whole, are quite overwhelming—more so than for any other civilization yet examined herein. Many of these resemblances can clearly be supported by anthropological studies; others seem overly general, a few seem somewhat distorted or thin. Over the years the attempt to prove Israelite characteristics in ancient America has been so ambitious that in searching the vast literature it is difficult to discern even one missing trait.

Seemingly Solid Evidence

Not all of the Israel/American issue hinges on concepts alone. In the last two centuries, interest in the Hebrew supposition has grown as a result of various archaeological discoveries. Russell Burrows reports that among the thousands of 2,000-year-old carved stones he found in a cave in Southern Illinois (Chapter. 10) were several Menorahs, Jewish ceremonial candelabras. Of the many other related finds, four will be mentioned. The first, a stone now sitting in the Veracruz wing of the National Museum of Mexico displays two native men—near life-size, wearing what appear to be false beards. One figure bows before the other. The taller figure wears some kind of cord, "Tefillin," wound around his arm seven times; it then surrounds his fingers. This strange practice was also used by the Hebrews. The author Von Wuthenau in *Unexpected Faces in Ancient America* (1975, 42), translates an entry from the Mexican *Judaic Encyclopedia* (1958) describing a similar performance by Jewish priests at early morning prayers: "A cord is wound around the arm seven times and three times around the middle finger." Above the head of the Veracruz figure, like the Jewish priest, can be seen a possible phylactery, or scroll upon which the Israelites wrote words from their law.

Phylactery Stela Tepatlaxco, Veracruz
(Nat. Mus. Mexico City A.D. 100-300)

Another intrigue comes from the
father of the author/historian, Bancroft,
who in 1860 describes seeing the results
of a strange discovery near Newark,
Ohio. Twenty feet into an earthen
mound were buried three small stones,
one resembling a carved coffin with a
smaller stone settled in it: "Upon the
face of the smaller stone was the carved
figure of a man with a long flowing
beard, and a robe reaching to his feet."
Around the head of the figure was a
curved line of characters, and others
neatly carved down the sides and on the
reverse. The local Episcopal clergyman
of Newark correctly identified the writings as ancient Hebrew with nine of the
Ten Commandments. The figure was
believed to be a depiction of Moses. The
accompanying stone also had Hebrew
inscriptions that spoke of the "Law of
God" and "Jehovah." These curious
stones, called the "Newark Holy

"Newark Holy Stone"
(Moses and 10 Commandments)
(Coshocton, Ohio)

Stones," can be seen today in the Johnson-Hummickhouse museum in Coshocten,
Ohio.[24] Other artifacts found with these stones are common to the Hopewellian
period near the time of Christ.

The third example comes from Cyrus Gordon, whose challenging book,
Before Columbus (1973, 179), reviewed in chapter 10, displays photos of Hebrew
coins from the Bar Kokhba rebellion that caused Jewish refugees to flee Rome
around A.D. 132-135. These coins, surprisingly, were dug up in this century in
Kentucky. Scholars at the Universities of Louisville and Chicago have verified
their authenticity, although, according to Gordon, one may be modern. Gordon
also displays a curious stone carved with an ancient Mediterranean script found in
1889 in a burial mound at Bat Creek, Tennessee. Located under the head of one of
nine skeletons, the stone was unearthed by John Emmert under strict archaeological conditions, and published in 1894 with a photo by Cyrus Thomas, director of
the Smithsonian project. Curiously, it was initially published upside down and
declared to be written in Cherokee.

Gordon reports that nothing more was thought about the stone until someone turned it around, and scholars identified the script as Phoenician and
related Canaanite. Dr. Gordon, a Semitic languages specialist, pronounced it

paleo-Hebrew from the first or second century, A.D.. He translates it, "A comet (star) for the Judeans," referring to the anticipated Jewish savior. Additional support for possible ancient Hebrew influence in the area comes from the Yuchi Indians who once lived in the same valley, and who, according to anthropologist and author George Carter, preserved the Hebrew harvest festival of Sukoth in every detail.[25]

Bat Creek Stone
(Indian Burial 2nd Century A.D.)

The last example of conceivable Jewish presence is the most dramatic. On a volcanic mesa called "Hidden" or "Mystery" Mountain, thirty miles southwest of Albuquerque, New Mexico, along the Rio Puercos, exists a puzzle which, if authentic, would leave no doubt about someone with Hebrew background visiting the Americas.

On top of the 400' mountain lie the ruins of what appears to be an ancient encampment with man-made dugouts encircled by rocks that might have once secured tents. Also, there are what may be chieftain's quarters and a large, rectangular stone enclosure which could have contained animals—similar to military encampments in the Middle East. Inscriptions found at the site are in ancient Hebrew, and one reads, "Yahweh is our Mighty One." All of this alone would cause reflection, but a far greater shock awaits!

On the winding path leading to the encampment stands a large basalt stone. Chiseled into the stone are ancient Hebrew letters identified by Dr. Robert Pfeiffer of Harvard to be an abbreviated version of the Ten Commandments. Sightings of the stone reportedly date as early as 1800, and Indians of the area insist it was there before they arrived, much earlier that that. The writing is in a style that was used between 500 to 100 B.C., and much of it was not known until the end of the 19th Century, which would eliminate forgery or fraud.

David Diel, in his *Discovery of Ancient America* (1984), insists this is an ancient Israelite encampment created to celebrate the holy feast of tents. Israelites traditionally sought out high places for an eight-day worship, and afterwards left behind a holy monument. Of course, he admits, they didn't come all the way to the Americas just to find a high place; they would have already been here.

So, what about these alleged evidences? Do they convince us that Israel infiltrated the Americas? Scholars, with their cautious approach, are not easily swayed. Authenticity of the first stone has never been questioned: it is undoubtedly from the Veracruz, Mexico area, near the time of Christ. And there is no denying the

Author with 10 Commandment Stone
(Rio Puerco, N.M.)

cord is wound around the arm seven times, in Jewish fashion. But it is on the wrong arm, for the Hebrews wrapped the left arm. The same geographical area had a seven-headed figure that may have more to do with the stone than with Jewish phylacteries. It could be a preparation for the native ballgame, but to pronounce it Jewish at this point is pure speculation.

The second, or "Moses Stone," is impressive, and has had many inquisitive visitors since its appearance. But it is considered by most scholars to be a clever hoax. Whether perpetrated by its discoverer, David Wyrick, or upon him by others, is not known. Stones of the same composition, a Hebrew Bible, and tools for carving were reportedly found in the closet of Wyrick's home shortly after his death. Circumstantial? Yes. Did some skeptic place them there? Perhaps. Wyrick may have tried his hand at carving *after* finding the stones. Recent archaeological evidence has prompted a reevaluation which indicates the square Hebrew letters were done by someone with a working knowledge of Hebrew not fully known in 1867. The case looks better, but a conclusive answer still looks unlikely.[26]

The so-called "Bat Creek Inscription" and Bar Kokhba coins are considered by some scholars to be authentic finds, but their time and means of arrival on the continent have not been determined. Gordon claims the coins have received little attention because they were not excavated by professionals. Many scholars have looked at the inscribed stone and find closely related Hebrew or Phoenician letters, but not all agree on the interpretation.

For years the burial was thought to be ancient, but with the stone were found some copper bracelets which at first testing seemed to be eighteenth or nineteenth century Indian trade goods—not Semitic. Thus the stone was discredited from being ancient. More precise tests done later by the Smithsonian, however, established that the bracelets were not native copper at all, but an alloy of copper, zinc, and lead, commonly used anciently in the Mediterranean. Recent carbon dating of the tomb and Wooden ear spools found in the same grave tested out to be most likely the same age as the bracelets and stone—45 B.C.-A.D. 200.[27] Skeptics suggest the objects may have been placed in the grave at a much later date, thus negating contact. One of the skeptics, Kyle McCarter, Jr., proposes evidence for a brilliant archaeological hoax.(McCarter, F.A.R.M.S..) The controversy continues.

Mystery Mountain with its Ten Commandment stone still remains a mystery. Boy Scouts and others have cleaned the stone, so the age of the carving is difficult to detect. When Dr. Hibben from Albuquerque first saw it in 1936 he reported it was half buried with sand and lichens. Along with other inscriptions on the mountain, there was a stone showing what appeared to be Semitic figures of the zodiac. By putting these figures into a computer, Deal arrived at the date of September 15, 107 B.C., the known date of a lunar eclipse—reason enough to record a date. He therefore assumed the commandment stone was done at that time. Others have challenged him and insist the petroglyphs are not Semitic.

Still, even if these relics are authentic, they do not explain how—or why—ancient Semites would manage to cross an unknown ocean, sail into the Gulf, up the Mississippi, Ohio, Tennessee, or Rio Puerco rivers, and end up in remote areas of Tennessee and New Mexico. One highly vocal scholar with a compelling name, Cyclone Covey, proposes that latin inscriptions, stone carvings and artifacts found in Arizona describe a voyage from the Mediterranean of a Roman Jewish colony that maintained several cities in that western desert until A.D. 900.[28] A more recent possibility is offered by the Jewish people themselves.

Expelled from Spain the same year Columbus set out for the New World, 200,000 Jews had to convert to Catholicism or find a new home. Half of them converted, but many allegedly found their way to the New World where they eventually worked their way into New Mexico and joined with Spanish Catholics, but kept their Jewish faith underground (or if they carved the commandment stone, far above ground). Many modern-day Catholic converts claim to be descended from these Jewish immigrants in what is termed a "fantasy heritage."[29]

Knowing who created these various objects, when, under what conditions, and what, if any, influence they might have had on native cultures, would be of considerable interest. At any rate, the few examples considered here demonstrate the perplexing difficulties involved in trying to affix authenticity to foreign relics allegedly found on native American soil.

The Controversy Continues

The first Spanish writers did not have clear sailing with their attempts to establish Jewish/American contact either, for very early controversy began to churn up the waters. Father Torquemada is credited with being the first to suggest the Ten Tribes theory, followed by Gómara, Oviedo, Durán, and later, the most intense advocate, García. Their sometimes naive evidence for an Israelite presence was often vehemently challenged by critics who, like Bancroft, insisted they colored some traditions and suppressed others.[30] Critics complain that if the Jews were there, why did they leave no Hebrew writings? Resolutions are often just beyond reach: Durán (1977, 63) claims that an old Indian told him of a book left in ancient times in a nearby town. Led to believe it contained Hebrew, Durán sought to track it down. Local Indians affirmed it existed, but since the writing was different from theirs and unintelligible to them, they had burned it six years previously. Father Francisco Ximenez tells of finding Indian books as late as 1696 in Yucatan, which he claims were written in "Hebrew and Chinese characters."[31]

The "Chinese" was probably a wild guess, and so might the "Hebrew" have been, except that Spain had been supporting Jewish colonies for centuries. They were a visible part of Spanish life until Queen Isabella, in 1492, succumbed to Inquisition and church pressures to banish the conversos, the "converted Jews." Kingsborough writes that the Queen even went to great lengths to suppress incoming knowledge that Jews were anciently in the New World. The queen even forbade visits to those colonies by learned priests who might discover the secret of ancient visits and "shake the sacred institutions of Europe" which found no place for Indians in the Bible.[32]

In spite of the queen's attempts to suppress knowledge, the learned Spanish priests did make visits, and recorded their impressions. Many Europeans at the time were glad to think of Indians as Jews for, in their thinking, it put them both on the same miserably low cultural ladder. In doing so, they ignored or were unaware of the previously brilliant accomplishments of both races. Others believed that discovering the house of Israel in America after thousands of years showed God's great compassion and that whom the God of Israel loves, "He loves unto the end."

Not all agreed. Robert Wauchope, presents an entertaining view of writers who rejected any ancient American visits by Israelites. Responding to writers like Las Casas who believed one Indian dialect was corrupt Hebrew, he repeats their protests that Indian languages, mixed with imagination, could be thought to sound like "Greek, Latin, French, and many other tongues." Early writers, he insists, had travelled very little and were therefore unaware of how native traditions found in any country can often appear similar to those of another with whom they had no communication.[33]

Another skeptic, Acosta, in his *History of the Indians*, felt that if Jews had visited in ancient times, any preservation of their language, customs and traditions would be obvious. Others agreed with him that conclusive Jewish elements were missing, and that the idea that a people as conservative as the Jews would lose all their traditions and customs is absurd. On this basis, they concluded no Jews ever came. Others insisted that a strong mixture of Jewish blood would have produced distinct customs which "are not to be found."[34] It does seem curious that in order to create the impressive list of Israelite characteristics written down by early Spaniards, one would have to borrow isolated instances from numerous tribes scattered all over the Americas. No one culture possesses them all or even has an abundance of them, as would seem likely if they colonized at all.

Still, heated arguments insist that Hebrews were "fickle" and "unbelieving," and did not push religion on others. Instead, they often regressed into the ways of the pagan. It is speculated that they could easily have merged with Indians, giving up many old traditions and leaving only a few traces after such a long time. Such believers have religiously demonstrated that such distinct Israelite customs and traditions could still be found. Unfortunately, overenthusiastic advocates, like Adair, stretched every Indian trait to make it fit some Hebrew custom. Again, Wauchope relates how Adair heard an Indian chant *Schiluhyu, Schiluhe, Schiluhva* and selected out the last syllables to create the word, "Jehovah." The Indian name for a guilty person, "Haksit Canaha, " became to him "a sinner of Canaan." Under this liberal system, so-called "evidence" could mount rapidly.

The search for support extended to a very personal level. Kingsborough says Mackenzie observed the Jewish practice of circumcision among all the Dog-ribbed Indians. The same practice was reported by Peter Martyr in Yucatan where natives said it was introduced by a former visitor.[35] Wolff, a Jewish traveller among

Drawing from Temple of the Warriors, Chichen Itzá; White-skinned, Circumcised Prisoners Led by Dark-skinned Captors.

the North American Indians, followed reports of the practice of circumcision among the Sitkas on the Missouri to see if he could discover ancient kin. If they were kin, they were not circumcised, for he reports, "a strict examination proved it to be a mistake."[36] One wonders how he managed that.

One opponent to theories of ancient Jewish immigrations, John Baldwin, doubted that subjugated Israelites ever left southwest Asia, and believed most of them simply stayed in Palestine. He called the whole idea of lost tribes a "wild idea," and felt it "scarcely deserves so much attention." Another skeptic, James Kennedy, questioned whether the tribes were ever lost at all.[37]

Many writers felt that the search for lost tribes was inspired by fanaticism and that Christian influences were being projected into the Indian stories in an attempt to provide "new meanings for old traditions." In support of this, Diego Durán, a Spanish priest who believed Israelites came, admits that when he asked an aged Indian what he knew about the departure of Quetzalcoatl from Mexico, he was quoted the fourteenth chapter of Exodus, stating that when "Papa" (the hero) had reached the sea, "he had stricken it with his staff. The waters then dried up, and a road appeared." His followers were swallowed up when the parted waters returned. Durán suspected that the old man was merely quoting from the book of Exodus and quit the interrogation.[38]

Indoctrination of Indians by Christians in the sixteenth century moved rapidly, and some intermixing of the religions would seem inevitable. The Abbé Brasseur de Bourborg, a nineteenth-century scholar and advocate of pre-conquest influence, says that by the time the *Popol Vuh* was written, Guatemalan Indians were already under the influence of the paintings, books, and chants which the Spanish missionaries used to instruct them in Christianity.[39] Following the Conquest, Catholic Indians were undoubtedly well indoctrinated into the basic concepts of the Old as well as the New Testament.

Ancient Manuscript Emerges

Now back to the earlier story of Bible parallels discovered in the Quiché and Cakchiquel manuscripts of Guatemala. Although the young missionary did not succeed in his attempt to locate the Totonicapán document, another missionary and close associate, Robert Carmack, did. Equally intrigued with the possibility of hidden manuscripts, he returned often to the Clan leaders of Totonicapán and tried to convince them to release the mysterious document for publication. They resisted. Continued attempts got no results, but the challenge nagged, and he cultivated their trust.

Carmack remained undaunted, and in 1973, armed with a newly-earned degree in Ethnohistory from UCLA and hard-won fluency in Quiché, he finally succeeded in convincing the town leaders of his sincere interest in their clan. He wished to help them preserve what he feared would be a deteriorating record. The past twenty years of waiting now seemed but a moment when, to his delight, they produced a large, ancient, leather-bound book written in the Quiché language. It contained seven documents, including a bonus: the lost manuscript of the *Titulo de Totonicapán* itself.

He sought permission to copy the works, and his description of their final relenting is worth quoting: "They agreed, and together we marched to the photocopying machine in the town center. They personally cut the binding holding the book together, and handed over and received in turn each page as it was copied." It took about three hours, after which he took them to dinner, and then bid them farewell.[40] One can only imagine the exhilarated emotions he must have felt as he carried off the precious treasure. He has returned many times since and feels certain there are still more records to be obtained.

Of the part of the record never before translated, Carmack says it gives an account "similar to that of the Old Testament, from the Creation to the Babylonian captivity." Is this, then, new evidence that Israelites were a part of ancient Indigenous traditions? Carmack believes not. It merely demonstrates, he says, "one of the first attempts by native Guatemalans to synchronize their own historical traditions with the Christian ones." Identical excerpts found in the catechism of the time have convinced him that "this reference in the *Titulo de Totonicapan* to the Israelites was borrowed directly from missionary teachings." As to how much of these Christian-like doctrines, if any, may have already been a part of Indian traditions in pre-Conquest times, he wisely refuses to speculate.

On the reverse side of this unsettled coin, Max Muller, a German scholar, argues that in spite of certain similarities between the *Popol Vuh* and the *Bible*, "its content was a true product of the intellectual soil of America." Bandelier saw some adjustment of Indian mythology with Christian, but arrived at the same conclusions as Müller, that "the bulk is an . . . evident collection of original traditions of the Indians of Guatemala."[41]

It seems only fair to recognize that in many cases there seems a conscientious attempt on the part of priest and Indian to record accurately. Goetz, who translated the *Popol Vuh*, said Ximenez translated the Quiché manuscript "with impartiality and with care designed to give his readers a faithful version of the traditions and beliefs of these people." He did this in spite of his judgment that they were full of "error and superstition." Las Casas claimed the Indian chroniclers and historians knew the origin of everything pertaining to their religion and had recorded it well, that the accuracy of Spanish writing was not an improvement over theirs.[42]

Similarly, historians like Acosta, Clavijero, Ixtlilxochitl and Torquemada claim that ancient traditions handed down from pre-Conquest ancestors were the basis for the information received from their native informants. These Indians were trained from childhood to memorize carefully and were repeatedly corrected by their teachers until they had it right. Is it presumptuous to assume that Indians so thoroughly schooled before the Conquest were well enough acquainted with their native histories and hieroglyphics that no amount of Christianizing would erase it from their minds? People today are able to separate their personal beliefs from the foreign traditions they study, should they not afford the native a similar capacity?

Likewise with the Spaniard recorders. No doubt errors in judgment were made, but since they provided most of the information available on the natives, one cannot afford to reject all of their statements, no matter how over-zealous some may appear. If it were not for that zeal, Bancroft suggests, there is little probability that the work would have been done at all.

So the fascinating pot of cultural parallels continues to boil with its claims and rebuttals of similar traditions, legends, speech and even personal characteristics. Von Wuthenau believes the thousands of clay faces and monuments carved before 300 A.D. show no similarities to the Indians of the conquest. Instead, he displays in *Unexpected Faces* angular features, long noses, bearded faces, pointed toes, long robes and turbans. Could these be silent witnesses that sometime in the distant past, a colony of Israelites came to America seeking their promised land? Perhaps, yet some of the most intriguing possibilities of discovering a bearded white visitor to the Americas still lie ahead, as will be seen in the next chapter.

12

CHRIST BEFORE COLUMBUS

A Lonely Scribe

Of the many speculations concerning the identity of the mysterious visitor to the Americas before Columbus, none has captured the imagination or stirred the waters of controversy as much as the next prospect. High upon a prominent hill in the state of New York stands a solitary statue unique in the Americas. Located just outside the town of Palmyra, it was erected in the twentieth century to honor a person believed by millions to have actually lived on this continent nearly 1600 years ago. His name was Moroni, and he is said to have been a great American warrior who fought to save his people in their last great battle. His incredible story reflects upon the search for a fair, bearded culture hero.

The story recounts that Moroni alone survived the total destruction of his race. He then recorded the tragic history on tablets he had formed of thin sheets of gold and buried them in a stone box in the hill where his statue now stands, to await discovery by some future generation. The record remained hidden until 1823 when a young lad named Joseph Smith uncovered the treasure and secreted it to his home. Insisting that the same Moroni had appeared to him earlier in angelic form and directed him to the plates, Smith, through mystical means, translated the document for publication in 1830.

The published book was named after another great warrior, Mormon, father of the man who buried the plates. Although Smith eventually suffered a martyr's fate, some ten-million people today, world-wide, honor him and accept the *Book of Mormon* as an account of God's dealings with an immigrant branch of Israel. To them, the *Book of Mormon* is as sacred a record for the remnant of Israel in the Americas as the Holy Bible is for the main body remaining in the Old World.

This curious New World record begins about 600 B.C. with a migration of several Hebrew families from Jerusalem fleeing the coming Babylonian captivity. Taking with them the first five books of the Old Testament and other histories of their people, they are directed by God into the wilderness. Traveling over a several-year period, they finally arrive at a seacoast where they build a ship and sail across the Pacific ocean for the "Promised Land" in the Americas.

In the new land these people discover the surviving record of an earlier but extinct people, the Jaredites, who had left Mesopotamia in the third millennium B.C., during the great confusion at the tower of Babel. The Hebrew colony, along with still another group called the Mulekites, who crossed the ocean to escape the same Babylonian conquest, struggle for existence in the new land. One of the biggest challenges for these immigrants is to minimize the pagan elements that continually creep into their cultures—whether from remembered traditions of the Old World or from the New is not clear, for curiously, nowhere in the Book of Mormon are native Americans mentioned.

All of these people go on to great heights, creating large cities complete with temples, palaces, extensive roadways, rich apparel, jewelry, and carefully kept histories. The Jaredites fade out shortly before the arrival in the Americas of the Hebrew families, which shortly divide into two groups. One of these groups follows their righteous leader, Nephi, becoming the culture bearers of the tribe. The more troublesome ones support Nephi's rebel brother, Laman, receive from God a darker skin, and wander off into a nomadic existence.

Much of the book deals with endless religious conflicts between the two groups, including preparations for wars, battles, struggles with evil inclinations, and calls to repentance by their prophets. Finally, around A.D. 400, the usually more wicked Lamanites (considered by Mormons the ancestors of at least some of today's Indians) become more righteous than the prosperous and proud Nephites (ill-fated preservers of the Hebrew traditions) and completely obliterate them in one last, great battle. Mormon, the revered Nephite general, compiles the accumulated records of his people; after which his surviving son, Moroni, writes a sad epitaph, then hides the metal plates in the hill Cumorah. There they remain until Moroni directs Joseph Smith to remove them 1,400 years later.

Claim of Claims

Thought-provoking as *Book of Mormon* claims are that colonies of Hebrews came to the Americas, they are not nearly so startling as another of the book's assertions—that following his resurrection in the Old World, Jesus Christ visited the Americas. As a background to why he would visit the New World, Mormons quote the Bible message in John given by Christ to his followers while he was yet in Palestine:

I am the good shepherd, and know my sheep, and am known of mine. As the Father knoweth me, even so know I the Father: and I lay down my life for the sheep. And other sheep I have, which are not of this fold: them also I must bring, and they shall hear my voice; and there shall be one fold, and one shepherd. (John 10:14-16)

This, they maintain, is a reference to Christ's anticipated visit to those Hebrew colonies in the Americas, which by then had expanded into an extensive civilization. According to the Book of Mormon, prophets on the American continents had been foretelling the Old-World birth of Christ and were preparing their people for his inevitable resurrection there, and his subsequent visit to this hemisphere. They were not to be disappointed.

At the time of Christ's death in Jerusalem, Matthew (27:51) and Luke (23:45) relate a series of frightening events: rending of the temple veil, earthquakes, rocks splitting apart, and a darkening of the sun. Similarly, the Book of Mormon (3 Nephi: 8) records terrifying events at the same time on the American Continents: a great storm, earthquakes, lightning, upheavals of the earth, broken rocks, and terrible destruction for about three hours. After that, it says, came "darkness for the space of three days over the face of the land," and there was "great mourning and howling and weeping among the people continually."

The Mormon record (3 Nephi: 11) says that at the end of all of this confusion in the Americas there was silence for many hours. Then there came a voice from heaven saying, "Behold my Beloved Son, in whom I am well pleased . . . hear ye him." Casting their eyes towards the skies, the frightened people saw "a Man descending out of heaven; and he was clothed in a white robe; and he came down and stood in the midst of them; and the eyes of the whole multitude were turned upon him." The people were astonished and speechless, but he stretched out his hand to them and said, "Behold, I am Jesus Christ, whom the prophets testified shall come into the World. And behold, I am the light and the life of the World." And the account says simply that they "fell to the earth before him."

Following this memorable event, the book relates that the resurrected Christ delivered to them many of the same teachings he had imparted to his followers in Palestine. After reassuring them that they were also of the house of Israel (the tribe of Joseph), he gave them these insightful words:

Ye are they of whom I said: Other sheep I have which are not of this fold; them also I must bring, and they shall hear my voice; and there shall be one fold and one shepherd.

And they understood me not, for they supposed it had been the Gentiles . . . But behold, ye have both heard my voice and seen me; and ye are my sheep. (3 Nephi 15: 21-24)

In the *Book of Mormon* account, Christ appears repeatedly for several days, walking among the American people, teaching them to pray, blessing their children, healing their sick, and working miracles. He instructs them and requires them to record his word. He also commissions twelve men, as he had done in

Palestine, to go forth in the land and teach the others. In departing, he commands them to always remember him; then he ascends into the heavens. The people express sorrow to see him go, but he assures them he will return.

This, then, is the central, controversial message of the *Book of Mormon.* While millions of Mormons have accepted it, many other Christians consider it a threat to traditional beliefs. Few people have received the message indifferently. In this work this singular claim to a New World visitation by Jesus Christ will be investigated as still another intriguing prospect (certainly the most dramatic so far) in the search for the bearded, white hero of ancient America.

The Resurrected Lord

In the New Testament, Luke (24:39) relates that, following Jesus's resurrection in Palestine, he manifested himself to various individuals, including his apostles and several congregations. On the evening of his resurrection, he suddenly appeared to his disciples in a room where the doors had been closed "for fear of the Jews." They were frightened and thought he was a spirit. But to ease their minds, he said: "Behold my hands and my feet, that it is I myself: handle me, and see; for a spirit hath not flesh and bones, as ye see me have."

Eight days later he made a similar appearance, although the doors were again guarded. And to the doubting Thomas, who had not been present at the previous gathering, he said: "Reach hither thy hand and thrust it into my side: and be not faithless, but believing." The response given by Thomas indicates his skeptical attitude was instantly changed: "My Lord and my God." Christ responded, "Because thou hast seen me, thou hast believed: blessed are they that have not seen, and yet have believed."[1]

Such events attest to the resurrected Christ's ability to move around at will, with total disregard for barriers such as walls, in spite of the fact that his body was such that it could be seen and even touched. Among the proofs he gave of his resurrection was the eating of a fish before his apostles along the shore. The list of witnesses to this miraculous condition extends beyond his immediate associates. A quarter of a century after these events, the apostle Paul recalls that the resurrected Christ had been seen of "above five hundred brethren at once." (1 Cor. 15:6) Most of these people, he says, were still living at the time he wrote about it.

Following several appearances over a period of forty days, Christ met with his apostles for the last time on a mountain and affirmed his supreme authority: "All power is given unto me in heaven and in earth. Go therefore and make disciples of all the nations." He further informed them that whereas before, the gospel was only for the "lost sheep of the house of Israel," now it was to be offered freely to everyone. His commission to them was "Go ye into all the world, and preach the gospel to every creature."[2] It was clear that his word, previously confined to Palestine, would now be offered to people everywhere.

When he finished speaking to his apostles, they watched as a cloud took him up out of their sight. And while they were looking toward the heavens, two men stood by them in white clothing and said, "This same Jesus, which is taken up from you into heaven, shall so come in like manner as ye have seen him go into heaven" (Acts 1:10,11). From that time on, his Old World return was anticipated.

Since Christ was with his followers in Palestine only intermittently following the resurrection, many students of the scriptures have pondered his whereabouts in the intervals between periodic visits during that forty-day ministry, and even after his ascension The question often arises, could he have gone then to visit his "other sheep?" To his apostles he had given the responsibility to teach the rest of the world, but as an Israelite himself, of the tribe of Judah, his direct mission was only to the "lost and scattered sheep" of the House of Israel. He had spoken of these "other sheep" who were not of the Palestine fold, dwelling in some unknown place, and that they too would hear his voice. It would appear his mission was not to end in Jerusalem nor on Calvary.

Peter indicates that it did not end there by providing some insight to the vast extent of Christ's calling when he recorded that the Savior "went and preached to the spirits in prison." However, that visit was only to the disobedient of Noah's time, long before there was a "House of Israel." Christ's promised visit to the lost sheep also had to be fulfilled. Various world locations would qualify but, it might be argued, if Israelites managed to cross the oceans to the Americas and become a large nation, and since Christ said his mission was to visit the House of Israel, would not the American branch also qualify as lost sheep? And if so, would they not, as a large body of believers, be entitled to hear the voice of their awaited Savior as well? On this the Bible is mute. The question must be asked: what evidences can be found in ancient America to indicate that Jesus Christ visited the people of these lands, and what indication exists that his voice may have been heard among them?

Fair Gods in Far Lands

No Indian legend or Spanish retelling gives a complete story, but by considering similar tribal tales from widely scattered areas, one can obtain an overall view of those unsettling incidents believed by early Spanish and Indian writers to have occurred on the American Continent at the time of Christ's death and resurrection.

Mexico's sixteenth-century Indian historian, Ixtlilxochitl, relates an ancient occurrence on American soil which he approximates to be near the time of the death of Christ. He says it was when all nations were at war with one another and no one could find peace or rest from the turmoil. There was darkness, for the sun and moon refused to shine, "and the earth trembled, and the rocks broke, and many other things and signs occurred."[3] Near Lima, Peru, in 1608, a resident priest, Francisco de Avila, recorded similar traditions of an event he believed to be an eclipse on this continent at the death of Christ: "A long time ago the sun disappeared and the world was in darkness for a space of five days; that the stones knocked one against the other."[4]

Natives of Mexico had a tradition that at the city of Teotihuacan, shortly before the appearance of the god Quetzalcoatl, "the world was in darkness . . . when no sun had shone and no dawn had broken."[5] They seem to borrow elements of that story when they tell of the later 11th-century Quetzalcoatl, Topiltzin, whose disappearance, or death, was followed by both the sun and moon being covered in darkness. A similar condition occurred in ancient Peru when hills became valleys and valleys became great hills.[6] Along with the darkness, they recall, came terror, and in the middle of the night, according to the Indian Salcamayhua, great grandson of the Inca, there were "mournful complaints, and crying out." In their fear the people made vows and supplications, praying publicly to their gods for relief.

Then, according to Herrera, who fills in more of the story, a miraculous thing happened. From Lake Titicaca the sun arose, and there appeared about midday "a white man of large stature and of venerable presence whose power was boundless." He called them his sons and daughters, and they called him "The beginning of all created things" and "Father of the Sun." He performed wonderful things, giving life to mankind and to the animals, and "by his hand great benefits came to them."[7]

In these accounts he is fair of appearance, has a full beard and wears a long, flowing robe. "Speaking to them with great love and kindness," he walks the land, "admonishing them to be good and . . . to love one another and show charity to all." Passing among the people, he gives them wise counsel and teachings, works many miracles, heals their sick by his touch, and brings sight to the blind. In one of his miracles, he kneels to the ground, raises his hands to heaven, and is surrounded, along with the people, by a fire which does not consume them. During his travels he encounters many languages, yet speaks each better than the natives themselves. He shows the people how to put their lives in order and encourages them to meet often.[8]

Although they called him *Ticci Viracocha*, the true and highly sacred name of this unforgettable visitor was unknown, or unspeakable, but some of the numerous titles they bestowed upon him were "Infinite Creator," "Wise Ruler," "Lord of the Wind and of the Light," "He who is Successful in all Things," "He who Controls all Things," "Teacher of the World," "The Ever Present One," "Final Judge," and "The One." The titles, Ila Ticci Viracocha and Con Ticci Viracocha refer to his designation as "God" and the "ancient cause" or the "first beginning."[9]

A selection from various prayers in Quechua (KEH-chu-ah), the official Inca language, recorded by the Spanish chronicler Christoval Molina, give a good idea of the reverence and various titles accorded Viracocha.

> O Creator! 'Ever present Viracocha! Thou who art without equal unto the ends of the earth! Thou who givest life and strength to mankind . . . Thou who dwellest in the heights of heaven, most fortunate, most merciful and mighty, who doest wonders and marvels, grant our prayer, keep us in health and safety. Grant prosperity to the people, give them peace and eternal life. Bring us near to the Creator as Thou art, O Creator![10]

So moving was his message that they accepted a challenge to spread the word. So deeply imbedded became these traditions that even in Pizarro's time the Inca people still considered themselves "apostles of a new creed and teachers of a new way of life . . . sent by their divine parent to bring to a darkened and barbarous world a more pure faith and a more enlightened conduct."[11]

According to the Peruvian historian Cieza de Leon, this unforgettable man "travelled along the highland route toward the north, working marvels as he went, and that they never saw him again."[12] His path can't be followed with precision, but, as was seen in chapter 4, about the same time a mysterious, bearded person passed through the Oaxacan area of Mexico, having come from the southern sea. It is not surprising, then, that even farther to the north where unsettling occurrences of a physical nature similar to those in Peru were reported, Ixtlilxochitl, among others, records, "There arrived in this land a man whom they called Quetzalcoatl and others Hueman, for his great virtues, being just, holy and good, teaching them by works and words the path of virtue, and forbidding them vice and sin, giving them laws and good doctrine; and in order to restrain them from their gratifications and dishonesties he introduced the fast."[13]

Ixtlilxochitl makes no distinction between Quetzalcoatl the god and Quetzalcoatl the man, for some of these events apparently refer directly to the ancient god of the air, "he of the large and powerful hand," while others seem to fit the later Toltec, Topiltzin. Still, many of the events in the life of Topiltzin were borrowed directly from the ancient hero, and, as in the legends of Viracocha, Quetzalcoatl, whether god or man, was often described as fair and bearded.

Similar accounts of the fair, bearded visitor in northern and southern hemi-spheres indicate he may have established himself in both areas. In Peru and Mesoamerica, the memory of this great leader would be passed on to the descendants of those who experienced these events. And in both places he leaves with the memorable promise that other white, bearded disciples would fol-low him and rule the lands until the day when he would return to bring a golden age to the people.[14]

Christians and Natives on Common Ground

It would seem that anyone examining these amazing native traditions would naturally be moved to wonder on the similarities to the resurrect-ed Messiah, yet, strangely, in none of the earliest Spanish writings is this ever considered. To make such an obvious, yet heretical, comparison during the Spanish Inquisition would have been dangerous and foolish. Still, the sixteenth-century Dominican priest, Diego de Durán, recognizing the remarkable nature of the Indian hero stories, comments, "These deeds are of such renown, and remind one so much of miracles, that I dare not make any statement or write of them." He bravely admits his fear to be that of submitting himself to the correc-tion of the Holy Catholic Church.[15] Still, fully aware of the startling similarities, he and others cautiously get around the issue by suggesting that in ancient times America may have been visited by one of Christ's apostles, fulfilling the assign-ment to take the gospel to all the earth.

Many Spanish writers equate Quetzalcoatl with the apostle Saint Andrew. Bancroft gives the arguments presented by Góngora and Tanco for a visit by the "glorious apostle St. Thomas," claiming that his Greek name "Didymus" and the name "Quetzalcoatl" both refer to a "precious twin." Early Christian missionaries and Indians of Peru made the same identification with the culture hero of Lake Titicaca. And in Cuzco, the great Indian temple of Viracocha, later converted into a Catholic cathedral, contained a marble statue of that god, described as being "both as to the hair, complexion, features, raiment and sandals, just as painters rep-resent the Apostle, St. Bartholomew."[16]

To counter the obvious parallels, the Catholic church often attempted to replace the local native traditions with Christian ones. This effort more often resulted in an admixture of both, or at least it would seem so on the surface, for many natives then, as now, merely went along with the new traditions while secretly harboring the old. Colorful examples of this strange compromise can be seen today in the market town of Chichicastenango, Guatemala, where Indians still burn copal incense on the steps of the church (a practice both pagan and Catholic), light can-dles to the Catholic "santos" inside, and then make pilgrimages up the mountain outside of town to placate their old, traditional gods.

Nearby, in the ancient Guatemalan capital of Antigua, a photographer's delight nestled precariously at the foot of the perfectly sculpted but menacing volcano Agua, tourists gather every Easter. In this colonial atmosphere, devout Indians reenact Christian ceremonies that are not unlike more ancient ones practiced before the Conquest, in the hopes of receiving great blessings. Local citizens pay to carry large statues of Christ and the apostles—Christian adaptations of old tribal deities—through elaborate, handmade murals of pine needles, sawdust, and flower petals that carpet the cobblestoned streets. In addition to the influx of foreign tourists, the faithful Guatemalans come from miles around to witness the procession and pay homage to these sacred images.

Although this haunting and somber ceremony, with its pungent incense, purple-robed image carriers, and monotonous drumming, was introduced to the Indians by the Catholic fathers to replace the deeply ingrained pagan rituals that had already been in use for centuries, these devout natives surprisingly found acceptance not too difficult. Sixteenth-century Christian practices were in many ways similar to what they already had been doing. In her book on Mexican mythology, Irene Nicholson suggests that the reason the Maya could accept Christian doctrine so readily was "that it was not incompatible with their own."[17] Durán, a Catholic who grew up among remaining natives of the conquest, puzzles that "The ancient beliefs are still so numerous, so complex, so similar to our own . . . "[18] Could the reason for this be that in the distant past someone had already brought in teachings similar to those now provided by the Catholics?

It seems reasonable to suggest that had Christ, or his apostles, appeared in the New World shortly after his ministry in the Old World, followers of both continents would have the same number of centuries to transform and embellish the religion. In Europe, the expanding Christian church was continually influenced by and absorbing the lingering pagan traditions of ancient Rome and Greece. Likewise, if Christianity were ever taught in ancient America, a similar change could have occurred from the well-established and more extensively practiced paganism here. Whatever the reasons, and if existing accounts are accurate, by the year 1500 the resultant beliefs and pageantry in both worlds were remarkably similar, at least on the surface.

Even among the most remote and primitive of American tribes, early writers noted resemblances to Christianity which are difficult to explain by mere coincidence. This unexpected phenomenon unsettled the priests, who, if they did not subscribe to the "Apostle theory," attempted to explain it away as Satan's influence upon the natives to confuse them when the true faith should appear. In their concern, many priests chose to ignore or destroy the legends. Others, fortunately, preferred to collect these amazing parallels. Durán laments that the task of discovering and making them known is overwhelming. Still, he faced the task and produced many pages of remarkable commonalities between Catholic and Aztec priests.

Among the similarities, Duran describes native use of incense and rites practiced to commemorate the great sacrifice once made for them by a divine being.
Like Catholics, they chanted, did penance, wore elaborate robes, fasted, made
vows of celibacy, lived in communities, observed holy days, exhorted the people
to do penance for their sins, and wore their hair in a tonsure (shaved spot). They
also had boys who assisted at the altar; kept cloistered women, like nuns, who
lived chastely; offered unleavened bread to their god; blessed the children; took
confession; and practiced a rite similar to baptism. They even taught the unusual
doctrine of a "war in heaven" found in the Book of Revelation (12:7).[19] Such practices, although not entirely unique to Christianity, were so close they convinced
Durán that at some time in the past someone had come to the New World and
"preached the Bible to the natives."[20]

Christian Doctrines and Native Traditions

One of the strongest arguments for Christian teachings in ancient
America would be the presence of one of Christianity's most enigmatic doctrines, the belief in one God who forms a trinity. Even
devout Christians have never been able to explain fully how *one* God is also
three. To find such a parallel among native beliefs would be remarkable indeed,
yet it exists, as we will see. But first, among ceremonies all over the Americas
to highly esteemed Sun gods, rain gods, underworld gods and a thousand other
gods, it is most surprising to find native belief in *one* "unknown" god, supreme
over all the others.[21]

The Peruvians, according to Brinton, were essentially monotheistic, and
although they worshiped the Sun, even it was considered an object created by the
supreme "Creator." To the ancient Maya, the creator of the world was a god named
Hunab Ku (meaning one God). Sahagún said the Toltecs had only one god, and
he was named Quetzalcoatl. He also records that although the Aztecs had many
deities, with idols to them all, only Quetzalcoatl was looked upon as the son of the
one Supreme God, Camaxtli, or Tloque-Nahuaque (God or Lord). Pre-Aztec tribes
(Chichimecs), he relates, believed in one god called Yoalli Ehécatl, "God invisible, impalpable, beneficent, protector, omnipotent, by whose strength alone the
whole world lives." Several writers mention that the first inhabitants of Chichen
Itza were not idolaters, and Bancroft, summing up a discussion of Mexican and
Yucatecan divinities, writes, "The knowledge of one Supreme Being appears to
have been among the first dogmas instilled into the minds of their people."[22] As for
North American Indians, scholars have reviewed the religions of the major tribes,
and report a prevailing belief in One Supreme Being

Discovering that native Americans worshiped one god seems confusing when
their pantheon of gods and numerous culture heroes also said to be gods are
recalled. But it becomes clearer when it is understood that the Supreme God is not

one of the subordinate gods and that he is not the culture hero. The Supreme God was invisible and unknowable, the god of heaven for whom, Kingsborough reports, they made no images. This was the god of whom the Zapotecs said, "He was the creator of all things and was himself uncreated."[23]

However, even though there is only one God above all others, a second god-like figure emerges when the Supreme God sends his son down to the earth to reform it. It is that son who becomes the great mediator or culture hero to his people.[24]

To compound this already complex situation, a third god emerges who is often identified with the other two. This puzzling god is even less tangible, a sort of "spirit-merchant" who brings gifts to god's children. Thus, in these three, the Father, the Son, and a Spirit, an American trinity exists. This unexpected concept of a trinity may have been known all over the Americas, according to Squier, who maintains that it comes not from the Spanish, but from a study of the Indians from California to Peru. Of the many examples collected by him and others, the following selection is typical. This statement comes from Francisco Hernandez, chaplain to the Spanish government, who was sent by Las Casas, Bishop of Yucatan, to preach to the Mayas in the interior where Spaniards and Christianity had not yet been. Las Casas describes a letter Hernandez wrote him after a year there:

> . . . he had found a chief principal lord, who, when he was asked about his belief and the old religion which they had been accustomed to have in that kingdom, the chief told him that they knew and believed in God who lived in heaven and that this God was Father and Son and Holy Ghost, and that the Father was called Izona, and had created men and all things, and the Son had for a name Bacab, who was born from a virgin called Chibirias, that she was in heaven with God, . . . and they called the Holy Ghost Echuah . . . When he was asked what these names of the three persons meant, he said that Izona meant the great father, and Bacab the son of the great father, and Echuah the merchant and in truth the Holy Spirit sent down good merchandise into the world, since it filled the earth . . . with its gifts and its grace.[25]

Although the letter displays an unmistakable Christian flavor, which may have been added by Las Casas or Hernandez, the Indian names lend authenticity. Duran's lament that "so much was similar is appropriately recalled in this context." In the same letter, Hernandez says he asked the Mayan lord how he had knowledge of these things and was given the answer: "The lords taught their sons and thus this doctrine descended from hand to hand." At least he felt it was authentic.

Trials and Perfection of a God

The allusion to the birth of Christ in Hernandez's report that the son Bacab was born of a virgin is common to many American hero legends. In company with Bacab, heroes such as Quetzalcoatl, Viracocha, Nanabozho, Ioskeha and the North American Montezuma were said to have been born of virgin mothers. The stories of conception are numerous, and vary according to the tellers, but in the case of Quetzalcoatl, the chronicler Mendietta reports that Chimalma, the hero's mother, swallowed a precious green emerald. Torquemada attributes the conception to a ball of white feathers falling from the sky and kept in her bosom, and Kingsborough relates that it was by the breath alone of the Supreme deity.[26]

Like Christ, the culture heroes were often involved in a battle between darkness and light. The evil one was ominously present and provided temptations. Since most of the heroes were already considered gods, and their lives were very private, no insights into the details of those temptations are available. But as a man, Topiltzin Quetzalcoatl struggled with the appeals of sex, strong drink, power and personal riches in order to achieve self-mastery, reach perfection, and attain ultimate godhood. So strong were these enticements, says Kingsborough, that

Author in Alleged Baptismal, or Ritual Bathing Font.
(Chichen Itzá, Yucatan)

Quetzalcoatl went on a forty-day fast. Only when he attained his position as a puri-fied deity, one who had ultimately triumphed over the powerful forces of evil, was he then able to bring his people to perfection.[27]

In the process of perfecting his people, he was not without assistance. Both Christ and the culture heroes had apostles and disciples-followers who took upon themselves his name, prayed, offered sacrifices, and preached his message.[28] As Durán and de Landa both pointed out, these priests declared days of fasting and performed a cleansing ceremony of baptism called "caput-sihil," which translates "re-birth." [29]

There are examples of the baptism rite all over the Americas, from immersion to sprinklings, and in Mexico, children were baptized in special water in the name of Quetzalcoatl. Considered necessary for everyone, this one-time ceremony was preceded by a special confession of sins to the priests, and it was believed that those who died without it would suffer more in the next life. For those who were baptized, there was a ceremony of remembrance, much like the Christian com-munion, in which images of his body were made of dough, broken and eaten.[30]

The accumulated teachings of the culture heroes, as recorded by early Spaniards and Indians, manifest a concern for life lived on an unfulfilled level. They offer a new religion about God's love, with instructions to practice brother-ly love towards each other and to cultivate other virtues. These ennobling teach-ings encouraged the natives to clothe the naked, feed the hungry, care for the sick, and practice charity whatever the cost. They discouraged violence and admonished the people against war, stealing and killing. They forbid the practice of human sac-rifice. Contrary native practices would indicate that at times those teachings were blatantly ignored.

The culture hero introduced the temple and altars, and taught the priests who officiated there to pray, teach, and to practice the traits he embodied: chastity, virtue, and temperance. By his example they also introduced confession, penance and fasting as means for purification.

He was called the "dew of heaven" and was said to have introduced maize, the "bread of life" as a form of communion. He was identified with "light and knowl-edge," for he knew all things and gave wise counsel. He was known everywhere as a worker of miracles, for he possessed all power. He could heal with the touch of his hand. And although he would sit and discourse with the people, he was looked upon as more than a man; he was seen as saintly, a "sacred human being." He was to them a teacher of great wisdom, who spoke of the rewards of heaven and the sufferings of hell while promising eternal life—a god who would one day return to rule again and usher in an age of great peace. From the time of his depar-ture onward, all rulers, kings, and priests, anxious to share in his divine qualities, claimed direct descent from him.[31]

Death and Rebirth

Like Christ, the culture hero also suffered persecution. Of the many memorials that remain to the culture hero all over the Americas, temples, pyramids, and bearded statues, the most remarkable of these emblems, in a Christian context, is the native cross—the symbol of ultimate persecution. This cross is amply represented in native wood, stone, and legend. Roys summarizes crosses found in Yucatan, where the Mayan prophet Chilam Balam prophesied the arrival of the Spaniards shortly before their coming. The old prophet also predicted they would bring the sign of their religion, the cross, with them: "Receive your guests, the bearded men, the men of the east, the bearers of the sign of God, lord." Calling it the "First Tree of the World," he placed stone crosses in the courtyards of their temples as a remembrance of his prophecy and told them, "Let us exalt his sign on high."[32]

Balam was not the first to introduce the cross. Metal crosses were reportedly discovered in tombs in Yucatan. The first Spaniard to mention them, Bernal Diaz, noticed them on the backs of idols. Even Columbus, in 1492, found a beautiful cross on one of the Bahama islands. This would indicate that the symbol was already old before the Conquest. Bearded culture heroes of both Peru and Ecuador bore crosses, and in North America the Micmac Indians had great esteem for the cross passed down in tradition from their ancestors.[33] In Mesoamerica, the most ornate crosses are those seen in the temples at Palenque. Whether they are true crosses, "trees of life," or both, is somewhat nebulous, for the cross and "tree of life are often synonymous.[34]

According to Ixtlilxochitl, Quetzalcoatl was the first to set up the cross as a symbol for adoration. Many descriptions of Quetzalcoatl include red crosses sewn onto his flowing robes, and round temples to him are adorned with crosses (e.g., Ixtlán del Río, near Guadalajara). Quetzalcoatl, like Christ, is a savior-god, and one of his representations, Nanautzin, is noted for self-sacrifice to save all mankind from destruction. Kingsborough, who was convinced early Christians had influenced New World inhabitants, quotes various native sources claiming that Quetzalcoatl was scourged and died upon a cross for the sins of mankind. He sees in Mexican codices representations of Quetzalcoatl as a crucified person bearing the prints of the nails in his hands and feet, and in another with a spear in his side and water flowing from the wound.[35] In observing these drawings, Spaniards were eagerly seeking parallels with Christianity, and found them. Sahagún felt threatened by such parallels, and told the natives it was Christ who reformed the world "by doing penance and by dying upon the cross for our sins; and not the wretched Quetzalcoatl, to whom these miserable people attributed this work."[36]

The most dramatic native record of crucifixion comes from the remote interi-
or of Yucatan to Las Casas in the letter already quoted by Herrera. Along with his
statement about native beliefs in a Father, Son, and Holy Ghost, supposedly collected before any Spanish/Christian indoctrination, he includes this stirring information received from a native:

> About Bacab (who is the son) they say that Eopuco killed him and had
> him whipped and they placed a crown of thorns upon him and they placed
> him with his arms stretched upon a beam, and they did not understand that
> he was nailed to it, but only tied and there he died, and he stayed three days
> dead and on the third day returned to life and went up to heaven and there
> he sits with his Father.[37]

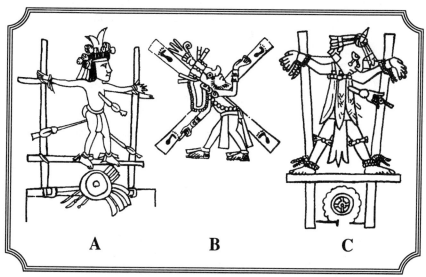

A: Codex Vatican (Kingsborough III); *B: Lord of the Vanguard, Codex
Hungary, Plate 8* (Kingsborough III); *C: Codex Nuttal*

Kingsborough laments that the correlation is not known with certainty, but he
suspects, with good reason, that Bacab and Quetzalcoatl are the same person.

Christian concepts of whipping, thorns, crucifixion, blood sacrifice and resurrection are not unusual in American lore. Bancroft reports that Itzamna was
scourged and crucified, and that a crown of thorns was reportedly worn on the
head of one of the ancient heroes in California. Native Mesoamerican priests
commonly practiced a bizarre ritual in which they pierced various parts of their
bodies with thorns, drawing blood in penitence and sacrifice to God. This custom, they believed, was instigated by Quetzalcoatl, whose body was also once
pierced. The culture hero of the Iroquois, Ioskeha, was said to have been wound-

ed in the side and from it blood flowed. The ceremonial and sacrificial blood-
letting of the Maya is done in remembrance of the god who gave his blood and
his life for his people.[38]

Of all the god-like qualifications Christ possessed, none was greater than his
claim of power over death—resurrection. As resurrected Lord, he then is able to
lift others from the grave and offer them new life. Christians believe that the greatest message of hope ever proclaimed was that of Christ to Martha found in the
book of St. John (11:25), "I am the resurrection and the life: he that believeth in
me, though he were dead, yet shall he live" Similarly, resurrection and ascension
appear in native American legends, and this hope for new life may have been considered the greatest message from American culture heroes. Brinton records that
the Tarascans, neighbors to the Aztecs, celebrated with a great feast the resurrection of their great god Surites. And of Quetzalcoatl it was said that his body lay
four days in a stone box, then arose to heaven.[39]

Not only do the heroes conquer death, but, like Christ, are able to rescue others as well. A Catholic priest, Lizana, recorded in 1633 that in the city of Izamal a
great king (Izamná) was scourged and crucified, and then lived again. Following
that, he cured the sick, and the dead were taken to him, and "he brought them back
to life."[40] Following his earth life, Quetzalcoatl, like Christ, also went into the
underworld for several days to dwell among the dead. In Peru it was believed the
dead would remain undisturbed in their graves until the day of resurrection, when
Viracocha would return in bodily form to restore them to life.[41] All over the Maya
world one can observe monuments to the apotheosis (death and expected resurrection) of the royal families. Full details have not been unravelled, but this expectation of new life is always associated somehow with the power and authority of
ancestors descended from ancient gods and kings, whose symbols, as was
observed in chapter 4, point to an ancient, bearded culture hero. The fullest insight
to this phenomenon is found in Schele & Miller's *Blood of Kings* (1986).

The Light With a Promise

A ztec legends say that following Quetzalcoatl's ascension to heaven,
he was reported to have miraculously become the morning star.
Sejourné records the story from the annals of Chauhtitlan: "They say
that when he died dawn did not appear for four days, because he had gone to
dwell among the dead; . . . in eight days there appeared the great star, Venus,
called "Quetzalcoatl." And they add that he was enthroned as Lord."[42] It was a
fitting symbol, for that planet-star periodically "dies " and is "resurrected."
Sejourné interprets this event as a demonstration of the King's light and
"absolute purity," his "abandonment of the things of this world, and return to the
heavens whence he came." The sun is a symbol for the father of Quetzalcoatl,
and now, the light of the morning star (the son) can be reunited with the light of

the sun (the Father) from which the Indians believed Venus was broken off when Quetzalcoatl came to earth. As a god, Quetzalcoatl will once again be in the presence of the father who is god over all.

And how might all of this relate to Jesus Christ? Like Quetzalcoatl, Christ is similarly identified as "the light of the world" (John 8:12). His birth is symbolized by a light shining in the darkness. Echoing Quetzalcoatl's return to his father/god, Christ said to Mary Magdalene, "Touch me not; for I am not yet ascended to my Father: but go to my brethren, and say unto them, I ascend unto my Father, to my God, and your God "(John 20:17). Even the transformation of Quetzalcoatl into Venus is surprisingly mirrored in Christ's words to the Apostle John in the Book of Revelation (22:16): "I am . . . the bright and morning star."

In the Book of Revelation (22:20), Christ's very last words, "I come quickly," anticipate his return. Matthew 24:29, 30 portrays vividly the ominous conditions that are prophesied to exist at that time—much like those at his death: darkness, tribulation, and mourning. But then, what a glorious return is to follow while all the earth looks on, "For the Son of man shall come in the glory of his Father with his angels; and then he shall reward every man according to his works" (Matthew 16: 27).

The expected return of the American culture hero was just as eagerly anticipated by native Americans as was Christ by the Christians, or the Messiah by the Jews. Torquemada describes the Mexican Messiah as "perfect in moral virtues" and says that the Aztecs believed he is alive and is to return. Carrasco quotes the ill-fated Montezuma, who told Cortez, ". . . the elders of Tula are certain that Quetzalcoatl told them he would return to rule at Tula and all parts of the world."[43] Carrasco, who is unmoved by stories that the Spaniards invented the "Quetzalcoatl myth," insists there is ample proof that belief in a returning king predated the arrival of Europeans. He claims the appearance of the Spaniards merely revived the ancient promise. Sahagún, who abhorred Quetzalcoatl for his similarities to Christ, records that when the Spaniards arrived on the shores, natives entered the water and kissed the prows of the boats, "For they thought that Quetzalcoatl Topiltzin had come."

South American legends contain a similar promise in Viracocha who, Brinton says, "The Quichuas [Incas] expected . . . not merely as an earthly ruler to govern their nation, but as a god who, by his divine power, would call the dead to life."[44] Among numerous North American peoples, Algonquins, Iroquois, Tlingit, Mojaves, Piutes, and Hopis also awaited the return of a beloved culture hero.[45] Their legends, and legends from other civilizations all over the Americas are clear that one day, when the people reach their greatest need, a mighty culture hero, who once had been among the tribes, will return from the land of the rising sun to relieve the oppressed and bring them a better life, a golden age.

It is apparent that early writings about the various culture heroes of ancient America record numerous parallels to Jesus Christ of Nazareth. These culture heroes undoubtedly did many more things than the few remaining records on them contain. There is, however, one more piece of evidence that must be considered. This time instead of measuring the culture hero against Christ, Christ will be compared to the culture hero.

Searching For a Symbol

It is singular that many of the major features which set Christ apart from other men are also found among the American culture heroes. Still, one additional trait sets the American culture heroes even further apart from other men and gods—the extensively carved, painted and worn symbol of a feathered serpent with its connected cross and world tree. It must now be determined whether Christ relates with those distinguishing characteristics.

Best known of all feathered serpents are those identified with Mexico's hero, Quetzalcoatl. The "quetzal" is a richly-colored bird of the highlands with long, green, iridescent feathers and a bright red breast. "Co" is a generic Maya name for the menacing serpent, and "atl" is Nahuatl for water. Thus, the term Quetzalcoatl means, literally, a feathered water snake. Not only did this highly visible symbol represent the revered lord, Quetzalcoatl, and other related culture heroes of the Mexican and Mayan areas, but the ubiquitous feathered serpent symbol is identified with the white, bearded culture heroes of South and North America as well. No symbol is more prevalent in native America, and none is given more significance than that of the feathered serpent and the legendary, bearded figure behind it.

In considering a fitting symbol to represent Christ, no image could at first seem so inappropriate as a bird or a serpent. But the bird and serpent placed together create an image and concept which are far more complex and profound than the mere objects they portray. This metaphor for the foreign visitor is quite complex. In summarizing it this work will borrow from several writers, including Laurette Séjourné (1976) and Irene Nicholson (1968).

Briefly, the feathered-serpent figure is a unique creature able to probe the depths of man's world, yet capable of soaring to communicate with the Gods. Deemed to be the wisest of creatures, the serpent in the third chapter of Genesis is devious, but also imparts wisdom to open men's minds to their potential and the ultimate possibility of becoming God-like. Moses lifted a fiery serpent up on his staff (Numbers 21:8, 9), and early Hebrews saw in it a symbol of God's salvation.

Considered by most cultures a place of mystery, the underworld represents man's darker side where the ongoing struggle against temptation and even death must eventually be met. The serpent cunningly leads man's spirit into that lower realm which it inhabits. Essential to man's progress is matter and a tangible form (a body) for the spirit to work out the processes of regeneration—the main purpose of creation. This fusion of body and spirit is often represented by water—the blood of the land without which there would be no life. The rhythmic quality of water is represented in the sinuous movements of the serpent as well as in the long, undulating feathers of the bird.

The other half of the feathered serpent, the bird, flies to the sky, the source of light and life. The bird represents man's eternal soul searching for celestial origins and heavenly aspirations. These elusive pursuits, like the shy and retiring Quetzal bird, are treasured but difficult to grasp.

Humans are complex beings, continually torn between what is interpreted as evil and good. The serpent, with its connection to the underworld, recalls the depths to which man may slip. But at times, the serpent sheds its weathered scales and emerges new in a symbolic triumph over sin and death. Scales now become feathers, which allow the serpent to lift itself metaphorically from the curse of crawling forever upon the earth. As a feathered-serpent, free from the restrictions of mortality, it is able to soar toward the heavens in a rebirth of spirit and matter. This complex symbol, then, includes preparation for death, a standard for life, and finally, a glorious expectation for rebirth, in which mankind may be united with god. Campbell says the act of a serpent shedding its skin is a symbol of victory over death. In the Americas it is the feathered serpent from the sea who introduces all of the advantages of civilization, and at the same time offers hope for a higher life. Sejourné calls the plumed serpent the "key image in Nahuatl religion." For Christ to be the original source for American culture heroes he must also have much in common with this complex figure.

More Than a Tree

Another closely related symbol for eternal unity of matter and spirit is nearly as common as the feathered serpent—the tree of life, or the world tree, symbol of the universe itself. Examples are found on codices, walls, and monuments all over the Americas. Especially dramatic are those of the temples at Palenque in Chiapas, Mexico (Chapter 4). At their base is the ominous earth monster, symbol of death and struggle. In his headdress he wears the symbols of life, death, and resurrection. A tree extends from the underworld to the heavens, a means of ascension from the lower regions of the earth into the upper realms of the universe. And at the top of the tree sits a bird, the glorious sun bird of resurrection—symbol of the heavenly origin and destiny of mankind. As Quetzalcoatl left the cares of earth life, went into the underworld, wrestled with the gods of night and overcame them, and then ascended into the heavens in a glorious apotheosis, so might others follow.

The tree which nurtures and gives life eventually becomes another step in the journey of discovery: the cross—symbol of the knowledge of life and death. The heart of man is at the center. At times the center is represented by the sun which gives life to man, the energy source through which, Campbell says," God assumes the life of man and man releases the God within himself."[46] The points of the cross reach out in all four directions to people everywhere. Above, it points to the heavens, and below the earth. The four directions, the four seasons, the four ages of creation are there. Life, death and resurrection are represented, and the whole world drama is brought together in the simple cross.

In these three interrelated symbols, the plumed-serpent, the tree of life, and the cross, the message and mission of the culture hero are defined: to bring the people of the earth to a knowledge of who they are and what they may become. Sejourné (1976, 142) expresses it as "the salvation each individual can try to achieve for himself," through the redeeming sacrifice of Quetzalcoatl. Thus the culture hero, with strange and wonderful symbols, represents the son who gives mankind desires and reason; then leaves them to war with both until one should win. The son comes to earth in the midst of this conflict to provide strength, instill hope, and show the way. The symbols of the feathered-serpent, tree of life, and cross, represent to Howey the "crucified serpent which will cast off the worn-out skin and arise in renewed vigour and beauty." These rude symbols point to the mysterious visitor, a god who descended below all things that he might rise above all things, and at the same time build a bridge for mankind to pass through on a similar journey, with the promise of a rich reward at the end.

Biblical Symbols

Thus, for Jesus Christ to be the original source for legends of an American culture hero, he must also closely relate to the complex symbols of cross, tree and feathered serpent identified everywhere in the Americas with them. In spite of their abstract forms, it is surprisingly easy to relate these nature symbols to the Nazarene who lived so far across the sea. In Christianity, the significance of the cross is well known. But this excruciating means of punishment, used by the Romans long before and after Christ's crucifixion, becomes in him not just an instrument to end life but a vehicle for new life, a symbol of the passion of crucifixion suffered willingly in order to bring about the ecstasy of resurrection. But what of the other two symbols, the tree of life and the feathered serpent?

Every year Christians greet the return of the sun at the winter solstice by ornamenting a tree and placing a shining star on top. With this colorful tradition they celebrate the birth of their savior and hope for a joyous season and good life in the coming year. Although this more recent custom of Christianity seemingly defies the admonition of the Biblical prophet Jeremiah (10:1-4) against the heathen practice of decorating a tree, the tree of life and the tree of knowledge are recurrent in the scriptures, and have long been a positive part of the religion (Genesis 2:9, Revelation 2:7).

In the purest sense, Christ died upon a tree—the tree of redemption. Although it is generally looked upon today as mere decoration and for merchants an assured seasonal sale, the Christmas tree, for the devout, can represent not the pagan custom Jeremiah opposed, but the felled trunk upon which Christ died. Now it is seen in its resurrected form—ornamented and resplendent, surrounded by colorful lights and gifts, alive once more—the greatest gift of all, rebirth.

The loathsome serpent has long been considered a symbol for evil and deviousness, but it has a positive side less often recognized. Not only does it present temptation in the garden, but by encouraging the partaking of the fruit of the tree of knowledge, it provides the beginnings of wisdom and man's search for meaning. In this aspect, according to Jung (1964, 267), it appears as Lucifer—literally, the "light bringer." In Greek mythology, the serpent was considered to have medicinal properties. Wrapped around a staff in the left hand of the Greek god Mercury and with the addition of wings, it became the caduceus—emblem of medicine and healing. In his attempt to convince Pharaoh to let his people go, Moses threw down his staff, which then became a serpent that devoured the serpent-staffs of the court magicians. Thus the serpent represents power and authority from the highest source. In the wilderness, Moses, witnessing his people being poisoned by snakes raised a brass serpent upon a pole, and those who looked upon it with faith were spared a deadly fate. In this context the serpent represents not only the power of healing, but the ability to overcome the flesh and to strengthen one's faith. It even goes beyond that.

Maurice Farbridge, in his studies of Biblical symbolism, refers to the brass serpent on a pole as a "principal symbol of the hoped-for Messiah, which he claims was kept "in the chief temple of the Israelite nation for approximately 500 years time."[47] Francis Robiscek (1978, 74) points out that among the Hellenized Jews, Jehovah once appeared as the snake-footed sun god. The prophet Isaiah (30:60) speaks of "fiery flying serpents." Even in the Bible, then, wings were added to the lowest of creatures that otherwise must crawl upon its belly. Howey records that "The cross was an evolution from the tree and the serpent, and thus became the salvation of mankind."[48] Paradoxically, then, the serpent symbol, which to many had represented sin and evil, now becomes a tribute to the rewards of rising above them—new life and salvation.

Although the feathered serpent is not a symbol that Christians today equate with Christ, he, like the American culture heroes, has traits that can be identified with the positive aspects of the feathered serpent. New Testament reference to such a creature, however, can only be implied. The only time Christ mentions the snake and the bird together is when he admonishes his apostles to be "wise as serpents, and harmless as doves"(Matthew 10:16). Although the Bible gives few hints,

Campbell notes that early in Christianity there were Ophitic (Serpent) Christian sects, which honored the serpent in the garden as a "first appearance of the Savior." They taught that "no one can be saved and rise up again without the Son, who is the Serpent." Their favored symbol, he claims, was a winged serpent.[49]

Thus it is seen that Christ effectively embodies all of the ennobling qualities attributed to New World symbols of cross, tree, and feathered-serpent, along with the message of hope they suggest. The apostle, John (3:14-15), comes the closest to making the connection when he sums it up in one proclamation: "And as Moses lifted up the serpent in the wilderness, even so must the Son of Man be lifted up: that whosoever believeth in him should not perish, but have eternal life." The parallels between Christ and the New World heroes appear remarkably compatible.

A Time of Times

In an attempt to determine approximately when the feathered serpent or culture hero began his reign in the Americas, many early writers agree with Sejourné that: "just as our era began with Christ, so that of the Aztecs and their predecessors began—approximately at the same time—with Quetzalcoatl."[50] In South America, the long line of Peruvian kings was compiled by the historian Montesinos, who places the beginning of these royal lines at about the dawn of Christianity. Since the South American culture hero, Viracocha, is at the very beginning of the noble list of all Peruvian kings, that would place him around the time calculated for the first Quetzalcoatl in Mesoamerica—about the time of Christ.[51]

In light of this limited evidence, it would appear that the two most powerful culture heroes on the American continents, Viracocha and Quetzalcoatl, and possibly other similar heroes, begin their historic reigns and pervading influence in the Americas at the beginning of the Christian era. If they are not identical with each other and with Jesus Christ, they may at least be contemporaries.

Something to Consider

Examine the following list and determine, if you will, who it describes:

1. Born of a virgin about 2,000 years ago in the east.
2. Has a little-known childhood, identified with a star.
3. Appears as a holy man and teacher among men.
4. Is of fair complexion, and bearded.
5. Wears a long white robe and sandals.
6. Is tempted by the adversary and endures a 40-day fast.
7. Brings a message of peace, love, charity, and lives chastely.
8. Prays to his Father in Heaven and teaches others to pray.
9. Says feed the hungry, clothe the naked, care for the sick, avoid violence.

10. Creates all people and blesses his followers.

11. Works miracles: walks on water, heals the sick, cures the blind.

12. Instigates confession, communion, fasting, and baptism of water.

13. Has a body, yet is worshiped as a god by his followers.

14. Is identified with healing and with the serpent.

15. Is persecuted by his enemies, yet offers forgiveness.

16. Is scourged, wears a crown of thorns, and carries a cross.

17. Is crucified, his side is pierced, and water flows from it.

18. Sheds his blood for our sins, and darkness occurs at his death.

19. Visits the underworld of the dead, and speaks of heaven and hell.

20. Although he dies on Friday, he resurrects three days later.

21. Ascends to the heavens, where he now dwells.

22. Returns to the throne of his Father, who is the Supreme God of heaven.

23. Becomes a Savior and Redeemer for all. Resurrects the dead.

24. Is worshiped as One God, yet forms part of a trinity with his father.

25. Is called the life and the light of the world, omnipotent, omniscient.

26. Apostles and disciples continue his work building temples and altars.

27. Will return to reign and bring about a resurrection and golden age.[52]

It would appear that the list describes Jesus of Nazareth, for the list admittedly contains remarkable parallels with his life as depicted in the New Testament. But it is not Christ who is described here. It is, instead, the culture hero of the ancient Americas, as summarized in this chapter from traditional legends believed by natives from North to South America, and recorded by early scribes. As.Jesus Christ has been called the central figure in the history of the Western World, so the fair, bearded god is recognized as the central figure in all of the ancient Americas. Because of the perplexing similarities between the two, the unavoidable question follows: Are they one and the same person?

If Jesus, however inspired and profound, was a mere mortal there is no need to consider his coming to the Americas following death upon the cross. Like early Spanish priests, one still may have to consider that perhaps one of his apostles somehow brought the message. If, however, Christ's resurrection was literal, with the ability to transcend physical barriers and even to visit the realm of the dead and return, as scriptures indicate, it should not be difficult to imagine his appearance on the American continents. If Jesus Christ is indeed the divine Savior to all the world, then a visit to the millions of inhabitants in the Americas would seem almost required. How one responds to the possibility of a visit by Jesus to the New World depends largely upon how one views Jesus in his mission as The Christ.

The Apostle John (21:25) wrote, "There are also many other things which Jesus did, the which, if they should be written every one, I suppose that even the world itself could not contain the books that should be written." Some may argue that to recognize Jesus as Savior with a mission to the "lost sheep" in the "other half of the world" extends his ministry and influence beyond anything most Christians have ever allowed.

To consider a visit of Christ to the Americas is not to discredit all that has been examined in previous chapters. Egyptians, Romans, Greeks, or Phoenicians may still have brought lingering tales of visiting bearded white men, but the fair culture hero was far more than just a foreign explorer blown off course. One single visitation from the resurrected Jesus Christ in all his glory would establish miraculous stories of a god who appears in light from the heavens with power to transform whole civilizations and leave them with the promise to return one day, bringing a golden future.

The parallels between Christ and the Americas' fascinating visitor are remarkable. But whether or not one accepts a divine appearance by Jesus Christ on this hemisphere, one thing seems sure—the many legends of ancient America *as they have been recorded* clearly support such a visit.

Tangible Testaments

Having examined a substantial amount of external evidence for alleged visitors to the Americas from foreign lands in ancient times, it is not reasonable to also look for similar "ground support" for a visit from Christ and his followers? As in the case of Christ in the Old World, most evidence comes from tradition and history. In the Americas there is less tangible evidence than in Israel where one can at least point to a supposed shroud, pieces of the cross, paths walked by Christ with his followers, and traditional locations of his birth, sermons, crucifixion and burial.

What physical evidence is available is actually another baffling riddle that began late in the last century and ran through the 1920's, which if true, would definitely establish Christianity in the Americas long before its discovery by modern-day Europeans. The story—another complex controversy that can only be briefly summarized here—begins in Michigan with the appearance of thousands of tablets, coins, wooden boxes, bones, stone tools and other curious objects dug from ancient burial mounds from seventeen counties and five states.

Called the "Michigan Plates," or by some, the "Soper Frauds," the tablets are of clay, stone, copper and slate displaying hieroglyphic writings and simple illustrations which seem to come straight out of the Bible. Plate scenes include rain falling upon an ark while animals embark; a deluge and a dove, and animals disembarking. There is a large tower (Babel?) and the ten commandments. One tablet shows an elephant; another, a calendar. Others depict angels, a trinity, a robed man teaching a congregation, other robed bearded men, a cross, and a crucifixion with what look like Roman generals in the background. All of them contain the letters "I-H-S," whose precise interpretation is yet unknown.

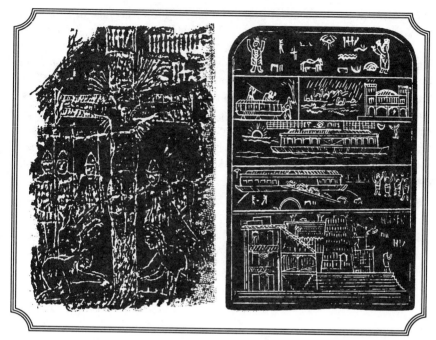

Michigan Plates, Allegedly 2nd Century A.D. (Courtesy Betty Sodders)
Christ-like Figure on Cross; Animals disembarking from an ark

Visual aids for a colony of early Christians? The plates have been examined by numerous experts, including Dr. James E. Talmage, apostle and geologist for the Mormon church, who, surprisingly, believed them to be forgeries. More recently they were examined by Dr. Henrietta Mertz, a brilliant scientist trained to identify forgeries, who after 30 years study pronounced them authentic, created by a people who lived in the area in the second or third century A.D. Sadly, perhaps 3,000 of the plates, when first branded frauds by the academic world, were destroyed. The rest of the split collection has over time resided at Notre Dame, the Smithsonian, Mt. Vernon, in private collections, and the bulk with the LDS Church in Salt Lake City.

So, are the plates concrete evidence of Christians in ancient America or just another perplexing mystery to add to the others? Williams, in *Fantastic Archaeology* debunks the whole collection. Mertz, in *The Mystic Symbol*, supports it. Others who have written about it, including Schaffer, in *Treasures of the Ancients*, and Sodders, in *Michigan Prehistory Mysteries*, I, II, present varying opinions. Professor Kelsey, quoted by Ken Moore in his article, "Michigan's Mysterious Tablets," believes the letters I-H-S, found on each plate, are the initials of an arrogant forger. Mertz, however, feels that would be absurd, and they are, instead, a mystic symbol referring to the name of God. Epigrapher and writer,

David Deal, in the same article states, "I think they [the Michigan Plates] are an extremely important piece of ancient American History. . . they are genuine."[53]

On most matters it can safely be said that neither belief (no matter how many embrace it), nor arguments (however convincing, or loudly, or often repeated), by themselves guarantee full truth. Strong as evidence may indicate that Jesus Christ visited lands beyond those which the Bible reveals, leaving behind New World colonies and disciples to spread his message, and that he alone fulfills the complex, super-human requirements as the fair, bearded god of the ancient Americas, this search is not over yet. Before any conclusions can be drawn, there still remain some demanding, and sometimes bewildering, alternatives which will be considered in the following chapters.

13

THE UNIVERSAL NATURE OF CULTURE HEROES

Thus far this pursuit of a mysterious, fair, bearded visitor reported to have walked the Americas before Columbus has followed two basic assumptions: that he was a real flesh-and-blood person, and that he was an immigrant from outside the Western Hemisphere. Old World prospects have been examined, and it would be romantic to envision a bigger-than-life heroic figure—a Greek, a Roman, a Christian—braving treacherous oceans to reach American shores and going forth to raise native life to a higher level.

But experience teaches caution about what is considered fact, and so it is necessary to turn for a time from previous explorations and examine a belief more commonly held by today's isolationist scholars: that the American culture figure did not arrive from some distant land but is completely native to this one and to the people who revered him so highly. Great heroes grew up in the Old World with no apparent interference from early Americans; could New World heroes have sprung from native soil and culture as well without foreign intervention?

The greatest aid to investigating American culture hero origins are the rich remnants of native American mythology. Many scholars have noted that as a preserver of basic truths, mythology is the principal door to the guarded inner world of primitive peoples. From seemingly simple tales come insights to the foundations of their worship and their approach to life's basic questions concerning origins, purpose in being, and ultimate destinies. These tales explain earth's creation, the appearance of plants and animals, and the peopling of both heaven and earth. They present both men and women who subdue nature to become heroes, then rise to rule, and in later times are remembered as gods. These hero-gods take on various forms and often descend to earth as humans to walk among their creations. To help us better understand the heroes and myths of the New World, and because the Americas' culture hero was said to come from across the sea, we will now examine culture heroes and mythology across the sea—the Old World. Perhaps there will be insights to the New World search.

Familiar Tales on Foreign Soil

In spite of alleged foreign origin of the American culture hero, most accounts treat him and circumstances surrounding him as unique to the Americas—at least the names "Quetzalcoatl," "Itzamná," "Kukulcan," and "Viracocha" seem unique. However, a review of world mythology demonstrates clearly that he may not be so unique. Basic stories and figures strikingly similar to those of the Americas can be found elsewhere. The Toltec god, Quetzalcoatl, descending from the heavens on a rope ladder, has a counterpart in Hebrew texts as well as in Egyptian pyramid writings and in the tales of Buddha.[1] Paintings and carvings of a serpent (or bird) in a sacred tree of life (or cross), making heaven accessible to earth, which are common in ancient Mexico, appear at various times in places like China, Japan, Babylonia, Persia, Egypt, Greece, Rome, Scandinavia, and Britain. They are also depicted in many religions like the Hindu, Buddhist, Druid, Christian, and Judaic. In his *Mythic Image* (424), Campbell shows both tree and serpent, along with the celestial ladder, together on rock paintings in far-off Rhodesia, South Africa.

Temples, as symbols of the sacred tree, and pyramids as the Cosmic Mountain or an image of the world or cosmos, can be seen universally. Many cultures outside the Americas display similar lion-masked men and sacred buckets of water overflowing eternally from both sides of a god-held vase. The resurrection theme, depicted in ceremonial serpents, the sun, and the morning star, is common to both hemispheres, as are stories of the "creation" and the "flood."

The calendar, which Aztecs attributed to Quetzalcoatl, appears first in Mesopotamia (today's Iraq) with similar names, numbers, and symbols. From there it spreads to all of Europe and Asia. Cosmic trees appear in most cultures, sometimes including the four cosmic directions and corresponding birds and colors.[2] Many calendars—Persian, Indian, Egyptian—also include a serpent-sphere similar to that surrounding the Aztec calendar.[3]

Symbols, traditions, and rites that seem so completely peculiar to the Americas that one would not expect to find them anywhere else, do indeed surface elsewhere. Both American and Babylonian gods create man by the immolation of one of the gods, or by molding him from clay mixed with their own blood.[4] Babylonian fires, like those of the Aztecs, were all extinguished at the end of certain time periods, and both cultures included traditions of a celestial eagle devouring an earthly serpent.[5] Maya, the name of America's highest civilization, is also the name of the mother of the Indian Buddha and of the fourteenth-century B.C. treasurer to Egypt's boy-pharaoh, Tutankhamen. Toltec symbols and Maya rites depicted on pottery, only recently understood by modern-day scholars, bear a remarkable resemblance to those of India (for example, the Indian deity, Shiva, like Maya royalty, dresses in tiger skins adorned with skulls and serpents). Like the Maya, followers of Shiva dedicate bloody sacrifices to their god and pierce various parts of their bodies. In a bizarre twist to a strange Maya practice of running a rope through the pierced tongue, Shiva priests perforated the tongue, and thrust live serpents through the hole.[6]

The grotesque and ominous statue of Coatlicue, mother of Aztec gods, has a close counterpart in Kali, the wife of Shiva: Both women are nature- and war-goddesses who instill feelings of fear and death. These hideous female monsters are depicted entwined by serpents. Their necklaces and belts consist of human skulls, hearts and hands. In earlier days, temples of both were smeared from bloody sacrifices, yet, paradoxically, both represented love and eternal motherhood.

Not only do many of these seemingly one-of-a-kind stories from the Americas have parallels elsewhere, but, surprisingly, even the most publicized of all the Americas' legends, the culture hero, is not unique. This great teacher of men, bringer of the arts and civilization, the bearded white visitor from across the seas, has surprisingly much in common with the many early hero myths of Europe and Asia, as will be seen.

Heroes Across the Sea

Coatlicue, Mother of Quetzalcoatl
(Natural Museum, Mexico)

The best known of these extraordinary stories about a "hero-god" outside the New World are, for Westerners, contained in the hymns, prayers and writings from the Mediterranean area about Christ. The more miraculous details of his life and teachings, as noted in chapter 12, remarkably mirror those of the culture heroes of the Americas including the common practice by followers of assuming his sacred name. But long before Christianity spread its message about the Son of God throughout Europe, there were other god-men in similar dress.

Among these, the greatest of Egypt's hundreds of deities was Osiris, whose father, the earth-god Geb (in some accounts), sends him to earth with gifts and blessings for his people. Osiris then, like the American heroes, bestows the arts of civilization: agriculture, architecture, writing, astronomy, laws, marriage, and religious practices. Like American culture heroes he is tall, handsome, bearded, and of a gentle and generous nature. He distributes his gifts not only to Egypt, but to all the world. He is later killed, but, like New-World heroes, is resurrected and ascends to the heavens where he judges the dead. Like Quetzalcoatl of the Mexican area, he is part of a trinity, is identified with a sun-serpent, and his followers adopt his sacred name.[7]

The Greek culture hero, Dionysus (Bacchus), is more than a god of wine as most people know him. Having borrowed traits from other Greek and foreign gods, he at times appears quite similar to New-World heroes. This son of Zeus (Jupiter) has a miraculous birth and is often depicted as wearing a long robe and beard. Arriving from the seas, sometimes from the east, he roams the world bringing great blessings, working miracles, and promoting civilization, laws, and peace. His travels take him into the underworld, and like New World culture heroes, after his death he is reborn and becomes a supreme god—a symbol of eternal life. In some narratives he is associated with the now-familiar serpent, and in New World tradition, followers anticipate his return.[8]

Other Old-World heroes possess attributes readily identified with those of the Americas. In addition to Osiris and Dionysus, Marduk and Tammuz of Babylonia experience death and new life as do Hay-Tau and Mot of Phoenicia; Adonis, Attis, and Virbius of Greece and Phoenicia; Mithra the Sun-god of Rome and Persia; and the Lydian hero, Tylon. Not only do the gods get new life, but resurrection rites were enacted for the commoner in many primitive societies.[9]

Like myths of the New World, Old World mythology shows a fascination for serpent figures as symbols of wisdom and authority. In the Gilgamesh epic the serpent steals the plant of immortality. The Egyptian, Typhon, is a serpent-man; Jason, a Greek, emerges from the mouth of a serpent; Zeus is adored as a serpent; Shiva is called "King of the Serpents;" The Hittites and Romans also had their serpent-gods. Serpents guard the sacred shrine of Buddha who, like the Persian Savior Mithra, and India's Vishnu, sits upon coiled serpents. Apollo, the Greek Sun-God, slays the serpent Python the oracle and mouthpiece of God. England's Stonehenge is considered a temple to the Serpent-Sun. Hu, of the Celtic nations, is identified with serpents. The role of the serpent in the Garden of Eden is well known in the Old Testament; and St. Patrick drives them not only out of Ireland's countryside, but from its worship.[10]

Wings and Things

At times these mystical creatures, like the prolific serpents of Mexico and Yucatan, even produce wings. Triptolemus, a Greek culture hero, drives a chariot drawn by winged-serpents. Mercury's staff, or caduceus, displays wings above the serpents. Azon, the Persian Sun-God, is depicted as a serpent with wings. Vishnu dances above a winged serpent. Zeus attacks the feathered-serpent, Typhon, and in the corner of a Greek temple (chapter 10) crouch three men in one winged serpent body.[11] Kneph, one of the fathers attributed to Osiris, is sometimes depicted as a winged-serpent, and all over Egypt temples display winged serpents as well as statues of Pharaohs who wear adjoining falcons and cobras on their headdresses (the winged cobra is the divine protector of pharaohs).

Not only Egypt, but Israel had serpents—"fiery flying serpents" (Moses' bronze serpent became a prefiguration of the coming savior): therefore, later Christian cults revered them. Like Mayan sky-bar depictions, these Old-World sky-born creatures on occasion have two heads and even comely beards.[12]

Further similarities between Old- and New-World culture heroes include a common acceptance by followers as saviors or as one in a trinity. Heroes from both sides perform blood sacrifices, and both appear in tales of creation and the flood. Like Kukulcan of the Maya and Christ of Christendom, both Orpheus-Bacchus and the Nordic Wodan die on a cross. Similarly, the Egyptian Ba-Tau hangs his heart on a tree, and Attis of Phyrgia is a savior who is crucified and resurrected.[13]

Contrary to nature, miraculous or virgin births are not unusual occurrences for culture heroes of either side. Among those of the Old World, according to which retelling one accepts, are Osiris in Egypt; Thamuz in Babylonia; Hermes, Adonis and Dionysus in Greece; Romulus in Rome; Buddha in India; Fo-Hi in China, and Mithra and Zoroaster in Persia. In Northern Siberia, virgin birth is attributed to the young hero, Muzykay. The Scandinavians make the same claim for Odin, and the Siamese attribute virgin birth to their Great Teacher and miracle worker, Codom.[14]

In the Old World even heroes arriving from across the seas are not so rare—the Celts and Greeks each had one. Anticipation of the hero's return—the fateful promise made by Quetzalcoatl, Kukulcan, Viracocha and others, that so stirred the American natives to receive the conquering Spaniards—was common of Old World gods of vegetation like Tammuz, Adonis, Dionysus, and Marduk. Parallels between culture heroes of the Old and New Worlds are numerous, and it is no exaggeration to state that in examining Old-World myths, one can discover nearly every basic characteristic existing in New-World mythology. In many cases, only the superficial details differ.

Nature of the Myth

On one thing isolationists and diffusionists agree: that many similarities between Old World and New World myths seem to be the result of ancient migrations of Europeans and Asians across the Bering Straits into the Americas. Still not explained, however, is if the Western Hemisphere experienced no contact with the Eastern Hemisphere following the last entry into the Americas from Asia some 10,000 years ago, as isolationist scholars insist, what accounts for the existence among New-World myths of so many similar characteristics and minute details in Old-World myths which have developed in remote regions since that time? As Joseph Campbell puts it in his *Hero of a Thousand Faces*, "Why is mythology everywhere the same, beneath its varieties of costume?"

Since Old-World myths are more fully documented than those of the New World, perhaps they can provide insights to possible origins of American myths, and especially to those of its culture heroes. Anyone who pursues the folklore of ancient Europe, Asia, and the Mediterranean soon discovers that one's understanding of New-World mythology is greatly enhanced by exposure to that of the Old, and, in fact, is incomplete without it.

At this point it might be well to ask, what is mythology? Scholars have proposed volumes of answers—often in conflict—and at best they can only be skimmed here. Summaries given by Eliot, Campbell, Eliade, and others vary from the skeptical nineteenth-century approach that myth is "anything opposed to reality" to the more generous contemporary acceptance that myths were believed by the tellers to be the "absolute truth."[15]

Briefly, myth has been defined as "fantasy repetition of a real act" (Freud); "collective unconscious " (Jung); "more like music than speech (Claude Levi Strauss); "an account of a 'creation'," in which the actors are "supernatural beings" (Eliot); "a sacred history," which "provides the pattern for human behavior"(Eliade); "a primitive, fumbling effort to explain the world of nature" (Frazer). To this, Campbell, who contends that mankind must have myth to survive, adds his own definitions: a "metaphor for what lies behind the visible world "(1988, xvii), and "getting into harmony and tune with the universe and staying there."(1990,1)

Myths can be called idealized stories which help people deal with the disorder that comes into their lives. Even more, they lift humans from the wretched to the sublime. Or, as Eliade puts it (1969,45), they help people to " find meaning to the precariousness and the contradictions of human existence."

Culture heroes are the personifications of mythology, and they appear in all societies. They show their followers how to achieve balance in their lives, and lead them through the process. They are the exalted tutors, who alone know the secrets of attaining oneness with the universe and accord with the divine. Their chosen priests and faithful devotees are the vehicles through whom the heroes recount or reenact great moments and insure they will be remembered. Anciently myths transported believers to distant times, places, and events as books and films do for us today. Except they believed that while they recited or reenacted the myth they entered into the presence of the gods or heroes involved—they were actually experiencing the event.

A Bottomless Pot

The question arises, why is mythology everywhere? And the answer glares: mythology is everywhere because people are everywhere, and people everywhere seek answers for their existence. The answers they find become foundations for their mythology, and though the results differ somewhat in detail, basics are remarkably similar. In stirring the ancient pot of myth, an endless assortment of culture heroes boils to the surface. As Jung pointed out, "the myth of the hero is the most common and best known myth in the world."[16]

And the pot is not just deep, it is bottomless. No one knows how far back these culture heroes extend, or precisely what roles they played in remote times. Writers have churned up countless theories about the origins of these inscrutable beings, but always the relationship of heroes to gods and mythology to religion is unclear. Scholars, like La Barre, believe the hero is a "mediator between god and man" and that the so-called "trickster, culture hero, and spirit-mediator [are] all related."[17] This complex mixing of gods, heroes, myths and religion becomes difficult, if not impossible, to sort out, and at such a distance through the mists of time, our vision of such things becomes hazy.

In spite of scanty knowledge about the ancients, Eliade and other scholars feel that they can be at least dimly comprehended from "fragments" preserved in the traditions of historical peasant societies. Among primitive cultures, he explains, the highest god creates the world and mankind, then abandons his creations and withdraws into the sky. Often, it is the hero who has a more direct contact with his people as he continues the work of the great god, who may be his father. At other times, he is the abandoned son of a king, who grows up to overcome great obstacles (monsters, demons, hell) and eventually wins semidivine status for himself. As has been seen in past chapters, he is, in this exalted position, often mistaken for the god.

A peculiar breed, these culture heroes work miracles, effect cures, teach peace, bring civilization, and are seen as superhuman individuals. Although they are said to descend from the gods, they can also have earthly or mixed parentage (god and human). Their births are unusual or miraculous, and they are often abandoned soon after. They travel widely and embark on daring adventures that win them great acclaim. At times they have unsurmountable difficulties or adverse influences to overcome; occasionally these forces defeat them.

As in the Americas, the hero is often considered the first ancestor of the race, even, at times, the creator. He is the founder of cities and introduces the benefits of civilization: agriculture, architecture, laws, the arts, writing, and religious rites. His life inspires dramatic reenactments or even athletic contests: great athletes were included on the Greek list of heroes.

Heroes' deaths are as unorthodox as their lives: they disappear into the under-world, are transferred to great distances, and often suffer violently in battle casu-alties: their bodies are torn apart, burned, crucified, devoured, or sealed up in boxes. Through death and resurrection, the heroes confirm their divine natures. They enjoy immortality, judge the dead, and are among the elite of heaven. Back on earth, their followers make sacrifices to them and build temples in their honor.

Heroes Looking For a Myth

To the question, what is the origin of these super-beings, there are as many answers as scholars to provide them. Some scholars have pro-posed that these heroes were "spirits of dead men, who live inside the earth," or persons who "descend from gods, really lived, or were invented by poets or scholars."[18] Primitives may see nature as possessed by spiritual beings (animism), thus giving natural elements different personalities. From this view-point in each rock and tree and stream, in the water, fire, rain, wind, and sun-shine, in every plant, animal, and natural occurrence, there is a god—thousands of them (polytheism). In due course all of these gods become *one* with the cre-ator (pantheism or monotheism).

In the Nineteenth century, Bancroft and others explained that people tend to revere what they fear or do not understand. Darkness and danger are continually present to the primitive, for whom foreboding images are never far away. Demons howl in the night, the moon disappears in stages—then reappears. Powerful forces hurl lightning bolts, gods speak out in the roar of the waterfalls and thunder, and sinister forms are witnessed slinking through the evening mists. At times the pow-ers of nature become unexplainedly violent, as murderous winds uproot trees and heave them like lances, raging waters engulf whole villages, roaring volcanoes belch forth their fury, and the incensed land ruptures to swallow the people.

Powerless under such cataclysms, the primitive mind attributes the unpre-dictable forces of nature to capricious gods whose favor they must win to gain con-trol. Not to do so would incur the wrath of these divine beings, who can decree great catastrophes: floods, drought, disease, pestilence, and death. In fear of these dramatic threats, man throws himself upon the ground and pleads for deliverance. To strengthen his pleas, he extends some kind of offering. In extreme cases, he makes the ultimate sacrifice, that of human blood or even life—preferably that of others. When the forces at last subside, the evidence is clear: The gods have heard.[19]

Twentieth-century writers have another approach to primitive thinking. Under great stress, the masses often seek security in figures whose power they trust and whom they can follow blindly. These potent figures, in many cultures, are referred to as shamans (medicine men). Shamans, intoxicated by the power placed in them, invent ways to retain and increase it (more than one writer has noted that the wise priest or shaman waits for storm clouds before appealing to the gods for needed rain). Years after the event, the actual incidents are forgotten or misinterpreted and distorted. But the figure who successfully supplicated the gods to avert the calamity remains fixed in the minds of later generations who see him, greater than life, as a powerful mediator to the gods. Not only did people believe the shaman could control the elements and animals, but that he "became" them. Again, although the shaman is not originally the god or hero, his followers may translate him into a divine image, making it difficult to separate them. La Barre believes the culture hero "derives from the shaman." Even more, he insists, "There were shamans before there were gods."[20]

At the polytheistic level, gods and heroes sometimes become identified with one another in a number of forms: sky gods, storm gods, vegetation gods and deities of fertility, life, and death. There are gods who, like the crops they preside over, are young and growing. Like the crops which are snatched from the earth or cut down at their prime, these young gods also die violent deaths but later come back to life. Like crops, they disappear during drought, intense heat of summer or cold of winter, then reappear in the spring, young again. In support of such beginnings, Campbell says: "These cults were very much associated with a cycle of death, descent into the underworld, and then life-reform [rebirth] again. By analogy, this was symbolized in the agricultural cycle of the harvest death, the planting of seed, and the plants coming to life again."[21]

In areas like the tropics where the seasons are not so clearly marked, stories differed. Before bringing rain to grow the crops, the hero may steal into the heavens and sneak back with the precious grain necessary for mankind.

Societies which grew tubers (potatoes, fruits), as opposed to cereals, often explained their origins with a primordial murder in which the hero is sacrificed so that the tubers might grow from his body. The plant is now considered sacred, and, in consuming it, one partakes of the divine being.[22] In the fields farming peasants ran shouting, dancing, and wielding torches to scare off evil and to goad the spirits of the field into production. In the high mountains away from the fields, cults, like those of Dionysus, seem to spring from some other sources, perhaps a more materialistic and "common sense" way of looking at things.[23]

Other societies built their gods around celestial objects like stars, or the sun and moon—"eyes of the supreme being." Venus appears in the night sky brilliantly—a god is born. Then, disappointingly, it disappears—the god dies. Several days later it reappears in full splendor in the morning sky—the god has been resurrected. The moon enters three phases—waxing, waning, and full—thus becoming a triad (not a trinity) of gods.

Oftentimes these gods are transformed into the sun, which, as long as it gives warmth and produces growth, is seen as a beneficent god. But when it burns and parches, it is regarded as evil or punishing. Thus it becomes a dual god, or even two separate divinities. As in Mexican myths, the daytime sun of the Old World can become one god and the fallen sun at night another. The nighttime sun faces great perils as it goes through the underworld. But in the morning, it is reborn a child who matures and grows older as the day progresses. Similarly, contrasting forces such as good and evil or death and life may be assigned to lightning, storms, winds, or waters, which all relate to the heroes. Such mysteries inspire the formation of opposing divinities who represent life's conflicts.

Myths Looking for a Hero

It is not always a god who becomes the sun but perhaps a great chief, warrior, shaman, or king who, in recognizing the sun's great powers and in retelling its mythological origins, goes out daily to worship as it rises. Later societies recall the stories and remember him imperfectly in close association with the sun. In time they may even revere him *as* the rising sun—thus he becomes their god or culture hero. (Egyptians said their sun deities were originally their kings.) This hero may also take on the alternating traits of dark and light, good or evil identified with the day and night sun. Because great birds like falcons and eagles can be seen flying across the sky, they too become connected with the sun and with the hero. Eliade points out that dynasties (like Egypt's) and military aristocracies (Melanesia's) often trace their origins to solar heroes who often identified with birds.[24]

The mythical conflict between the sun and the moon may be the origin for another common tale about two warring brothers: While the path of the sun (one brother) is predictable, disappearing regularly each night, the moon (the other brother) disappears slowly and reappears only after leaving the earth in darkness for three nights. Because Venus and the moon both disappear for several days before reappearing, they become sources for themes about death and resurrection, which are identified with the heroes.

Another popular theory is that religion, myths, and heroes originate with the worship of dead ancestors who, though departed, are believed still capable of working on behalf of or against their descendants. Savages reportedly fear the dead more than they fear the living, believing their powers increase in death. Thus they go to great lengths to control this "unseen power" over themselves. To win favor with these superhuman ancestors they place offerings in their graves, slay family members and favored animals to serve them, enact rituals to please them, and, at times, sacrifice messengers to approach them. A particularly memorable ancestor could eventually become a culture hero to his or her people, and if in life he or she identified with a certain animal, it too would be venerated. Other cultures may adopt this hero as well.

Animals are born with strengths and abilities men do not possess; nature demonstrates further enviable powers. Winter spreads a shroud of death over the land, but spring brings forth new life. The sleeping bear also seems dead through-out the winter, then comes forth in the spring. Birds fly to the heavens where they can communicate with the gods; other creatures invade the underworld. Thus men have sought to obtain these desired qualities for themselves and their gods through close identification. By adopting the names and characteristics of animals or nat-ural forces, one could, it was believed, share those powers. A swift runner might be called "lightning," "leopard," or "antelope." A powerful warrior might be des-ignated as "thunder cloud," "bear," "lion," or "bull." These metaphors, once attached, might become the adopted name for the whole clan or tribe—the off-spring of the Bear, Wolf, Eagle, or Serpent.

At one time or another most deities, many culture heroes, and all shamans were seen as animals thought to be the very soul of that individual: Horus, a falcon; Thoth, an Ibis; Sebek, a crocodile; Quetzalcoatl, a feathered-serpent. It is easy to see how a god or hero identified with death, birth, and resurrection could be con-nected with a bird or serpent which lay eggs (symbols of fertility). In addition, the serpent periodically emerges from underground after shedding its skin (symbol of rebirth following death). Both serpent and long-tailed birds display winding move-ments like a river, which brings life-giving waters to the fields. Thus any person who is lord over the rivers also becomes identified with the serpent. If wings are attached to the serpent, the metaphor becomes even more powerful: the hybrid can now rise from its underground retreat and fly upward like the birds that are iden-tified with the sun and the heavens (resurrection). Thus, by extension, the hero, like the winged-serpent and the rising sun, ascends above the restrictions of earth and soars to the heavens.[25]

Scholars Looking For Answers

Not everyone accepts these myths at face value. Early Greek philoso-phers rejected the Homeric myths as fiction. Euhemerus of the third century B.C. was more generous: he saw the early gods (culture heroes) historically as "ancient kings who had been deified." Even more diver-gence occurs in the nineteenth century when a rash of scholars began to study myths more scientifically. One of them, Max Müller, attributed the birth of gods to the "disease of language" in which similar names and objects become con-fused over time. Thus an object with a name possessing a feminine ending later becomes a goddess. A golden boat sinking into the sea, if it possesses a name similar to the sun, eventually replaces the setting sun.[26] Under this system a king or great leader with a "solar" name would in time be said to be fair, have gold-en hair, and to have come from the east like the sun (Egyptian Pharaohs called themselves the children of Ra, the name of the sun). Since at night the sun's path is replaced by a great sky-serpent of stars (the Milky Way), the hero might also take on that symbol, becoming a dual god of day and night.

Among hunters and food-gatherers Lang and Schmidt discovered "High Gods" (belief in an eternal creator, omniscient and beneficent). They propose that originally the concept of a "High God" was everywhere, but societal developments degraded and obliterated these beliefs. This god abandons his creations and withdraws into the sky. People later create gods and heroes to represent him, but they are merely substitutions.[27]

The possibilities are many, and combinations of gods, heroes, and symbols crafted by the ancients to explain the mysteries behind life as they experienced it are plentiful. But in matters so ancient—and modern research continues to stretch the distance—ultimate answers seem unlikely.

To summarize in simple form what has been covered thus far: earth, sky, water, celestial bodies, elements (wind, rain, fire, etc.), plants, animals, night/day, the seasons, time cycles—these and human beings with their complex needs, instincts, and imaginations, are the raw ingredients of mythology. Mixed thoroughly and given sufficient time, they produce similar results—including a generous supply of culture heroes. And where does all of this occur? It occurs wherever these ingredients come together—practically everywhere. People in all countries and in every age have sought to understand the origin of things; mythology is the result of that search—mankind looking for itself.

Historic Haze

It may never be determined precisely where or when in the history of mankind the first Old World culture heroes and gods appear, but the earliest intimations exist in ancient art and burial practices. Burials, especially if accompanied by funerary objects such as food, jewelry, and tools, suggest ceremony and belief in survival after death. Archaeologists will explain that orientation of the grave toward the east indicates an attempt to join the soul with the sun's course across the sky, thus expressing a hope for rebirth and continued existence in the celestial sphere. The earliest of these burials was of the Neanderthal, who flourished some 70,000 years ago. But with no written history to go by, organized religion and belief in a divinity or culture hero at that distant time can only be implied.

Art has always been the servant of religion and mythology, and the most ancient discovery consists of Eurasian statuettes made of bone, ivory, and clay (mainly of women, dating around 25,000 B.C). The exaggerated sexual features suggest, perhaps, that the creators were expressing the need of small tribes for fertile women to keep up their population. These may be the world's first religious symbols, and possibly the earliest precursors of the mother-goddess—who may be the first hero. But at this time there is not yet evidence of male culture heroes.

The next dramatic art objects—carvings, drawings, and masterful paintings—appear around 12,000-20,000 B.C. in the deep, dark recesses of hundreds of advanced Stone-Age, Cro-Magnon caves—considered by primitives to be the underworld. The most elaborate, found in Spain at Altamira, France at Lescaux, and more recently in an underwater grotto near Marseilles, seem to demonstrate a deep obsession with the animal world and the needs of the hunter—perhaps portraying the kill somehow assures the accomplishment of the event. Campbell speaks of the hunter as "identified with the sun, his javelin with its rays, and the herds of the field with the herds of the sky (nighttime stars)."[28] Even at this early date, Eliade assures us, there is certain evidence for a shaman who travels to the gods to ask for favors.

From this time rock carvings, painted plaster murals, carved figures of humans and animals, painted pottery, and tool decoration continue to appear and spread out all over Europe, Asia and Africa. From these early periods archaeologists have discovered divinity masks, religious altars, ceremonial structures, fertility goddesses, and "big heads." They also see lunar cycles in calendars, writing, math, and symbols involving woman, water, vegetation, serpents, dancing men with beards, fertility, death, and rebirth.[29] All of this, according to Eliade, indicates a well-organized religion. What myths and religious traditions relating to heroes and gods may have accompanied these prehistoric representations, and how much of them were carried over into succeeding cultures—or across the Bering Straits—one can only speculate, but many of these themes also appear in later historical religious practices suggesting similar meanings.

Such extensive depictions indicate that continuing through the Stone and Ice Ages (ending about 8,000 B.C.) and beyond, religious ideas were fermenting and growing. Much of the cultural banquet that later surfaces was in preparation for countless millennia, for the ancients, like us, must have had their dreams and fantasies and religious beliefs put into some ritual practice. Apparently, only the specifics remain a mystery. But for the truly dramatic manifestations of civilization in the art and architecture, said to have been the gifts of the early hero-gods, and for the appearance of the heroes themselves, history would have to wait thousands of years more.

Gestation of the Gods

Apart from a few brilliant and unexplainable advances in civilization, as at Jericho (8,000 B.C.), and Çatal Hüyük, Turkey (6500 B.C.), the earliest and most dramatic results of community effort and culture heroes occur in ancient Mesopotamia (today's Iraq) around the fourth millennium B.C., between the Tigris and Euphrates rivers which pour into the Persian Gulf. There, most scholars concede, civilization and mythology were born. Sumerians were the first to invent the wheel and plow, making it possible to till the earth and produce grain surpluses that freed the non-farmer and gave him time necessary to become a specialist in weaving, fired pottery, house building, trading, and selling. The resulting increase in wealth allowed for eventual development of a government that introduced many powerful city states and a nation presided over by kings whose deeds were recorded by scribes in a newly-devised script, the world's first writing.

By 3500 B.C. this area was so rich its abundance and influence eventually spilled over to inspire other great river areas: the Nile in Egypt (c. 2800 B.C.), the Indus of Pakistan (c. 2600 B.C.), and the Yellow River of Eastern China (c. 1600 B.C.). Campbell (1987, 149) calls this migration of high civilization "the limbs of one great tree whose root is in heaven." Along with Sumer's civilization came the first known developments of fully organized religion, complete with professional temple priests, sacred towers and buildings (where heaven and earth meet), divine images, and ritual ceremonies. And although they were no doubt gestating for millenniums, it appears that here too were born the first great culture heroes.

Observing the complex birth of culture heroes at the cradle of civilization helps one understand the development of similar figures in the myths of the Americas. In the trip through origins of Old World heroes from ancient times, watch for situations that may have parallels in the early New World.

Birth of Culture Heroes

For millenniums the Sumerian and Semitic peoples had struggled together against the elements along the rivers of Mesopotamia. In order to deal with beliefs in the divine bestowal of vegetation and spring floods that brought rich soil over the banks, every village and town created gods—it has been estimated there were over 3,000 of them. They evolved deities of the rain, sun, moon, crops, life, death—virtually every aspect of natural and human involvement. These gods, although immortal, took on the characteristics of families, with spouses, children, human emotions, and needs. They ate, drank, loved, battled, kept servants and soldiers, and lived in palaces. To scholars like Campbell, these very human practices indicate that the gods originated from early kings: "The queen or princess of each city was in those earliest days identified with the goddess, and the king, her spouse, with the god."[30]

In more remote times these countless deities from each city had little connection with one another. But as the nation began to solidify, villages unified, rulerships merged, and so did the gods. By the time of the first great ruler of Mesopotamia, Sargon (c. 2250 B.C.), there had already been many kings, and the protracted list of complex gods had long since been established. Along with merging of gods, Campbell (1987, 403) sees a "hodge-podge of differing mythologies being coordinated, synthesized, and syncretized by the new professional priesthoods." This fusion also appears in amazing combinations of creatures as well: "bull-horned serpents, fish-tailed bulls, lion-headed eagles," and feathered serpents. The difficulty in explaining the origins of these gods and heroes is compounded by their existence in at least four different narratives—which suggests various traditions, and as Eliade points out, a seeming Sumerian indifference toward logic or chronology.[31]

Briefly explained, creation to the Sumerians was a great war fought in the heavens by the gods against the evil forces of the mother, Tiamut, who produces monstrous sky serpents. One of the younger gods, Enlil, destroys the mother and, aided by the winds and hurricanes, splits her in two. From the two halves he forms heaven and earth. Enlil, now god of the earth, along with his father, Ea, god of waters, and Anu, the supreme sky god, form a powerful male triad.

To get things going on earth, Enlil creates mankind from the blood of one of the gods, and Ea, his father, excited by the presence of the Lady of the Land, Nintur, fertilizes the swampy land with his semen. Enlil and Ea control the fertilizing waters, and they organize the world, send the rains, make the plants grow, and produce the great rivers and animals. As if that weren't enough to keep them occupied, they fertilize the fields and flocks, stock the rivers with fish and reeds, bring forth the plow, yoke, axe, and brick mold. Then they blanket the fields with vegetation, establish governments, introduce the arts, guard justice and law, and decree men's fates. A fair day's work.[32]

It is not difficult to see the roles of nature and the elements in all of these activities, for, like the rains and the winds he represents, Enlil comes from the heavens. After bringing rain to the crops, like them, he dies and is resurrected. Identified with the sun god who drives his chariot across the sky, he regulates the courses of heavenly bodies, forms the earth, installs the stars, determines the length of a year, and organizes the universe. In him an explanation for nature's extremes is seen, for his benevolent nature calms the tempestuous sea while his violent nature brings hurricanes and a deluge upon mankind.

Earthly kings were merely representatives of Enlil, and receive their authority from him. His followers built temples to him and, yearly, carried his statue through the crowds in anticipation of his seasonal return. He was considered without rival among all the gods, so when the Babylonians borrowed the gods of Sumer they combined Enlil with their god Marduk who had, in turn, absorbed all of their previous gods. Enlil/Marduk became the Supreme god of the Universe with an accumulation of over fifty titles found in numerous writings. Among them are "Lord of Life," "The Wise," "Creator of All Things," "The First," "Lord of Kings," "Shepherd of the Gods," and "The Great Healer."

A Hero Named Tammuz

As if the powerful Marduk were not dynamic enough, along came another hero, a beautiful young man of such charisma he was the essence of Sumerian mythology. This god, Tammuz, presides over vegetation and the harvest and, like the seasonal crops that are plowed under, dies and is forced into the underworld. His voluptuous sister and lover, Ishtar, goddess of love and fertility, employs a choir of weeping men and women to lament his passing. This becomes a tradition reenacted yearly when the earth becomes parched under the summer sun. Ishtar then braves the threatening underworld to retrieve him, but before she can do that, he is resurrected and ascends to heaven as a god.

There is evidence that Tammuz was originally a deified king, but some writers represent Tammuz as a human being who died at the hands of a king so that the earth might be restored following its fallow period of withering plants and drying soil. He rises again yearly as the crops begin to appear with the spring sun and descending rains. Thus he resurrects and becomes a "perpetual atonement," the symbol of the annual triumph over death.

The myth of the beautiful young king who died to save the world found universal and lasting appeal. In the sixth century B.C., Ezekiel decried the women who were weeping over Tammuz at the temple of Jerusalem (Ezekiel 8:14). And history shows they hadn't stopped weeping for him as late as the Middle Ages, for according to Eliade and others, the Christians borrowed some of the myth for their stories of Saint George and the Dragon. Kings were said to be Tammuz incarnate, and some of their sons were sacrificed to share his annual fate. The cult of Tammuz was the most important in Mesopotamia, and is considered by many writers to be the greatest of all ancient myths.[33]

Marduk and Tammuz are generally treated as separate heroes, with different legends to tell. But the borders of their identities get blurred, and in them, over time, various legends merge. In some accounts they are seen as the same figure. Tammuz is the first-born of Ea, and so is Marduk. As dynamic and memorable heroes, they extend far beyond their confined beginnings. Over the centuries, Babylonians assumed many of the Sumerian myths, and Assyrians took over most of the Babylonian ones. Eventually the combined myths travelled beyond both areas.

Since Marduk's first title was Asari, scholars have suggested a connection between the Babylonian Asari and the Egyptian Osiris: Like Marduk and Tammuz, Osiris is a vegetation god who dies and goes into the underworld at the time of harvest and the receding of the Nile. He is reborn yearly as the river overflows, bringing rich soil and new crops. It is extremely possible, scholars believe, that Osiris-Isis have their prehistoric origins in Asari-Ishtar. Although most of Egypt's myths came from the people and the land and were well developed in ancient times, the similarities of their myths with those of Sumeria would make it appear that Egypt borrowed more than writing and culture from its neighbors in Mesopotamia.

The cult of Tammuz was accepted at an early period by the Phoenicians and later by the Greeks, who called him Adonis, the beautiful vegetation god who dies and later lives again. Eventually this spreading cult of a dying god, found in early

Sumerian, Babylonian, Assyrian, Egyptian, and Greek mythologies, was also adopted by Arameaens, Canaanites, and Hebrews. Even Christians, as has been seen, used the myth and kept it alive.

Absorbing Mythology

The spreading of Near-Eastern mythology was not limited to the west or to early civilizations. Buddhism later adopted much from these pagan cults, as did the Shinto in Japan and Taoism in China. Even Christianity, in absorbing the pagan nations, clearly adopts or parallels many of their ancient traditions, like burning of incense; chants and ceremonies; water baptism; ritual use of bread and wine; a cup of the god's blood; death of the god to save the world; use of the cross; world darkness and destruction upon death (as with Buddha); resurrection of a man who then becomes god; a savior such as Dionysus who turns water to wine; Sargon, who like Moses is placed in a basket as a baby to float down the river; a Babylonian world flood; Venus crowned with stars (like Mary's diadem of twelve stars), and Pagan association with divinity and plants later transferred to Mary, "Our Lady of the Plants."

Solar discs of ancient rulers became halos for the Christian Saints, and like ancient sun-gods, Christ is depicted on an early mosaic driving a chariot across the sky with rays of light behind his head. Thus, for pagans, the "Sun's birth" becomes the "Son's birth," and the Sabbath is changed to "Sun's day." In addition to these pagan practices which parallel Christian ones, there were others like altars, vestments, feasts, nuns, indulgences, Easter eggs, fasting, lent, and statues.

Most fascinating of the parallels between Christian traditions and those of paganism are the numerous similarities to Christ's birth and childhood. The virgin birth, as seen earlier, is found in all cultures. The term *Divine Child* was given to most ancient culture heroes. December 25 is a date borrowed from the birth of the Persian Savior Mithra. The word *yule* in Chaldean meant *infant*, and December 25 was Yule Day or *child's day*. Yule logs and decorated trees were used anciently to release the old year and usher in the new. The ass and ox of Jesus' nativity also appear in stories of Seth and Osiris. Shepherds at the birth of Christ were also present for the birth of several pagan heroes. Best known today of mythological additions to the birth of Christ are stories of the religious saint who becomes a superhero wearing a red suit and a beard. Reindeer and chimneys were added as recently as the nineteenth century.[34]

All of this does not infer that Christ was not historical, or that all Christian parallels with paganism are direct implants; there are substantial differences. Osiris resurrected yearly; Christ resurrected only once. Osiris was mythical; Jesus Christ was real flesh and blood. Stories about early heroes, although perhaps based in some fact, are accepted as myth; much of what is written about Christ may be factual. Followers attributed divine status to their heroes; Christ declared it for himself. But to keep it in perspective, Christ's story was written long after his death, and inasmuch as Eastern myths infiltrated the lore of Egypt, Greece, Rome and other areas, how could Christianity avoid them, growing up in the center of it all and absorbing so many pagan believers? From what we have seen, it didn't.

The Evolution of a God

The past few pages have shown that from remote times people in a hostile world find security in gods who they believe hear them, and extraordinary beings (culture heroes) to mediate in their behalf. These gods and heroes evolve slowly until each city has its own. Born of unclear history, elements, and forces of nature, they become powerful influences in stories, religions, and lives of their followers.

The first people to record world mythology, the Mesopotamians, generated an impressive number of these super-beings who spread throughout all the ancient world to a greater or lesser degree. Their pervading influence resulted in a fusing with other local deities and heroes. Finally, they were blended by over-zealous priests who mixed tales about nature, kings, heroes, and great events from local as well as from foreign sources. Eventually, all peoples of Europe and Asia shared these rich legacies, or as Campbell puts it, "The arts of cultivation spread, and the myths accompanied them."

To better understand the enigmatic heroes of ancient America, many characteristics of Old World culture heroes, have been described, and their development over long periods of time and a wide range of locations have been observed. It is clear that heroes of the world are strikingly alike, and many traits appear to have been borrowed from one another. Still, each fulfilled a particular need for a particular people at the time, thus each can be considered an original product of the culture and land that created him.

Traits of a Culture Hero

Chapter 12 examined a list of parallel attributes between Christ and New World culture heroes. Now . . . another list. Determine, if you will, who is described by the following:

1. Identifies with the sun—a sun god.
2. Arrives from the East across the sea.
3. Is said to be fair, and bearded, and wears a long robe.
4. Descends from a heavenly ladder, has a miraculous birth.
5. Is symbolized by a feathered-serpent.
6. Is identified with the tree of life and bird of resurrection.
7. Is identified with vegetation, thunder, lightning, rain, and wind.
8. Is associated in some areas with the name Maya.

9.   Is related to traditions of an eagle devouring a serpent.
10.   Visits various cultures across the country.
11.   Introduces civilization: the calendar, language, arts, agriculture, writing.
12.   Possesses great wisdom. Brings laws and a higher way of life.
13.   Is first in a long line of kings who claim descent from him.
14.   Lends his name and power to later priests and kings.
15.   Has great monuments erected to him.
16.   Has abundant temples adorned with serpents.
17.   Has priests who pierce their body parts and perform blood sacrifices.
18.   Has ceremonies which use a sacred bucket of copal.
19.   Is a god of peace, a healer, and a worker of miracles.
20.   Is a great visionary visited by angelic beings. Is one of a triad of gods.
21.   Has an evil counterpart who opposes him.
22.   Dies and visits the gods of the underworld; judges the dead.
23.   Is resuscitated and becomes a Supreme God.
24.   Identifies with the star Venus.
25.   Is expected to one day return to his people in a golden age.

It would seem we have just described Quetzalcoatl or Kukulcan of Mesoamerica, or perhaps Ioskeha of the Northeast, Viracocha of Peru, or a number of other New World culture heroes. However, this list just as easily describes the numerous culture heroes found all over Europe, Asia, and the Near East long before the time of Christ, or even before the alleged appearance of most heroes upon the Western Hemisphere. Several Hero-Gods of the Old World possess a majority of the characteristics found on this list, but together they include them all. It is clear that bearded, white culture heroes and feathered-serpents are not unique to the Americas. Surveying these amazing parallels between Old and New World heroes brings an appreciation of how very similar ancient people have been all over the world. Given similar needs and similar resources, solutions are often similar in all countries.

Having concluded a review of the birth of the gods of Mesopotamia and their subsequent spread across Europe and Asia, a logical question is, did these mythological figures also work their way into the Americas in ancient times? Opinions differ, and diffusionists would say they did, brought across the seas by followers, or inspired and created in native minds by newly-arrived visitors. Isolationists, on the other hand, would maintain that if New-World heroes didn't come with the first immigrants across the Bering Straits, they would have evolved in a manner much like their counterparts in the Old World.

Still, most Pre-Columbian scholars in either camp consider the Toltec Topiltzin most likely a real, flesh-and-blood, historic king revered as a deity. But he borrowed his god-like traits from a more ancient hero, Quetzalcoatl . . . was that

Quetzalcoatl a real person? What of others like Kukulcan, Itzamná, Viracocha and Ioskeha? Were they real?

The next chapter moves to New World territory and its familiar heroes. Because America's heroes are not as well documented as those of Europe and Asia, light gathered from Old World mythology should dispel some shadows from that of the New World and help weave some meaningful conclusions into this complex tapestry.

14

THROUGH THE LOOM

The last chapter recalled myriad Old World myths and heroes who evolved and were revered since distant times. In reviewing these fanciful heroes, one does not expect to ever meet in the annals of history a real Osiris or Zeus or Dionysus or Tammuz: they were beloved allegories which served human needs. Should one, then, look for real persons in the culture heroes of the Americas? Many scholars would suggest not, that they too were allegorical inventions of the ancient imagination created to serve aboriginal needs.[1] They believe that as in the Old World, so in the New: to discover the mysterious bearded white visitor to the Americas before the Conquest, look to the Americas. They believe he came not from some distant land; he was the product of his own. He was always here.

Like Old-World peoples, New-World natives have for millenniums woven tales about their culture hero in rich supply and with great variety. But in this complex native weave, a number of familiar Old-World patterns emerge. Comparing them with New-World myths may help determine whether the Americas' heroes evolved in similar fashion, as isolationists insist, without foreign aid.

In Old-World fashion, the Americas' hero often descends from the sky gods, from old chiefs, or may simply just appear—usually from the east. He may assist the great creator or even be a creator himself—at times creating mankind from his own blood. He identifies with the sun, moon, Venus, vegetation, the elements, or a combination of these. In many tales he is born of a virgin. He may have offspring or be solitary, be an only son or, in some accounts, have a twin. He is always mysterious.

His inventive means of travel may include a ride on the rising sun, or the sea, or a descent from the heavens by a rope, a ladder, or a cosmic tree. He may arrive by wind, by rain, on a square-sailed ship, or (in North America) in a copper canoe. Then he disappears. Like the crops at harvest time, he may die. But he returns to life in the spring. Most tales have him enter the underworld and in many cases overcome that dreaded place to rise to the heavens as a god. Reminiscent of heroes of the Old World, he sometimes (like Quetzalcoatl) sneaks into heaven to steal life-giving food, fire, or light for mankind.

As an intelligent being he brings civilization and a higher, more spiritual way of life. He may be a messenger of peace or an antagonizing trickster capable of taking on strange forms. He may be a great lord or king. At times he walks the land or remains with the tribes. He may be youthful, or he may grow old and disappear daily with the setting sun. Upon death, he sometimes becomes the evening star, Venus.

In the Americas, the culture hero is usually of fair complexion, tall and bearded. He wears a long robe. The memory of him is held sacred, and followers build large cities and monuments to his honor; kings and priests claim descent and power from him. A future return is generally anticipated.

Earlier chapters considered a difussionist list of possible foreign visitors as candidates for the fair god. Now, the search examines the isolationist concept presented in the last chapter—that New World culture heroes, like those in Europe and Asia, originated not from bearded foreign visitors but from purely native sources.

A Different Breed

As in the Old World, New-World culture heroes seem to be different from mere commoners—no shipwrecked sailors washed up on the shore. They were revered and accepted as gods. In attempting to discern where and how such grand and mysterious figures originated, three possibilities will be considered:

1. They arrived in the New World, at least in concept, with the earliest immigrants across the Bering Straits, and from there spread into every part of the land.

2. As in Europe, similar heroes developed independently out of people's similar needs, ancient imaginations, and responses to overwhelming forces of nature.

3. They evolved from ancient local ancestors, tribal chiefs, kings, or gods. Ambitious aristocracies, aware of the stronghold of these legends upon the people, took full advantage of them and identified themselves with the heroes to obtain further power. Missionary efforts, trading, and conquests spread the legends.

New-World Heroes in Old-World Dress

Because tales of culture heroes exist all over the world and in every age, it would be strange indeed if the Spaniards had arrived upon American lands to discover none among its natives. But, as expected, they were here. Columbus encountered them and so did Cortez, Pizarro and others. It appears that every native tribe, village, and civilization had tales to tell, tales which go back to very remote times. The question is, how remote?

In the New World, as in the Old, scholars have presented numerous theories about the origins of myths and heroes. Some, like Brian Fagan (1987), would have them immigrate across the Bering Straits as early as 36,000 years ago, or as recently as 10,000, with one basic cultural and religious root which then branched into a variety of beliefs and cults all over the Americas. Others believe that each of three waves of immigrants brought a variety of traditions with it.[2]

In chapter 13, Old-World culture heroes and myths were shown to be obscurely connected with religion and gods. In the Americas, because so few records have been preserved, the attempt to separate myth from religion and heroes from gods grows even more difficult than in the Old World. However, the Americas of the Conquest had one great advantage over Europe and Asia: there were still-living examples of archaic periods and peoples much like those lost to the Old World in pre-historic times. What was later recorded about them and their mythological traditions demonstrates amply that in the basic elements explored in chapter 13, myths of North, Central, and South America have remarkable parallels. This causes many modern scholars to accept a common mythical origin for both American continents in remote times.

Initial influence may well have come very early from the Old World, for the first wanderers into the American continents no doubt brought with them intelligence, imagination and emotional responses to their environment and spiritual world in some tangible form. Scholars still debate the arrival time of those first immigrants, but recent finds in a cave near Orogrande, New Mexico, indicate at least 36,000 B.C.[3] As in Europe and Asia, America's earliest rock art, fertility figures, and paintings—none yet as dramatic nor as early as those at Lescaux and Altamira—indicate advanced, rather complex religion, magic, and involvement with a shaman. Shaman activities in South America today resemble very closely those in Alaska and Siberia, and recent discoveries in Chile place people there before 12,500 B.C.[4] High-quality copper objects were being created all over Northeastern America by a people who distributed their wealth and, no doubt, their beliefs and practices by 7500 B.C.

From modern-day discoveries it appears that paintings and carvings continued to spread among the peoples, and along with them, no doubt, religion and mythology. But the appearance of more familiar and clearly recognizable expressions in the Americas awaited the establishment of plant domestication and village life around 2500-1500 B.C., as they did in Mesopotamia centuries earlier. By 2,000 B.C. North American burials included copper, marine shells, jewelry and corpses covered with red ochre—strong indications of beliefs in the afterlife.[5] By that time, earliest Maya ceremonial centers were devoted to ritual, and it appears reasonable, although unproved, that the hero had already made his appearance.

The Nature of Heroes

If myths and heroes did not arrive in the Americas with the early hunters across the Bering Straits (consideration #1), they still could have evolved here later (consideration #2). Art and fragments of mythology left by the more advanced of early New World civilizations give ample support to the belief that myths and heroes developed here much like those of the Old World. Many of the same theories seem to apply, although insights from one culture do not always fully explain another. From the same human needs, ancestor worship, unexplainable forces of nature, and fertile imaginations, similar traditions could emerge.

Native tribes all over the Americas, no matter how remote and distant from other tribes, have their origin stories which involve a god, a hero, some mystical animal, or natural forces. With chapter 13 in mind, many of these tales resemble stories found throughout the ancient world (e.g., The gods Quetzalcoatl and Tezcatlipoca transform themselves into serpents and, like the Babylonian, Marduk, tear apart the threatening sky monster; from the two pieces they form heaven and earth).[6] In spite of the parallels with the Old World, these stories are often millenniums apart, with no known contact between the storytellers.

Like people along the Tigris and Nile rivers, American natives lived by an overwhelming variety of religious practices and mythologies which involved every aspect of their lives. As in Europe and Asia in earlier times, one finds here animal and monster effigies, human/animal depictions, and fabulous tales of men who become were-jaguars, thunderbirds, bird-serpents, or grasshopper-men. Serpents swallow the rivers, eagles bring the rains, and dogs lead you through the underworld. Believers dress in the skins of these animals and mimic their movements and sounds.

As in the Old World, myths of native America assert that everything has life and there is life in everything. Stones have spirits, plants have souls, and the winds and rains are to be reasoned with. Fire, lightning, floods, day, night— each is a god, and each has the power for good or evil. These early natives were not idle: they discovered their gods in the skies, on the mountains, in the deserts, in the waters, and under the earth. There is a god of fishing, a god of the hunt, a god of the harvest, a god or goddess of fertility, and a god over the gods. A living plant is presided over by one god, and the dead one by another. Like Old World gods who die so that plants can grow from their body, Pachacamac (Chapter 5), in South America, does the same. Cannibalism was sometimes practiced with this in mind. The dead are not really dead and through ritual can be approached: in South America, mummies were included in processions and social activities.

Celestial bodies inspired many New-World as well as Old-World myths: moon, sun, stars, earth, planets, and comets each have their roles and identities.

Everywhere in the Americas the sun is god , and most other gods demonstrate some aspect of the sun, which is usually male, with the moon as his consort. At times, however, they are enemies or even brothers. The sun in the Western Hemisphere, as in Egypt, may be the supreme god, or secondary to the omnipotent creator-god. Just as in the Old World, conflicts seen in the rising and setting of the sun and the waxing and waning of the moon find expression in mythological stories. Often these astral bodies take on human characteristics: the Aztec sun, Tonatiuh, sticks a tongue out of its human face, and the face of the Inca sun-god, Inti, peers out of a golden disc. Venus is seen as the son of the sun, and rulers are also called the "children of the sun."

From all of these ingredients emerge worship and possibilities for culture heroes to rise in a fashion similar to that of the Old World. People's needs and nature gradually evolve from native thought into human form and personality. In tribes far removed from one another, and with no apparent contact, traditions of heroes and myths appear nearly identical. Contradictions found in the myths of both Old and New Worlds can be explained in part by similar contradictions in nature (e.g. calm and violence, birth and death, light and dark), for any being born of nature's diverse aspects will abound in them.

Heroes on High

Once nature and man's imagination provide a culture hero, a variety of situations may follow (consideration #3). As in the Old World, it is possible that over time some of these traditions would become identified with actual persons of high rank or achievement within the tribe or village. The Algonquins of North America recalled that their great culture hero, Michabo, was a mighty hunter of old. As tribes later mingled or merged, so did their myths. Over-ambitious chiefs or rulers were not slow to see personal advantages in identifying with these extraordinary beings. Proclaiming descent from great culture heroes and demonstrating power over the elements through cleverly devised rituals and symbols insured loyalty and support from the believing subjects. Tribal support brought riches to the presiding family who did not labor for their living.

Kings, hungry for more control, identified with powerful heroes, and people eager for objects to worship elevated both king and hero to the position of gods, as is seen so graphically in the art of the Maya. Kings sometimes traced their lineage to beings who once were human, but who later became heroes who became kings who became gods. A clear example of this is Viracocha of Peru, said to have been a human who ascended to the highest pantheon. He was also first in a long line of later Inca kings who claimed descent from him. In Mexico, Topiltzin-Quetzalcoatl, the Toltec culture hero, also claimed authority from a distant king, and natives claimed Quetzalcoatl was the only one of their gods who once had a human body.

It is not known, exactly, when the more famous New World culture heroes became prominent and were identified with rulers, but this no doubt occurred among various cultures at various times. Clues come from the first advanced civilizations like the Chavín of South America (c.1500-400 B.C.) and the Olmec of Mesoamerica (c. 1200-300 B.C) who fixed the images of their mythical ancestors in stone. Their use of many of the same religious symbols which later cultures used to validate the king's descent from earlier ancestors and culture heroes suggests a long history of hero worship. At Chavín, elaborate temples with projecting stone heads and serpent-jaguar-eagle monsters probably represent ancient chiefs, rulers, or deities, as they did in later cultures. Ritualistic images indicate that the shaman, who is often related to gods and heroes, is present also.

The Olmecs, whose influence pervades all later Mesoamerican cultures, display large human heads and animal human being combinations as well as serpents, jaguars and birds that somehow relate to their ancestors, deities and heroes. Similarly, later cultures with Olmec influence identified eagles with the day sun, jaguars with the night, and both with the god or hero.[7] Huge stone altars with depictions of a jaguar-like creature emerging from a cave while holding a baby may graphically portray mythological stories about the race's origins. The question of the presence of an Olmec feathered-serpent, which would strongly indicate their belief in the culture hero, still has scholars in disagreement.

It is unfortunate that none of their myths are known now, for both Chavín and Olmec religions seem to be the foundations for most advanced New World cultures, even up to conquest times. According to Schele and Freidel, the Classic Maya remembered the Olmecs as "the great ancestral civilization" which developed "many of the symbols, the rituals, and the styles of artistic presentation that would be used by their successors for millenniums."[8] In Peru, no doubt, the Chavín served the same purpose. How much of all this they inherited from still earlier cultures, is not known.

Both the Olmec and Chavín undoubtedly had their heroes—they would be totally different from all other cultures on earth if they did not—but nothing of them is known. Lost with these obscure civilizations were undoubtedly valuable insights to the origins and myths about the Americas' mystery man.

Although these heroes could evolve anywhere with a remarkable degree of similarity, their wide distribution would certainly be assisted by cultural expansion. While powerful empires like the Aztecs and Incas, and great civilizations like the Maya, the Olmecs and Chavín traded goods, conquered lands, and subjugated people, they also implanted local beliefs. The creation of great monuments, temples, and other works of art dedicated to leaders who identified with the heroes, who, in turn, represented the gods, served to unite the people and to strengthen their devotion to these beings. Impressive works could also serve as powerful missionary tools, as did prolific art of the Counter-Reformation in Europe, to pull nonbelievers into the faith and to spread the word. In the Americas the big question is, what was the word?

In seeking origins for these mysterious figures it is obvious that the creation of culture heroes is a long and involved process. Three possibilities have been considered: (1) they arrived with the first immigrants, (2) they evolved from spiritual needs, universal elements, imagination, and (3) their legends were expanded by rulers to assure their positions and to control other fellow beings.

Now the search returns to where it began—with Quetzalcoatl—to see how the best documented of the Americas' bearded heroes fits these three categories. In light of what is now known about Old-World heroes, it will be shown that his general characteristics are quite universal. In him and his counterparts, Kukulcan and Gukumatz (chapter 3), one finds as well, the basics—but in greater detail—found in all the heroes of the Americas. And through him the others can be better comprehended.

Quetzalcoatl—Close Up

Chapter 3 examined a great native American, Topiltzin, believed to have lived among the Toltecs in the ninth century. Although he was a man of many accomplishments, the highest of high priests, one who identified with the beloved hero, Quetzalcoatl, he was not the original. He merely followed a centuries-old practice of borrowing traits from a more ancient source. Although chapter 3 pursued him through centuries of tradition and art, it is difficult to say when the original Quetzalcoatl/feathered-serpent hero first appeared. Was he once a great warrior, a hunter, or high priest? Did he once lead migrations down the Bering Straits, bringing traditions retained by descendents of those first colonizers? Did later generations, anxious to have a more powerful god, identify him with forces of nature and significant tribal gods, giving him further god-like status? Or was he brought by visiting foreigners from across the sea?

Early civilizations like the Chavín and the Olmecs possibly inherited him or similar heroes, then magnified their images and refined their symbols—serpents and eagles are rampant in the art of Chavín, and birds and serpents appear in Olmec stone carvings. Both have ceremonial sky bars. Later cultures must have also consolidated and enlarged the traditions, because by early Christian times Quetzalcoatl appears as the most elaborate of Mexico's feathered-serpent images grandly displayed on his temple at Teotihuacan (chapter 4). Myths and rituals surrounding this hero image were no doubt by that time equally as impressive as the monuments they inspired.

During Classic times (A.D. 250-900) in Mesoamerica, there seems to be an almost fanatic devotion to serpent visions, if not to feathers and serpents. If they in fact represent Quetzalcoatl, then he is one of the principal sources of large sculptured monuments, imposing structures, and other art containing depictions of rituals and symbols which establish royal connections with heroes and feathered serpents. This worship of a culture hero apparently culminated with Topiltzin Quetzalcoatl and the peak of civilization attributed to the Toltecs around A.D. 1000. By Aztec times, four-hundred years later, the influence of Quetzalcoatl was still present but waning, as other gods now demanded more attention. Because natives made no distinctions between the legends about Topiltzin and the more ancient Quetzalcoatl, neither can we.

Had Quetzalcoatl not arrived with immigrants across the Straits, or with visiting seamen, it is easy to imagine these myths born of natural phenomena. Many of the principal traits of Quetzalcoatl begin with the sun. The *Popol Vuh* says "The sun arose, like a man." "All the tribes worshiped the sun."[9] He comes from the east, youthful but bearded; he is god of the sunrise. The sun, as it is born in the east each day, sends forth rays of light—his beard. The hero's golden hair, which at other times is black, mirrors the sun, which is golden by day, but a shadow by night. He is fair of complexion, for he radiates the light of dawn. Like the sun, the hero travels extensively across the earth, filling every space with warmth and light. He makes things grow and gives life to the earth. He grows older as the day progresses. And by evening, as shadows lengthen, he becomes a white-haired, wise old man with a longer beard; then he dies.

As the sun plunges into the western ocean and enters the threatening underworld, so Quetzalcoatl, the "serpent-sun," follows and returns through the night to the east from whence he came. Both Quetzalcoatl and the sun fight life-challenging battles, and both, having won, are resurrected in the morning. In one version (chapter 3), Quetzalcoatl dies by fire and rises from the ashes as a bird which becomes the morning star, Venus, which also dies and is resurrected. Because Venus disappears in darkness for days at a time, so must Quetzalcoatl remain in the underworld for three or four days. The conflict between Quetzalcoatl and his dark opponent, Tezcatlipoca, represents the fight between the powers of light and darkness—the bright daytime sun versus the dark sun hidden at night—well being and dilemma, the daily human struggle.

As in the Old World, the New World daytime sun is seen as a bird flying across the sky. At night it becomes a serpent-creature of the underworld (the Milky Way). Or the bright Mexican sun may be seen as a feathered-serpent by day and a jaguar—a creature of the dark with stars as spots—by night. What Spaniards saw as a "Mexican Trinity" is easily explained: The sun is the father. He sends out light and warmth—his son. Nourishment and growth from these two are the mysterious gifts to mankind—seen as the spirit. The three then, the sun, the warmth, and the benefits form a "Trinity."

The sun is readily identified with serpents, vegetation, and the moon, which are all symbols of death and new birth. The hero is like the plants which die and are turned back into the earth. But the rains and warmth of the sun—aspects of the hero—bring them forth again stronger than before; therefore, he is a healer. Serpents emerge from the underworld, lay eggs—symbols of fertility, and renew their skins much like seedling plants. Like emerging serpents and daily risings of the sun, and like the "new moon," renewed life and resurrection are added to the hero's attributes. The sun descends nightly into the mouth of a serpent from which it also rises the next day, providing another symbol for Quetzalcoatl, the two-headed sky-serpent—symbol of authority and power.[10]

The letters A-T-L of Quetzalcoatl signify water or rain, and the first Quetzalcoatls were, according to Carrasco, "mythical serpent beings who symbolized the moisture and life produced by the new rains that poured after the long dry season."[11] Quetzalcoatl's mythical association with water and life connects him to many other natural phenomena as well. Since he presides over the waters he also becomes god of the winds that precede the coming rains. It follows that he must therefore come in from the sea on the winds or with the rains. Like wind and rain, he descends from the sky. And as the parched earth absorbs the welcomed waters into the underground, so Quetzalcoatl enters the underworld with the same purpose as the water, to bring forth new life.

While Quetzalcoatl the creator is in the underworld, he steals the bones of the dead and covers them with his blood, blood drawn from his penis—divine semen—so that mankind might come forth.[12] Later, priests drew their own blood in remembrance of his great gift. At night the sun turns red and gives its blood in order to sustain the world. Thus blood sacrifice was required of humans to replace that lost by the sun.

He will return. As the sun and the new moon return, as the night and the tides return, as the winds and the rains and Venus and the crops return, Quetzalcoatl will return. Because the natives saw in him the elements and forces of nature, his periodic return, like that in nature, was predictable and certain. Early in the development of the hero his daily arrival with the sun could have lengthened in some places to a yearly return with the crops. Fifty-two yearly returns became a native century (Quetzalcoatl was looked for every fifty-two years). Or, as he acquired more human traits, it could stretch into an indefinite expectation.

In their obsession for immortality, generations of kings identified with Quetzalcoatl, for like Osiris of Egypt he is king of kings. He descends from ancient legendary ancestor-kings, and as their proven successor, is crowned king by his people. He has dual parentage: his earthly father, Mixcoatl, was a king who, following death, became the patron of hunting. Quetzalcoatl's celestial parent, the sun, is also the royal deity over other celestial bodies. This dual parentage from earth and sky is not so unusual, for Earth and Sky were called "twins;" day and night are twins, and the name "Quetzalcoatl" is often translated as "precious twin." Crowns worn by royalty represented the rays of light from the celestial parent, the sun. This light, combined with truth, was also manifest in the arts of civilization which he brought the people. Where one culture hero introduces agriculture and another writing, the fusing of many heroes into one produces a culture hero who provides all benefits. He becomes, Carrasco points out, the "creator of life, ceremony, ceremonial structures, and social authority."[13]

Was Quetzalcoatl totally unique to the Mexican area, or was he the local adaptation of a basic myth found everywhere? Perhaps some of both, for similar and varying versions were found all over the Americas. The Hopi culture hero, Pahana, for example, not only parallels Quetzalcoatl in many ways, but was expected to return at the same time. This is not so strange since the Hopi believed their ancestors came anciently from Central America, the home of Quetzalcoatl.[14] If the legend did not come from an early common origin with sufficient time to filter into each tribe and village, the many similar tales could have evolved independently in various times and places from people's similar encounters with their similar worlds. Eventually, centuries of native traders, travelling missionaries, and migrations would have blended tribal myths just as they did in the Old World, filling gaps and making them even more alike.

It is easy to see in Quetzalcoatl a blending and lending of many traits found in neighboring heroes: Kukulcan, Gucumatz, Itzamná, Votan, and the Mayan Hero Twins of the *Popol Vuh*. Just how much borrowing and mixing took place over the millenniums is unknown, for according to Davies, changes came slowly. Conversely, Michael Coe believes that "great new advances were registered throughout the land within quite brief intervals of time."[15] Whether they moved fast or slowly, they combined with other influences which today are perhaps unknown, and fantastic tales about Quetzalcoatl and other like heroes were the result. Jacques Lafaye suggests that even into modern times, "historical memory and myth-making processes were woven together to make Quetzalcoatl a symbol for political and social legitimacy."[16]

An Old Friend—Almost

As one becomes more acquainted with world mythology, the American hero—at first mysterious and remote—now seems less so. Granted, he is still shrouded in mystery and will probably never reveal himself fully, but, at least, he has become approachable. Although the figure of the bearded white visitor to the Americas will always remain intriguingly elusive, one can begin to fathom in him that which once seemed unfathomable.

In having examined heroes and myths across the ocean, their New World cousins now can be accepted as old friends—not just from the introduction to them in previous chapters, but from having met their counterparts in distant lands. In both worlds, myths and heroes walked similar paths, played similar roles, and were likely born of similar ingredients. It has been shown that wherever culture heroes appear, they bear a strong family resemblance. This may be the result of some cultural sharing and intermingling, but it may also occur in isolation, the result of resemblances in the family—the human family.

This search has demonstrated that although they may have begun as bearded lords or kings or highly respected warriors of a tribe, American culture heroes ended up as mythological beings, a breed apart from the people who revered them. It is also believed that this process began very early in the history of the Americas, and that by the time higher civilizations like the Chavín and the Olmecs arrived, these heroes were probably fully established. This is not to say that later peoples and events did not add to them, for like the humans who served them, they were also subject to change. Over the centuries, monuments and rituals to them were created and enlarged upon, and no doubt some periods of native history gave them much more attention than others.

Bearded Visitors

Although the isolationist argument for emergence of New World heroes from native soil seems reasonable enough, still so many legends speak of "bearded visitors" from across the sea. Without conceding to diffusionism, even isolationists must be ready to ask, if foreigners (from overseas or other parts of the Americas) are conclusively shown to have infiltrated a culture, would they not be woven into the already existing fabric of legends? The process of confusing heroes with gods and with each other, and of intermixing both with humans and bearded visitors was well demonstrated by Topiltzin, leader of the Toltecs. Although his Mexica parentage was well known, he assumed divine characteristics and lineage from the earlier hero, Ehécatl Quetzalcoatl. Adding those familiar legends to his deeds increased his own importance. Like the Aztecs who changed Toltec history, Topiltzin did the same to make himself look good. It seems to be an ancient tradition: if your neighbor's culture hero looks better than your own, you simply borrow his superior traits.

It is easy to see how if a shipload of natives from say, Cuba, with an already established tradition of a culture hero, sailed into Mexican shores and somehow managed to establish a colony, the more dramatic exploits of their own culture hero would eventually merge with those of local legends. Years later, in the minds of natives who had no written records, this colony would have been said to be the beginning of their civilization, brought in remote times from across the seas by a revered culture hero. In this case, the hero tradition would include a whole company of foreigners.

Such a situation occurred in Mexico, where Topiltzin Quetzalcoatl, "the feathered serpent," leaves the shores near Veracruz with his bearded followers, and although it was previously clear that he was born on the Aztec mainland we are now told that he returned to the place he came from, "across the seas."

Shortly after the departure of Topiltzin Quetzalcoatl from Mexico a great hero, Kukulcan, also a " feathered serpent," arrives in Yucatan with his bearded followers from "across the seas." The contradiction appears to be a fusion of two stories: Topiltzin comes from Mexico, and the more ancient Quetzalcoatl comes from Yucatan, across the gulf. As Topiltzin Quetzalcoatl he does both. The departure from one area and the arrival at another, then, could be aspects of the same event, and those legends would then be speaking of the same person.

"Across the seas" could simply mean "across the gulf." (Any ship sailing down the coast, beyond the horizon, and then heading toward the shore would appear to be coming from "across the sea.") Arriving in Yucatan, Topiltzin would not have created for the Mayas a brand new myth about a "bearded hero," but would merely have added colorful details to an already established one. Similar migrations may have occurred elsewhere, contributing to other bearded-foreigner stories all over the Americas as well, for the Maya apparently had cultural exchanges with Mexico, and Mexico appears to have had limited contact with North and South America.

Previous chapters have considered intriguing possibilities of intruding Romans, Greeks, Phoenicians and others who may have contributed to the stories of bearded visitors. Although these possibilities are admittedly gaining some acceptance with scholars, foreigners need not have arrived from distant lands to inspire hero stories. As already seen, the hero's coming from across the sea could have already been established from events like the daily movements of the sun. His beard could evolve from the shining rays. Even so, beards were not especially foreign to native Americans, for contrary to popular belief, Aztec priests reportedly wore full beards, and Montezuma had a sparse one. Tozzer says that native children burned their faces to avoid bearded growth, but when they did grow them some had good ones, although like horse hair. Even today, some natives grow beards. Whether these are natural to them or a result of cross-breeding is difficult to say.

The big question today does not seem to be: did foreigners get to the Americas, for evidence is mounting (recent discoveries indicate a later introduction of the non-Asian blood-type B over the earlier Asiatic type O of many Indians),[17] but, what would foreigners contribute to the American way of life? If they arrived, what of them would get blended into existing myths? What of Romans, Greeks, Orientals, Phoenicians, or Israelites would become an enduring part of native tradition? Scholars are continually working on this question, and answers vary.

The only documented cases of foreign visitations are those of the Vikings and the Spanish. But, Vikings who colonized Greenland and even Northern America for centuries never made it into native legends. Only recently, with artifacts to support their brief records (and granted there may be other records still unknown), has it been possible to prove they were ever here. Any other foreigners are dated with even less-accepted evidence, and there is no more guarantee of their influence upon native cultures and legends than for the Vikings.

If Spaniards had returned to Spain after 27 years of cruising the American coasts without conquering, what of their visit would have remained in Indian legend? Perhaps there would have been rumors of square-sailed ships, perhaps a few unimpressive artifacts ceremoniously buried by natives, tales of bearded men with thunder and lightning in their hands—little the myths didn't already have.

When Juan de Oñate penetrated New Mexico in 1596, the Cibolan Indians had already forgotten the Coronado expedition of 1540. Fathers Crespi and Junipero Serra, in preparing to set up a chain of missions along the California coast in 1769, found the Indians so impressed and fearful of Spaniards what they thought they were gods. Yet, among them there was no native memory of Cabrillo's 1542 voyage or of the landing of Sir Francis Drake in 1579.[18] Again, it seems that the mere presence of bearded white men among natives, however impressive, does not in itself create lasting heroes. It can also be concluded, conversely, that the absence of records does not necessarily prove the absence of visitors.

Many writers have suggested that the success of the Spaniards was not so much due to being white and bearded as to being equipped with horses and guns. These were admittedly a great advantage and quickly demonstrated to the Indians a superior power. Without them, the Spaniards and any other foreign visitors would probably not have survived. Examples in which some did not survive include Schoolcraft's telling of a tale among the Iroquois of a vessel landing on their southern Atlantic shores in pre-Columbian times. The floundering crew was temporarily saved by the natives, only to be killed later and eaten. In Yucatan one of the early Spanish vessels wrecked on the Maya coast, and except for two of the men who joined with the natives and became like them in nudity and speech, all others were killed, and some devoured.[19]

If superstitious Indians, already anxious about gods from across the seas and eager for sacrificial subjects, received any sailing party with hostility, travel-worn sailors with depleted supplies and no fire-arms would hardly be a match for the Indians on their own territory. If earlier visitors to these shores received cannibalistic treatment similar to that previously mentioned, then the only changes Europeans would bring the native Americans would be in their diets. On the other hand, early English settlers at Jamestown and Plymouth most likely survived because of the generous hospitality and wilderness knowledge of the Algonquian-speaking Indian tribes who saw in them not gods, but people in need of assistance.

Oceans of Hazards

The strongest arguments against Europeans and Asians visiting the Americas are the overwhelming obstacles presented by the tempestuous oceans themselves. Anyone who has crossed either of the great bodies of water knows the difficulties even today. Why would anyone brave unknown and treacherous waters for weeks and months without instruments, maps, known destinations or adequate supplies? And who would finance such an insane journey to nowhere, and why? That they were blown off course seems the most likely answer (since 1600, over sixty voyages adrift to American shores have been reported—some with survivors). In the past, a few sailors or fishermen might have explored past the straits and down the lengthy American coasts—which would be a distance equal to crossing the sea, but with land in sight. Because the oldest known Amerind cultures are found in South America, archaeologists believe they may have gotten there not by land but by boat down the coast. Still, over the millenniums the incidents would be few, and sailors and fishermen seldom carry with them the great advances of civilization, an absolute requirement for culture heroes.

Most writers on this puzzle note the additional problems of getting back, for winds and currents are deceptive. If some did make it both ways, why did they not record it or at least return with some evidence such as artifacts, codices, maize, potatoes, tobacco, a few natives, and exciting tales—all highly marketable items? (There have been unconfirmed reports of tobacco found among mummified Pharaohs.) Why, if the oceans were so readily crossed, do the records of Europe and Asia not speak of a reverse situation where ships full of native Americans came across the seas to the Old World? If they did, why didn't people there add them to their hero myths? The questions continue.

Earlier chapters considered a number of Old-World civilizations which could possibly have provided a New-World culture hero. The past two chapters suggested that instead of looking to Old-World myths and peoples, many scholars believe that all myths can just as easily be seen as a "pattern" witnessed in cultures throughout the world.[20] No doubt myths of both hemispheres have come down distorted and changed, but in them lies universality. Those who recorded them may have recreated them to suit some purpose now lost, and original versions may have dimmed with time, but the basics still remain. Tempting as it might be to attribute the remarkable parallels between Old- and New-World mythology as proof of pre-Columbian contact, isolationist scholars would insist that they merely validate the similarity of the races. Look "not to ancient migrations" for similarities in myth, said Brinton, "but to great events of nature. . . ."[20]

However, just as there are unresolved aspects to all culture heroes, there still remain many perplexing differences and intriguing parallels between the Old World and the New not fully explained by either universality, or by a totally isolated native America. That myths from both hemispheres contain worldwide elements of truth is obvious, yet no proposed solution to this absorbing coincidence is sufficiently satisfying to assume that all answers are in and the mystery totally solved.

Too many New-World myths speak of bearded foreigners from across the seas for one to dismiss them all as mere products of nature, imagination, or psychic unity. Natives said that the hero would return "some day," not "every day," or "seasonally," as the sun, Venus, crops, and Old World vegetation gods do. The Aztecs had awaited Quetzalcoatl for five centuries, and even predicted the years for his return. The Inca had expected the return of Viracocha for over fifteen centuries. Would that not indicate specific beings? If culture heroes are merely personifications of the sun, why do so many of them return toward the East instead of continuing West with the setting sun? And how do traditions of a whole colony of bearded visitors come from the daily rising and setting of one sun? The questions haunt, and previous considerations cannot yet be eliminated.

The next, and last, chapter will review the multicolored threads thus far worked through the vast loom of mythological intrigue. In the search for a bearded visitor to the Americas in ancient times, many compelling images have emerged, and an attempt will be made to bring them all into focus.

15

THE FINAL FABRIC

Guatemalan Weavers

Anyone who has watched a weaver at work marvels at the patience required to insert countless strands, one at a time. Each carefully placed thread seems to add very little to the all-over design, but upon returning weeks or months later, one sees the finished work—a complex meshing of delicate fibers creating a rich tapestry. In the obscure looms of time, native Americans have woven fascinating legends about a fair bearded visitor—a culture hero or god—who with his symbol of a feathered serpent, reportedly walked the Americas long before Columbus. Past chapters have reported many quests to discover who this mystery man might be, and in so doing have followed thin threads of evidence through the annals of history.

The potential candidates have been impressive: Vikings, Welsh, Celts, Orientals, Romans, Greeks, Atlanteans, Egyptians, Phoenicians, and Israelites. Also considered was a possible visit by Jesus Christ or one of his Apostles.

To keep the perspective balanced, the previous two chapters (13 and 14) followed an idea commonly accepted among isolationist scholars that heroes of the world usually are of purely native origins, born of universal elements, human needs, enlarged egos, and forces at work.

Every proposal has been tantalizing and persuasive, but never quite conclusive. Arguments have been given for and against each theory, allowing the reader to draw conclusions, while at the same time increasing the chance for bewilderment. Still, somewhere in this web there must be a recognizable pattern, a satisfactory answer to the questions, who was the fair, bearded god and culture hero of the Americas, and where did he come from?

The great challenges facing anyone trying to fathom this complex tapestry are bewildering. There are too many visitors, they appear in too many locations, and they arrive over too many periods of time too long ago. Legends speak of one visitor or a whole company. Compounding the stories, the visitors come from the East or they come from the West—from the sea or the sky. They arrive about the time of Christ or they arrive earlier . . . or later. They may be kings, priests, great men or gods. They are bearded or they are not. Their hair may be light or it is dark. Following their arrival, they stay for years or they depart suddenly. They will someday return or they won't. They promise life eternal or they don't. Can any sense be made out of all these contradictions?

In the absence of sufficient historical data, we may never fully comprehend the final intricate design that has taken millennia to weave, but an attempt can be made. Like creating a tapestry, the best chance of weaving or of unravelling is to deal with one strand at a time. And when the picture is completed it should be clearer, and much of the mystery should be resolved.

Of Bearded Visitors and Culture Heroes

As observed earlier, America's early immigration laws were quite relaxed for anyone seeking to fill the position of "visiting bearded stranger from across the sea." One needed only to be a foreigner—preferably white—wear a beard and white robe—both preferably long—and in most cases, agree not to stay around too long. The applicant could arrive alone or in company with others. Nationality was no issue, and his place of appearance could be anywhere in the Western Hemisphere.

The position of culture hero, on the other hand, was far more demanding. Like the visitors, the culture hero had to be bearded and fair and could come from East or West—preferably West. He must demonstrate a highly cultured mind—far above those he visits, and be proficient in all languages—from Alaska to South

America. But if he is a god he must also possess mystical powers—miracle workers were given preference. His character must be impeccable—god-like, with charm and charismatic leadership, able to establish new traditions and gain followers everywhere. He must control power over life and death—for himself and others, but with a gentle approach—teaching love and peace. Finally, he must be willing to return someday—even centuries later. Commoners need not apply!

Whoever the mysterious hero was, it can safely be concluded that he was not a typical blanket-selling, pot-making, incense-burning Indian. Neither was he a commonplace fisherman, marooned sailor, nor the usual invading and conquering explorer—he was not just any white, bearded stranger. He also was not the typical king, priest, shaman or warrior. No, the American hero was far from common. He exceeds all abilities of humans, and it seems logical that no unheralded appearance of a mere Roman, Greek, or Phoenician upon native shores would infiltrate every native village inspiring stories of such grandiose events and attributes as those reported about the culture hero. Besides, how could one mortal visit all the locations in North, Central and South America, and appear in the many time-periods that culture heroes and bearded foreigners have reportedly visited? Herein lies a fundamental clue for discovering his origin and identity.

Another challenge to understanding the hero is that myths about him do not agree on details. Not all visitors to the Americas bring culture, not all provide miraculous events, not all arrive from the sea nor infiltrate the land and lifestyle, and not all promise to return. These seeming inconsistencies, among other reasons, may arise from the misleading assumption that the many different legends in diverse locations apply to only one person. From the sheer number of heroes, god-like attributes, locations, and time-periods found in the Americas, it would seem that the mysterious visitor is more than a human being, and that he may be more than one individual or Being. How can all of this be sorted out?

In order to work through this complex mythological mesh, it seems necessary to separate native stories into at least two distinct categories: (1) bearded visitors, and (2) culture heroes. Although most legends report that the culture heroes in the Americas were bearded visitors, it appears that not all the bearded visitors were culture heroes. Certainly the Spaniards were not, and as far as present evidence indicates, neither were the Vikings. Many legends, as has been seen, speak of bearded foreigners on the coasts of Florida, Mexico, and Peru who did not end up in the pantheon of heroes.

Even though the Aztecs and Inca, anxious to personify their ancient legends, at first accepted the Spaniards as divine, they quickly discerned that they were not gods and wished them gone. The Spaniards did not create in the native mind the concept of deity; the gods the Spaniards were at first thought to be were already fully established in the land, as evidenced by endless native representations in art and legend. With all the wonders they brought from Europe, The Spaniards did not maintain native esteem for long, demonstrating again that the mere appearance of bearded white men does not alone create culture heroes nor fair gods.

Although invading Spaniards, with their guns, armor, horses and canons would have been far more persuasive than Greeks, Egyptians or Romans, they still added but little to the hero legends, which indicates that the natives anciently were hesitant to accepted just any foreigners as gods. This strengthens the three propositions previously considered: (1) that culture heroes may have arrived, at least in concept, over the Bering Straits, and from there to all parts of the land; (2) that the culture heroes may have developed independently out of people's needs, imaginations, and responses to nature's forces; (3) and that the culture heroes may have evolved from ancient ancestors, tribal chiefs, kings, or divinities whose legends expanded greatly over time, and whose missionaries spread the word.

Each of these suggestions—and there may be others—seems logical, and from such a remote distance in time, hard to refute. Even more tenable is a gradual fusion or combining over the centuries of these three. In support of these conclusions, Isolationists might argue that the greatest of all myths about the Americas is one that has the natives sitting around idly for millenniums waiting for outsiders to bring them their myths: Ancient American mythology did not, they would assert, begin with European discovery nor with occasional foreign encounters. Native art indicates mythology and heroes were in America before many Europeans or Asians had fully developed their own. This argument is admittedly strong, and appears to be an inevitable and unavoidable part of the final answer. But not all!

Isolationist or Diffusionist?

Even though bearded Spaniards were discovered not to be gods, and even though they left no hero legends, the fact that they were initially accepted as gods seems to indicate that sometime in the past, other bearded visitors may have influenced already existing native legends. If, over the millennia, following the first migrations across the Bering Straits, culture heroes evolved and fused and spread all over the Americas, as happened in Europe, then would not any new tales or acts by alleged later immigrants or bearded visitors—whether by the Straits, or by the oceans—be woven over time into the already existing fabric of legends and myths? To allow the possibility of occasional foreign visits would not change the basics, but might account for diversity of detail and timing that appear in otherwise similar tales.

Isolationists correctly point out that diffusionists have often been too liberal in their identification of so-called evidence for trans-oceanic infusion, and that substantial proof of contact is needed. But to make an absolute pronouncement that between entrance from the time of the Bering Straits to arrival of the Vikings no foreigner *ever* came to the Americas, seems unrealistically limiting: there are too many problems not answered by isolation, and too many indications—even if inconclusively proved—to the contrary. To maintain the unwavering isolationist position that no one ever came to these shores, one would have to overturn every stone and examine every inch of native soil.

The diffusionist, on the other hand, need only search until such evidence is found. Fortunately, many isolationists are loosening up and admitting that evidence shows some contacts may have been made. Diffusionists, at the same time, are beginning to tighten up their approach and to become more cautious and demanding with what they consider evidence. It is hoped that someday soon both might put pre-determined theories aside and work together to get to the real story.

In the final search for answers, we have separated native legends into two categories: culture heroes and bearded visitors. Culture heroes, it is strongly suggested, were already in the Americas and evolving from very remote times. Bearded visitors in the form of Romans, Greeks, or Egyptians, as the gold-encased mummy allegedly lying in a stone sarcophagus in Burrows' mystery cave may yet demonstrate, may have added later to the process of local hero evolution. The door to bearded visitors is open to new evidence, but until more is known, and although they were fascinating to study, we must at present dismiss most of them as culture heroes or gods . . . with one exception!

A Reconsideration

Because he was from a distant land, believed to be bearded and to possess the attributes of a culture hero *and* a god, we must reconsider once more one of our proposed visitors, the only one who filled every requirement—Jesus Christ.

Bestowed with divine qualities and mystical powers, the miraculous appearance of Christ in the Americas would have had quite a different effect upon the natives than that of other supposed visitors. We need not consider speculative visits by his Apostles from Israel, for as human beings they would no doubt have suffered similar difficulties from hostile natives as other foreigners. But with an appearance from the sky of the resurrected Christ in great light and majesty to an astonished people, followed by a ministry among them with miracles and gentle teachings such as those recorded in the New Testament, we can envision newly won disciples in the New World eagerly spreading the word to their own people.

What would a visit from Jesus Christ do for the already existing legend of a culture hero? Strengthen it. What would it do for the rulers? Validate them. What would it do for Christ? Expand his mission.

A heavenly visitation from the resurrected Christ would prove the death and rebirth (apotheosis) native kings had promised their people. Except for some details, the already-ancient legend of a fair god from across the sea would change very little; it would simply blend in with the memorable events surrounding

Christ's visit. Not only would incidents during his stay enrich the hero legends, but after his departure, stories would continue to grow and be added. This is the only proposal, out of all the possibilities considered thus far, that fits both bearded visitor and divine culture hero. It allows native culture heroes, bearded visitors, and Jesus Christ to influence one another and yet to exist independently.

If Christ and his New-World disciples preached his doctrine here, some natives would accept it and others, of course, would not. As in the Old World, many would not even hear it. Such a division would help explain later conflicts in the Indian religion over two deeply divergent philosophies, one requiring human sacrifices and the other forbidding them.[1] The unique majesty and power of Christ would also explain why later kings and priests continued to identify with him. Christ in the flesh would explain the native belief that Quetzalcoatl was the only one of their gods who ever possessed a body. Such an appearance would answer a host of other questions about the remarkable similarities Spanish writers claimed to have observed between the Indian traditions and Christianity. Most of all, the mystery of the illustrious bearded visitor from across the sea would at last be resolved.

As was seen in chapter 11, some ten million members of The Church of Jesus Christ of Latter-day Saints (Mormons) accept the visitation of Christ to the Americas as recorded in their *Book of Mormon*. They believe that following his resurrection in Israel he appeared to native Americans in a shaft of light, walked among the people, and performed miracles. He taught the natives the basic tenets of Christianity found in the New Testament, blessed them, requested that they record his visit, and left disciples to spread the word. For Mormons, this is an unquestioned fact, and a seemingly fitting conclusion to the search for a fair god from across the sea.

It would be comforting to stop here and declare the search over: look no further, the fair bearded god has been found! But, as so often has happened in the unravelling or weaving of this complex fabric, final solutions seldom come easily: there is always another point of view. Not only would the visit of Christ answer many questions, it would raise several more.

Some Demanding Questions

For the believer, nothing more is needed: Christ is the answer. But for others, and for general acceptance that Christ came to the Americas, several difficulties would have to be resolved. First, for the non-Christian, and there are billions, it must reasonably be established that Christ was divine and capable of the great miracles and events attributed to America's mysterious visitor. Some scholars—even Christian ones—insist that Christ was a great teacher, but that his "divine nature" was invented by his followers. The same scholars believe that Christ's expected "return" was also added later by believers who edited and selected that which has come down as scripture.[2] If

Christ did not promise to return to the Old World, then why suggest a similar promise for the New World? If he did, then New World expectations strengthen that promise. As for trying to establish what Christ would have taught in the New World, the existence of thousands of divergent Christian churches and sects today is a witness that even Christians could not totally agree upon that.

Next, one must ask, where in the New World would Christ have appeared? North America, Mexico, Yucatan, Peru? Mormons, who firmly attest to his visit, claim it was in the "land Bountiful," but where is that? No ancient American city has yet provided tangible evidence of such a visit, and Mormon archaeologists have so far been unable to specifically locate even Zarahemla, the key city of their *Book of Mormon*. However, there are several compelling theories.

What guarantees that Christianity would be accepted here any better than it was in the first few centuries of Europe, where it proceeded cautiously under the menacing shadow of persecution and pagan cults? It took the fourth-century Roman Emperor, Constantine, to bring Christianity into the light when he proclaimed religious freedom, sponsored Christianity, and made it possible for that faith to become the state religion—a needed boost. Where in the New World is a Constantine?[3]

The *Book of Mormon* records the majestic visit of Christ in only one location—the land Bountiful. But native legends all over the Americas say the hero visited them personally, lived with them, and, in some cases, died with them. In life, Christ limited his ministry to the small country of Palestine, and after death, he reappeared as a resurrected being for forty days only there, and finally ascended to heaven in majesty above the hills of Jerusalem. Why would Christ appear in more than one location in the Americas? A commission by Christ in the Americas for followers to spread the word might account for bearded visitors and fair gods in many other places, but unless all natives everywhere were converted, what would keep them from destroying those disciples? In Europe it took centuries to spread the message, and many nations never accepted. Would it be different in the Western Hemisphere?

If Christ descended in a cloud of light, bringing culture and the arts to each village, as natives claim of their culture hero, why did civilization in the Americas not develop equally everywhere? Why did it become so highly complex only in Mexico, Yucatan and Peru? An even more penetrating question is, If Christ is the hero, who would have brought the advanced culture natives attributed to the hero? Jesus of Nazareth did not build pyramids or temples, nor did he provide science, arts, agriculture, language and other refinements of civilization for the Old World; why would he for the New? Besides, most of the refinements seen in the arts and technology of New World cultures existed long before the Christian era.

Anyone attempting to establish that Christ visited the Americas must be prepared for other demanding questions. Indian legends say the hero came from the east across the sea (as the sun rises in the east so the hero arrives from the east). But natives observing a sudden radiant appearance of Christ in the sky high above them would not know what direction he came from. And why would a God over all things, with power to appear and disappear, need to cross an ocean? Especially in a copper canoe.

Legends often do not make it clear whether their hero was a white-bearded man or a bearded, white man. White beards represent age, and "white" can also refer to a glowing countenance, not skin color. To many Indian tribes, the word "white" referred to the coming light of dawn with which Quetzalcoatl and other heroes were identified.[4] Quetzalcoatl was associated with death, also the color white. Nowhere does the Bible say that Jesus was fair-skinned or blond, or that he had long hair. Even among his own tribe, Judah, there were dark-haired, dark-skinned people. And the bible doesn't even tell if he was bearded. The custom of the Roman world at the time of early Christianity—including Palestine—was for men to have short hair and be clean-shaven. Not until the emperor Hadrian, much later, did beards regain popularity.[5] What would a clean-shaven Christ contribute to the image of America's bearded hero?

One might argue, if Christ did not come here, how does one explain the religious use by New World natives of vestments, the cross, chants, rituals, incense, ceremonial objects, infant baptism, and great works of religious art: statues and paintings, also identified with Christianity?[6] Clearly, all of these were recorded by Spaniards to be found among native Americans, and seemingly point to Christian influence. Yet, surprisingly, none of these objects was used in the Old World by Christians until centuries after Christ's death when they were added by pagan converts anxious to dress up the rather plain Christian services. If Christianity in its pure state came to the Americas and gradually grew pretentious under pagan pressure, as it did in Europe, then were Spaniards who saw "Christian traits " in the natives centuries later merely judging them by similar pagan adornments that were now standard practices in their own religion? If true, that would be one of the great ironies of history.

More perplexing yet, many native practices and depictions surrounding the best known of America's heroes, Quetzalcoatl, seem to have nothing in common with Christianity. Some native statues showed the hero as being not fair-skinned and bearded at all, but black, with an ugly face spattered with blood.[7] Others were painted black and yellow, with protruding lips like a duck. In some stories he becomes drunk and performs sexual acts. Legend depicts him as a twin, or sometimes with offspring. Some say he was "very old."

Quetzalcoatl was said to have a virgin mother, Coatlicue, but her hideous, two-serpent-headed statue is covered with other serpents and dismembered human hearts and hands. No more powerfully repulsive relic remains from Aztec times (a "nightmare in stone," Griffin calls her).[8] But to accept Quetzalcoatl as Christ, would one then have to consider his loathsome mother, Coatlicue, as a representation of the Virgin Mary? (See page 237.) That would be a real test of faith. And if Christ is the original culture hero, where did all the feathered serpents that long preceded him come from? They do not appear on Old-World cathedrals or statues, why are they so prevalent in the Americas? If they truly represent Christ, how does one explain their New-World existence long before the advent of Christianity, and what would they have meant?

Then there are the grisly Indian traditions and practices which are totally unrelated to Christianity, yet identified at one time or another with the culture heroes: ritual piercing of the tongue and penis, ceremonial head chopping, the use of drugs in ritual enemas, the sacrificing of babies and enemies, the tearing out of human hearts, eating the victim's corpse, reading of the future in entrails and nasal discharges, burning the dead corpse, and burying live slaves and members of the family at the death of a god/king. Would Christ introduce these, or were they merely vestiges of an ancient religion he came to replace?

Perhaps, for these pagan practices, so abhorred by the Spanish, continue back in an unbroken chain to remote times, while at the same time at least one other milder religious tradition runs concurrently—as today the modern and the Maya still exist together. Of course, the presence of such pagan practices does not negate the arrival of Christianity, for as has been seen, Europe also failed to avoid them. The atrocities of Old-World Inquisitions, holy wars, burnings at the stake, indulgences, Crusades, Conquests, and modern-day fund raisers, religious T.V. scandals, and much of Christmas have little to do with Christ's ministry. Similarly, it might be argued that corruptions and apostasy may have plagued an early church in the Americas as well.

In explaining the similarities between Christ and the culture heroes, some people feel that God implanted in mankind from the beginning a desire for the divine and the curiosity to seek it. They would argue that he then instilled a need in people of every time and place for a Savior, and for all civilizations to respond to that need in various ways. In the universal rise of culture heroes they would see a response—albeit distorted—to that need. Christ's mission, as many see it, is to all people everywhere, and those same people believe that "Satan," in order to frustrate the plan, introduced duplication and deception.

Christ, as millions accept him today, is not seen as a myth. Similarly, Christ's chief apostle, Peter, said, "We have not followed cunningly devised fables, when we made known unto you the power and coming of our Lord Jesus Christ, but were eyewitnesses of his majesty" (2 Peter 1:16). Culture heroes, according to this reasoning, could be merely misleading copies or prototypes of the Christ to come. These beliefs, for those who accept them, would help explain the many similarities in world myths and culture heroes as well as the differences. For those who do not accept them, they are simply more myths to consider.

So, what can one conclude about Christ in the Americas? It might first be asked, what can one conclude about Christ in Israel? Great changes in history and in the lives of people, a dramatic chain of events, and later imposing monuments of art and architecture—all connected with the life of Christ—proclaim that something extraordinary happened in Israel. Admittedly, the same might be said of ancient America.

History is replete with problems, and no person can resolve them all. Not all answers come through reason, and there's little progress if one always awaits final solutions. In believing that Christ came to the Americas, Latter-day Saints rely instead upon a promise at the end of the *Book of Mormon* made by one of its ancient native authors and prophets, Moroni, that those who read the book and ask with "faith" and a "sincere heart " will receive a witness that it is true.[9] Skip the questions, a "Mormon" might advise you, and just apply Moroni's promise. Millions claim to have tried it, and millions testify that it works.

In considering a visit to the Americas by Jesus Christ, what seemed to be the solution now becomes the question—a complex question that only individuals can answer. That a culture hero (or heroes) "walked" the Americas is a matter of record; that Christ walked the Americas is a matter of faith.

Distorted Legends

Before winding up this complex weaving, one more consideration must be presented. Although belief in a visit from Christ to the Americas is left up to individuals, European scribes upon their arrival in the Americas recorded so many parallels between native American and sixteenth-century European traditions, Old World civilizations and Christianity—why do all the amazing similarities exist?

At first glance, the New-World native legends and traditions recorded by early Europeans do appear strikingly similar to those of the Old. But it must be admitted that in collecting and retelling their surviving legends native scribes—both pre-Conquest and post-Conquest—as well as Spanish chroniclers—sometimes poorly understood, distorted, and edited what they heard. Cortez noted profound differences in thought and practice, and Wenke suggests that some native views of life and the world were "unlike the Spanish who first met them, and probably from any of the other Western European traditions."[10] Similarities revealed in this search were recorded by over-zealous scribes who sometimes edited out differences and magnified similarities. Wenke and others have expressed the opinion that Europeans of this era "were among the greatest egotists and ethnocentrists the world has known."[11]

Believing Europe to be the geographical and cultural center of the world and Christian thought to be the ultimate truth, some sixteenth-century Christians were uneasy at discovering a new people in a land not mentioned in the Bible, and were anxious to fit them into the Biblical lineage. Nicholson reports that some early

writers "repeatedly revised, reorganized, embellished, cut, even consciously distorted," Indian traditions.[12] Brinton, writing of the same distortions, claims that
early works on native religions included mistranslations and inaccurate interpretations of native words because of preconceptions and "habits of thought" of some
early missionaries. He says, "Writers, anxious to discover Jewish or Christian
analogies, forcibly construed myths to suit their pet theories."[13] John Carroll, in
Search For Quetzalcoatl, says, "Copyists were also editors, and from generation
to generation textual changes occurred."[14] Thus, what was learned about America's
natives was sometimes done by observing them through "Western" (European)
glasses. Unfortunately, some Indians trained in "Western" ways and anxious to
please the foreigners occasionally wore the same "glasses" in reporting their history, giving the questioners what they wanted to hear.

　　Non-native scribes sometimes put their findings into a style familiar to
Europeans. Chroniclers, according to Davies, even added Biblical touches.
"Accounts of how Viracocha healed the sick and gave sight to the blind," he says,
"read exactly as if they had been taken from the New Testament."[15] He further
adds that tales of fair gods were literally "whitewashed" and seemed to bear the
stamp, "Made in Spain." Some of those stories, having been transposed into a language and tradition more comprehensible to a European reader not versed in
Indian lore, if translated directly back into their original language, would probably
be incomprehensible to the native storyteller.[16]

　　Because of European hostility toward native ways and abysmal ignorance of
ancient world mythology, much of the unique strangeness of these cultures was
eventually edited out. Had the first writers just recorded what natives told them
without interpreting for the European reader, and without presenting leading questions, they might have discovered that the native environment was, as Eliade puts
it, "radically different from that of the West."[17]

　　How then does one explain such close similarities between Christ and culture
heroes on the lists found in chapters 12 and 13? Simple. The lists are close because
they were selected with closeness in mind. Items used are authentic, but only parallel items were listed; what didn't fit was disregarded. Spaniards—and natives
anxious to counter the accusation that their religion was pagan—sometimes chose
to record only what they found similar.[18] Granted, there are many Christian-like
elements in the basics of New World mythology to choose from, but history will
forever ask: did the early Spaniards find them there, or put them there? That question cannot be answered fully, but if one considers the broader picture, and especially the unique details of American and European myths, there is much in practice that is not parallel at all.

　　An example of this confusion comes from a Peruvian chronicler, Cieza de
Leon, who upon hearing that a statue of Viracocha closely resembled a Christian

saint, went to see the figure for himself. He concluded that "only a blind man could believe that it bore any relationship to one of Jesus' apostles."[19]

The belief that Indian gods resembled Christ could be partly due to European misinterpretation as well. Father Lalemant among the Huron Indians in 1640 tells of the alleged appearance to one of the local Indians of the beautiful, imposing Huron god Ioskeha, whose message was, "The French wrongly call me Jesus, because they do not know me."[20] Brinton reports that several writers who had lived with American natives for up to eighteen years insisted that the idea among natives of a devil, hell, or One God, was totally unknown among natives until implanted by European missionaries.[21]

Pointing to similarities as proof of contact fails when farms, families, homes, roads, devotions, temples, priests, art, royalty, kingdoms, wars and power struggles show evidence of the basic sameness of mankind. At the same time, togas, armor, leiderhosen, sombreros, and feathered headdresses point to superficial differences. One might ask, If Old-World visitors had as much influence on New-World natives as diffusionists claim, why don't they look more alike?

As well as differences between Christ and American heroes, there are basic dissimilarities between American heroes and those of Europe and Asia also. One example should do. In chapter 13, the Greek hero Dionysus appears much like the American culture hero or even like Christ. Although he first appears as a god of wine, he evolves into a god of vegetation and moisture; he afterwards becomes a god of pleasures and civilization, and finally he's regarded as a kind of supreme god. But consider his other traits left off the list and found in most tales about him: he has a wild spirit, his troops use loud music, he drives his followers mad, he brings death and destruction upon all who follow him, mothers of his cult tear apart their children, he lusts for raw flesh and introduces orgiastic rites, he tears apart male victims, turns women into rocks, and he is called a mad man. Does that sound like Christ, or like the New-World culture hero? Similar contradictions (although not as extreme) exist for Osiris, Marduk, Tammuz, and other Old-World heroes as well. If New-World myths were merely transported from the Old World, as many diffusionists claim, why were these gruesome traits not included?

To assume that the whole picture of Indian traditions can be reassembled from the scattered fragments and carefully selected parallels handed down is misleading. One wonders what view we would have of the hero if the Spanish had reported the whole panorama of Indian traditions more objectively; It might be quite different.[22] Such complexities should signal to diffusionists and isolationists to suspend conflicting judgments and to work together for a more accurate picture.

Bearded Figure with Serpent Crown
(Teotihuacán, Mexico)

Off the Loom

In this search many challenging theories have been pursued—some highly speculative, and others seemingly reasonable. For lack of space, many have been left out. Final conclusions about whether bearded foreigners came anciently to the Americas are left to scholarly arguments and future discoveries and studies. Bancroft, in the nineteenth century wrote, "No one at present day can tell the origin of the Americans; they may have come from any one of the hypothetical sources. . . , and here the question must rest until we have more light upon the subject."[23]

Over one hundred years later, with some added light, the only additional statement one can make with confidence is that given current evidence, and strong human drives and capacities to explore the unknown, along with the great number of stories about bearded visitors and modern claims of foreign writing and burials discovered on American soil, it is easier to believe that a few must have made it than to believe they didn't.

But considering the odds of powerful natural and native forces against an occasional boat load of weakened mariners, and with some understanding of how ancient hero traditions emerge, it also is easier to believe that foreign visitors would not greatly influence nor change native tales than it is to believe they would.

Enthusiasts will continue to debate these issues, and the picture is destined to change. If there is ever accord, it will come from strong and convincing evidence, not from clever or emotional arguments no matter how often or how intensely they are declared. The culture hero is still another matter.

Real persons or real gods may once have been the inspiration for the heroes, for natives made no distinction between gods and culture heroes. No doubt historic persons like Topiltzin appeared on occasion to personify the hero and added to or modified the details, but the resulting myths probably bear little resemblance to them. The hero of origin may once have dwelled in the huts and mounds of his people, but the hero of legends lives on in their hearts and minds.

That native heroes need no outside influence does not negate the possibility of occasional foreign contacts which may have added color and details to the legends, but is indifferent toward them. If foreigners are clearly demonstrated to have arrived later in the Americans, or if Jesus Christ truly walked the land, they would likely have been added to existing tales, and the basic legends about New World heroes will not have changed significantly. If Old World peoples never brought culture heroes to the Americas, native people would still have invented them.

In conclusion, the many stories about bearded heroes in America are much more than a collection of isolated instances of a people's belief in some mysterious stranger from across the sea. They are the personification of man's basic struggles with himself and his challenging world. They demonstrate the fundamental longings in all races to rise above the limitations of the flesh and to identify with the sublime. The culture heroes were the embodiments of higher ideals and refining principles people sought to cultivate in their own lives so that they might live more fully on a daily level and more perfectly on an eternal one. They are the symbol of hope for the regeneration and respiritualization of the human race.

Of the American culture hero in general it can be said that millenniums could not suppress him, Indian rulers dared not ignore him, the Conquest failed to obliterate him, and hundreds of years since have not diminished his image. The legends of an American hero, the mysterious visitor from across the sea, are among the greatest dramas of history, and they continually recur in art, music, dance, theater, literature, and in the emotions and imaginations of the people. Yet, the hero still remains inscrutable, a shadowy figure seen obscurely through a shroud of legend and mystery. And as some have observed, perhaps that is where his followers prefer him to stay, for therein lies much of his intrigue.

Native myths rightly say the hero will come back, for as each generation awakens to his existence, he returns anew. And when he does, in whatever form, one can hope that new discoverers will heartily welcome the ancient hero, the fair god and feathered serpent—the unforgettable mystery man of the Ancient Americas.

Temple of the Warriors, Chichen Itzá

ENDNOTES

Chapter 1:
Fair Gods and Fallen Empires

1. Men from heaven: Thatcher 1903, Vol. 1, 534-7.
2. Native reception: Colón (in Huddleston 1967), 3; Honoré 1964,15.
3. Ruler distressed: Prescott 1843, 313 n. 8; (Modern Library), 171.
4. Sister resurrected: Prescott (Modern Library), 172 n. 11.
5. Serpent temple: Gómara 1964, 165.
6. Bloodthirsty god: Bancroft 1883, Vol. 5, 482.
7. 50,000 sacrifices: Prescott (Modern library), 48.
8. Passage to Paradise: Prescott (Modern Library), 51.
9. Thunder and Lightning: Gómara 1964, 58.
10. Year Prophesied: Carrasco 1984. 194-5.
11. The Gold Cure: Gómara 1964, 58.
12. Scuttles Ships: Castillo 1972, 110.
13. Canopied Beds: Prescott (Modern Library), 301; Castillo 1972, 194-6.
14. Doña Marina: Gómara 1964, 56.
15. Return: Prescott (Modern Library), 305-6; Castillo 1972, 204; Pagden 1992, 85,98.
16. Rule with Thunder: Pagden 1986, 85, 86, 98; Gómara 1964, 141.
17. Rule in Name of King: Prescott (Modern Library), 306.
18. Atahualpa: Prescott (Modern Library), 917.
19. Viracocha to Return: Von Hagen 1961, 207; Mason 1975, 135.

Chapter 2: A Lingering Legend

1. Nothing left standing: Castillo 1972, 191.
2. Golden age: Spence 1945, 147.
3. Higher civilization: De la Fuente 1968, 17.
4. Florentine Codex: Edmonson 1974, 111-49.
5. Books burned: Blom 1971, 109.
6. Questionnaires: Carrasco 1982. 16. Early traditions are recorded in letters by Columbus, Cortez. Vespucci, Xeres, and others. First-hand accounts by Conquistadores were published in four volumes as early as 1511 by Peter Martyr de Angleria. Throughout the sixteenth century and into the next, many other Spaniards discussed and wrote about the origins of the Indians: the most prominent being Motolinia, Olmos, Del Castillo, Oviedo, Las Casas, Gómara, Acosta, and Garcia. In South America, early Spanish writers like Cieza de Leon, Galvao, and Zárate preserved information about the Inca. Juan de Sarmiento, Polo de Ondegardo, and Christoval de Molina lived close to conquest times and carefully extracted material directly from the natives. other contributors who were even closer to the sources were Garcilaso de la Vega, an Inca prince, and Salcaymahua (Sahl-caee-MAH-wah), great, great grandson of native chiefs. Both passed on much valuable informa-

tion, although at times the material seems suspiciously distorted to favor illustrious ancestors.
7. Held in reverence: Bancroft 1883, Vol. 5, 23.
8. Culture-heroes: Squier 1851, 184-192. Many of the above are given here, but others will be found throughout the book.
9. Burning of books: Squier 1851, 224.
10. Reading discouraged: Sanders 19??, 183.
11. Quetzalcoatl obliterated: Tozzer 1966, 43 n. 214.
12. Sahagún rejects Quetzalcoatl: Nicholson 1957, 43.
13. Quetzalcoatl descends: Tozzer 1966, 158.
14. Mendieta and Sahagún: Nicholson 1957, 85; Carrasco 1984, 192.
15. Myths before Conquest: Brinton 1882, 29, 203.
16. Quetzalcoatl real: Hermann 1954, 171-2.
17. Greatest figure: (quoting Spinden) Sejourné 1976, 25.
18. Central figure: Sejourné 1976, 25.
19. No mere invention: Davies 1979, 127.
20. Prominent figure: Nicholson 1957, i, 314, 322, 359, 360.
21. Not a rumor: Carrasco 1984, 192-193.
22. Most famous figure: Coe 1984, 124-5; 1994, 132.
23. Correct understanding: Brinton 1882, 27.
24. Debunking the myth: Davies 1979,125-139.
25. New appraisals: Mason 1975, 207.
26. Dialogue with other cultures: Eliade 1975, 8-10.
27. Cannot suppress myths: Campbell 1973, 4.
28. Analysis: Wenke 1990, 604.

Chapter 3: Mystery Men in Mexico

1. Tula: Prescott (Modern Library), 39; Bancroft 1883, Vol. 3, 241.
2. Quecadquaal: Nicholson 1957, 139,140.
3. Legend holy: Burland 1968, 151.
4. Mythological elements: Nicholson 1957, 301.
5. Everything under sun: Nicholson 1957, ii.
6. Description of Quetzalcoatl: Carroll 1994, 35,36; Nicholson 1957, 82, 84-5, 150; Bailey 1973, 56.
7. Crosses, staff, and book: Bancroft 1883 Vol. 3, 274; Carroll 1994, 40; Ferguson (quoting Veytia) 1958, 146
8. Calendar: Bancroft 1883, Vol. 3. 274.
9. Light and life: Alexander 1964, Vol. 6, 68-9,89.
10. First Quecalcoatle: Carroll 1994, 25.
11. Dead rulers in his costume: Nicholson 1957, 113.
12. Give up throne: Pagden, 85-6.
13. Celestial parents: Séjourné 1976, 56.
14. Heard for miles: Burland 1968, 155.
15. A composite of many sources: Sahagún (14 journals), Bancroft 1883, Vol.3, 274-5, Vol. 5, 258-9; Nicholson 1957; Squier 1851, 190; Coe 1984, 124-5; Campbell 1987, 459.
16. Cholula: Carroll 1994, 33-4.
17. Cacaxtla portrait: Gillett Griffin, (personal interview 12-3-89).
18. White men to come: Nicholson (quoting Mendietta)1957, 83.

19. Resurrected: Nicholson 1957, 356; Carroll 1994, 63-6.
20. List of great men: Brinton 1882, 312, n 1.
21. Arrives from the west: Roys 1967, 194.
22. Bearded followers: Tozzer.1966, 22-3.
23. De Landa: Roys 1967, 4.
24. Born again: Carroll 1994, 49.
25. Quetzalcoatl departs: Gómara 1964, 141.
26. Idolatry unknown: Roys 1967, 15.
27. Idolatry: Tozzer (quoting Seler) 1966, 23.
28. Well of the Itza: Thompson 1970, 134.
29. Erasing memory: Bancroft (Quoting Torquemada) 1883, Vol. 3, 258.
30. Tezcatlipoca of Yucatan: Coe 1984, 104.
31. Feathers: Squier 1851, 216.
32. Sun symbol: Squier 1851, 155-8.
33. Thirteen heavens: Nicholson (in Wauchope 1971), Vol. 10, 407
34. Winding like water: De Leonard (in Wauchope 1971), Vol. 10, 218.
35. Lightning: Alexander 1964, Vol. 10, 288; Brinton 1976, 118.
36. Serpents and birds: Alexander 1964, Vol. 10. 300.
37. Divine: Séjourné 1976, 84,53.
38. Green bird shall come: Roys 1967, 133.
39. Foreigners to rule: Roys 1967, 187; Tozzer 1966, 43.
40. White robed priests: Tozzer 1966, 43.
41. Bearded guests, cross: Brinton 1974, 204.
42. Uxmal burial: Carrasco 1984, 55.
43. Tradition to myth: Nicholson 1957, 107.
44. *Popol Vuh*: Goetz & Morley 1969, 78-84.
45. Quiche hero: Cordell Anderson (Transcript on file.)
46. Pilgrimages to honor Kukulcan: Goetz 1969, 69.

Chapter 4:
The Serpent Sheds an Ancient Skin

1. Ehécatl: Nicholson 1957, 320,355, 360; Brinton 1986, 196-197.
2. Christian era: Nicholson 1957, iii.
3. Would return: Prescott (Modern Library), 305-6; Pagden 1992, 85,86.
4. He will come: Dibble 1961, Vol. 10, 190-1.
5. Ancient temple: Kingsborough 1831-38, Vol. 6, 140.
6. Seven ships: Bancroft 1883, Vol. 5, 21; 3, 270.
7. Panuco visitor: Bancroft 1883, V, 257-260.
8. Cholula: Bancroft 1883, Vol. 3, 260, 261.
9. Earthquake: Ixtlilxochitl, pp. 20-21.
10. Chilam Balam: Roys 1967, 3, 4, 120.
11. Second time: Tozzer 1966, 22-3; Roys 1967, 161.
12. A.D. 780 Seler (in Tozzer 1966),22,23.
13. A.D. 299 Bancroft 1883, Vol. 5, 199,200.
14. Flood and creation: Nicholson 1957,277; Bancroft 1833, Vol. 5, 200.
15. Secrets: Kingsborough 1831-8, Vol. 6, 162.
16. Maya/Toltec influence: Coe 1989, 137.
17. Venus: Closs, (in Robertson 4) 1978 pp. 151; Thompson 1972, 68, 69.
18. Greatest figure: Spinden (in Hunter 1972), 35.
19. Wind gods: Roys (in Wauchope 1971), Vol. 3, 674

20. Great Lord: Benson 1977, 112; Tozzer: 1966, 146.
21. Votan: Nicholson 1957, 213-21; Brinton 1882, 213.
22. Four brothers: Brinton 1882, 212-20; Dibble 1961, 191.
23. Tower: Alexander 1964, Vol. 2, 131 -3.
24. Votan deified: Brinton 1882, 212-15; Bancroft 3: 450-5.
25. Men from the east: Brinton 1882,219-20.
26. Only two: Bancroft 1883, Vol. 3,451.
27. Serpent bar: Schele and Freidel 1990) 415.
28. Vision quest: Schele & Miller 1986,46, 175-6.
29. Throat of the divine: Robicsek 1978,77.
30. Patterns: Nicholson, Irene 1968, 123.
31. The mask of god: Markman 1989, xxi.
32. Palenque Tomb: Blom 1926,178.
33. Pacal: Robertson 1973, Vol. 1, 77; Matthews & Schele, 63-5.
34. Rebirth: Robertson 1973, Vol. 1, 81; Schele & Friedel 1990, 268-9.
35. Tree of Life: Schele & Friedel 1990,90,129.
36. God K: Robiscek 1981, 47,67-80.
37. Gods K and B: Spinden 1975, 64.
38. Tezcatlipoca: Robicsek 1978,105; Squier 1851, 186.
39. Descent from God K: Robicsek 1978, 68.
40. A god is born: Robertson 1983, 59.
41. Legitimizing the throne: Schele 1984, 9-31
42. He is god: Robertson 1978, 138
43. Xbalanque: Kelley (in Coe 1987), 168.
44. Serpent-hero: Spinden 1975, 32.
45. Japanese Emperor: *L.A.Times*, Monday, June 4, 1990.
46. Teotihuacan: Coe 1984, 89.
47. Sacrifices: Carlson 1993, 60-9.
48. Feathered Serpent: Griffin (Personal conversation 12-3-89).
49. Serpent learns to fly: Sejourné 1976, 86.
50. Ehécatl: Carrasco 1984, 28.
51. Cross: Bancroft 1883, Vol. 3, 454-5; Nicholson 1957. 209- 10.
52. Cult of Quetzalcoatl: Covarrubias 1947, 186.

Chapter 5:
Bearded Visitors to South America

1. Source of legends: Hamlyn 1968, 32-4
2. Fair, bearded hero: Mason 1975, 135.
3. White men to come: Brinton 1882,199-201.
4. Bochica: Osborne 1968, 112-114; Brinton 1882,220-1.
5. 2,000 years: Bancroft 1883, Vol. 3, 269.
6. Crosses and serpents: Alexander 1964, Vol. 11, 202-7,241.
7. Amalivaca: Alexander 1964, Vol. 11, 270.
8. Tamu: Brinton 1974. 199.
9. "Ackawaoi": Alexander 11, 269-70.
10. Wako: McGovern (in Hunter 1972), 44.
11. Zumé, Paye Tome: Bancroft 1883, Vol. 5, 24.
12. Tupa: Brinton 1974, 200.
13. Watauinewa: Eliade 1987, Vol. 13, 491-2; Osborne 1968, 117.
14. Big Foot: Morison 1974, 367.

15. Temaukel: Eliade 1987, 505.
16. Elal. & Heller: Osborne 1978, 117.
17. Chilean miracle worker: Bancroft 1883, Vol. 5, 24 n. 56.
18. Thunupa (Tonapa): Alexander.1964, Vol. 2, 239; Osborne:1968, 86-7.
19. Medieval Kingdoms: Mason 1975, 100.
20. "Naked giants": Alexander ll: 205-6, Osborne, 1968, 90.
21. Bearded giants and others: Alexander 1964, Vol. 2, 206-7.
22. Taycanamo: Moseley and Mackey 1973, 322-35; Meggars 1974, 181-3
23. Desert empire: Moseley and Mackey 1973, 344.
24. Naymlap: Lumbreras 1976, 181; Alexander 1964, Vol. ll, 208-9.
25. Con: Osborne 1968, 107; Brinton 1882, 195.
26. Pachacamac: Brinton 1976.
27. Pachacamac: Prescott (Modern Library), 953; Osborne 1968.
28. Tiwanacu: Alexander 1964, Vol. ll, 233; Lumbreras 1976, 139-45.
29. Tiwanacu: Mason 1975: 91-95.
30. White race: Brinton 1882, 188-92.
31. Calendar figures: Posnasky (in Verill 1967) 204.
32. Power and authority: Lathrop (in Benson 1971), 75-7.
33. Chavín influence: Patterson (in Benson 1971), 29-47.
34. Chavín from the jungle: Lathrop (in Benson 1971), 73-97.
35. White race before Inca: Brinton, 1882, 188.
36. Four brothers: Osborne 1968, 42-6; Eliade 1978, 503.
37. Manco Capac: Alexander 1964, Vol. 2, 242-52.
38. Worship me: Markham 1873, 5-7.
39. Viracocha/Thunupa: Markham 1873, 72; Osborne 1968, 72-82.
40. Viracocha/Sea: Alexander 1964, Vol. 2, 239-48
41. Other white Viracochas: Brinton 1882, 199-201.
42. Summing up: Brinton 1882, 172-3.
43. Appearance: Osborne 1968,78,81; Markham 1873, 70-2.
44. Feathered Serpent: de la Vega (in Markam 1873, 12; Marcos (in Sorenson 1990), M-087; Brinton 1976, 125.
45. Atahualpa expects the return: Brinton,1882, 199-200.

Chapter 6:
Fair Gods in North America

1. Foolish beliefs: Campanius 1834, 112-13
2. Satan's inventions: Brinton 1882, 238.
3. White ancestors: Schoolcraft 1884, Vol. l, 19; Spence, 1975: 119-20.
4. Ascends to the sky: Brinton 1882, 51-3.
5. Light and knowledge: Brinton 1882, pp. 46-51; 1976, 178-9.
6. Brothers; Death to life: Burland 1975, 53.
7. Golden age: Spence 1975, 147.
8. Morning Star: Hamilton,1977, 76-7.
9. Big mouths: Campanius 1834, 140.

10. Similar legends: Brinton 1882, 61.
11. Hiawatha: Alexander 1964, Vol. ll, 51; National Geographic, September. 1987, 380.
12. Confederation: Marriott, Rachlin 1968, 33; National Geographic, Sept. 1987, 398-9; Hamilton 1977. 118-9.
13. Ioskeha: Brinton, 1975, 186-90; Brinton 1882, 53-7; Morgan 1851, 210.
14. Winnebago hero: Radin 1972, 125.
15. Glooskap: Spence 1975, 147.
16. Yehl: Bancroft 1883, Vol. 3, 99-103,146,151; Brinton 1882, 228-9; Oswalt 1966, 293,299.
17. Old man above: Bancroft 1883, Vol. 3, 151.
18. Carocs: Bancroft 1883, Vol. 3, 161 -77.
19. Olchones and Matevil: Bancroft 1883, Vol. 3, 161,171-5.
20. Chinigchinich: Bancroft 1883, Vol. 3, 161-9.
21. White Sands: Santa Ana Register, March 21, 1977.
22. Montezuma of the Pueblos: Bancroft 1883, Vol. 3, 171-5.
23. White brothers: Winnemucca 1883, 5-7.
24. Pahana, Quetzalcoatl: Waters 1963, 308, 411.
25. White men with tools: Schoolcraft 1884, Vol. l, 19.
26. White ancestors: Brinton 1976, 94, 188-9.
27. Hopis sea crossing: May 1971, 132.
28. Race of white giants: Bancroft 1883, Vol. 3, 153-4.
29. Seneca marry whites: Deacon 1966, 154-5.
30. Almost white: Catlin 1973, vol 1, 93-4.
31. Parchments: Armstrong 1950, 105.
32. Ancient white man: Catlin 1973, Vol. l, 177-8.
33. Chaco Canyon: Lekson 1997, 52-5.
34. Hopewell & Adena: Wenke 1990, 565-6.
35. Newer cultures: Silverberg 1968, 41; Williams 1991, 321-45.
36. Majestic people: Maxwell,1978, 35.
37. Great mound at Cahokia: Wenke 1990, 573.
38. Great sun: Maxwell, 1978, 72-5; Oswalt 1966, 472-85.
39. Thunder, lightning: Bancroft 1883, Vol. 3, 132. 171-2.
40. Serpent skins: Spence 1975, 1975: 217.
41. Snake dances: La Barre 1970, 628.
42. Feathered serpents: Wenke 1990, 574.

Chapter 7:
Culture Heroes and Colonies

1. Beyond Greenland: Magnusson 1966, 24-5.
2. Odin: Hyerdahl 1978, 131-2.
3. Independent state: Ashe 1971, 98.
4. Greenland colonized: Magnusson , 19.
5. Festive Yule: Harvard Classics , Vol. 43, 5-8.
6. Viking settlement: National Geographic (November1964), Vol. 126, No. 5, 726-34.
7. Kukulcán: Carroll 1994, 88.
8. Viking feathered serpents: Nelin (in Sorenson 1996).
9. Hostile natives: Carroll 1994, 98.
10. No Indians: Morrison 1971, 184.
11. Skraelings: Magnusson 1966, 59-60.
12. Freydis: Harvard Classics Vol. 43, 20; Morison 1971, Chapter. 3.

13. Lost at sea: Harvard Classics , Vol. 43, 11.
14. Many ships lost: Taylor (in Riley) 1971, 244.
15. Nude sailors: Gillett Griffin, (personal correspondence), Sept. 3, 1990.
16. No Christians, no Skraelings: Holland 1956, 124.
17. Bjorn: Morison 1971, 27; Carroll 1994, 91-8.
18. Horse or litter?: Carroll 1994, 97-102.
19. Fair natives: Holland 1956, 128.
20. Not Eskimo: Holland 1956, 128.
21. White Eskimos?: Hougaard 1914, 49.
22. Blond Eskimos and Greenlanders: Holland 1956, 50,153.
23. Race of giants: Rink 1875, 47.
24. Traditions lost: Rink 1875, 75.
25. Viking artifacts: Morison 1971, 37.
26. Leif Ericsson: Morison 1971, 28.

Chapter 8:
Fair-skinned Natives
and the Welsh

1. Not Indians: Catlin 1973, Vol. 1, 93.
2. Catlin on the Mandan: Catlin 1973, Vol. 1, n. 9, 87, 93, 94.
3. Man Dan Ark: Billiard, ed. 1974, 281.
4. Twig and flood: Catlin 1973, Vol. 1, 105.
5. Great Spirit: Catlin 1973] Vol. l, 135. 159-81
6. Divine Being: Maximillian 1843, 360.
7. People of the pheasant: Catlin 1973, Vol. 2, 260.
8. Up the Missouri: Maximillian 1843, 335.
9. Welsh language: Deacon 1966, 223.
10. Madoc: Morison 1971, Vol. 1, 84-7, 106-7
11. Great waters: Armstrong 1950, 105, 185.
12. Daniel Boone: Deacon 1966, 132.
13. Lives spared: Deacon 1966, 111,116.
14. Welsh Indians: Williams 1979, 191; Deacon 1966. 157-8. 133-6
15. "White Beards": Neill 1890, 116-23; Deacon 1966, 115.
16. Not idealized: Abel 1939, xxxiii.
17. Fair-skinned Paduacas: Deacon 1966, 146./ Nasatir 1952, 493.
18. Gentle and Peaceful: Abel 1939, 127.
19. Cowardly dogs: Chardon (in Abel 1939), 28.
20. Cruel, lying, thieving: Abel 1939 ,172.
21. "Good savages": Nasatir 1952, 285.
22. "Seldom aggressors": De Voto 1953, 65.
23. Lewis and Clark: Gwyn 1979, 188; Biddle 1962, 75.
24. Greatest villains: Abel 1939, 172.
25. Early discrepancies: Maximillian 1843, 353.
26. Almost white: Maximillian 1843, 337.
27. Ribbons and hospitality: Nasatir 1952, 258; Biddle 1962, 65-7.
28. White lovers: Maximillian 1843, 340, 350.
29. Venus' country: Nasatir 1952, 258, 300.
30. Differ little: Nasatir 1952, 452
31. No Welsh: Morison 1971, 86; Williams 1979, 183.
32. Last word?: Morison 1971, 87.
33. Blended language: Biddle 1962, 82.
34. Spanish Governor: Deacon 1966, 149
35. Remove all traces: Deacon 1966, 148.
36. Notion unfounded: Maximillian 1843, 351-9.
37. Prove the truth: Nasatir 1927, 442-8.
38. A good myth: Williams 1979, 202.
39. In Memory of Prince Madoc: Morison 1971, 85.
40. Flood and Eve: Neill 1890, 120-3.
41. Christian and Indian: Eliade 1987, Vol. 10, 544.

Chapter 9:
Contacts from East and West

1. St. Brendon: Morison 1971, 14,15; National Geographic (December 1977), 78.
2. Irish exploration: Ashe 1971, 23.
3. Fell, Farley and a Basque King: Fell 1977, 19-23.
4. More like Ireland: Fell 1977, 39.
5. Ogam and Phoenician: Fell 1977, 151.
6. Write on the ceiling: Fell 1977, 13.
7. Wild claims: Fell 1983, 23-4.
8. Basically correct: Fell 1977, 288-9; 1983, 12, 24.
9. Mystical island: National Geographic (May 1977), 590; Graves 1982, 234-5.
10. Sons of God: Alexander 1964, Vol. 3, 211; Graves 1982, 234.
11. Wheeled carts: National Geographic (May 1977), 627.
12. Horse murals: Marx 1992, 91,112.
13. Celtic art: Celtic World, (author, year?), 125.
14. Early Asiatics: Ashe 1971, 244; Reed (in Riley & Kelley 1976), 107,108.
15. Japanese objects in Washington: Fingerhut 1994, 126-7.
16. One migration: Benson 1977, 11.
17. Type B Blood: Fingerhut 1994, 128.
18. Rafts across the Pacific: Doran (in Riley & Kelley 1976), 135
19. Shang and Chavín: Davies (quoting Wiley) 1979, 100.
20. Similarities: Estrada & Meggars (in Fingerhut 1994), 122.
21. Tajin and the Bronze age: Coe 1984, 109.
22. Wild theories of crossings: Wauchope 1962, 88-101.
23. Fusang: Wauchope 1962, 90-91; Mertz 1972, 1-19.
24. Chinese anchors: Fingerhut 1984, 73; 1994, 121.
25. Chinese compass: Mertz 1972, 15.
26. Hard to credit: Davies 1979, 122.
27. Buddha: Fingerhut 1994, 129.

Chapter 10:
Visiting Seamen
from the Mediterranean

1. Mystery Cave: Burrows 1992; May,1996, vol 3, #16.
2. Atlantis: Ashe 1971,17-8.
3. Thera: Pelligrino 1991, 3-8, 44-5.
4. All gods from Atlantis: Wauchope 1962, 32,48.
5. Roman coins: Peterson (Tel. conv., 6-28-88); Gordon 1973, 68,175.
6. Roman coins in Iceland: Marble 1980,176.
7. Romans made it: Peterson (Telephone conversation,6-28-88).
8. Beached coins: Monson 1971,135.
9. Romans in Oregon?: Dodi (Telephone conversation, 6-28-88).
10. Guanadara Bay: Marx 1976,156,159; 1992, 306-26

11. Greeks in the Atlantic: Gordon 1971,38 49
12. How to Get Back: Monson 1971,12.
13. Homer: Ashe 1971,17.
14. Boldest of Voyages: Monson 1971, 6.
15. Isle of the Blest: Hesiod (in Monson 1971),4,5.
16. Lack of provisions: Monson 1971,8.
17. A Real Continent: Gordon 1971,43.
18. Alexander's tomb lost: Rybnikar (in May,1996), 2-11
19. Alexander's Fleet: Gladwin 1947, 232-3, 270-73, 322; Irwin 1963, 243-57.
20. Tomb of Alexander: Schaffranke (in May 1996), 44-5.
21. Sunken Palace: Covey 1997,14.
22. Put up or Shut up: McGlone 1993, 54-60.
23. Godlike race of hero-men: Morison 1971,4.
24. Greek plumed serpent: Gordon 1973, 51; Pinsent 1987, 90
25. Egyptian tale of a feathered serpent: Gordon 1973, 54-67.
26. Osiris; Graves 1982,16,17; Grimal 1977, 34-7.
27. Ancient pyramids: Billiard 1978, 73-100.
28. Mexican Tower: Bancroft 1883, vol. V, 17, 89; III, 67-69; Kingsborough 1831-8, vol. V,164-5.
29. Egyptian/New World links: Jairazbhoy (In Sorenson 1990), J-012-J-017.
30. Hatshepsut: Honore,1964, 171, 204.
31. From all over: Gordon 1973, 30.
32. Pointing the way: (Archaeology Jan./Feb. 1990, 20.) Finish!
33. Sources for all the above: Matthews, Nat. Geo. Aug. '74, 149-89.
34. Dubious destination: Morison 1971, 8-9.
35. Cabral crossing: Gordon 1973,126.
36. BRZL= Brazil: Gordon 1973,119-27
37. Phoenicians in Brazil: Gordon 1973,124-5; Morison 1971,11-12.
38. Amazon tablets: Savoy (S.L. Tribune, Sun. Dec.10,1989).
39. Helmeted carving: Coe 1968, 39,75.
40. Currents to the Olmec area: Irwin 1963, 216-7.
41. Foreign visitors: Gardner 1986, 130.
42. God Bes: Von Wuthenau 1975, 32-3.
43. Purple paint: Coe 1984, 77.
44. New light: Stuart (in Nat. Geog. Nov. 1993), 88-115.
45. Phoenicians off course: Gordon 1973, 39-40.
46. Piri Re'is map: Hapgood 1979,I-36.
47. New World Phoenicians: Thompson (in Coe 1984), 104.

Chapter 11:
Lost Tribes in a Promised Land

1. Hidden record: Groesbeck 1956, (Personal Journal).
2. Ten Tribes of Israel: Recinos & Goetz 1974, 165, 170.
3. Light from across the Sea: Tedlock 1958, 55, 71, 204.
4. Old Testament traditions: Goetz & Morley 1969, 90-2.
5. A path opened: Recinos & Goetz 1967, 55, 170.

6. Persecutors drowned: Durán, 1977, 24, 62.
7. Descendants of the Jews: Tozzer 1966, 16-17.
8. Israelite descent: Bancroft 1882, Vol. 5, 77.
9. Israel survives: Dimont, 1962, 14-16.
10. David's wealth: Josephus, 1967, 170, 172, 181.
11. Lost tribes: Josephus 1967, 211, 222.
12. Fled to Egypt: Ben Gurion 1974, 67.
13. Blondes in China: Whitehead, 1972, 97.
14. J.S. and the North Star: Brough 1979, Chapter 3.
15. Jewish theories: Bancroft.1883, Vol. 5, 77-90.
16. Four-cornered altar: Ferguson 1958, 87.
17. Psalms 106:37-38.
18. Boys in the temple: Sahagún (in Burland 1968), 152,153.
19. Native Ark: Durán 1977, 23-4.
20. Ark among Cherokees: Adair (in Williams 1930), 229.
21. Jehovah and Hebrews: Kingsborough 1831-8, Vol. 9, 179.
22. Scalping: Numbers 25:4, Bancroft 1883, Vol. 5, 95; Psalm 68:21.
23. Smoke signals: Gordon 1973, 199 n. 78.
24. Moses Stones: Bancroft 1883, Vol. 5, 94-5; McGlone 1992, 7-9; Williams 1991, 171-4.
25. Yuchis and Sukoth: Carter (Personal correspondence June 1991).
26. Holy Stones: Altruz; Williams 1991, 171-4; McGlone 1993, 8, 9.
27. Dating: Fingerhut 1994, 18; McGlone 1993, 5-7.
28. Roman Jewish colony: Covey 1975.
29. Jewish colonizers: Valle 1988 (L.A. Times, July 15), 40R.
30. Writings colored: Bancroft 1883, Vol. 5, 144.
31. Hebrew and Chinese: Goetz 1969, 10.
32. Jews in ancient America: Kingsborough 18321-38, Vol. 6, Chapter 3.
33. Rejected theories: Wauchope 1962, 50-68.
34. Not to be found: Bancroft 1883, Vol. 5, 96-7.
35. Circumcision in Yucatan: Huddlestone 1944, 8.
36. No circumcision: Schoolcraft (in Bancroft 1883, Vol. 5, 96).
37. No lost tribes: Wauchope 1962, 56.
38. Borrowing tales: Durán 1977, 62.
39. Christian influence: Goetz 1969, 18,19.
40. Ancient record obtained: Carmack (Personal interview 8-6-88, Personal correspondence, 8-20-90).
41. Original traditions: Goetz 1969, 19.
42. No improvement: Goets 1969, 7,54.

Chapter 12:
Christ Before Columbus

1. "Reach thy hand": John 20:24-9.
2. Various statements: Matt. 28: 18,19; Matt. 10:5, 6; Mark 16:15.
3. Signs occurred: Ixtlilxochitl 1891, Vol. 1,14.
4. Darkness for five days: Avila (in Markham 1873), 5,131-3.
5. World in darkness: De Roo 1900, 431.
6. Hills and valleys: Osborne 1968, 74.
7. These legends are a composite of the following: Carrasco 1984, 96-7; Bancroft 1883,Vol. 5, 23-4, 258-60; Brinton 1882, 189-93,233; Osborne 1968, 74-81; Markham 1873, 5, 6, 70, 71, 131 -2.

8. Miracle worker: Alexander, Vol. 1l, 239-41; Osborne 1968, 74-81.
9. Titles: Brinton 1882, 170-3; Osborne 1968, 41.
10. Prayers: Markham 1873, 28-33; Brinton 1882, 172-3.
11. Apostles & teachers: Means 1968, 142; Alexander 1964, Vol. 1l, 238-42.
12. Worked marvels: Osborne 1968, 74-81.
13. Teaches by works: Ixtlilxochitl 1891 ,20; Durán 1977, 23, 30, 27-60.
14. Bearded followers: De Roo 1900, 440-3; Osborne 1968, 74,78,81; Bancroft 1883, Vol. 3, 260,267, 5: 258-60; Nicholson 1957, 82-3,159.
15. Fear of the church: Durán 1977, 59.
16. Twin/ Statue: Bancroft 1883, Vol. 5, 25; Alexander 1964, 293; Brinton 1882 193; Durán 1977, 59.
17. Not incompatible: Nicholson 1968, 21.
18. Similar to our own: Durán 1977, 54.
19. War in heaven: Bancroft 1883, Vol. 3, 169.
20. More similarities: Durán 1977, 27, 28; Tozzer 1966, 207; Kingsborough 1831-38, Vol. 6, 107.
21. One God: Dibble 1961, 169; Durán 1977. 29; Tozzer 1966, 146; Squier 1851, 181-2.
22. More on one God: Bancroft 1883, Vol. 3, 451; Brinton 1882, 172-5; Morley 1956, 188, 194-5; Dibble 1961, Vol. 10, 169; Roys 1967, 115; Morgan 1851/1969, 152-4.
23. Uncreated: Alexander 1964, Vol. 2, 87; Osborne 1968, 64-5.
24. Second God: Bancroft1883. Vol. 3, 272, 451.
25. Trinity: Hernandez (in Tozzer 1966), 207 n. 1154.
26. Virgin birth: Carrasco 1982, 79; De Roo 1900, 428-9.
27. Trials and Perfection: Kingsborough 1831-8, Vol. 6, 100; Nicholson 1968, 94-111; Carroll 1994, Chapter. 4; Nicholson 1957, 18, 36-7, 304-5.
28. Apostles and followers: Alexander 1964, 242; Carroll 1994, 35; Durán 1977, 60.
29. Rebirth: De Landa 1978, 42-4.
30. Baptism and communion: Tozzer 1966, 102, 142, 207; Sejourné 1976, 61.
31. Accumulated teachings: Carroll 1994, 44-51; Alexander 1964, 1l, 69, 87, 89, 239; Squier, Serpent, 52-3; Brinton 1882, 189; Nicholson 1968, 127; Bancroft 1883, Vol. 3, 381, 383, 439-40, 439; Vol. 5, 23-4; Osborne 1986, 74, 86,112.
32. The cross: Roys 1967, 167-8.
33. More crosses: Alexander 1964, Vol. 1l, 142,238-9; Markham 1873, 72; Bancroft 1883, Vol. 3, 273; De Roo 1900, 440-9.
34. Tree of Life: Brinton,1972, 97, 98.
35. Nails, spear, crucifixion: Kingsborough 1831-8, Vol. 6, 118, 156, 165; De Roo, 1900, 430-3; Bancroft 1883, Vol. 3, 462; Vol. 5, 27.
36. Christ, not Quetzalcoatl: Bancroft 1883, Vol. 3, 273.
37. Crucified and resurrected: Tozzer 1966, 207.
38. Blood-letting: Brinton 1882, 56,129; Schele & Miller 1986. 175-6, 181-4.
39. Resurrection: Brinton 1882, 208; Sejourné 1976, 58.
40. Raises the dead: Alexander 1964, Vol. 1l, 134; Willard 1941, 151-2.
41. Calls the dead to life: Brinton, 1882, 200-1, 208.

42. Morning Star: Sejourné 1976, 54,58-9; Carroll 1994, 82, 86-7.
43. Quetzalcoatl to return: Carrasco. 1984, 150,197.
44. Viracocha to return: Brinton 1882, Z00.
45. Return of Northern heroes: Boissiére 1990, xvi; Spence 1975, 147.
46. God within: Campbell 1973, 260.
47. Kept serpent: Farbridge 1928, 75.
48. Salvation of mankind: Howey 19--, 132
49. Winged-serpent: Campbell 1974, 297-8.
50. Christ & Quetzalcoatl: Sejourné 1976, 25.
51. Time of Christ: Alexander 1964, 216; Osborne 1968. 112.
52. Each of these references is found in the text of the chapter and in the end notes above.
53. Michigan Plates: Deal, Moore, Ancient American Vol. 2, n. 9, 36.

Chapter 13:
The Universal Nature of Culture Heroes

1. Rope and ladder: Campbell 1974,184.
2. Cosmic trees: Campbell 1974,141-165; Eliade 1960. 65; Cook, 1988, 9-17.
3. Serpent sphere around calendar: Howey,17
4. Man from god's blood: N. Larousse, 62.
5. Eagle and serpents: Graves 1982,.65.
6. Shiva: Howey, 64,65; Squier 1851,197
7. Osiris: Frazer 1981, vol. 1, 301-20.
8. Dionysus: Graves 1982, 155-60; Pinsent 1987, 52-4.
9. Resurrection of gods: Campbell 1973, 73,143.
10. Serpent gods: Campbell 1974, 281-302; Pinsent 1987, 73; Eliade 1987, vol. 13, 370-73.
11. Feathered serpents: Pinsent 1987. 17,26,73, 90:
12. Much about serpents: Alexander 1964, vol. XII, 180; Howey 19—, 21.
13. Crucifixions: Ba-Tau and Odin: Graves 1982, 75; Cook 1988, 22; Attis: Campbell 1973,93.
14. Virgin births: Squier 1851,184-5; Campbell 1962,39, 40.
15. Summaries of myths: Eliot, .1990,14-23; Campbell 1973, 382; Eliade 1960, 23-29
16. Most common: Jung 1964,.11 O.
17. All related: La Barre 1970,186, 187.
18. Origins of Heroes: in Eliade 1978, vol. l, 284.
19. Origins: Bancroft 1883, vol. III, 30,31.
20. Shamans before gods: La Barre 1970, 161, 186-87
21. Cycle of death and crops: Campbell 1990, 191.
22. Tubers from body: Eliade 1975,45; Eliade 1969, 19, 20.
23. Dionysus in the forest: Otto 1965,129.
24. Solar heroes and birds: Eliot p. 36.
25. Animal gods: Loosely based on Bullfinch 1979, 293; Bancroft 1883, vol. III, 32-39; 227; Brinton 1974, 112; Eliot 1990, 36.
26. Disease of language: Eliot 1990, 16.
27. High gods: Eliot 1990, 34; Eliade 1969, 14-15, 24.
28. Hunter identified with sun: Campbell 1987, 377
29. Lunar symbolism: Eliade 1978, 22-23.

30. Gods=kings and queens: Campbell 1987, 144
31. Indifference: Eliade 1978, vol. I 59
32. Tiamut: Eliade 1967, 67, 98-108; 1978, vol. I, 71
33. Tammuz comes from: Eliade 19—, vol. 10, 276; Alexander, 1964, vol. V, 336-351; Eliade 1978 vol. I, 66-67; 1987, vol. 4; 1967, 21-24, 97-109
34. Christian/Pagan sources: Campbell 1974,239, 243,248; Graves 1982, 58-60; Alexander 1964, vol. V.19,24; Campbell 1973, 33,143; Religions of the World, 56-61; Campbell 1990,196-98; Eliade 1978, Vol III, 221-225; Otto 98-103; Eliade 19— vol. 7, 1749.

Chapter 14: Through the Loom

1. Scholarly views: Carrasco 1984, 56-60.
2. Bering Straits immigrations: LA Times, Mar. 1, 1994, front p.
3. 36,000 B.C.: L.A. Times, May 2,1991.
4. 12,500 years: NY Times, Feb. 11, 1997, C-4,
5. Copper: Gardner 1986, 175.
6. Sky monster: Eliade 1987, Vol. 13, 370; Nicholson 1968, 26-7.
7. Races origins: Schele and Friedel 1990, 56-7.
8. Olmecs remembered by the Maya: Schele & Freidel 1990, 254.
9. Sun worship: Goets 1969, 71.
10. Serpent Sun: Squier 1851, 186-7; Portilla, Eliade, Ed., 1987, Vol.9, 395.
11. First Quetzalcoatls: Carrasco 1984, 59.
12. Bones: Carrasco 1984, 99-100.
13. Quetzalcoatl, creator of life: Carrasco 1984, 32.
14. Pahana and Quetzalcoatl: Waters 1963, 308; Boissiere, 1990: 69.
15. Changes, slow or fast?: Davies 1979, 15; Coe 1986, 13.
16. Symbol for legitimacy: Lafaye (in Carrasco 1984), 62.

17. Non-Asian blood: Fingerhut, 102.
18. Spaniards forgotten: Bancroft 1883, Vol. III, 27.
19. Spaniards eaten: Schoolcraft 1851, 125,198.
20. Hero Pattern: Campbell 1973, 35; Eliade 1975, 23-34.
21. Similarities in myths: Brinton1882, 202.

Chapter 15: The Final Fabric

1. Two divergent philosophies: Sejourne 1976, 35.
2. Christ's return: L.A. Times, March 5,1989, p. 1.
3. Constantine: Moore 1994, 56-59
4. "White": Brinton 1976,184-189: Spence 1975, 120.
5. Short hair, no beards: Boswell 1980, 102.
6. Late religious use of cross: Clark 1969, 29.
7. Quetzalcoatl statue ugly: Davies 1979,133.
8. Nightmare in stone: Gillett Griffin, personal correspondence, Sept. 1990
9. Book of Mormon, Moroni 10:4.
10. Native views different: Wenke 1990,520.
11. European egotists: Wenke, 1990, 557
12. Writers distorted: Nicholson 1957, 3O2.
13. Construed myths to fit theories: Brinton 1976, 63.
14. Copyists were editors: Carroll 1994, 23.
15. New Testament similarities: Davies, 1979, 136.
16. Native stories changed: Carrasco 1984, 15.
17. Radically different from the West: Eliade 1960, 9.
18. Recorded only what was similar: Carrasco 1984, 38.
19. Statue of Viracocha: Davies 1979,136.
20. God Ioskeha/Christ: Brinton 1882, 57.
21. Devil, Hell, one God: Brinton 1976, 57-67.
22. Spanish changes: Carrasco 1984,15,19-23,41,47.
23. More light: Bancroft 1883, vol. V,132.

WORKS CITED

Abel, Annie Heloise, ed. 1939. *Tabeau's Narrative of Loisel's Expedition to the Upper Missouri.* Norman, Oklahoma: University of Oklahoma Press.

Acosta, José. 1972. *Natural and Moral History of the Indies.* 6th ed.

Adair, James. 1968. *The History of the American Indians.* New York and London: Johnson Reprint Corporation

Alexander, Hartley Burr. 1964. *Mythology of All Races.* 13 Vols. New York: Cooper Square Publishers

Allen, Joseph Lovell. 1970. *A Comparative Study of Quetzalcoatl.* Provo, Utah: BYU Doctoral Dissertation.

Altruz, Robert W. *Newark Holy Stones.* Grandville, Ohio: Dennison University

Armstrong, Zella. 1 950. *Who Discovered America? The Amazing Story of Madoc.* Chatanooga: Lookout Publication Co.

Ashe, Geoffrey, et al. 1971. *The Quest for America.* New York: Praeger.

Avila, Francisco de. 1608. *Narrative of the Errors False Gods, and other Superstitions and Diabolical Rites, in Narratives of The Rites And Laws of The Incas.* Translated by Clements R. Markham, 1873, London.

Bailey, James. 1973. *The God-Kings & The Titans.* New York: St. Martin's Press.

_____. 1994, *Sailing to Paradise.* New York: Simon & Schuster.

Bancroft, Huber Howe. 1883. *The Native Races.* 5 Vols. San Francisco.

Ben Gurion, David, ed. 1974. *The Jews in Their Land.* Garden City, New York: Doubleday and Company.

Ben Khader, Alcha Ben Abed. 1987. *Carthage: A Mosaic of Ancient Tunisia.* American Museum Natural History. New York: W.W. Norton, Company

Benson, Elizabeth P. 1977. *The Maya World.* New York: Thomas E. Crowell.

_____. ed. 1981. *The Olmec and Their Neighbors.* Washington D.C. Dumbarton oaks.

Bernal, Ignacio. 1969. *The Olmec World.* Translated by Doris Hey den. Berkley, California: University California Press.

Biddle, Nicholas, ed. 1962. *The Journals of the Expedition under the Command of Capt's Lewis and Clark.* 2 Vols. New York: Heritage Press.

Billiard, Jules. 1974. *The World of the American Indian.* Washington D.C. *National Geographic Society*

Blom, Frans. 1927. *Tribes and Temples.* 2 Vols. New Orleans: Tulane University

_____. 1971. *The Conquest of Yucatan.* New York: Cooper Square.

Boissoiere, Robert. 1990. *The Return of Pahana.* New Mexico: Bear & Co.

Boland, Charles Michael. 1961. *They All Discovered America.* Garden City, New York: Doubleday.

Boulanger, Robert. 1979. *Mexico. Guatemala.* A.C. Mexico: Fomento Cultural Banamex.

Brinton, Daniel G. 1882. *American Hero Myths.* Philadelphia: H.C. Watts & Company

_____. 1974 (1896). *Myths of the New World.* New York: Multimedia Publishing.

Brough, Clayton R. 1979. *Lost Tribes.* Bountiful, Utah: Horizon.

Bulfinch, Thomas. 1979. *Bulfinch's Mythology.* New York: Crown.

Burland, Cottie A. 1968. *The Gods of Mexico.* New York: Capricorn.

Campanius, Holm Thomas. 1834. *Description of the Province of New Sweden.* Philadelphia.

Campbell, Joseph. 1973. *The Hero With a Thousand Faces.* New Jersey: Princeton University Press.

_____. 1974. *The Mythic Image.* New Jersey: Princeton University Press.

_____. 1986. *The Inner Reaches of Outer Space.* New York: Alfred Van der Marck.

_____. 1987-a. *Occidental Mythology.* New York: Penguin.

_____. 1987-b. *Oriental Mythology.* New York: Penguin.

_____. 1987-c. *Primitive Mythology.* New York: Penguin

_____. 1988. *The Power of Myth.* New York: Doubleday.

_____. 1990. *Transformations of Myth Through Time.* New York: Harper & Row.

Carlson, John B. 1993. "Rise and Fall of the City of Gods." *Archaeology,* November, December, Vol. 46.

Carmack, Robert M. & James M. Mondlock. 1983. *El Título de Totonicapán.* Mexico: Universidad Nacional Autonoma.

Carrasco, David. 1984. *Quetzalcoatl and the Irony of Empire.* Chicago: University of Chicago Press.

Carroll, John Spencer. 1994. *A Search for Quetzalcoatl.* Santa Barbara, California: Stonehenge Viewpoint.

Castillo, Bernal Diaz Del. 1972. *The Discovery and Conquest of Mexico.* Translated and edited by A.P. Maudslay. New York: Noonday Press.

Catlin, George. 1973. *North American Indians.* 2 Vols. New York: Dover.

Ceram, C.W. 1971. *The First American.* New York.

Charnay, Desiré. 1973. *The Ancient Cities of the New World.* Cambridge.
Clark, Kenneth. 1969. *Civilization.* New York: Harper & Row.
Coe, Michael, et. al. 1989. *Atlas of Ancient America.* New York: Facts On File.
————. 1968. *America's First Civilization.* New York: American Heritage.
————. 1973. *The Maya Scribe and His World.* New York: Grolier.
————. 1984. *Mexico.* Hungary: Thames & Hudson.
————. 1986. *The Maya.* London: Thames & Hudson.
————. 1992. *Breaking the Maya Code.* New York: Thames & Hudson.
Coffer, William E. 1978. *Spirits of the Sacred Mountains.* New York: Van Nostrand Reinhold.
Cook, Roger. 1988. *The Tree of Life.* New York: Thames & Hudson
Covarubias, Miguel. 1947. *Mexico South.* New York: Knopf.
Covey, Cyclone. 1975. *Calalus: A Roman Jewish Colony in America From the Time of Charlemagne
    Through Alfred The Great.* New York: Vantage.
Daniken, Erich von. 1969. *Chariots of the Gods.* London: Souvenir Press.
Davies, Nigel. 1979. *Voyagers to the New World: Fact or Fantasy?* London: Macmillan.
De La Fuente, Beatriz. 1968. *Palenque en la Historia y en El Arte.* Mexico: Fondo de Cultura
    Económica.
De Leonard & Carmen Cook. 1971. "Minor Arts of the Classic Period in Central Mexico."
    H.M.A.I. vol.10, Wauchope, Gen. ed. Austin, Texas: University Texas. Press.
De Roo, Peter. 1900. *History of America Before Columbus.* 2 Vols. Philadelphia: Lippincott.
De Vaux, Roland 1965. *Ancient Israel.* 2 Vols. New York: McGraw-Hill.
————. 1953: *The Journals of Lewis and Clark.* Boston: Houghton & Mifflin.
————. 1980. *The Course of Empire.* Boston: Houghton & Mifflin.
Deacon, Richard. 1966. *Madoc and the Discovery of America.* London: Frederick Muller
Deal, David Allen. 1992. *Discovery of Ancient America.* Irvine, Ca.: Kherem La Yah Press.
Diego de Land a. 1978. *Yucatan Before and After the Conquest.* William Gates, translator. New York: Dover.
Dimont, Max 1. 1962. *Jews. God and History.* New York: New Am. Lib.
Durán, Fray Diego de. 1977. *Book of the Gods and Rites and the Ancient Calendar.* Translated and
    edited by Fernando Horcitas and Doris Hey den. Norman: Oklahoma Press.
Edmonson, Munroe S. 1974. *Sixteenth Century Mexico. The Woek of Sahagún.* Albuquerque:
    University New Mexico Press.
Ekholm, Gordon F. 1964. "Transpacific Contacts" In *Prehistoric Man in the New World.* Chicago:
    University Chicago Press.
Eliade, Mircea, ed. in Chief. 1987. *The Encyclopedia of Religion.* New York: MacMillan.
————. 1967. *From Primitives to Zen.* New York: Harper & Row.
————. 1969. *The Quest. History and Meaning in Religion.* Chicago: University Chicago Press.
————. 1975. *Myths. Dreams. and Mysteries.* New York: Harper Torchbooks.
————. 1978. *A History of Religious Ideas.* 3 Vols. Chicago: University Chicago Press.
————. 1994. *Man, Myth and Magic: The Illustrated Encyclopedia of Mythology, Religion And
    the Unknown.* 21 Vols. Revised by Richard Cavendish
Eliot, Alexander. 1990. *The Universal Myths.* New York: Meridian.
Estrada, Emilio and Meggers, Berry J. 1961. "A Complex of Traits of Probable Transpacific Origin
    on the Coast of Ecuador." *American Anthropologist.* 63.
Fagan, Brian M. 1977. *Elusive Treasure.* New York: Charles Scribner's Sons.
————. 1987. *The Great Journey.* New York: Thames & Hudson.
————. 1997. "The First Americans." *Archaeology,* Mar./Apr., 1997. New York.
Farbridge, Maurice H. 1928. *Studies in Biblical and Semitic Symbolism.* New York.
Fell, Barry. 1977. *America B.C.* New York: New York Times Books.
————. 1982. *Bronze Age America.* Boston: Little, Brown and Company.
————. 1983. *Saga America.* New York: New York Times Books.
Ferguson, Thomas Stuart. 1958. *One Fold and One Shepherd.* Salt Lake City. Olympus.
Fingerhut, Eugene R. 1984. *Who First Discovered America?* Claremont, California: Regent Books.
————. 1994. *Explorers of Pre-Columbian America?* Claremont California: Regina Books.
Frazer, James G. 1981. *The Golden Bough.* 2 Vols. New York: Avenel.
Gardner, James L. Proj. ed. 1986. *Mysteries of the Ancient Americas.* New York: Pleasantville.
Gladwin, Harold S. 1947. *Men Out of Asia.* New York: McGraw-Hill.
Goetz, Delia & Sylvanus Morley. 1969. *Popol Vuh.* Norman: University Oklahoma Press.
Goetz, Delia, trans. 1953. *Title of the Lords of Totonicapán.* Norman: University Oklahoma.
Goldstein, David. 1980. *Jewish Folklore and Legend.* London: Hamlyn.
Gordon, Cyrus H. 1973. *Before Columbus.* New York: Crown.
————. 1974. *Riddles in History.* New York: Crown
Gómara, Francisco Lopes de. 1964. *Cortez, The Life of The Conqueror by His Secretary.* Translated
    and edited by Lesley Simpson. Cal: University Cal. Press.
Graves, Robert, Intro. 1982. *New larousse Encyclopedia of Mythology.* New York: Hamlyn.

Grimal, Pierre, ed. 1977. *Larousse World Mythology.* New Jersey: Chartwell.
Groesbeck, C. Jess. 1956. Personal Journal. Utah: Springville.
Grosvenor, Gilbert M., ed. 1978. *Ancient Egypt, Discovering its Splendors.* Washington D.C.: National Geographic Society.
Hackin, J., et. al. *Asiatic Mythology.* New York: Crescent Books.
Hamilton, Charles, ed. 1977. *City of The Thunderbird.* Norman: University Oklahoma Press.
Hapgood, Charles H. 1979. *Maps of the Ancient Sea Kings.* New York: Dutton.
Harvard Classics. 1910. Vol. 43 "The Voyages of Vinland." N.Y.P.F. Collier.
Hawkes, Jacquetta. 1976. *The Atlas of Early Man.* New York: St. Martin's.
Her Mann, Paul. 1954. *Conquest by Man.* New York.
Hodge, F.W. 1910. *Handbook of American Indians North of Mexico.* 2 Vols. Washington D.C.: Smithsonian.
Holland, Hjalmarr. 1956. *Explorations in America Before Columbus.* New York: Twayne.
Honoré, Pierre. 1961. *!n Quest of the White God.* New York: Putnam's Sons.
Hougaard, William. 1914. *The Voyages of the Norsemen to America.* New York: American Scandinavian Foundation.
Howey, M. old field. *The Encircled Serpent.* Philadelphia: David McKay.
Huddles ton, Lee E. 1967. *Origins of the American Indians.* Austin: University Texas.
Hunter, Milton R. 1972. *Christ in Ancient America.* Vol. II. Salt Lake City: Deseret.
Hyerdahl, Thor. 1979. *Early Man and the Ocean.* New York: Doubleday.
Ilxtlilxochitl, Don Fernando de Alva. *Relaciones.* Vol. I of *Obras Historicas.* Alfredo Chavero, editor. originally published in Kingsborough, 1838. Mexico.
Ingstad, Helge. 1964. "Vinland Ruins Prove Vikings Found the New World." *National Geographic* November 1964: 708-734.
Irwin, Constance. 1963. *Fair Gods and Stone Faces.* New York: St. Martin's.
Joralemon, Peter David. 1976. "The olmec Dragon," In *Origins of Religious Art and Iconography in Preclassic Mesoamerica.* H.B. Nicholson, ed. Los Angeles: UCLA Latin American Center.
Josephus, Flavius. 1967. *Josephus' Complete Works.* William Whiston, trans. Grand Rapids, Michigan: Kregel.
Jung, Carl G. 1964. *Man and His Symbols.* New York: Doubleday.
Kings borough, Edward King, (Lord). 1831-1838. *Antiquities of Mexico.* 9 Vols. London.
Kipper, Philip. 1986. *The Smithsonian Book of North American Indians.* Washington D.C.: Smithsonian.
Kirk, G.S. 1970. *Myth. its Meaning and Functions in Ancient and other Cultures.* Los Angeles: University California Press.
La Barre, Weston. 1970. *The Ghost Dance.* New York: Doubleday.
Lathrop, Donald W. 1968. "The Tropical Forest and the Cultural Context of Chavin." In *Dumbarton Oaks Conference on Chavín.* 1971. Elizabeth Benson, ed. Washington D.C.: Dumbarton Oaks.
Lekson, Stephen H. 1997. "Rewriting Southwestern Prehistory." In *Archaeology.* Jan vary 1997: 52-5.
Lumbreras, Luis & Betty Meggars, trans. 1976. *The Peoples and Cultures of Ancient Peru.* Washington D.C.: Smithsonian Institution.
Mac Cana, Proinsias. 1985. *Celtic Mythology.* New York: Peter Bedrick Books.
Mac Nutt, Francis A, Trans. and ed. 1908. *Letters of Cortez.* 2 Vols. New York. MAC
Magnusson, Magnus and Herman Pals son. 1966. *The Vinland Sagas.* New York: New York University Press.
Marble, Samuel D. 1980. *Before Columbus.* New Jersey: A.S. Barnes.
Markham, Clements R., ed. 1873. *Narratives of the Rites and Laws of the Incas.* London: Hakluyt Society
Markman, Roberta and Peter Mark man. 1989. *Masks of the Spirit.* Los Angeles: University California Press.
Marquina, Ignacio 1964. *Arquitectura Prehispanica.* Mexico: Instituto Nacional de Antropologíae Historia.
Marriott, Alice and Carol K. Rachlin. 1968. *American Indian Mythology.* New York.
Marx, Robert F. 1976. *Still More Adventures.* New York: Mason/Charter.
_____. 1992. *In Quest of the Great White Gods.* New York: Crown.
Mason, J. Alden. 1975. *The Ancient Civilizations of Peru.*
Maximillian, Alexander Phillip (Prince). 1843. *Travels in the Interior of North America.* London.
Maxwell, James A., ed. 1978. *America's Fascinating Indian Heritage.* New York: Pleasantville.
May, Charles Paul. 1971. *The Early Indians.* New York.
May, Wayne N. Publishers *The Ancient American.* (Monthly) Pittman N.J.: Carlton Dunn.
McGlone, William R., et. al. 1993. *Ancient American Inscriptions: Plow Marks or History?* Sutton, Massachusetts: Early Sites Research Society.
Means, Phillip A. 1968. *Ancient Civilizations of Peru.* Harmondsworth: Penguin
Meltzer, David J. 1993. *Search for the First Americans.* Washington D.C.: St. Remy Press and Smithsonian.
Mertz, Henriette.1972. *Pale Ink.* Chicago: The Swallow Press.

Molina, Christoval De. 1873. *Narratives of The Rites and Laws of The Incas.* Translated by Clements R. Markham. London: Hakluyt Society.

Morgan, Lewis Henry. 1851/1969. *League of the Iroquois.* New York: Rochester.

Morison, Samuel Eliot. 1971. *The European Discovery of America (The Northern Voyages).* New York: oxford University Press.

Morison, Samuel Eliot. 1974. *The European Discovery of America (The Southern Voyages).* New York: Oxford University Press.

Morley, Sylvanus G. 1956. *The Ancient Maya.* Cal.: Stanford University Press.

Moseley, Michael and Carroll Mackey. 1973. "Chan Chan, Peru's Ancient City of Kings." *National Geographic* March 319-337.

Nasatir, A.P. 1952. *Before Lewis and Clark.* Vol. 1. St. Louis.

_____. 1927. "Spanish Exploration of the Upper Missouri. Missouri." In *Missouri. Valley Historical Review.* XIV. Missouri.

Neill, Edward Duffield. 1890. "The Development of Trade on Lake Superior and its Tributaries During the French Regime." In *Macalester College Contributions.* St. Paul, Minnesota.: Pioneer Press.

Nicholson, H.B. 1957. *Topiltzin Quetzalcoatl of Tollan: A Problem in Mesoamerican Ethnohistory.* Dr. Dissertation. Massachusetts: Harvard University

_____. 1971. "Religion in Pre-Hispanic Central Mexico." In *H.M.A.I.* Vol. 10. Wauchope, Ben. ed. Austin: University Texas Press.

Nicholson, Irene 1967. *Mexican and Central American Mythology.* New York: Hamlyn.

Nuttall, Zelia, ed. 1975. *The Codex Nuttall.* New York: Dover.

Osborne, Harold. 1968. *South American Mythology.* Middlesex: Hamlyn.

Oswalt, Wendell H. 1966. *This Land Was Theirs.* New York.

Otto, Walter F. 1965. *Dionysus, Myth and Cult.* Bloomington: Indiana University Press.

Pagden, Anthony, Trans., ed. 1992. *Hernan Cortes, Letters From Mexico.* New Haven: Yale University Press.

Patterson, Thomas C. 1968. "Chavín: An Interpretation of Its Spread and Influence." In *Dumbarton Oaks Conference on Chavín.* Washington D.C.: Dumbarton Oaks.

Pearce, Kenneth. 1985. *The View From the Top of the Temple.* Albuquerque: University New Mexico.

Pellegrino, Charles. 1991. *Unearthing Atlantis.* New York: Random House.

Perowne, Stewart. 1984. *Roman Mythology.* New York: Peter Bedrick Books.

Pidgeon, William. 1853. *Traditions of The De-Coo-Dah.* New York.

Pinsent, John. 1987. *Greek Mythology.* New York: Peter Bedrick Books.

Prescott, William H. *History of the Conquest of Mexico and History of the Conquest of Peru.* Modern Library. New York: Random House.

Radin, Paul 1971. *The Winnebago Tribe.* Lincoln: University Nebraska Press.

_____. 1972. *The Trickster, a Study in American Indian Mythology.* New York.

Recinos, Adrian & Goetz, Delia. 1967. *Annals of the Cakchiquels & Title of the Lords of Totonicapán.* Norman: University of Oklahoma Press.

Riley, Carroll & Charles Kelley, ed. 1971. *Man Across the Sea.* Austin: University Texas Press.

Rink, Henry. 1875. *Tales and Traditions of the Eskimo.* London: William Blackwood & Sons.

Robertson, Merle Green 1983. *Sculpture of Palenque.* Vol. 1 . New Jersey: Princeton University Press.

Robertson, Merle, Chair. 1973. *Mesa Redonda.* Vol. lll. Cal if. Herald Printers.

Robiscek, Francis. 1972. Cop an. Home of the Mayan Gods. New York: Museum of the American Indian Heye Foundation.

Roblscek, Francis. 1978. *The Smoking Gods.* Norman: University Oklahoma Press. .

Roys, Ralph L. 1938. "Fray Diego de Landa and the Problem of Idolatry in Yucatan." *Cooperation in Research.* Washington D.C.: Carnegie Institute

Roys, Ralph L. 1967. *Book of Chilam Balam of Chumayel.* Norman: University Oklahoma Press.

Rybnikar, Horatio. 1997. "The Greatest Discovery in the History of Archaeology." *Ancient American,* Vol 3, Issue 16, January 1997: 2-11.

Saenz, Caesar A. 1962. *Quetzalcoatl.* Mexico: Instituto Nacional de Antropologia e Historia.

Sahagún, Fray Bernardino de. 1950-69. *The Florentine Codex.* Edited by Arthur J. Anderson & Charles Dibble. 12 Vols. Santa Fe, New Mexico: School of American Research & University of Utah.

Salcamayhua, Don Juan. 1620. "An Account of the Antiquities of Peru." *Narratives of the Rites and Laws of the Incas.* Clements R. Markham, trans.1873. London: Hakluyt Society

Sanders, Ronald. *Lost Tribes and Promised Lands.* Boston: Little Brown.

Schele, Linda & David Freidel. 1990. *Forest of Kings.* New York: William Morrow.

Schele, Linda & Mary Miller. 1986. *Blood of Kings.* New York: George Braziller.

Schoolcraft, Henry R. 1851. *History of the Indian Tribes of the United States.* Lippincott, Gambo & Company, Philadelphia

Schoolcraft, Henry R. 1884. *Indian Tribes of the United States*. 2 Vols. Philadelphia.

Schoolcroaft, Henry R. 1855. *Information Respecting The History, Condition and Prospects of The Indian Tribes of the United States*. 5 Vols. Philadelphia.

Scofield, John. 1975. "Christopher Columbus." *National Geographic* Vol. 148 No. 5, November Washington, D.C.

SeJourné, Laurette. 1976. *Burning Water*. Berkeley: Shambhala Publishers

Shaffer Stephen B. 1996. *Treasures of the Ancients*. Utah: Cedar Fort.

Shao, Paul. 1976. *Asiatic Influences in Pre-Columbian American Art*. Iowa: Iowa State University Press.

Shao, Paul. 1983. *The Origin of Ancient American Cultures*. Ames: Iowa State University Press.

Silverberg, Robert. 1968. *Mound Builders of Ancient America*. Connecticut.

Smith, William. 1967. *Smith's Bible Dictionary*. New Jersey: Pyramid Publishers

Snyder, Graydon F. 1985. *Ante Pacem: Archaeological Evidence of Church Life Before Constantine*. Mercer University Press

Sodders, Betty. 1990-91. *Michigan Prehistory Mysteries*. 2 Vols. Autrain: Avery Color Studios.

Sorenson, John L. & Martin H. Raish. 1990. *Pre-Columbian Contact With the Americas Across the Oceans*. 2 Vols. Utah: Research Press.

Soustelle, Jacques. 1984. *The Olmecs*. New York: Doubleday.

Spence, Lewis. 1975. *Myths and Legends of The North American Indians*. New York.

Spinden, Herbert Joseph. 1947. "New Light on Quetzalcoatl." *Congreso Internacional de Americanistas*. Paris.

_____. 1975. *A Study of Maya Art*. New York: Dover Publications.

Squier, Ephraim George. 1851. *The Serpent Symbol and the Worship of the Reciprocal Principles of Nature in America*. New York: Putnam.

Stuart, George. 1993. "New Light on the Olmec." *National Geographic*. November 1993: 88-115.

Tedlock, Dennis. 1985. *Popol Vuh*. New York: Simon & Schuster.

Thatcher, John Boyd. 1903. *Christopher Columbus—His Works, His Life, His Remains*. New York: G.P Putnam and Sons.

Thomas, Hugh. 1994. *Conquest: Montezuma, Cortes, and the Fall of Old Mexico*. New York: Simon and Schuster.

Thompson, Gunnar. 1992. *American Discovery: The Real Story*. Seattle: Argonauts Misty Isles Press.

Thompson, J. Eric. 1970. *The Rise and Fall of Maya Civilization*. Norman: University Oklahoma Press.

_____. 1972. *Commentary on the Dresden Codex*. Philadelphia: American Philosophical Society.

Thompson, Stith. 1928. *Tales of the North American Indians*. Bloomington.

TIME/LIFE. 1987. *Age of God-Kings*. Time Frame. Alexandria, Virginia.

Torquemada, Juan De. 1943. *Monarquia Indiana*. 3 Vols. Ed. by Salvador Chavez Hay hoe. Mexico, D.F.

Tozzer, Alfred M., ed. 1966. *Land a's Relacion de Las Cosas de Yucatan*. New York: Kraus Reprint Corporation

Trump, David H. 1980. *The Prehistory of the Mediterranean*. New Haven: Yale University Press.

Underhill, Ruth M. 1965. *Red Man's Religion*. Chicago: University Chicago Press.

Valle,Victor. 1988. "The Exodus of New Mexico's 'Hidden Jews.'" In *L.A. Times*, July 15, 1988.

Verrill, Hyatt and Ruth. 1967. *America's Ancient Civilizations*. New York: Capricorn.

Von Hagen, Victor. 1961. *Realm of The Incas*. New York.

Von Wuthenau, Alexander. 1975. *Unexpected Faces in Ancient America*. New York: Crown.

Waters, Frank. 1977. *Book of the Hopi*. New York: Ballantine.

Wauchope, Robert, Gen. ed. 1971. *Handbook of Middle American Indians* (H.M.A.I.). 12 Vols. Austin: University Texas Press.

_____. 1962. *Lost Tribes and Sunken Continents*. Chicago: University Chicago Press.

Weaver, Muriel Porter. 1972. *The Aztecs, Maya, and Their Predecessors*. New York: Seminar Press.

Wenke, Robert J. 1990. *Patterns in Prehistory*. New York: Oxford University Press.

Whitehead, E.L. 1972. *The House of Israel*. Salt Lake City.

Willard, T.A. 1941. *Kukulcan—The Bearded Conqueror*. Hollywood: Murray and Gee.

Williams, Gwyn A. 1979. *Madoc. The Making of a Myth*. London: Eyre Methuel.

_____. 1979. *Madoc. The Making of a Myth*. London: Fakenham Press.

Williams, Samuel Cole. ed. 1930. *History of the American Indians*. (Journal of James Adair). Tennessee: Watuga Press.

Williams, Stephen. 1991. *Fantastic Archaeology*. Philadelphia: University of Pennsylvania

Winnemucca, Sarah Hopkins. 1883. *Life Among the Piutes*. Boston.

Woodruff, Sir John. 1931. *The Serpent Power*. Madras.

Worsley, Israel. 1928. *The View of the American Indians*. London.

Wright, Esmond. General ed. 1985. *History of the World*. London: Hamlyn.

INDEX